"You're scared:

"Aren't you?"

"Sure, but I've been scared before. I wouldn't mind getting a little extra something." Judith pointed to her empty plate. "How about you?"

Renie waved her cigarette. "I'm good. But I'll be your bodyguard. It's probably not wise to go off by ourselves."

The lights in the corridor had been dimmed. In the vacant lobby, a single lamp glowed in the corner by one of the sofas. The wind moaned in the big chimney, and the pennants that hung from the rafters rustled gently above the cousins' heads.

The dining room was dark, but Renie found the switch. A pale, sallow patch of light followed them into the kitchen. Judith started to feel for the on/off button by the sink, but stopped abruptly.

Something was wrong. She could make out the marble-topped counter and the glass dessert plate. She could also see that someone's face was lying in what was left of the angel food cake.

In memory of Katharine Dawson Marshall, the last of the Dawson clan to enter eternal life on January 30, 1998, joining Monica Richardson Dawson, Louis Dawson, Frances Dawson Webster, Thomas Dawson, and Helen Dawson Shelley. We will always love you.

ONE

JUDITH MCMONIGLE FLYNN stacked twenty-four pancakes on a platter, grabbed the syrup pitcher, and opened the swinging door with her hip. Just behind her, the kitchen phone rang.

"Damn!" Judith cursed under her breath, then sheepishly smiled at the eight hungry, curious faces seated around the old oak dining room table. The phone kept ringing. "Sorry," Judith apologized, as she set the pancakes and syrup on the table, "I don't usually get calls this early unless they're reservations from the East Coast."

The bed and breakfast guests made various incomprehensible sounds, then began dishing up pancakes. Judith returned to the kitchen just as the phone trunked over to the answering machine. After delivering bacon, eggs, and extra butter, she checked the message.

"I know you're there, you twit!" Cousin Renie's voice had an early-morning croak. "Call me! Quick!"

It was 7:36. Judith's cousin never, ever got out of bed before nine and almost never achieved full consciousness until ten. Apprehensively, Judith dialed Renie's number.

"Are you okay?" Judith asked in a breathless voice.

"I'm terrible," Renie replied crossly. "I'm up the creek, in the soup, down the toilet."

1

The exaggerated response relieved Judith's mind. If Renie had been held hostage or was lying at the bottom of her basement stairs, she wouldn't describe her plight so vividly. Judith poured a mug of coffee and sat down at the kitchen table. "So what's really wrong?" she asked, more intrigued than alarmed.

A big sigh rolled over the phone line from the other side of Heraldsgate Hill. "It's the OTIOSE conference—you know, the Overland Telecommunications and Information Organization of Systems Engineers."

"It's called OTIOSE for short?" Judith asked in surprise. "Do they know what it means?"

"Of course not. They're engineers. Anyway," Renie went on, still sounding vexed, "they used to be part of the local phone company before the Bell System got broken up by the Justice Department. Remember I told you I was putting together a really big graphic design presentation for their annual winter retreat? I'm redoing their logo, their colors, everything right down to the cheap pens they hand out to lucky customers and members of their board. But there's a problem—the caterer backed out at the last minute and they've asked me to find a sub."

"So? There are a zillion caterers in the Yellow Pages. If they're telephone company people, why can't they let their fingers do the walking?"

"Because they *are* telephone company people. Their brains aren't attached to their fingers. Plus, these are the top executives. They're not used to doing things for themselves." Renie was clearly exasperated. "Anyway, I opened my big mouth and told them I knew a topnotch caterer. Believe it or not, I was referring to you. What do you say?"

"Ohhh . . ." Judith set her mug down with a thud and splashed coffee onto the plastic table cover. Running a B&B was hard enough, especially with the holidays so recently behind her. Of late she'd been trying to phase out the catering arm of her business. For several years it had been a joint venture with Judith's friend and neighbor, Arlene Rankers. Her husband, Carl, had retired two years earlier, and their family of five had expanded. The quiet leisure years they'd anticipated had turned into a merry-go-round of grandchildren crawling around in the laurel hedge that separated the Rankers and Flynn properties. Arlene no longer had the time or the energy to help run a full-scale catering service, and Judith couldn't do it without her.

"I really don't think I can manage on such short notice," Judith said at last. "Isn't the retreat this weekend?"

"Right, over the three-day Martin Luther King holiday." Renie paused. "It'd be for only a day, actually. All you have to do is set up the first meal on Friday, then stock the fridge and freezer and whatever. The rest of the weekend is . . ."

"More coffee please," came a request from the dining room.

"Do you have powdered sugar?" called another guest.

"There's something gruesome crawling around under the table," complained a third, rather frantic voice.

Judith hadn't heard the last part of Renie's explanation. "Coz, I'll get back to you in half an hour," she said, feeling a touch of panic.

The coffee and powdered sugar were delivered, then Judith dove under the big oak table to retrieve her cat, Sweetums. The cat arched his back, hissed, and began rubbing against the sheer stockings on a pair of rather hefty legs.

"Eeek!" cried a voice somewhere over Judith's head. "My hose! I'm being attacked by an animal! I feel fur and disgusting warmth!"

"What is it?" inquired an anxious male voice. "Not a porcupine, surely."

Judith grabbed Sweetums with both hands and dragged him out from under the table. "Sorry," she apologized again. "My husband must have let him in when he went to work."

"I hate cats," said the woman who had first complained.

"Cats carry all kinds of dread disease," stated a man at the end of the table.

"That cat looks mean," remarked a woman who was sprinkling powdered sugar on her pancakes. "Is he rabid?"

Sweetums was now sitting by the swinging doors, his long, fluffy tail curled around his large orange, white, and gray body. The yellow eyes narrowed and the whiskers twitched.

"He's a very healthy cat," Judith declared in a defensive tone. "I'll take him outside. Come on, Sweetums. Let's go eat some birds."

A gasp went up from some of the guests. Judith immediately realized she should have kept her mouth shut. But this time she didn't apologize. Nudging Sweetums with her foot, she guided him into the kitchen, down the narrow hall past the pantry and the back stairs, and out onto the porch.

Sweetums balked. It was extremely cold, as befitted the third week of January. Heavy dark clouds hung in low over Heraldsgate Hill. Despite the budding camellia bushes and the green forsythia shoots, Judith sensed that winter was far from over. She didn't blame Sweetums for not wanting to stay outside. Maybe he'd be satisfied visiting Judith's mother in the converted toolshed. Gertrude Grover was probably champing at the bit, awaiting her own breakfast.

Judith went back into the kitchen to prepare her mother's morning repast. Then she and the cat trudged down the walkway to the small apartment. Gertrude opened the door and offered her daughter a knuckle sandwich.

"You're late, you moron," Gertrude snarled. "It's seven-forty-nine. I'm practically ready to keel over from starvation." Her small eyes brightened as Judith uncovered the plastic tray. "Flapjacks, huh? You got any little pigs?"

"Not today," Judith replied as Sweetums sniffed around the legs of Gertrude's walker. "Bacon, not too crisp, just the way you like it, swimming in its own grease."

"Mmm." Gertrude seemed appeased. "Did you warm the syrup?"

"Of course." Judith began setting the breakfast things on Gertrude's card table, which was littered with magazines, jumble puzzles, candy boxes, candy wrappers, and half a chocolate Santa. Gertrude had already eaten the head and shoulders, and was obviously working her way through the little round belly. Though bacon, eggs, and pancakes might not be the most wholesome of foodstuffs, Judith consoled herself that at least they weren't sweets. In recent years, Gertrude had begun to reject such items as fruit, vegetables, and almost anything else that was healthy. The problem had been exacerbated by the holidays. Gertrude had stockpiled sugary treats given by friends, relatives, and neighbors. If her mother had had any of her own teeth left, Judith guessed that they would have fallen out by New Year's Eve.

Returning to the house, Judith tended to her guests' latest, not always reasonable requests, and tried to keep smiling. She knew she was suffering from the usual post-holiday doldrums. Traditionally, January was a slow month in the hostelry business, but this year had proved to be an exception. For the first time since Judith had converted the family home into a B&B almost eight years earlier, Hillside Manor was booked through the twenty-first. Following on the heels of the holiday season with its professional and personal hustle-and-bustle, Judith could have used a respite. But there was none, and she was tired, cranky, and drained of her usual cheerful enthusiasm.

It was eight-thirty by the time the guests had finished breakfast. Two couples had drifted into the living room to drink coffee in front of the fireplace, and the others had gone upstairs to prepare for checkout. Judith dialed Renie's number, propped the portable phone between her shoulder and ear, and loaded the dishwasher.

"You're late," Renie snapped. "I was ready to drive over to see if you'd died."

"Just busy, coz," Judith replied in a listless voice. "Anyway, the answer is no. I've got a full house this weekend and I'm really beat. Today's Tuesday, and if this event is set for Friday, that doesn't give me much time to put together a menu that'll last through the long weekend.''

"Oh. Okay. Bye.''

"Wait!'' Annoyed with herself for letting Renie goad her, Judith slapped a hand against the dishwasher lid. "I mean, you're not mad?''

"Huh? No. That's fine. See you.''

"But what will you do?'' Judith asked anxiously. "You said you were in a bind.''

"I'll kill myself. I'm getting a noose out of the broom closet even as we speak.'' Renie's voice was unnaturally placid. "Now where's a box I can stand on?''

"Dammit, you're making me feel guilty.''

"That's okay. You'll forget all about it when Bill keels over from grief and you and Joe end up with our three kids. They may be adults legally, but they're still a financial drain. Unlike you, we haven't been able to marry ours off.''

Judith's mind flashed back to Mike and Kristin's wedding the previous summer. It had been wonderful; it had been terrible. Judith had felt the wrench of parting with her only son, and had somehow temporarily buried her feelings by trying to help her homicide detective husband catch a murderer. But during the months that followed, the sense of loss had deepened. Even though Mike hadn't lived at home for several years, his marriage had been a major life change for Judith. He and his bride worked as park rangers some four hundred miles away in Idaho, but they were due to be transferred. The new posting could take them almost anywhere in the fifty states, and Judith feared she wouldn't see her son and his wife more than once a year. The hollow feeling wouldn't go away, and Judith knew it was another reason she felt not only tired, but suddenly old.

"When do you make your presentation?'' Judith asked, forcing herself out of her reverie.

"Friday,'' Renie answered, no longer placid. "I told you, it's just for a day. Can't Arlene Rankers help you throw some crap together for these bozos? Bring her along. You'll be up at the lodge for about six hours, and they'll pay you three grand.''

''Arlene's getting ready for her annual jaunt to Palm Desert with Carl, and . . . *three grand*?'' Judith's jaw dropped.

''Right.'' The smirk in Renie's voice was audible. ''OTI-OSE pays well. Why do you think I'm so anxious to peddle my pretty little proposals? I could make a bundle off these phone company phonies.''

''Wow.'' Judith leaned against the kitchen counter. ''That would pay off our Christmas bills and then some. Six hours, right?''

''Right. We can come and go together, because my presentation should take about two hours, plus Q&A, plus the usual yakkity-yak and glad-handing. You'll get to see me work the room. It'll be a whole new experience. I actually stay nice for several minutes at a time.''

Judith couldn't help but smile. Her cousin wasn't famous for her even temper. ''How many?'' she asked, getting down to business.

''Ten—six men, four women,'' Renie answered, also sounding equally professional. ''All their officers, plus the administrative assistant. I'll make a list, just so you know the names. Executives are very touchy about being recognized correctly.''

Judith nodded to herself. ''Okay. You mentioned a lodge. Which one?''

''Mountain Goat,'' Renie replied. ''It's only an hour or so from town, so we should leave Friday morning around nine.''

Judith knew the lodge, which was located on one of the state's major mountain passes. ''I can't wait to tell Joe. He'll be thrilled about the money. By the way, why did the other caterers back out?''

There was a long pause. ''Uh . . . I guess they're sort of superstitious.''

"What do you mean?" Judith's voice had turned wary.

"Oh, it's nothing, really," Renie said, sounding unnaturally jaunty. "Last year they had a staff assistant handle the catering at Mountain Goat Lodge. Barry Something-Or-Other, who was starting up his own business on the side. He . . . ah . . . disappeared."

"He *disappeared*?" Judith gasped into the receiver.

"Yeah, well, he went out for cigarettes or something and never came back. Got to run, coz. See you later."

Renie hung up.

Joe wasn't excited about Judith's bonanza. Indeed, Joe didn't really hear her mention the OTIOSE catering job. He was uncharacteristically self-absorbed and depressed, though the reasons had nothing to do with his wife.

"It's these damned drive-bys," he complained, accepting a stiff Scotch from Judith. "They're always kids, both victims and perps, and sometimes they're innocent bystanders. The victims, I mean. God, it's such a waste." He loosened his tie and collapsed into a kitchen chair.

Judith came up behind him and massaged his tense shoulders. "It's sad. What are they trying to prove?"

"That they belong." Joe sighed. "It doesn't matter that it's a gang of punks just like themselves. They fit in somewhere, there's a place for them, a niche they can't find with family, because they don't have any. Not a real family, I mean. They're the new outcasts, and they can only prove their worth by blowing some other poor kid away."

"It's an awfully stupid way to prove anything," Judith said, turning back to the stove where mussels boiled in a big pot. "You usually catch them, though."

"That's the frustrating part," Joe said, taking a deep drink. "The perps end up in the slammer for fifteen, twenty years, wasting their young lives. What's even worse is that the rest of them don't learn by what happens to the ones we send away. There are times when I hate my job. Do you realize I could retire in three years?"

Judith, who was draining the mussels into a colander, almost dropped the pot. She'd never heard Joe mention retirement before. "Do you want to?" she gulped.

Joe sighed again, his green eyes troubled. "I've been thinking about it lately. Hell, I've been on the force for thirty-three years. Plenty of guys burn out by fifty-five. I'm past that already. I figure I'm lucky to have lasted this long."

So was Judith. Only in the five and a half years of her marriage to Joe had she been able to count on financial support from a spouse. During her nineteen years with the unemployed and unemployable Dan McMonigle, Judith had worked two jobs. By day she had served as a librarian, and at night, she had toiled behind the bar at the Meat and Mingle. The daytime and evening clientele neither met nor mingled. Most of the hard-fisted drinkers were lucky they could read the bar specials posted on a chalkboard set next to the blinking sign depicting a hula-skirted chipmunk.

"Well," Judith said, tossing the mussels into a bowl of vermicelli and rice, "it's your decision." She gave her husband a quick, keen look. The red hair had more gray in it, the forehead was growing higher, the laugh and worry lines were etched more deeply. Joe was still the most attractive man in the world to Judith, but he *was* getting older. She'd hardly noticed. After a twenty-five-year separation, their time together had seemed so brief. "You'll know when it's time to quit," she added a bit lamely.

"Hmm." Joe sipped more Scotch. "The retirement package is fairly good, all things considered."

Which, Judith realized, Joe *had* considered. "Medical, dental?"

"Right. I'd have Social Security, too."

There had been no security with Dan, social or otherwise. At over four hundred pounds, her first husband had offered only verbal abuse and demands for more vodka, Ding-Dongs, apple fritters, and whatever else he could stuff into his fat, lazy face.

"I guess we'll have to think about it," Judith said, sounding slightly wistful.

Joe didn't reply. *He has thought about it. Plenty. Why hasn't he mentioned it to me?* Judith felt betrayed.

Maybe this wasn't the time to discuss the three grand for the OTIOSE conference. Maybe Judith should start building her own little nest egg. Certainly she wasn't prepared to give up the B&B. She'd worked too hard to turn it into a successful venture.

"Did you hear me say I'll be gone most of Friday?" she asked, spooning green beans onto a plate for Gertrude. "I'm catering a phone company conference for Renie."

Joe had picked up the evening paper and was reading the sports page. "Since when did Renie go to work for the phone company?"

"She's freelancing, as usual." Judith was getting exasperated.

"Bill's retiring next year." Joe turned a page of the newspaper.

"What?" Judith gaped at her husband.

He nodded, but didn't look up. "Thirty-one years in the university system. Why shouldn't he?"

"Renie hasn't said a thing!" Now Judith's annoyance spread to her cousin.

"Maybe Bill hasn't told Renie. Where the hell is the Hot Stove League news? I heard there was a big trade brewing." Joe riffled the pages, in search of baseball reports.

"Bill wouldn't *not* tell Renie," Judith seethed. "Bill and Renie *communicate*."

"Maybe she forgot to mention it to you. Ah, here we are . . ." Joe disappeared behind the paper.

Judith marched out to the toolshed with Gertrude's dinner. For once, she put the covered plate outside the door, knocked twice, and raced back to the house. Gertrude hated mussels. Judith wasn't in a mood to hear her mother gripe. Judith, in fact, was feeling mutinous. Joe wasn't usually secretive, especially not when it came to making decisions that affected them as a couple. And Renie *always* told Judith everything. The cousins were as close as sisters, maybe closer, because they hadn't been forced to grow up under the same roof. Judith felt like slugging Joe, shaking Renie, and giving Bill a boot just for the hell of it.

Judith would never admit it, but she was in the mood for murder.

TWO

FRIDAY DAWNED COLD and cloudy. Renie was driving the Jones's big blue Chev, which was fitted with snow tires, and carried chains in the trunk. The cousins set out at nine on the dot, heading east toward the mountain pass that was located about an hour outside of the city.

"I made a list," Renie said, patting an envelope that lay on the seat between them. "It's on top. Take it out and go over the names. When—and if—I introduce you, it won't be so confusing."

Judith perused the single sheet of typewritten paper as they crossed the floating bridge that led out of the city. "You should have included descriptions," she complained. "These names and titles don't mean much. The only one I've ever heard of is the CEO, Frank Killegrew. I've seen his name in the newspaper."

"Good, that leaves only nine, and four of them are women. Don't worry about it," Renie counseled. "With any luck, you won't have much contact with them."

Judith scanned the names: After Franklin Killegrew, president and CEO, there was Ward Haugland, executive vice president–network and customer services. Judith made a face. "What's with these complicated titles? Why can't Haugland just be an executive vice president?"

"Because telecommunications *is* complicated these days," Renie replied. "It's still in a state of flux. First came the big Bell System divestiture, sixteen, seventeen years ago, along with the revolution in technology. Independent companies like OTIOSE are still trying to find their niche."

"Is that why I get four phone bills instead of one?" Judith asked.

"Yep. You've got your local carrier, your long distance company, your leased equipment, your . . . what?" Renie shot Judith an inquiring glance.

"My pager," Judith said. "It's really Mike's pager, but he doesn't use it anymore. The problem is, neither do I. I only took it from him so Mother could get me in an emergency."

"Has she ever paged you?" Renie asked as they reached the mainland and flourishing suburbia.

"Never. She swears she lost the number and wouldn't use it if she found it."

"Then get rid of the thing. It must cost you twenty bucks a month."

"Arlene has the number," Judith said. "Like now, she could page me if she has a problem taking over for the day at the B&B."

Renie shrugged. "Then maybe it's worth it."

They drove the interstate past industrial complexes, car dealerships, fast-food chains, trendy restaurants, and gas stations the size of a mini-mall. It never ceased to amaze Judith that what used to be vacant rural areas where the family gathered hazelnuts, blackberries, and Christmas trees was now a thirty-mile stretch of commercialism. At last they began to climb, but even where tall trees still grew, there were large swaths of housing developments. The city had sprawled, almost to the pass itself.

"Joe says Bill's going to retire." Judith finally broached the subject that had been on her mind since Tuesday night.

"He's talking about it." Renie pulled into the fast lane, passing a big semi-truck.

Judith noticed that some of the taller trees were dusted with fresh snow. "Really?" she remarked. "You haven't said so to me."

Renie gave a little shrug. "It won't be final—or real— until he hands in his retirement application to the university administration. I never anticipate, you know."

"Joe's talking about it, too." Judith tried to keep her tone light. "Of course he wouldn't retire for another three years."

"Good for him," Renie said, moving back into the right-hand lane. "Both of our husbands have had long careers. They need to kick back and enjoy themselves."

"Yes." Judith's tone was dubious. "Yes. I suppose they do." A vision of Dan McMonigle, supine and blimplike on the sofa, rumbled through her mind's eye. "It's just that I've been through quite a bit of change lately. With Mike married and now being transferred, he and Kristin could end up in Alaska or Hawaii or Florida where I'd hardly ever see them."

"So Joe retires and you travel." Renie shrugged. "That's what people do. Frank Killegrew's retiring, by the way," she added as they drove further into the forest and away from civilization. "Haugland's his heir apparent, but I've heard you can't count on it."

Judith glanced at the list Renie had given her. She wasn't terribly interested in OTIOSE's career paths. All she could think of was trying to live on Joe's retirement and Social Security. Would he insist she give up Hillside Manor and retire with him?

"Doesn't retirement make you feel *old*?" Judith finally asked.

"Huh?" Renie seemed puzzled. "No, why should it? It's a natural act, like eating or shopping for shoes. Besides, I won't give up my graphic design business. I do it at home, we can use the extra money, and I'd be bored stiff if I didn't work."

"I agree," Judith said as low clouds drifted across the

divided six-lane highway. "I'd like to keep the B&B going for another ten years. But I'll definitely dump the catering part in the next few months. Say," she went on, changing gears, "speaking of caterers, what about the guy who disappeared last year?"

Renie frowned. "I told you. He left on some errand and never came back. End of story."

Judith, who possessed a very logical mind, wanted details. "He never came back to the lodge? Or he never came back, period?"

"Period." Renie was exhibiting a touch of impatience. "This Barry . . . Newsom or Newsbaum or . . . Newcombe, I think it was, had forgotten something for his catering stockpile. He went off that Friday afternoon, presumably to the nearest store which is at the summit of the pass, and never came back. When he didn't show up for work the following Tuesday after the long weekend, his co-workers back at the company weren't concerned. They figured he was tired out from his catering duties. But later, one of the executives asked about Barry because they hadn't seen him after he left the lodge Friday afternoon. I guess he was listed as a missing person, and that's what he still is— missing."

"The executives didn't miss him that Friday?" Judith was incredulous.

"I guess not," Renie replied, negotiating the wide, sweeping switchback turns. "They probably thought he hadn't been able to find what he was looking for at the summit grocery and had gone all the way back into the nearest town. It had started to snow hard by then, so maybe they figured Barry couldn't get back up the pass. Bear in mind, coz, these big business types are all wrapped up in themselves. They don't pay much attention to underlings."

The executive suite was a world that Judith didn't understand. The B&B, the Thurlow Street branch of the public library, and the Meat and Mingle hadn't prepared her to face an officer corps. Renie, however, was accustomed to captains of industry. It seemed to Judith that her cousin regarded them much as she would observe animals at the zoo. They were interesting, they were different, they could even be amusing, and only upon rare occasions did they do something vulgar in public that would be better done in private.

As they approached the summit, driving conditions worsened, with deep piles of snow alongside the road. Not once had they glimpsed the mountains. The clouds were low and heavy, creating a foglike atmosphere that kept the Chev down to a crawl.

"We take a side road at the summit," Renie said, again pointing to the envelope on the seat. "Check the map. I've never been there before, but the directions looked easy."

It was a few minutes after ten when they reached the turnoff. Renie pulled into a service station that also featured a small grocery store. "This is where Barry supposedly went," she said. "As you can tell, they don't carry much beyond the basics. That's why he might have gone back down the pass. I'm going to fill up now because I didn't take time to stop at the BP on Heraldsgate Hill."

While Renie pumped gas, Judith got out of the car and walked around the wet tarmac. The area around the station had been plowed, but there was snow everywhere, perhaps as much as twenty feet. Judith spotted the main ski lodge through the drifting clouds and managed to catch sight of some of the chalets utilized by winter sports buffs.

Having used her credit card to pay at the pump, Renie got back in the car. "It can't be more than a mile from here," she said as Judith refastened her seatbelt. "Let me see that map."

The road was easy to find, not quite a quarter-mile from the service station, and on the north side of the interstate. It, too, had been recently plowed, and the going was relatively easy. Or seemed to be, for the first half-mile. Then the pavement suddenly ended. Renie found herself driving on bare gravel.

"This is stupid," she complained. "If they can pave half of the damned thing, why not the rest?"

"Maybe it's a matter of jurisdiction," Judith suggested. "The state or county may keep up part of it and the rest is Forest Service. I'd guess this was originally a logging road."

"Probably." Renie had dropped down to under ten miles an hour. "I wish Bill were here. I don't like driving in snow."

"You're not in snow. It's plowed."

"So far. But who knows what's up ahead?"

The narrow road zigged and zagged, climbing higher into the mountains. During the brief intervals when the cousins could see more than a few feet, they noticed that the trees grew more sparsely, and were of a different variety than the evergreens below the snow line. Judith counted lodgepole pine, western larch, Engelmann spruce, and Noble fir.

"You should have let me drive," Judith said. "I could have taken the Subaru. What if we get into a snowstorm on the way home this afternoon? You'll panic and kill us."

"I'll panic and let *you* drive," Renie responded, already looking rather grim. "Bill said the Chev would hold the road better because it's so big."

Heavy iron gates stood directly in front of them. Fortunately, they were open. Renie drove through, accelerated up a little rise, and hit pavement again. "Thank goodness," she murmured.

They were no longer on a road but in a sweeping drive which lead to the lodge and a large parking area. "Who owns this place?" Judith asked, peering through the foggy clouds at skimpy views of weathered logs and stone chimneys.

"It's privately owned," Renie said, heading for the nearest parking spot. As far as the cousins could tell, no other vehicles were present. "It used to belong to the park service years ago, but it's changed hands several times. Some group in the city owns it, and at one time, Frank Killegrew was involved in a partnership with other downtown investors. Now, it's mostly doctors and dentists who rent it out to private parties. Not just conferences and retreats like the previous owners, I gather, but ski groups and church organizations and whoever else is willing to pay the freight. This new bunch shut it down last summer and did some renovations to bring everything up to speed. I don't think the lodge rental comes cheap.''

Judith understood why after they carried the first load of comestibles inside. The lobby was vast, with a high, arched ceiling hung with multicolored banners. Built entirely of pine logs, the old wood gleamed under the lights of a half-dozen cast-iron candelabra suspended from the rafters. Animal skins and stuffed heads decorated the walls, and the huge stone fireplace was filled with cedar and fir, awaiting the touch of a match.

''It's grand,'' Judith said, smiling in appreciation. ''Where's the staff?''

''I told you, nobody's here but us and the OTIOSE gang,'' Renie said, setting a carton of groceries down on the hardwood floor. ''The staff was due to take off about nine this morning. The caretaker lives in a cabin about a half-mile from the lodge, but he won't be around, either. I was told he'd leave the door open so we could get in. I don't think the phone company folks will be here much before noon.''

''Where's the kitchen?'' Judith turned every which way, taking in the rustic furnishings, all made of wood and covered in rich, dark nubby fabrics.

Renie gestured to french doors on her left. ''That looks like the dining room, so I assume the kitchen is off of that. Let's finish unloading, and then we can snoop around.''

Three more trips were required to deposit Judith's weekend supplies. As Renie had guessed, the kitchen was at the far side of the dining room. While the lodge appeared to have been built during the thirties, the kitchen facilities were state of the art. Judith rubbed her hands in glee as she ogled the stainless-steel American range, the Belgian cook-ware, the German cutlery, and the French skillets.

"This is wonderful!" she exclaimed. "I'm going to start right in on lunch. Ham-filled crepes, raddicchio salad, a fresh fruit medley, four kinds of cheese, and puff pastries with a blackberry and cream filling."

"Go for it," Renie said, turning toward the door. "I'm going to the conference room on the other side of the lobby to set up my stuff."

"Okay," Judith replied, still distracted by all the latest appliances and gadgets. Then, as Renie exited, it dawned on Judith that something was out of kilter. "Coz!" she called. "What's with you? Aren't you hungry?"

Renie turned in the doorway. "No. I've got work to do. That's why I'm here."

Judith stared. Renie was always ravenous. She ate often and in large amounts. It never ceased to amaze Judith how her cousin could consume so much food and stay slim. Metabolism, Judith told herself, and envied Renie's gene pool. All her life, Judith had fought to keep weight off, and only now, in her fifties, did she feel comfortable with a couple of extra pounds on her tall, statuesque figure.

"Do you feel okay?" Judith finally asked.

"Yes. Yes, I feel fine." Renie sounded cross. "It's going on eleven. I've got to get organized. Good luck." She disappeared from sight.

Judith didn't have time to worry about her cousin's sudden lack of appetite. For the next hour, she immersed herself in making crepes, dicing ham, rolling out puff pastry, and cutting up fruit. It was a joy to work under such splendid conditions, and best of all, with no interruptions from guests, the telephone, or her mother.

The bus arrived at ten to twelve. Judith didn't hear it pull in, but Renie came to alert her. "It's actually a big van," she told Judith from the doorway. "The driver won't stay, of course. He's already headed back to the city."

Judith, who was in the middle of fashioning her puff

pastries, merely nodded. "Lunch at twelve-thirty, right?"

"Right." Renie left again.

The lodge's staff had already set up a large round table for ten in the dining room. Judith checked the table settings, admired the centerpiece of yellow gladioli, purple freesia and white lilies, then returned to the kitchen. She was filling the industrial-size coffeemaker when a small woman with big glasses and a platinum blonde pageboy entered the kitchen.

"Are we on schedule?" the woman asked, tapping a huge wristwatch that looked as if it could weigh down her arm.

"We are," Judith replied with a smile. "My name's Judith Flynn." She wiped her hands on a cloth and reached out to the other woman.

"Nadia Weiss, administrative assistant," Nadia replied with a faint New York accent. She didn't budge, let alone shake hands. "If you have any problems, come to me." With a swish of cashmere skirts, she departed.

Judith uttered a self-conscious little laugh and went back to work. Two minutes later, another woman appeared in the doorway. "You must be the caterer," she said.

Judith looked up from the crepe pan she was heating on the stove. A slim, plain woman of Chinese ancestry fixed mesmerizing dark eyes on Judith. "Yes," she gulped. "I'm Judith Flynn."

"The caterer," the other woman said in a tone that indicated Judith wasn't a person, she was merely a service. "My name's Margo Chang. If a Ms. Weiss contacts you, ignore her. I'm the vice president in charge of public relations, and I handle jobbers like you."

Judith imagined that a small smirk tugged at Margo's tight, thin mouth. "Okay," Judith said, still subdued. "If I need anything, I'll ask you."

"You shouldn't need anything. You should have come prepared." Margo's voice dropped a notch in what sounded to Judith like a threat.

"I'm fine. Everything's fine," Judith said hastily.

Margo gave a curt nod and left. Judith's wide shoulders relaxed. She stiffened again when she heard someone else enter the kitchen. To her relief, it was Renie.

"Thank heavens!" Judith cried. "I've just been visited by two of the three witches."

"Which ones?" Renie asked. "By my count there're four."

Judith winced. "Are all the women who work for this outfit like Ms. Weiss and Ms. Chang?"

Renie's round face grew thoughtful. "I'm not sure. By chance, I've dealt mostly with those two. You have to realize, coz, that I don't know most of these people very well myself. I've only done a handful of smaller projects until now."

"But you've actually worked with the ones I just met?" Judith was aghast.

Renie nodded as she surveyed her cousin's handiwork in the kitchen. "I'm used to it. You have to remember that all these executive types must be fairly tough to get to the top. The women have to be even tougher."

Judith, who was slicing kiwi, looked a bit puzzled. "But Whatshername—Weiss, right?—isn't a vice president or an officer. Or is she?"

"That's the problem," Renie said, leaning against the marble countertop. "She feels she should be. As administrative assistant, she wields a lot of power, but she doesn't get the same perks or the big salary. In the last few years that I've dealt with Nadia and the p.r. v.p., Margo, I haven't seen any love lost between them. Nor with Andrea and Ava, if it comes to that."

"Andrea and Ava? They sound like a dance team." Judith tried to visualize the list Renie had given her. "Which ones are they?"

Renie smiled indulgently. "Ava Aunuu is vice president–information technology services. Andrea Piccoloni-Roth is vice president–human resources, which used to be known as personnel. I've never understood the name change in a world that keeps dehumanizing people.''

A quick glance at the digital clock on the stainless-steel range told Judith that it was 12:25. "I'd better start serving the food. When are you going to eat?"

Renie shrugged. "Later. I don't like to make presentations on a full stomach."

Judith started to say, *since when?*, thought better of it, and began dishing the fresh fruit onto heavy brown earthenware plates. "I'm surprised they didn't ask for a buffet."

"Everything else will be buffet," Renie said, rummaging in her big purse. "Since you're here only for one meal, they decided they'd like it to be a sit-down event." Renie took out a package of cigarettes and lighted up.

"Coz!" Judith almost dropped a crepe. *"What are you doing?"*

"Smoking," Renie responded through a thin haze.

"You don't smoke! You haven't smoked since we went to Europe where we *had* to smoke!"

"Well, I'm smoking now." Renie sounded unnaturally calm. She exhaled a large blue puff.

Judith was flabbergasted. She herself had quit smoking almost ten years earlier, and had never quite gotten over her desire to start again. Renie, however, was another matter: She had been what Judith called a party smoker, enjoying cigarettes only when accompanied by reasonable amounts of adult beverages and loud decibels of rock 'n roll.

But there was no time to discuss her cousin's newly acquired vice. "I could use some help with these plates," Judith said, picking up two of them.

"Can't." Renie puffed some more. "It'd ruin my image."

"Very funny," Judith said, heading for the dining room. "Hold the plates steady. I don't want to screw up the presentation."

"I'm not kidding," Renie called after her. "I can't help you."

Judith stopped at the door and turned to look at her cousin. "What on earth are you talking about?"

"I'm serious." Renie had put on what Judith referred to as her cousin's boardroom face. "I can't be a waitress one minute and a graphic designer the next. Those people out there would think I was nuts."

For the first time, Judith had a glimpse of Serena Grover Jones, graphics specialist to the stars. Or whatever. While she'd watched Renie at work in her basement office, she'd never actually seen her deal with clients. Judith wasn't sure she liked her cousin in this other guise.

"Fine," said Judith, annoyed. "I'll manage without you."

The OTIOSE executives were clustered in little groups of twos and threes. Judith tried to place them, but recognized only Nadia, who was chatting with a self-possessed African-American man, and Margo, who had been cornered by a wildly gesticulating male whose thinning fair hair stood up in several places on his very round head.

On the third and fourth trips, Judith managed to carry four plates at a time. The conferees still seemed absorbed in their various conversations. Not wanting the crepes to get cold, Judith picked up a spoon and tapped a water glass.

"Luncheon is served," she announced.

No one paid any attention. Judith tapped the glass again and raised her voice. Nothing happened. Judith hesitated.

Then, at precisely twelve-thirty, Nadia Weiss glanced at her big watch. "Lunch!" she bellowed.

A stampede of conservatively dressed animals headed for the table. Judith back-pedaled out of the way just before a very large man with a completely bald head and a wizened little fellow with buck teeth almost ran right over her. A moment later, everyone was seated. No one so much as looked at Judith.

Feeling humbled, she returned to the kitchen where
Renie was lighting another cigarette. "Coz!" Judith cried.
"What *is* all this? You're smoking, you're not eating,
you've turned into a stranger!"

Renie examined her fingernails. "I'm working. You're
not used to it, that's all. Don't you behave a bit differently
with your guests than you do when you're with me or Joe
or your mother?"

"Of course," Judith replied. "But it's not just that. It's
. . . this." She jabbed a finger at Renie's cigarette. "And
. . . that." She pointed to the untouched leftovers on the
marble counter.

Renie expelled more smoke and a big sigh. "Okay, okay.
We haven't seen much of each other since the holidays
because I've been putting this presentation together and
you've been really busy with the B&B. You know my eggnog diet?"

Judith knew it well, though she was skeptical about how
it worked. Renie claimed that from Thanksgiving until New
Year's, she lived on eggnog, the richer the better. It was
one of her favorite things, and she refused to dilute it with
milk or liquor. Because she was so busy with holiday prep-
arations and annual report designs, there was barely time
to eat. Thus, she fueled herself with eggnog from morning
until night, and insisted that since she wasn't eating many
regular meals, she actually lost instead of gained weight
over the holidays.

"I flunked it," Renie declared. "The eggnog diet finally
failed me. Or I failed it."

Judith couldn't help but laugh. "Coz! You mean you
didn't lose weight this year?"

Renie shook her head. "Not only that, I gained seven
pounds. I'm wearing my fat suit."

The tailored brown wool with the faux fur collar didn't
look like a fat suit to Judith. "I can't tell you've gained
anything," she said.

"I have," Renie insisted, patting her midsection. "This

outfit is just camouflage. I should be wearing Armani for the presentation, but trying to get into my other suits is like squeezing toothpaste back into the tube. It just doesn't quite make it.''

Judith's amusement faded. "So you're starving yourself *and* smoking? That's dumb, coz.''

"Only until I lose seven pounds. Two are already gone or I wouldn't have gotten into this suit, either.'' Renie stubbed her cigarette out in a saucer. "I had to do something with my mouth and hands before I went to the post-holiday sales and bought up all the Russell Stover chocolate Santas I could find.''

Judith recalled how Renie had eaten her way through seventy-eight dollars worth of chocolate bunnies during an infamous Lenten season a few years earlier. Her cousin loved Russell Stover's chocolate almost as much as she loved eggnog.

"I certainly hope you can quit smoking when the weight's off,'' Judith said darkly. "God knows, it was tough for me to give it up.'' Her dark eyes strayed to the open cigarette pack Renie had left on the counter.

"I will,'' Renie said complacently. "I'll do it for Lent.''

Judith was about to mention the chocolate bunnies when the cousins heard a commotion in the dining room. Renie remained in place, but Judith went to see what was going on.

At first, she thought it was a food fight. Then she realized that only two people were involved: A plump, pretty woman with upswept silver hair had just thrown a handful of raddicchio salad at Margo Chang. The white wine vinegar dressing and the hand-shredded magenta leaves clung to Margo's flat chest.

"Now, now,'' said a jovial voice. Judith recognized the speaker. She had seen Frank Killegrew's picture in the newspaper often enough to realize that he was the broad-shouldered, balding man in the well-cut charcoal suit who had a slide rule next to his place setting. "We're steering

this ship on a steady course. Let's not get personal, ladies,''
Killegrew urged good-naturedly.

Margo whirled on Killegrew, who was seated two places
down the table on her left. "I'm not a lady! I'm a *person*!''

"You're a slut!'' the silver-haired woman shouted,
plump shoulders shaking with wrath.

"That's kind of mean,'' said a tall, lean man on the
woman's right. "Couldn't we all sort of simmer down?''

"Why should we?'' demanded a handsome woman who
looked as if she might be Samoan. "Don't we come on
these retreats to air our differences?''

"Now, now,'' Killegrew repeated, though not quite so
jovially, "we don't have that many differences. We're a
team, a seaworthy crew.'' The gray eyes suddenly took on
a steellike quality as he gazed at the silver-haired woman.
"Andrea, pull yourself together.'' His gaze shifted to
Margo. "You'd better clean up, what do you say?''

Margo said nothing, but got up from the table, threw her
napkin onto the floor, and marched past Judith to the
kitchen. Judith followed.

"Hi, Margo,'' Renie said, revealing only a flicker of
astonishment at the spray of salad on the other's woman's
chest. "How's it going?''

Margo glared at Renie. "Terrible! Andrea Piccoloni-
Roth is such a bitch that I can hardly stand to be in the
same room with her! See what she did?''

"Owie!'' Renie said in a sympathetic tone. "That's an
oil base. You'd better not try to spot it or it'll set and
stain.''

"I know,'' Margo replied. "I'll have to change. For now,
I just want to scrape off the garbage.'' She went to the big
enamel sink and carefully began removing the raddicchio
from her pinstripe coat dress.

"Basically, I went with your colors for the corporate
logo,'' Renie said. "I only tweaked them a little. You've
got a good eye, Margo.''

"You can't go wrong with black on red,'' Margo replied,

grimacing as she took in the damage to her outfit. "You *did* keep that concept, didn't you?" Her almond eyes pinioned Renie.

Renie, however, seemed unperturbed. "I reversed it. OTIOSE isn't a firefighting unit, it's a telecommunications company. You use a red background, you're stuck with it for everything. It's too hot, it lacks class. Black is much more versatile. You'll like it when you see it. Your basic colors were a great idea."

If Margo was taken aback, she didn't show it. "Okay, we'll see. I still think red is vivid and eye-catching. I've got Ward Haugland's vote on that. Max Agasias is in my corner, too."

Renie chuckled softly. "I didn't realize it was a democratic process."

Margo's smooth skin darkened. "It should be." With great thoroughness, she wiped her hands on a towel. "You're on in thirty minutes," she said to Renie. "I hope you're ready."

Renie smiled and inclined her head. Margo left the kitchen. Judith started putting the puff pastry on dessert plates.

"She's dangerous, coz," Judith said. "Don't these people scare you?"

"Not anymore. I don't know what went on out there in the dining room, but I'd guess that one or more of them was acting like a big brat. That's what they are—spoiled children. You have to treat them like that. Let them have their little tantrums and allow them to show off a bit and give them an occasional ego-massage. Then yank the chain. Every so often, they have to get a dose of reality. If they don't like it, I peddle my wares someplace else."

Judith didn't try to hide her admiration of Renie. "You don't worry about losing clients?"

Renie shook her head. "That's bound to happen. But the marketplace is vast these days. If I lose somebody, two more pop up. Besides, I don't intend to lose this bunch.

Unless," she added with a little laugh as she reached for another cigarette, "they die on me."

It didn't occur to Judith that Renie's little joke might not be so funny.

THREE

As SHE'D PREDICTED, Renie's presentation went well. "There were the usual glitches," Renie reported to Judith three hours later, "and of course they got to arguing among themselves. But Killegrew still has the last word, and he seemed very pleased."

Judith gave Renie's shoulder a congratulatory pat. "Good for you, coz. I was worried, especially after that scene in the dining room."

"You can tell me about that now," Renie said, opening a duffel bag and pulling out a pair of old slacks and a Georgetown University sweatshirt. "I didn't want to know about it before I went onstage. It might have distracted me."

While Renie changed, Judith recounted what she knew of the incident between Margo Chang and Andrea Piccoloni-Roth. "Mr. Killegrew took charge, and everything sort of calmed down. There was another man who intervened, a tall, lean guy with a faint drawl."

"Ward Haugland," Renie said promptly. "He's the executive vice president, remember?"

Judith did, vaguely. "The only other one who spoke up was a woman who looked as if she was Samoan. I guessed her to be Ava Aunuu."

"Exactly." Renie slipped into thigh-high boots.

"Ava's a computer whiz. Frank Killegrew raided her from one of the big computer companies about four years ago and immediately made her a vice president. She's only in her thirties, but I've been told that she's the person most responsible for bringing OTIOSE up to speed in terms of technology. Frank's strictly from the old school of engineering. That's why he keeps his trusty slide rule at his side. I don't think he's figured out how to use a computer, let alone apply the new technology to modern communications."

Judith only half-heard Renie's comments. It was a quarter after four, and she was taking final inventory of the foodstuffs she'd arranged for the rest of the weekend.

"Just before we leave, I'll set up the supper buffet," Judith said, removing the soiled apron she'd worn since arriving at the lodge. "They plan to eat at seven, right?"

"Yes." Renie reached for her cigarettes, saw Judith's disapproving glance, and began to nibble for the first time. A slice of peach, a chunk of cantaloupe, and a plump strawberry seemed to satisfy her. "Right now, they're taking a breather, then they'll gather for cocktails around six. You've got chafing dishes, so you can put the hot food out around six-thirty. Then we can head home." Renie yawned and stretched.

"Sounds good to me," Judith said. "Is there any reason why we can't have a look around now?"

Renie considered. "We probably shouldn't go upstairs where the guest rooms are located. But we could snoop around the main floor. Oh, when I carted all my presentation materials back to the car, the clouds had lifted, and you could see the mountains. It's beautiful outside."

"Great," Judith said, putting on the dark red three-quarter coat Joe had given her for Christmas. "Let's have a look before it starts getting dark."

The cousins went out through the dining room, where Judith had cleared away the luncheon debris and reset the table for the buffet supper. In the lobby, they paused to examine some of the art works more closely. There were soapstone carvings, Native American masks, and a few pieces of jade, which were kept under glass. The only painting was a large, rather abstract mountain scene hanging above the big stone fireplace.

Judith smiled wistfully when she saw the swirling signature in the lower left-hand corner. "It's a Riley Tobias," she said to Renie. "Doesn't that bring back a few memories?"

Renie, however, made a face. "Not good ones, seeing how we found him dead next door to the family cabin."

Judith inclined her head in assent. "His art lives on, though. He did some wonderful work at one time."

"Let's skip the body count," Renie said. "You and I have had our share of stiffs over the years."

It was true. But Judith rarely marveled at her encounters with premeditated death. She was married to a homicide detective; she was engaged in a business which brought together all sorts of people, with all kinds of passions and quirks; she had a natural curiosity and a penchant for the unusual; she lived in a violent world. To outsiders, her daily routine of personal and professional domesticity should have invited calm. But coping with husbands, children, relatives, in-laws, neighbors, and friends brought not only joy but conflict. And the B&B guests ran the gamut from amiable to zany. If Judith didn't exactly live life in the fast lane, she was accustomed to traveling a bumpy road with unexpected detours.

"Here's the library," Renie said, standing in the doorway of a room off the far side of the lobby. "It's nice."

Judith agreed. Unlike the rest of the lodge, the room was paneled in knotty pine. Tall, open bookcases reached almost to the ceiling. With her librarian's eye, Judith took in the collection, from some of the classics to the latest bestsellers.

There was also a combination game- and sunroom, which faced what was probably a terrace when the snow melted.

Renie showed Judith the main conference room, though it lay in darkness and they couldn't find the lightswitch.

"You get the idea," Renie said dryly. "Chairs, tables, a viewing screen, sound system, etc. Seen one big conference room, seen 'em all." She started to close the double doors.

Judith put one hand on Renie's arm and signaled with the other for her cousin to be silent. A faint rustling noise could be heard from somewhere deep within the room.

Renie's face puckered with curiosity as she stared at Judith. The rustling stopped, only to be replaced by what sounded like heavy breathing. Transfixed, the cousins waited.

At last, there was silence. Renie slowly and quietly shut the doors. "What was that?" she whispered. "People? An animal? A gas jet?"

"They don't have gas up here," Judith murmured. "It's all electric. Whatever it is, I don't think it wants to be interrupted."

"OTIOSE sex?" Renie put a hand over her mouth to stifle a giggle. "Why in the big conference room? These people have private bedrooms, for heaven's sake!"

"How would I know?" Judith retorted. "You're the one who has them all figured out."

"I'm drawing a blank this time," Renie admitted. Rapidly, she opened the doors to the three smaller conference rooms, including the one where she'd made her presentation. "Shoot," she said, espying a folder on the podium. "I must have forgotten to collect all my stuff." Hurriedly, she marched down the aisle between the folding chairs. "This isn't mine," she called back to Judith. "I guess I'll leave it here. Whoa!"

Judith straightened up from where she'd been leaning in the doorway. "What is it?"

Staring down at the open folder, Renie shook her head. "I'm not sure. It's a list, sort of like a racing form."

Judith's curiosity got the better of her. "Let's see."

Renie hesitated, then picked up the folder and brought it

to Judith. "Look. It's a bunch of names, with comments. 'Heady Amber—light on her feet; Willy-Nilly—slim, trim, ready to roll; Algonquin Annie—new to the game.' "

Judith grinned. "You're right, it's some sort of handicapping. Which one of your OTIOSE pals plays the ponies?"

"It could be any of them." Renie closed the folder. "I'll leave this on that big coffee table in the lobby. I wonder how it got up on the podium. I was the last to leave."

Having completed their exploration of the lodge's main floor, the cousins went outside. During the half-hour since Renie had finished her presentation, the clouds had begun to settle in again but there were still spectacular views. The tips of evergreens poking out of the snow looked as if they had been covered with great dollops of spun-sugar frosting. The elevation was so high and the mountains so close that the great peaks loomed above the landscape, their sharp crags pocketed with new snow.

The afternoon sun apparently had warmed to just above freezing, for there were signs of thaw. Icicles dripped under the eaves of the lodge and ice chunks flowed freely in a creek that tumbled among big boulders. The footing was just a trifle soft, forcing the cousins to walk with care.

They followed the creek, not down toward the parking area, but up a bit where they could see a small waterfall caught between two large outcroppings of snow-covered rock. The sun was setting, and the mountains' long shadows reached far across the silent world of white.

"This is when I wish I'd learned to ski," Renie said, puffing a little with exertion.

"You did try," Judith responded. "That's more than I ever did."

"I quit after I skied between some tall guy's legs," said Renie, stopping and leaning precariously against a fallen evergreen limb. "It was up here, at the pass. Gosh, that must have been thirty-five years ago."

Judith gazed upward, taking in the majesty of winter.

"Doesn't it seem weird to talk about things that happened so far back in the past? I remember hearing our mothers mention things they'd done when they were young and thinking how old they'd gotten. That was years ago, when they were a lot younger than we are now."

Setting her gloved hands on her hips, Renie glowered at Judith. "What's with you? Suddenly you're obsessed with getting old. For God's sake, coz, you're two years younger than I am, and it never even occurs to me! Besides, we took a vow. Remember?"

Judith looked puzzled. "What kind of vow? A suicide pact? Or is it the promise I asked your daughter Anne to make, that when I got old and impossible like my mother, she'd put a pillow over my face, slip a *Gone with the Wind* video in the VCR, and wait for me to peg out?"

"Jeez!" Renie threw up her hands. "No! It was a few years ago, when our kids were teenagers, and they were accusing us of not acting our age. We told them we never would, because we might get *older*, but we'd never get *old*."

"What did the kids say?"

"Who cares? That's not the point." Renie began tramping around in the snow, leaving a circular pattern of footprints between the fallen branch and the tree. "It was our *attitude* that mattered. I remember, we looked at each other as if to say, *This is a solemn promise*. Except that being solemn wasn't part of it. We would always keep our sense of humor and our slightly screwy perspective on life and uphold the old Grover mantra of finding something to laugh about even when things got really grim."

Judith knew what Renie meant. Grandma Grover, who had endured her share of tragedy, had never, ever, lost her ability to laugh. "Keep your pecker up," she'd advised. "It's always better to laugh than to cry." Such homely, even trite counsel had been the family by-word, and it worked because it was practiced rather than preached.

"I guess it's this retirement thing," Judith admitted.

"And Mike getting married. Those are big life changes. You can't just shrug them off. You have to stop and think what it all means."

"You think I never think?" Renie was still trudging awkwardly, if gamely, around in the snow. "I think plenty. I couldn't be married to Bill if I didn't think now and then. He'd shoot me. Bill thinks all the time. But what I think now is that you . . . Ooops!"

Renie slipped in the snow at the edge of the creek and tumbled into the cold, swift-flowing water. Her shoulder struck the steep bank on the other side, dislodging a great chunk of snow. Judith rushed to her cousin's aid.

"Damn!" Renie wailed. "I'm soaked!"

Judith tried to grab Renie's hands, but their heavy gloves impeded them. They grappled for several moments, with Renie finally trying to gain some purchase on a boulder in the creek. The water rushed past her knees as she struggled into an upright position. Then a piece of loose ice hurtled into her, and she fell into the opposite bank. This time a veritable cloud of snow came loose from above the creek, pelting Renie and showering chilly particles on Judith.

Renie swore, resurrecting every curse she'd learn at her seagoing father's knee. But she'd managed to get to her feet and was slogging toward Judith.

"I'm going to catch pneumonia!" she shrieked. "I'll die before I can collect ten cents from OTIOSE!"

Judith, however, barely heard her cousin's lamentations. Her eyes were fixed on the far bank which now revealed a gaping hole above the creek. Broken branches protruded from each side, like long wooden fangs. Hazily, Judith thought of the ice caves she and Renie had explored in their youth a few miles from the family cabin. But this opening wasn't quite the same. It was much smaller, no bigger than a hall closet, and not quite as high.

What made it remarkable was the body inside.

*   *   *

Judith tried not to scream. She succeeded, and just stood there while Renie collapsed against her shoulder. "Do you have any spare underwear?" Renie murmured through chattering teeth.

Judith didn't respond. She was transfixed. "Coz," she finally gulped, "I hate to mention this, but . . ." Gently, she held Renie by the shoulders and turned her around. "Look."

"Good God." Renie sagged against Judith. "I don't believe it."

The cousins stood together in silence for what seemed like a very long time. The sun was setting, the clouds were rolling in, and it was beginning to grow dark. At last, Judith and Renie moved.

"I might as well get wet, too," Judith sighed. She waded into the creek and crossed the four-foot gap to the other side.

"Dare I ask what you're doing?" Renie inquired in a bleak voice.

"Ohhh," Judith replied, sounding weary and haggard, "just the usual cursory check. Whoever these poor bones belonged to still possesses remnants of clothing."

"Don't touch anything!" Renie shouted. "Come on, get back here! I'm turning blue!"

But Judith's curiosity overwhelmed caution and consideration. "We can't just run away. Besides, I wondered if . . . ah!" She held up a wallet. "There's more, scattered around the ground." Despite her aversion to being in such close quarters with skeletal remains, Judith dug around in the snow and ice. She found a keychain, a watch, a coin purse, and a soggy notebook. Unable to convey so many small items in her big gloves, she tossed each in turn to Renie, who stuffed them into the pocket of her all-weather jacket.

Judith had kept the wallet in her own coat. After she was satisfied that there was nothing else in the little cave except the body, she recrossed the creek and stood next to Renie, shivering and shaking with cold.

"Let's not dawdle," Judith said. "I feel like a freaking popsicle."

"I'm already dead," Renie replied through stiff lips. "Can we make it back to the lodge?"

The lodge, in fact, was less than a hundred yards away. Still, it took the cousins over five minutes to get there. They arrived in a numb, half-frozen state.

The fair-haired man with the round head that Judith had noticed before lunch now stood in front of the stone fireplace which he'd apparently just lighted. He turned jerkily when the cousins entered the lobby.

"Sorry," he said, waving both hands as if to shoo Judith and Renie away. "This is a private gathering."

"It's me, Russell," Renie said in a feeble voice. "Serena Jones, remember?"

Russell whipped off his rimless glasses and peered at the cousins. He was still wearing the glen plaid suit he'd had on earlier in the day. Vaguely, Judith noticed that the suit was blemished with grease spots. "Oh! Ms. Jones!" Russell exclaimed in astonishment. "Why are you so wet?"

"It's a long story," Renie said with an inquiring glance at Judith. "We were . . ."

Judith's response was to shove Renie toward the dining room and kitchen. "First things first," she muttered. "I can barely walk or talk."

There was a washer and dryer in an alcove off the kitchen. The cousins undressed, rubbed themselves down with big towels, and proceeded to do their laundry.

"I didn't bring any extra clothes," Judith said, the feeling in her feet starting to return. The cousins were sitting in the kitchen, each wrapped in the biggest towels they could find in the supply room.

"I've got my good suit, but that's it." Renie fluffed up her short, straight chestnut hair. "We can't leave until our clothes are dry."

"We can't leave anyway until I get the food out," Judith said in frustration. "How am I going to do that wearing a towel?"

"Nobody's around. I'll help. My stint's over, and they won't see me. We could do it in the nude."

"Yeah, right, and scare the OTIOSE executives half to death." Judith grimaced. Only now that her teeth had stopped chattering and her limbs were responding was she able to face up to their awful discovery. "None of the above are the biggest problem, though."

Renie sighed. "I know. I've been trying to forget about it. Maybe we were hallucinating."

"We weren't." Judith's eyes wandered over to a telephone that was set against the far wall. "We'll have to notify the authorities."

"We could do that now," Renie said, clumsily lighting a cigarette. The raw redness in her skin was beginning to fade and she had almost stopped shivering.

Given the circumstances, Judith refrained from criticizing Renie's newly acquired habit. Indeed, she could have used a cigarette herself, not to mention a stiff drink. "Hang on for a minute," she said, gathering the towel around her and walking over to the counter where she'd put the items she'd collected from the little cave. "Maybe we can read some of this stuff."

The plain leather wallet was soaked, but Judith pried it open and saw that most of its contents were either plastic or encased in plasticene. "Here's a driver's license," she said, holding the laminated item under an overhead light above the counter. "It's in pretty good shape."

"Better shape than its owner," Renie remarked, rubbing at her feet.

"I'm afraid so . . . Ohmigod!" With a stricken expression on her oval face, Judith turned to Renie. "This belongs to Barry Albert Newcombe!"

Renie slid off the tall stool where she'd been perched. "Barry! The disappearing caterer! Holy Mother!"

With shaking fingers, Judith rifled through credit cards and other personal pieces of ID. "It's him, all right. Some of this stuff is paper, and it's unreadable, but here are his OTIOSE employee card, credit cards, gas cards, medical enrollment card—the whole lot." Still clutching the wallet and the towel, Judith leaned against the counter.

"I guess," Renie said in a subdued voice, "Barry's not missing anymore."

Judith gave a single nod. "Are you going to call the cops or shall I?"

"Why call the cops?" Renie objected, puffing frantically at her cigarette. "We need an undertaker. Barry must have gotten caught in the middle of a snowstorm and froze to death."

"We need a cop because he was a missing person," Judith persisted. "Besides," she began, then made a face, "we need a cop, because that's what you do when you find a body."

Renie winced. "I wonder if we should tell the rest of them about Barry first. I mean, he belonged to them, not us."

"We found him." Judith chewed her lower lip. "Let's call and then you can tell them about Barry."

"Me?" Renie placed a hand on her semiexposed chest and gulped. "*I* didn't find him. You did."

"You fell and knocked down that big snow pack," Judith countered.

"I didn't go crawling around inside the cave."

"This is *your* big project." Judith was beginning to get annoyed. "Where's all that bravado you were showing off an hour ago?"

"I don't know," Renie replied, gazing around the kitchen. "Where is it?"

"Oooh . . . We'll do it together. As usual." She marched over to the phone. "I'll even call the cops." She punched in 911.

A quavery voice answered on a crackling line. Judith

could barely understand the woman—she guessed it was a woman—at the other end. "I'm calling from Mountain Goat Lodge," Judith said, speaking more loudly and precisely than usual. "We've found a corpse."

"You want a Coors?" the voice said, sounding slightly stronger. "This isn't a tavern, it's the county sheriff's emergency line. Please hang up at once."

The line went dead. "She thinks I'm a nut. Now what?"

"What?" Renie, who hadn't heard the other half of the conversation, looked bewildered.

"Never mind." Irked, Judith redialed. The same voice answered. "This isn't a joke," Judith shouted. "We have a dead body at Mountain Goat Lodge."

There was a long pause. Judith figured the woman in the sheriff's office was trying to figure out if this was a genuine call. "Mountain Goat?" the woman finally said. "That's not our jurisdiction. Try the next county to the east." She hung up again.

"What *is* the next county to the east?" Judith demanded of Renie.

"I don't know what you're talking about," Renie replied in an irritated tone. "I'm going to put our wash in the dryer while you figure out how to call the cops. You're married to one, for God's sake, you ought to know."

"I'll try the forest service," Judith said, trying to put a check on her impatience. "Their number is posted by the phone. If they used to own this property, they ought to know what county it's in."

Renie's eyebrows lifted in mock amazement. "A government agency knowing where they are? Who they are? What they're . . ."

As the connection was made, Judith made a shushing gesture with her hand. But the voice on the other end was a recording. The staff was out of the office, but if the caller would care to leave a name and number . . .

Judith hung up before the message droned to its conclusion. "What staff? I'll bet there's only one person in a snow shelter next to the nearest restaurant."

She was looking for a phone book when the man that Renie had called Russell poked his head in the kitchen. "Excuse me," he began, then gasped as he saw Judith adorned in the towel. "Sorry, I didn't realize you were . . . ah . . . um . . ."

"Russell?" Judith made a reassuring gesture with her free hand. "You work for the phone company. Do you know where I can find a phone book?"

The ordinary question seemed to calm Russell. "Of course. There's one in the . . . er . . . surely it would be . . . um . . . have you looked . . . ah . . . I've no idea." His face began to turn a deep red.

Judith put a hand to her shoulder-length silver-streaked hair and rubbed furiously at her scalp. "Okay, okay. Tell me this—how can I reach the local sheriff?"

Russell's eyebrows rose above his rimless glasses. "You dial 911, just as you would in the city."

Judith shook her head. "It doesn't work that way. Maybe the lines are crossed. Have you got another suggestion?"

"Ohhh . . ." Russell seemed at an utter loss. "I'm R&D, not operations. Really, I'm not what you'd call . . . practical."

Judith would have held her head with both hands if the effort wouldn't have caused her to drop the towel. "R&D? What's that? I know R&B is rhythm and blues, but . . ."

"Research and development." Renie was back in the kitchen. "Russell Craven is vice president–R&D." She nodded at Russell. "Hi again. What county are we in?"

"County?" Russell's thin fair hair seemed to twitch. "Well, I really couldn't say . . . We *are* in one, though . . . I mean, we have to be, don't we? Counties are like that, sort of next to each other and all . . . ah . . . Do you ladies need some clothing?"

Renie gave Russell a toothy grin. "Now there's a helpful

idea, Russell. We wouldn't mind borrowing a few items for just a bit. Let me see . . .'' Renie glanced at Judith. ''How about asking Ava and . . .'' She paused, gazing down at her own towel-wrapped figure. ''. . . Nadia. I think.''

''Yes. Yes.'' Russell nodded enthusiastically. ''Ava and Nadia. Shall I . . . ?'' He gestured at the door.

''You shall. And we thank you.'' Renie cocked her head.

Russell started out the door, then turned back. ''Oh! This business about the sheriff . . . is it urgent?''

''It'll keep,'' Renie replied dryly.

Russell left. Five minutes later, Ava Aunuu was in the kitchen, hand-tooled leather suitcase in hand. ''What happened?'' she asked, evincing what Judith took for actual concern.

Renie introduced Judith to the woman who served as OTIOSE's vice president–information technology services. The long-winded title didn't mean much to Judith, but she recalled that Ava was some kind of computer genius.

''We fell in the creek,'' Renie explained. ''You and my cousin are about the same size, so when Russell Craven suggested we borrow some clothes, I thought of you.''

''Sure,'' Ava said, undoing the straps and flipping the locks on her suitcase. ''I brought extra everything along. There's underwear, too. I'm not really into clothes, but you never know what can happen on one of these retreats.'' Her brown eyes danced with what might have been amusement—or something less pleasant.

Judith picked up the first items she saw. A high-necked blue sweater and navy slacks, almost exactly like the dark green outfit Ava was wearing. ''This'll be great. Are you sure . . . ?'' She gave Ava a questioning look.

''Well . . .'' Ava reached into the suitcase and a removed a red crewneck sweater and matching slacks. ''How about these? I'll bet red's your color.''

''It is.'' Judith smiled. ''Thanks a lot.''

''Don't worry about returning them right away.'' Ava's strong, handsome features seemed to radiate good will.

"I'll probably be seeing your cousin at corporate headquarters in a week or two."

Judith grabbed the garments and headed for the laundry room to dress. She had just slipped into her own boots when Renie joined her.

"Nadia's stuff is going to be a squeeze," Renie said, shaking out a gray cashmere sweater that had been carefully wrapped in tissue paper. "But Margo's too thin and Andrea's too plump. It was Nadia or nobody, unless I wanted to wear one of Russell Craven's soup-stained suits."

"Let's go back," Judith said abruptly.

"Back? Back where?" Renie's head poked through the sweater's mock turtleneck. "We can't go home until you've set up the buffet."

Judith was searching the drawers in the laundry room. "I know, plus we have to wait at least a half-hour for our clothes to dry. Ah, here's a flashlight."

Renie stared at Judith. "What are we doing?"

"We're going back to the cave." Judith was now at the linen closet. She tossed a blanket at Renie.

"Come on!" Renie cried. "It's almost dark! What's the point?"

Judith was covering herself in a striped Hudson Bay blanket. "Are you coming or not?"

"Not." Renie planted both feet firmly on the floor.

"Okay." Judith swept out into the kitchen, the blanket trailing behind her.

It wasn't quite dark, but it was very cold and a few drops of snow were drifting down. The wind had picked up, blowing from the north. Judith had to hold up the pants legs of Ava's slacks while trying to keep the blanket wrapped around her. She didn't try to cross the creek this time, but squatted on the opposite bank and turned on the flashlight.

"Has he moved?" The voice belonged to Renie, who had crept up behind Judith.

Judith gave a little start. "He's still there." She handed

the flashlight to Renie. "Look. See if you see what I thought I saw."

Renie, who had only glimpsed the skeletal remains of the dead man, steeled herself. "I see a really convincing Halloween costume. Except this is January, and it's not very funny." She shuddered, then tried to give the flashlight back to Judith.

Judith rebuffed Renie. "Look again."

Sighing, Renie complied. "I see what's left of his clothes—jacket, pants, shirt, whatever. It's hard to tell. Oh—he's got a watch on his left wrist." Starting to shiver again, Renie had trouble keeping the flashlight from wavering. "There's a leather thong around his neck, but I don't see any medal or jewelry or decoration."

"That's not what it's for," Judith said in a hollow voice.

As the snow began to fall harder, Renie steadied the flashlight with both hands. "Then it must be part of whatever he was wearing."

Judith took the flashlight from Renie. "No. I saw it from the back when I was in the cave earlier. It hasn't anything to do with apparel. It looks as if it's been twisted around something at the base of the neck. I believe you call it a garrote." She stood up and switched off the flashlight. "Barry didn't freeze to death, coz. He was murdered."

FOUR

"IT WAS ONE of those things you see, but you don't take in," Judith explained as the cousins trudged back to the lodge. "It was such a shock finding the body in the first place, and we were so wet and cold that the garrote didn't really register until much later, probably when Ava opened her leather suitcase. But it had been niggling at me all along."

"Incredible," Renie murmured. "Barry must have been murdered a year ago this very weekend." She stopped suddenly, a stricken expression on her face. "Oh, God—he may have been murdered by one of them!" Her brown eyes were riveted on the lodge.

"You're right," Judith said in wonder. "Let's hurry, coz. We've got to finish up and get the hell out of here."

They were met at the door by the African-American man who had exchanged his pinstripe suit for a turtle-neck sweater and corduroy pants. "I'd appreciate it," he said in a grave, concise voice, "if you'd tell me what's going on. It's not safe to have outsiders wandering around in the snow. OTIOSE isn't legally covered for such contingencies."

"Coz," Renie said, sounding tired, "meet Eugene Jarman, Junior, vice president–legal, as if you couldn't guess." She offered the attorney a small smile. "Gene, you honestly don't want to know."

Gene Jarman quietly closed the doors behind the cousins. Frank Killegrew and Ward Haugland were both in the lobby, wearing worried expressions and virtually matching outfits of plaid flannel shirts, tan khaki pants, and brown suspenders. Beyond them, Russell Craven huddled by the fire, his face averted.

"I'm afraid it's my business to know," Gene responded, his blunt features solemn. He was average height, but the self-assured way he carried himself made him seem much taller. "Let's sit down and discuss this."

Judith and Renie looked at each other. "Okay," said Renie, removing her blanket and tossing it over one arm. "Has anybody unlocked the liquor cabinet? This isn't going to be pretty."

"Liquor," Ward Haugland echoed, his lanky form twisting around. "There must be liquor somewhere."

Judith had spotted what might have been a wet bar in the dining room. "I'll check," she said. "Give me a hand, coz."

Five minutes later, the cousins had lined up bottles, glasses, mixer, and a bucket of ice on the big polished burl coffee table in the lobby. By then, other members of the OTIOSE executive corps were streaming in. It appeared that their master had spoken.

"Who's missing?" Killegrew asked, not bothering to look around. Judith guessed that others did that for him.

In this case, the task was performed by Ward Haugland, as befitted his executive vice president's status. "Ava and Leon," Ward said in his faint drawl. "They'll be here any minute, Frank. That dinky elevator can't hold but four or five people at a time."

"Persons!" snapped Margo Chang. "How often do I have to remind you *persons* that we're not just *people*?"

Judith nudged Renie. "Who's the big bald guy who

looks like number nine on the chart showing the Ten Steps From Ape to Man?''

"Max Agasias, vice president–marketing," Renie whispered. "He's sharper than he looks."

"I hope so. He practically mowed me down when lunch was served." Judith glanced at the elevator in the corner of the lobby which was discharging Ava Aunuu and the small, wizened man with buck teeth who Judith also remembered from the midday stampede.

"Leon Mooney," Renie murmured, "vice president and comptroller."

Judith's brain raced. Not only was she trying to put names to faces, but she couldn't keep from trying to figure out if one of the ten people—or *persons*—who congregated in the lobby looked like a murderer. Maybe they all did; certainly each of them seemed to have the killer instinct.

"Drink 'em if you got 'em," Frank Killegrew said, his usual jocular manner tempered by a hint of anxiety. "I believe Ms. Jones has some news for us."

"I thought she'd already made her presentation," Andrea Piccoloni-Roth said in a waspish tone. "And why is she wearing Nadia's castoffs?"

"They're not castoffs," Nadia declared with a malevolent look for Andrea. "Are you mocking me because I don't make as much money as you do?"

"Now, now," said Killegrew. "Let's get settled and hear what Ms. Jones has to say."

Margo, who had just accepted a very dry martini from Judith, stared at Renie. "You haven't reneged on my color scheme, have you?"

"*Your* color scheme!" Andrea exploded. "No wonder I didn't much like it!"

"It beats the crap out of the purple and pink you wanted, Andrea," growled Max Agasias, the simianlike marketing head. "What the hell do you think we are, a bunch of fruity florists?"

"It wasn't purple and pink, you idiot," Andrea retorted. "It was purple and *gold*. They're regal colors, fit for kings and queens."

"Speaking of queens," Ava began, "what do you suppose happened to . . . ?"

But Killegrew cut her off. He was standing in front of the fireplace, Scotch and soda in hand, looking less like a corporate CEO and more like a building contractor in the casual attire that tended to show off his impressive girth.

"As you know, the purpose of this retreat is to get away from the workplace, to put some distance between ourselves and what goes on in each of our shops, to reflect, to recreate, to . . ." He paused and leaned toward Margo who was sitting on a leather ottoman by the hearth. She whispered something to him and he resumed speaking. "To revitalize ourselves. Given those parameters and the current, often chaotic state of the industry, we . . ."

"It's an old speech," Renie said behind her hand. "Margo writes all of his public utterances. I actually got stuck listening to one last Memorial Day. You'd have thought Frank won the Korean War all by himself."

". . . feel compelled to do some soul-searching. But," he added, lowering his voice and apparently ad-libbing, "we can't accomplish much if we've got a bunch of distractions. The last hour or two should have been a time to relax in peace and quiet. I mean, you can't play golf in the snow." He paused to finger his belt buckle as dutiful laughter rose from members of the audience. "Anyway, some things have been going on around here that have gotten me a little frazzled. I want to keep the ship on course. Before we settle in for the rest of the weekend, I'd like an explanation. I'm sure it's nothing to worry about, but we're here at Mountain Goat Lodge because we don't want to get this train sidetracked. The moonshot's got to land on target, right?" The smile he gave Renie went no farther than his nose. "Ms. Jones, you're on."

Renie, who looked as if she'd been stuffed into Nadia's

sweater and slacks, moved in front of the fireplace. She hesitated, staring down at the flagstone hearth, then lifted her head and let her eyes take in the entire gathering.

"We found Barry Newcombe this afternoon. He'd been murdered. Thank you very much." Renie stepped aside and lit up a cigarette.

Frank Killegrew gasped; Nadia Weiss screamed; Max Agasias swore; Andrea Piccoloni-Roth sagged in her chair; Margo Chang protested Renie's smoking; Russell Craven asked, "Who's Barry Newcombe?"

"I don't get it," Ward Haugland said, scratching his head. "This sounds screwy."

"I think," Gene Jarman said carefully, "we need to have this situation clarified. Ms. Jones?"

Renie related how she and Judith had accidentally uncovered the ice cave by the creek. Judith, in turn, told how she had seen the garrote around the skeleton's neck. Some of her listeners reacted with skepticism.

"That's crazy," asserted Ward Haugland. "It must have been a joke. Somebody did that after poor Barry died."

"Hikers, probably," said Killegrew, though his fingers shook as he picked up his slide rule. "They can be strange. A lot of them are ex-hippies."

"Excuse me," put in Margo. "I don't think that makes sense, Frank. Who would find a body and make a joke out of it? Why didn't they call in a forest ranger? No, I'm afraid Ms. Jones's cousin is right."

"Poor Barry!" Andrea was still reeling in her chair. "He was so sweet! Do you remember the duck pate he left for us? It was divine."

"I'll take your word for it," Margo snapped. "You ate all of it."

"Did I ever meet Barry Newcombe?" Russell Craven asked in a bewildered voice.

Killegrew intervened before the two women could go at it again. "Let's not get derailed," he urged. "We don't want to go off on a sideline and miss the depot."

"What the hell happened?" Max demanded from his place behind a big wood and leather sofa. "Barry took off here around two in the afternoon. Did somebody jump him outside?"

"He didn't take the van." The speaker, who had been silent until now, was the gnarled little man Renie had identified as Leon Mooney.

All eyes turned to the vice president and comptroller. "That's true," said Ava. "Or if he did, he came back and then disappeared."

"We thought he'd walked to the store at the summit," Ward said. "It was a mighty funny thing to do, but Barry was a great walker."

A dozen questions flashed through Judith's mind, but it wasn't her place to ask them. Renie, however, possessed the corporate cachet. "How long was it before you realized he was missing?"

Glances were exchanged; several people shrugged. "A couple of hours?" Max finally offered.

"It was at dinner," Andrea said. "Actually, it was before dinner. We expected Barry to serve as bartender. When he didn't show up, Gene stood in for him."

Gene Jarman uttered a self-deprecating laugh. "I'd tended bar while I worked my way through Stanford Law School." He lifted one shoulder in a dismissive gesture, as if to suggest that those degrading days were far, far behind him.

Judith couldn't resist. "What did you do when Barry never showed?"

The others looked at her in mild astonishment. "We carried on," Margo said. "We figured he'd . . . had one of his whims."

"All that's behind us," Killegrew declared before Judith could speak again. "Let's get this tugboat hooked up to the barge. The question is, what do we do now?" His glance lighted on Gene Jarman.

Gene tugged at one earlobe. "The authorities must be notified." He gazed at Judith and Renie. "Or has that already been done?"

"We tried," Renie said. "There seems to be some confusion over jurisdiction."

"Really?" Gene gave a slight nod. "That's possible. This is something of a borderline location."

"Which district?" asked Ward Haugland. "Do we have supporters in the legislature from around here?"

"Screw the legislature," Max Agasias snarled. "It's the rate commission we care about. What the hell have our lobbyists been doing lately anyway? They're down there in the capital drinking high-priced booze out of some lowdown hooker's spike-heeled shoes."

"Cut the sexist remarks," Margo demanded in a shrill voice. "At least one of our lobbyists is a woman."

"So?" Max sneered at Margo. "If you ask me, she'd like to get in the sack with some cute little . . ."

"Now, now," reprimanded Killegrew, "let's keep our plane in its landing pattern. We'll skip all these local folks. I mean, persons. I'm calling the chief of police back in the city."

"Good idea," said Ward.

"You're damned right," agreed Max.

"Could somebody describe Barry Newcombe?" asked Russell.

"Call the chief," Killegrew ordered Nadia. "Explain everything. He'll know what we ought to do."

Judith knew what she had to do. It was after six, and she had to set up the buffet. Though no one heard her, she excused herself and headed for the kitchen. Renie followed.

"It serves the chief right," Judith said, getting a big ham out of the refrigerator. "He ought to have to put up with these self-centered morons. Joe says that under all that public bonhomie the chief is a stuffed shirt."

"I'll carve the turkey breast," Renie volunteered. "I

gather you've had enough of the OTIOSE crowd.''

"You bet. I don't see how you can work with people—
or should I say persons?—like them.''

"You get used to it. They're all alike.'' Renie selected
a knife from the wooden cutlery holder. "The problem is
that they get into these executive slots and they become
distanced from reality. They're pampered, protected—and
isolated. The same thing happens in government. They're
all out of touch.''

"So's the chief, according to Joe.'' Judith piled ham onto
a platter. "I suspect this crew is going to get a dose of
reality when they start investigating Barry Newcombe's
murder.''

"It'll serve them right, too,'' said Renie, aggressively
slicing the turkey. She suddenly paused. "As long as it
doesn't screw up their acceptance of my presentation.''

Judith shot her cousin a baleful glance. "Stop it. You
sound like one of them.''

"I'm not,'' Renie asserted. "I'm just a servile jobber
who wants to suck at the teat of corporate excess.''

Twenty minutes later, the cousins had the buffet set up.
The chafing dishes were lighted, the plates and utensils
were stacked, and the makeshift sideboard looked fit for a
king. Or a queen, or maybe even ten spoiled corporate executives.

In the laundry area, they found that their clothes were
dry. Hastily changing, Judith and Renie felt a huge sense
of relief as they put on their own garments.

"Let's go,'' Renie said. "We'll leave Ava and Nadia's
stuff on an empty table in the dining room where they can't
miss it. I'm not sure I want to talk to any of these people
again for a while.''

Judith had found a rear exit off the supply room. Feeling
liberated, the cousins headed through the door and into the
January night.

During the hour or more that they'd spent inside the
lodge, the snow had been falling steadily and heavily. The

wind from the north had now reached a high velocity. The blinding flakes whirled and swirled around the lodge, obliterating everything except the unsteady hands the cousins held before their faces to ward off the stinging cold.

"Jeez!" Renie cried. "It's a damned blizzard! I can't drive in this!"

"I can't either," Judith admitted in a stunned voice. "What shall we do?"

Renie stood stock-still, with the wind and snow blowing straight into her face. "We haven't got much choice. We're stuck, at least until the storm blows over and the roads get plowed. Let's go back inside before we end up like Barry."

"Don't say that," Judith cautioned. "The weather didn't kill him." She swallowed hard. "I've got a very ugly feeling that somebody inside that lodge that we are about to reenter was the person—yes, *person*—who killed Barry Newcombe."

"You sure know how to terrify a person," Renie retorted.

Judith gestured toward the lodge. "These people are risk takers, right?"

"Right. In one way or another." Renie kept her head down; her voice came out muffled.

"It required a big risk to kill Barry with the others around," Judith continued. "Whoever did it must have realized a storm was coming, but did you notice all those branches at the front of the little cave? I think the killer put them there to hide the body, just in case. Besides, when the snow melted—assuming there's ever a big thaw at this elevation—the branches would still provide some concealment. But then, the snow finally broke them down, probably when you fell into the bank."

"Lucky me," Renie sighed. "I'm a regular walkin', talkin' corpse detector."

"Lucky us," Judith echoed. "It isn't like it's the first time." Feeling bleak and bleary eyed, she entered the lodge.

They explained their forestalled departure plight to Nadia Weiss, who, surprisingly, was not without sympathy. "There are plenty of vacant rooms," she said. "I've already moved Frank once. Naturally, he wanted a corner room. But Mountain Goat Lodge can accommodate two hundred guests. We'll find you something in the main wing on the second floor, where the rest of us are staying."

Judith and Renie didn't find the idea particularly reassuring. But again, there wasn't much choice. "We'll share," Renie blurted. "We wouldn't want to mess up two rooms," she added hastily.

The arrangement was fine with Nadia. She led the cousins to the elevator via a back corridor. While waiting for the car to arrive, Judith overheard Killegrew expostulating on the deficiencies of the municipal police department.

"Lack of personal contact . . . city employees, not used to the bottom line . . . boondoggles . . . civil service . . . political pork barrel . . . favoritism . . ." The litany of complaints went on.

The three women got into the elevator. "Did you talk to the police chief?" Judith asked innocently.

Nadia leaned her slight frame against the upholstered padding of the elevator. "No! It's after six, he'd gone home. Frank had me call him there, but I reached his answering machine. We haven't heard back yet."

"Ah." Judith didn't know what else to say. She recalled how often Joe had tried to see the chief when he and his partner, Woody Price, were working a case. Unless the investigation was high profile, the chief usually shunted Joe and Woody off to his deputy or some other underling.

"This whole thing is very peculiar," Nadia said as they got out on the second floor. "I cannot—I simply *cannot*—imagine anything as seedy as murder being linked to OTIOSE. Whatever will our board of directors think? And our shareholders will be up in arms! This is simply terrible!"

"It's rough, all right," Renie agreed.

"It had to be some lunatic," Nadia declared. "Someone

wandering around the mountains. I've heard there are all sorts of strange types who live in the forest. Hermits, and other kinds of eccentrics. They often kill people. That's what must have happened to Barry.''

They had reached a door at the far end of the hall. Nadia sorted through a large key ring. ''Two-thirty-nine,'' she said under her breath. ''Here we are.''

There were twin beds, a small fireplace, a bathroom, and a wet bar. There were also two hooded bathrobes hanging on wooden pegs. Matching terrycloth slippers sat side by side on the polished hardwood floor. Judith and Renie both sighed with relief.

''Nice,'' Renie remarked. ''Thanks, Nadia. We're sorry to impose, but that storm out there is really something.''

Nadia's smile was tense. ''It should blow out in a few hours. That's what happened last year when we were at Mountain Goat.''

''You had a storm just like this one?'' Judith asked, setting her purse down on one of the twin beds.

''Oh, yes,'' Nadia replied. ''It was terrible. We weren't sure if we could get out by Monday afternoon. But it finally broke that morning, and we were able to leave.''

''Who drove?'' Renie had uttered the question from the fireplace where she was putting a match to the pile of wood and kindling.

''I did,'' Nadia replied. ''Barry had driven us up here, but when he . . . disappeared, it was up to me to get us back to the city. Fortunately, we were able to chain up at the summit.''

Judith sat down on the bed with its counterpane woven in a bright Native American design. ''Nadia, weren't you worried about what had happened to Barry?''

Nadia hung her head and clasped her hands. ''Not terribly,'' she replied in a sheepish tone. ''You see, Barry was gay. He was given to . . . following his special star.'' She paused, her thin face very earnest. ''It had happened before. Two summers ago at the company picnic, Barry was in charge of the food. About halfway through, he suddenly disappeared. He'd met someone on the adjacent tennis courts. Then at the Christmas party a year ago, he went off with Santa Claus.''

''I see.'' Judith took a deep breath. ''So you thought— what? That he'd met someone outside of the lodge or at the summit or down in the next town—or what?''

''Any of those things.'' Nadia now appeared to be on surer ground. ''Even here at the lodge, there are cross-country skiers who pass through. Not to mention snow-mobilers and hikers. It may seem isolated, but it really isn't, not when the weather is decent.''

''Except that you had a big storm last January,'' Judith pointed out. ''That would have cut down on the sports enthusiasts.''

''Y-e-s,'' Nadia said slowly. ''I suppose it did.'' She glanced around the room, her practiced mind taking inventory. ''I hope this will do. Everything seems to be in order. Now I should get back downstairs. I must see what's happening with Frank and the police chief.''

Judith locked the door behind Nadia and slid the deadbolt. ''We ought to be safe in here,'' she said, then gritted her teeth as Renie lighted yet another cigarette. ''Coz— must you? This is a small room, and it's too cold to open a window.''

Renie waved the cigarette. ''It's either this or we raid the buffet.''

Judith sniffed at the trail of smoke. ''That's not a bad idea. It just dawned on me that I'm starved. I haven't eaten since breakfast.''

''Then let's forage after they've finished. Meanwhile, we can check out the honor bar.'' She nodded at the compartment built between the room's two small windows.

The little refrigerator contained soda pop, sample-sized bottles of liquor, and water, both plain and flavored. There were also packets of various snack foods. The cousins

opened a bag of chips and a bag of pretzels before making
themselves a drink.

Sitting in a wooden chair with a comfortable padded
back and seat, Judith gazed around the room. "There's no
TV. Or radio. How are we going to hear about what's happening with the weather?"

Renie also studied their surroundings. "No phone, either.
I guess this is one of those places where you're supposed
to get back to nature or in touch with yourself or some
damned thing. Bill and I stayed at a lodge like this in
Oregon a few years ago. After an hour and a half, we were
ready to kill each other."

Judith got up and went to one of the windows. "All we
can do is watch what's happening outside. Once the storm
dies down, I suppose we could use the phone in the kitchen
to check on highway conditions."

Renie uttered a terse laugh. "Assuming we can reach the
right part of the state and don't end up with a report on the
ocean beaches."

"I've got a feeling that this blizzard is going to last well
into the night," Judith said, still peering through one of the
window's six small panes that were trimmed in bright red.
"I vaguely recall hearing a weather report at home yesterday that said we might get some snow in the city by Sunday, but of course I didn't worry about it because . . ." She
stopped, cupping her hands around her eyes. "What in . . . ?
I just saw a light."

Renie, who had been reclining on one of the twin beds,
went to the other window. "Where? I don't see anything."

"It's gone. Which way are we facing?"

Renie considered. "We're at the end of the hall, which
runs the width of the lodge. I'd guess that we're looking
out from the east, opposite from the parking lot and the
creek."

"That makes sense. The wind is from the north, and it's
blowing the snow right by us." Judith remained at the win-

dow, but the light didn't reappear. "Did you say there was a caretaker?"

Renie had returned to the bed. "Right, but he's at least half a mile away. I doubt he'd come out in this storm. Besides, he's under orders to keep away. The OTIOSE gang is very set on privacy."

"Where'd the staff go?" Judith asked, finally deserting her post and sitting down again.

"Home?" Renie gave a little shrug. "I understand some of them usually sleep over, up in dormer rooms on the third floor. But during the conference, they were all sent away. It *is* a three-day weekend, and they were probably delighted to have the time off."

Judith finished her bag of chips and sipped at her Scotch; Renie ate three pretzels, lighted another cigarette, and drank her bourbon. The fire, which Judith had lighted a few minutes earlier, burned in the small grate. They could hear the wind howl in the chimney, causing the flames to waver and dance.

"I should have mentioned to Nadia that we left her clothes—and Ava's—in the dining room," Renie said, breaking the sudden silence between them.

"They'll find the stuff," Judith replied, her eyes still on the storm that raged outside the window. She sat up straight and looked at Renie. "The folder was gone."

"Folder?" Renie was momentarily puzzled. "Oh, the one I found on the podium." She nodded once. "You're right. Somebody had picked it up off the coffee table in the lobby where we set up the bar."

Judith's high forehead was puckered in a frown. "I thought Ava acted kind of odd about which clothes she wanted to lend me."

"Maybe. So what? The blue outfit might be her favorite."

"Then why wasn't she wearing it?"

"I don't know," Renie replied, slightly impatient. "What difference does it make?"

Judith didn't reply immediately. "Would you know how to fashion a garrote?" she asked after another brief silence.

"I think I could learn," Renie said darkly. "Like about now. Forget it, coz. This isn't our problem."

"If you knew how, I don't imagine it would take much strength."

"I hope not. I'm feeling a little weak." Renie glowered at her cousin.

"But you need a stick or something, don't you? Where was the stick? I didn't see anything like that."

"If I had a stick, I know where I'd put it," Renie said between clenched teeth.

"What do you know about Barry Newcombe? Did you ever meet him?"

"Good God." Renie rubbed at one eye. "You're hopeless." She tossed her cigarette butt into the fireplace and regarded Judith with an indulgent expression. "Okay, I'll play the game if only because we can't amuse ourselves by watching *Crusader Rabbit* reruns on TV. Yes, I met Barry a couple of times, a year ago last December, when I got called in on the annual report. He seemed very nice, quite efficient, and otherwise utterly unremarkable. I also talked to him on the phone."

"Who did he work for?" Judith asked, adding more ice to her glass.

"He was assigned to Margo in p.r. then, as a staff assistant. But I think he'd been in human resources before that."

"Andrea Piccoloni-Roth?" Judith was finally beginning to put titles and departments with faces and names.

"That's right. But I honestly don't know much more about him," Renie admitted. "It appears that he didn't intend to make a career out of working at OTIOSE, or he wouldn't have started up the catering business on the side."

Judith grew thoughtful. "How old was he?"

"Mid-twenties, blond, medium height, nice-looking. I didn't know until today that he was gay, but then I wouldn't have given it a thought if I had," Renie said, slipping one more pretzel out of the little paper sack. "Quite a few of the guys who are employed at lower management levels in corporations are gay."

"So Barry wasn't in a power position?" Judith asked as the wind rattled the windows.

Renie ruffled her short hair. "Well—that depends. The salaries at that level aren't much, but somehow staff assistants, at least at OTIOSE, have some kind of abstruse clout. They answer the phones, they run personal errands for the bosses, they handle correspondence, they know all the gossip. They can be a great source of information, which means their importance goes far beyond their lowly titles and puny paychecks."

"Interesting," Judith murmured. "Maybe that's what got Barry killed."

Renie shuddered. "I hope not. I kind of like Nadia's hermit theory."

"It's comforting," Judith allowed, then turned a dour face to Renie. "The only problem is, I don't believe it."

FIVE

A FEW MINUTES before eight, the cousins went downstairs to get some food. They had snooped around on
the second floor until they found a staircase that led
from the west end of the main corridor to a small hallway off the laundry room and the rear entrance. A quick
peek into the dining room told them that the conferees
had finished eating. Judging from the hum of conversation, they had regrouped in the lobby.

"Who tidied up?" Judith inquired, noting that the big
round table had been cleared away and the sideboard
swept clean.

"Nadia, I suppose," Renie replied, opening the refrigerator. "Maybe someone was kind enough to help
her."

The cousins loaded plates with ham and turkey sandwiches, raw vegetables, and what was left of the potato
salad Judith had made from Gertrude's legendary recipe.
They were about to return upstairs when Ward Haugland
entered the kitchen.

"You're still here, huh?" His smile was off-center
and self-conscious. "I guess you can't get out in this
storm."

"That's right," Renie replied. "We're marooned. I
don't suppose you've heard a weather forecast?"

Ward shook his head. "Nope. There's no radio or TV at Mountain Goat. That's one of the reasons we pick this place for the retreats. Frank doesn't want any pleasurecraft bobbing around our corporate ship of state. Or something like that," he added with an uncertain frown.

Judith held up a hand, feeling like a grade-school pupil. "Did you ever get hold of the police chief?"

Ward winced. "Not yet. The deputy chief called but Frank won't deal with him. He wants to go straight to the top."

Judith bit her cheeks to keep from smiling. "I see. Well, good luck. With a three-day weekend at hand, I suspect the chief has gone off to ski in Canada. He usually does, during the winter."

Ward's pale blue eyes widened. "You know the chief?"

Embarrassed, Judith coughed. "Ah—sort of. It's a complicated story." It wasn't, of course, but Judith didn't think it was a good idea to mention that her husband was a homicide detective. "We've . . . um . . . crossed paths from time to time."

"Oh." Ward seemed satisfied. "I'm sorry you folks got stranded up here. I hope you realize that our meetings are real confidential." His off-center smile was apologetic.

Renie waved a hand. "Sure, Ward, I know how these retreats work. We'll stay in our little tiny room and amuse ourselves by watching each other's faces sag with age."

Ward didn't seem to see the humor in Renie's remark. His long bony fingers fiddled with the belt loops on his khaki pants. "I think there's a game room in the basement. You know—billiards, ping-pong, chess."

"What fun." Again, Renie's irony was lost on OTIOSE's executive vice president.

Judith, however, decided to take advantage of Ward's hesitation. "What do you remember about Barry's disappearance last year, Mr. Haugland?"

Ward, who had started for the refrigerator, paused in midstep. "Barry? Shoot, I don't recollect much about it.

He took off and never came back. The only thing I remember was the avocado dip.''

Judith frowned. "What about it?'

"That's what he went out for," Ward explained, opening the refrigerator. "We had all these chips, and he'd made a couple of special dips. But Margo or Max or somebody got a hankering for avocados. Barry volunteered to get some, so he took off and we never saw him again." Ward removed what was left of the ham from the fridge. "Personally, I'm not much for avocados. They're too danged squishy."

As Ward began to carve the ham, Judith leaned against the counter. "Weren't you shocked when you got back to the city and discovered he'd never shown up at all?"

Ward drew back, looking puzzled. "Well . . . not really. I mean, people can be kind of odd. Anyway, he didn't work for me."

Which, Judith thought with a pang, apparently made Barry a nonentity. "Now that Barry's body has been found," Judith began, carefully phrasing her words, "have you thought about why he was killed?"

Ward was pulling out various drawers. "Nope. It sounds kind of fishy to me." He extracted a knife and fork, then picked up his plate of ham. "I mean, we don't know for sure that he *was* killed. And," he added, heading toward the exit with his long, awkward strides, "we don't even know if it's Barry."

On that jarring note, Ward Haugland left the kitchen.

"You know," Judith sighed, "he's right. We won't know until a positive ID is made by the police."

"Shoot." Renie picked at the ham that Ward had left on the counter. "Are you saying Barry killed somebody else and made it look as if he was the victim?"

"It's been known to happen." Judith poured out a glass of cold apple cider. "If I had to guess —and you know I will— I'd say that's not the case. How many other people would have been wandering around Mountain Goat Lodge that Friday afternoon? I'm assuming the place was as dead—excuse the expression—then as it is now. It'd be a real stretch to have somebody show up that Barry wanted to murder.''

"Unless it was prearranged," Renie noted.

Judith reflected briefly. "No, I don't think so. If you were Barry, and there was someone you wanted to get out of the way, would you have that person drive to Mountain Goat Lodge, and then do him or her in less than a hundred yards from where your company's top executives were waiting for their avocado dip? I don't think so.''

"You have a point," Renie allowed, "though whoever killed Barry did just that.''

"I know," Judith said quietly. "As I mentioned earlier, that's what bothers me most.''

Before the cousins returned to their room, they each called home to let their loved ones know they were marooned. Bill, as usual, was terse on the phone because he firmly believed the instrument was a satanic tool. Joe was somewhat more talkative, if subdued.

"I cuffed a twelve-year-old today," he said after Judith told him about the storm. "He'd shot two other kids at a strip mall. Can you believe it?''

"Are the other kids dead?" Judith asked, lacing her voice with sympathy for Joe, the perp, and the victims.

"No, they'll probably make it," Joe replied. "But it still makes me sick. This kid—Jamaal—isn't a bad kid, really. At least I don't think he is. He just wants to belong. But it's been rough getting him to open up. He doesn't trust adults, especially not middle-aged white males.''

"Why don't you let Woody interrogate him?" Judith asked, referring to Joe's long-time partner, who was black.

"Because I'm the primary." Joe said. "And frankly, Woody can be pretty hard on black kids who get themselves in trouble. Sometimes it's almost like he takes it personally. Woody made it, and he can't understand why kids with the same ethnic background don't bother to try.''

"Woody was solid middle class,'' Judith pointed out. "I'll bet most of the gang members haven't had that advantage.''

"You're right,'' Joe agreed, "but tell that to Woody. He says that's all the more reason less fortunate black kids should try even harder.''

Judith could picture Woodrow Wilson Price, with his serious brown eyes and thick walrus mustache, lecturing disadvantaged youth. He would be solemn, eloquent, and somewhat pedantic. It was dubious that he'd make even the slightest dent on most of the bad apples Joe had described.

"By the way,'' Judith said, nervously clearing her throat, "you may hear something about an . . . incident at the lodge.''

"An incident?'' Joe sounded on guard.

"Yes. Ah . . . well . . . it seems that a body was discovered this afternoon not far from the parking lot. Um . . . it's not a *new* body, it's an *old* body. That is, it's . . . er . . . been dead for a long time. The OTIOSE president and CEO has been trying to get hold of the chief.''

Judith thought she heard Joe say an extremely naughty word under his breath. "The chief? *Our* chief?''

"Yes. Mr. Killegrew—the CEO—will only deal with his vis-à-vis.''

"Screw Mr. Killegrew,'' Joe growled. "The chief's in Hawaii. Besides, Mountain Goat is way outside our jurisdiction.'' He was silent for a few seconds, then exploded. "Jude-girl!'' The nickname was not spoken with affection. "How the hell did you get mixed up with another freaking body?''

Judith's voice came out in a squeak. "I'm just along for the ride.''

Renie, who been watching and listening with reasonable attention, yanked the phone out of Judith's hand. "Listen, Joe,'' she said in a sharp, querulous tone, "don't blame your wife. She's right, this is all my doing, and all she did was provide the food. We'll probably be home tomorrow, so go easy on her. It's been a long day.'' Renie handed the receiver back to Judith.

Neither husband nor wife spoke immediately, but it was Joe who broke the strained silence. "Okay, okay. It's not your fault. Am I to understand that this dead body met with an accident?"

"That's it," Judith said brightly. "It must have been an accident. A skier, a hiker, a . . . wandering minstrel. Be sure and tell Mother I'm okay, and let Arlene know what's going on. I trust she's still in charge?"

"Arlene was in the kitchen when I last looked about an hour ago," Joe said in a more normal voice. "If she's not there now, I'll call her."

"Thanks." Judith slumped onto the tall stool next to the counter. "I love you."

"I love you." Joe sounded just a trifle weary. "Keep out of trouble. *Please*."

"Renie and I are going straight to our room," Judith assured Joe.

The cousins didn't get any further than the door to the laundry room. Leon Mooney had tiptoed into the kitchen, a napkin tied around his scrawny neck. "Is there any more angel food cake?" he asked a bit shyly.

"I'll look." Judith removed the cover from the glass cake plate. "Yes, would you like some?"

"A thin sliver," Leon replied, seemingly unable to meet Judith's gaze. "You needn't add the strawberries. I'm allergic."

"Okay." Judith cut a piece of cake and put it on a dessert plate. "There you go, Mr. Mooney. How's the meeting coming along?"

"Oh!" Leon put a hand to his mouth. "It's top secret! I daren't discuss it!"

Judith smiled indulgently. "Of course you can't. How

stupid of me. Are all your annual retreats so very secretive?''

"My, yes." The little man nodded gravely. "But this year, it's even more so."

"I see," Judith replied, though of course she didn't. "I suppose you always make a lot of big decisions that determine how the company will be run in the coming year."

"Definitely, definitely." Leon wagged his head. "Executive decisions. Visionary decisions. Especially this time. The twenty-first century is at hand." OTIOSE's vice president and comptroller looked terrified at the prospect.

"It's not really an old company, is it?" Judith remarked with a quick glance at Renie, who had sketched in the corporate history earlier.

"My, no," Leon replied. "It was founded by Mr. Killegrew a few years after the big Bell System breakup. OTIOSE is an independent company, serving a fast-growing number of business and residential customers in the Pacific Northwest." Leon sounded as if he were reading from one of Margo's p.r. brochures. Indeed, he had to take a deep breath after he finished speaking.

"OTIOSE," said Renie, with a touch of irony, "is all Frank Killegrew. He'd worked for one of the Baby Bells as an engineering vice president. Then he decided there was room in the marketplace for a new independent, so he rounded up investors and put in quite a bit of his own money to get OTIOSE started. Isn't that right, Leon?"

Leon's gaze, which was always evasive, now seemed fixed on his angel food cake. "That's true. He bought up some very small independents as well. You know—family-owned, small-town firms without proper funding for the new technology."

Renie nodded. "His timing was excellent. He was able to buy out the little guys when they were faced with bankruptcy or getting in over their heads."

"Yes," Leon murmured, his buck teeth fretting his lower

lip. "Yes, Frank Killegrew is very astute." At last, he looked up at the cousins. "Excuse me, I must get back to the meeting. I shouldn't have sneaked away, but I'm very, very partial to angel food cake. My dear mother used to make it for me. Rest her soul." His withered face turned wistful.

The cousins watched him tiptoe out of the kitchen. "He's not like most of the others, is he?" Judith remarked.

Renie shook her head. "He's an odd duck. Actually, he's exactly what he looks like—the stereotypical bookkeeper who spends his days—and nights—hunched over his accounts."

"I can't see him using a garrote on Barry Newcombe," Judith said, again heading for the back stairs.

"Probably not," Renie agreed.

This time the cousins got as far as the rear door to the laundry room. That was when Nadia came tearing into the kitchen, screaming, "Help! Help!"

Judith and Renie backtracked, practically colliding with each other. Nadia's slight figure was running in circles, small hands waving frantically.

"What is it?" Renie demanded, setting her plate and glass of milk down on the counter.

"It's Mr. Craven! Quick, I need an ice bag!" Fighting for control, Nadia opened the freezer section of the refrigerator.

"What happened to Mr. Craven?" Judith inquired.

"Mr. Agasias attacked him with a soapstone Eskimo!" Nadia was grabbing handfuls of ice, spilling cubes all over the floor in the process.

"Here," Judith said, holding out a plastic bag to Nadia. "Fill this, then we'll take it out to Mr. Craven."

Nadia's hands were shaking so badly that she could hardly get the cubes into the bag. The autocratic demeanor Judith had seen earlier in the day had faded and fizzled into a quivering bundle of nerves. "Oh, dear," Nadia cried,

"I'm usually not such a wreck. But this weekend is turning out rather badly . . ."

"I'll take the ice bag," Judith said with a reassuring smile as Renie began to scoop up the fallen cubes. "Why don't you wait here and collect yourself?"

"I shouldn't," Nadia said, but collapsed onto one of the tall stools anyway. "Oh, dear. I do feel nervy."

The scene in the lobby was like a tableau on the stage. Andrea Piccoloni-Roth was bending over the prone figure of Russell Craven; Ward Haugland and Gene Jarman were restraining an irate Max Agasias; Ava Aunuu had a finger shoved into a bewildered Frank Killegrew's chest; Margo Chang held the soapstone carving at arm's length; Leon Mooney was scrambling around on the floor retrieving his angel food cake, which he'd apparently dropped.

"Excuse me," Judith called, trying to edge around Ava and Killegrew. "First aid!"

Grudgingly, the company stepped aside, except for Leon, who was still on his hands and knees. Andrea hovered over Russell, whose eyes looked glazed. Under the thinning fair hair, Judith could see a bump beginning to rise.

"Mr. Craven," Judith said softly as she applied the ice bag. "What's your first name?"

His eyes didn't quite focus, and he winced when he felt the ice. His mouth worked, but nothing came out.

"What's your first name?" Judith repeated.

"Barry," Russell replied, and passed out.

Max Agasias had finally simmered down, so much, in fact, that he and Ward Haugland carried Russell Craven to one of the lobby's three long sofas. Andrea, who had hurriedly helped Leon pick up the rest of his cake, took over from Judith. Her plump, motherly figure was perched on the sofa arm where she held the ice bag to Russell's head.

"I won't take back what I said," Max declared, pouring himself a single shot of Canadian whiskey from the makeshift bar Judith and Renie had set up earlier. "Craven and the rest of those R&D bastards don't know a damned thing about marketing."

"Now, now," soothed Killegrew, "let's not bore more holes in the corporate ship, Max. We all have to work together and try to understand what goes on in each other's shop."

"That's my point," Max railed. "Nobody in this company understands marketing! But R&D is the worst. You cut our budget for their sake, and we'll be out selling door-to-door!"

"You won't have anything to sell," Ava put in, "if R&D doesn't come up with new product. Put a sock in it, Max. You made your point."

He'd also made quite a lump on Russell Craven's head, but at least Max's victim had come around. Andrea offered him a glass of water or a snifter of brandy. Russell said he'd prefer coffee, strong and black. Judith started back to the kitchen.

She met Renie in the dining room. "What's up?" Renie asked. "Is somebody else dead?"

Judith shook her head. "Just wounded. I'm going to make coffee."

Nadia was still in the kitchen, fussing about, apparently trying to find busy work to calm her nerves. "Is Russell all right?" she asked when she saw Judith.

"He's got a nasty bump on his head, but I think he'll be fine," Judith replied, removing a regular-sized coffeemaker from one of the cupboards. "He should be checked for concussion, though. He seemed a bit confused."

"No wonder!" Nadia briefly closed her eyes. "Max hit him awfully hard. It was so unnecessary."

"Mr. Craven doesn't strike me as a combative type," Judith said, putting coffee into a copper filter.

"He's not," Nadia responded. "But he's very protective of his R&D people. When someone like Max calls them a bunch of dreamers and a waste of corporate funds, Russell

can become very mulish. Max resents all the other departments because he feels they don't understand marketing.
But he despises R&D most of all, because of the way they
work. Or don't, from his point of view.''

"You mean . . . ?" Judith frowned. "They just sit and
dream up things?''

"Yes." Nadia now seemed more relaxed, perhaps because she was discussing a subject she knew backward and
forward. It was beginning to dawn on Judith that many of
the OTIOSE conferees were like that. They felt on safe
ground only when dealing with corporate matters. The rest
of the world, even everyday occurrences, seemed to
threaten them. "You see," Nadia went on, "much of the
R&D work is conceptual. As Russell puts it, his people
have to dream a long time before they can even begin to
cope with reality.''

That, Judith thought, explained Russell himself, who
didn't seem quite plugged in. But it didn't explain his response to her question about his first name. "Did Russell
know Barry Newcombe?''

Nadia tipped her head to one side. The stylish platinum
pageboy had wilted during the past few hours. "I don't
think so," she answered cautiously. "In fact, I recall him
asking several questions about Barry today. As far as I
know, Russell probably never met Barry until he drove us
up to the lodge last January. Why do you ask?" Her blue
eyes hardened like sapphires.

Judith shrugged. "It's not important." The coffee was
almost ready and she didn't want to waste time bringing
Russell his cup. "You knew Barry, of course.''

"Oh, yes," Nadia replied, her expression softening.
"Such a well-mannered young man. I'd worked with him
before when he'd catered some of the other company
events. He was very good at it, even if he tended to . . .
become distracted." She lowered her eyes.

Judith and Nadia both returned to the lobby where Russell Craven was now in a half-sitting position on the sofa.

He seemed reasonably alert, and grateful for the coffee.
Judith offered to pour a cup for the others, but only Andrea
and Ward accepted.

"I'll get it," Andrea volunteered, taking Russell's hand
and placing it on the ice bag she'd been holding to his head.
"Easy does it," she said in a soothing voice.

Frank Killegrew had resumed his place of dominance in
front of the fireplace. His shrewd gaze traveled from Renie
to Judith. "We're going to get back down to business
now," he said, hands clasped behind his back. "It's been
a terrific session this evening, right up until the . . ." He
glanced at Russell, then at Max. ". . . the controversy. So
this train has to make up for lost time. It's just about nine
o'clock, and we can keep the old locomotive running until
say, ten-thirty. If you'll excuse us, Ms. Jones, Ms. . . ." His
voice trailed off.

"Flynn," Judith said, barely above a whisper.

"We're gone." Renie waved one hand, then trotted out
of the lobby.

Judith followed. In the dining room, they met Andrea,
who was carrying two cups of coffee. "I checked Russell's
eyes," she said. "They seem normal. Pay no attention to
his mention of Barry. Russell didn't know him."

"So I've heard," Judith replied, ignoring Renie's puzzled look.

Andrea's pretty face flushed slightly, an attractive combination with her silver hair. "I understand why he said
what he did. Russell is terribly sensitive. I'm sure the news
of Barry's death upset him. You know how creative types
tend to overreact." She bustled off to the lobby.

"I'm creative," Renie said in an ingenuous voice. "Do
I overreact?"

"It depends," Judith said, continuing on into the kitchen.
"I don't think I've ever described you as sensitive."

"What's with this about Russell calling himself Barry?"
Renie picked up her plate but dumped her milk into the
sink and poured out a fresh glass.

Judith explained as they went up the back stairs. Renie thought Andrea's rationale was probably correct. Judith didn't comment further.

It was after ten when the cousins finished their meal. The storm had not abated. Judith dared to open the window to get a better view.

"Brrr!" she exclaimed, closing the casement quickly. "It must be down in the teens, with a wind chill factor of minus about a hundred. Look at the way the snow is drifting on the windowsill."

"It's drifting, all right," Renie said without enthusiasm. "The fire's almost out. Do you want to stoke it or go to bed?"

Involuntarily, Judith yawned. "It's getting cold in here without the fire. We might as well sleep. I'm tired."

Renie tapped her fingers on the arm of the chair. "I'm hyped. I always get this way after a big presentation. Finding a dead body also makes me a little . . . edgy."

Judith was leaning against the honor bar. "You're scared?"

"Aren't you?"

"Sure. But I've been scared before. After nineteen years with Dan McMonigle, I can face almost anything."

"You do and you have," Renie said dryly. "Of course nobody wants to kill *us*. We're insignificant bugs on the corporate highway of life."

Judith smiled. "Roadkill?"

"That isn't what I meant." Renie got out of the chair and lighted a cigarette. "One for the road," she said. "Or should I say one for the corporate highway?"

"If you must," Judith responded, then turned to make sure she'd latched the window properly. "Coz!" she hissed. "There's that light again!"

Renie rushed to join her cousin at the window. This time, she, too, saw a faint, blurred light somewhere out in the swirling snow. "Jeez! Who could it be?"

"Maybe it's not a who," Judith muttered. "Maybe it's a what."

"You mean some sort of beacon?" asked Renie, all but pressing her nose against the window pane.

"Yes. Some kind of weather-related signal. Did you notice anything like that when we were outside today?"

"No. But I'm not even sure where we're looking," Renie pointed out. "We were on the other side of the lodge."

The light went out, or perhaps it was swallowed up by the thick flakes that blew past the lodge with renewed frenzy. Renie paced the small room, puffing and scowling. "Nobody in their right mind would be outside in this weather," she finally said. "Maybe there's a ski lift nearby. The storm might have shorted the wiring."

"That's possible." Judith moved away from the window. She tensed as she heard muffled voices in the hall, then the closing of doors. "The OTIOSE gang must be wrapping it up for the night. I hope nobody else got hurt. Say, do you know why Andrea got so mad at Margo this afternoon?"

Renie shook her head. "I couldn't guess. Women talk a great line about helping each other in the business world, but believe me, the sisterhood is a myth. Look at Nadia and Andrea—there's bad blood there, too, probably because Andrea is an officer and Nadia isn't. It's every girl for herself, just like it is with the boys. Maybe more so, because it's tougher for women. The old boy network still seems to function."

"They're sure a testy bunch," Judith remarked. "Frankly, I'm surprised. I would expect better of people in executive positions."

"Not so," Renie said, turning back the spread on the nearest twin bed. "These people are under tremendous pressure, from within and without. As a public utility, OTIOSE is watched closely by the state and federal commissions, not to mention the public and the media. So when they go off on a private retreat like this, they're supposed to vent and let their hair down. It's only natural that their emotions boil over and they behave badly."

"They sure do," Judith agreed.

"They're spoiled brats," Renie said. "I've tried to explain that."

"I know. I'm just not used to it," Judith said with a shake of her head. "I've never been involved in corporate life. Oh, there were politics and a pecking order within the library system, but it wasn't like this." Slowly, she wandered around the room, hugging herself to keep warm and absently taking in the modest decor: another mountainscape, a brightly colored Native American throw rug, a photograph of the lodge under construction. The handwritten date in the corner read August 21, 1936.

"This must have been a public works project," Judith mused. "You know—one of FDR's efforts to put the unemployed to work during the Depression."

"Probably," Renie agreed. "It has that look—spare, but functional. Of course the recent owners from the private sector have tried to jazz it up. Like the fancy kitchen, and the conference rooms."

"Speaking of kitchen," Judith said with a sheepish expression, "I wouldn't mind getting a little extra something." She pointed to her empty plate. "How about you?"

Renie waved her cigarette. "I'm good, but I'll be your bodyguard. It's probably not wise to go off by ourselves."

The lights in the corridor had been dimmed. Judith and Renie decided to use the elevator now that they assumed the lobby was vacant. Again, it appeared that Nadia—or somebody—had tidied up. A single lamp glowed in a corner by one of the sofas. In the grate, the fire had died down to a few crimson embers. The wind moaned in the big chimney, and the pennants that hung from the rafters rustled gently above the cousins' heads.

The dining room was dark, but Renie found the switch.

A pale, sallow patch of light followed them into the kitchen. Judith started to feel for the on-off button by the sink, but stopped abruptly.

Something was wrong. She could make out the marble-topped counter and the glass dessert plate. She could also see that someone's face was lying in what was left of the angel food cake.

SIX

NEITHER JUDITH NOR Renie screamed. Instead, they held onto each other so hard that their fingernails practically drew blood. Finally, after what seemed like hours, but was probably only a minute, they stood back and stared at their discovery.

"It's Leon Mooney," Renie said, stunned and hoarse. "What happened to him?"

Reluctantly, Judith went around to the other side of the counter. Leon's small body sagged against the counter, his knees buckled, his arms dangling at his sides.

"He *is* dead, I gather?" Renie still sounded unnatural.

Judith felt for a pulse in Leon's frail wrist. "I'm afraid so." Her own voice was shaking. "It *could* have been a heart attack."

But Judith knew better. As soon as Renie's fumbling fingers managed to turn on the lights, Judith saw the ugly bruise on the back of Leon's head. Then she spotted a heavy-duty plastic freezer bag next to his feet. The bag had something in it. Judith bent down for a closer look.

Through the transparent plastic, Judith could see the soapstone Eskimo carving. "Good God!" she breathed, wobbling on her heels. "It's that same carving Max used to conk Russell!"

"Poor little Leon!" Renie sounded genuinely moved. "I hardly knew him, but he seemed the most harmless of the bunch."

Judith sat down on the floor and held her head. "This is awful. I feel kind of sick."

Renie, who had propped herself up against the refrigerator, scanned the kitchen. "I hope whoever did this isn't lurking around here someplace. Is he still warm?"

Judith nodded, then tried to focus on the digital clock. "It's ten to eleven. Didn't Killegrew say they were going to cut the meeting off at ten-thirty?"

"I think so," Renie replied. "That's about when we heard the noises in the hall."

"Dear heaven." Judith rocked back and forth on the floor. "We have to do *something*."

Renie gestured at the phone. "Should we at least try to call for help?"

Judith hesitated. "Yes. We have to."

"I'll do it." On wobbly legs, Renie went to the phone.

Judith averted her eyes from Leon's pathetic body. If the little man had seemed wizened in life, he now appeared utterly wraithlike in death. But, Judith thought, that's what he'd become—a wraith. She felt an unaccustomed bout of hysteria surging up inside.

"Damn!" Renie slammed the phone back in place. "I can't get a dial tone! The lines must be down."

The announcement snapped Judith out of her emotional slide. She started to get up, still trying not to look at Leon. "We can't do anything about that," she said, using the counter's edge to pull herself to a standing position. "How do we deliver the bad news?"

Renie twisted her hands together. "Nadia, I suppose. We start with her. Or should it be Margo? She's p.r."

"Stop sounding like a corporate clone," Judith said, more severely than she intended. "Wouldn't it be better to go to Frank Killegrew?"

Renie considered. "Maybe. Yes, you're right. Let's do it."

But the cousins had no idea which room belonged to Killegrew. Bewildered, they stood in the dimly lit second-floor corridor and scanned the various doors.

"To hell with it," Renie finally said, and knocked at the one in front of her. There was no response; she knocked again.

"Maybe," Judith whispered, "that was Leon Mooney's room."

Renie grimaced. "You might be right." She moved on to the next door on the right.

Only a single knock was required before the cousins heard noises inside. Then Andrea Piccoloni-Roth, attired in a lavender satin robe, opened the door. Seeing the cousins, she blinked twice and gave a little start.

"What is it?" she asked in a low voice.

Renie swallowed hard. "It's Leon Mooney. I'm afraid— I'm really sorry, Andrea—but he's dead."

In a flurry of lavender satin, Andrea Piccoloni-Roth collapsed onto the brightly colored Navajo rug.

"It would have been nice," Renie said as Judith tried to rouse Andrea, "if they'd included the company medical chief on this trek. Not to mention their head of security."

Judith didn't respond. Her concern was for Andrea, who was beginning to move, though her eyes were still shut. At last, the heavy lids fluttered open.

"Oh," Andrea said in a lifeless voice. "It's you."

"Do you want to sit up?" Judith inquired.

Andrea's eyes, which were a light brown with flecks of green, wandered around the room "I don't know. I don't care." She pressed a plump fist to her carefully made-up cheek. "What happened?" Her voice was hollow.

"We're not sure," Judith temporized.

As usual, Renie was less tactful. "Somebody hit Leon

on the back of the head with that soapstone carving. I'm sorry, Andrea, but it looks like he was murdered, too.''

Andrea's mouth fell open, her eyes bulged, and then she began to hiccup. It was a struggle, but Judith managed to raise her to a sitting position.

"Get some water," she said to Renie.

Renie went off to the bathroom. Andrea's wide shoulders were heaving; the hiccups continued. Judith fought to keep the other woman upright.

Renie, wearing a curious expression, returned with the water. Andrea tried to drink, sputtered, hiccuped, and finally choked. The hiccups stopped. "Lord have mercy," she whispered, and crossed herself.

The cousins automatically followed suit. "Was Leon a Catholic?" Judith asked.

Andrea shook her head. The upswept silver hair had come loose, and strands trailed down her back. "No. But I am."

"So are we," Judith replied, hoping the religious affinity might somehow comfort Andrea. "Would you like to lie down?"

Together, Judith and Renie got Andrea to her feet and guided her to the nearest of the twin beds. The room was almost identical to the one shared by the cousins, except that the painting was of an alpine meadow, and the photograph showed the completed lodge.

"What's happening?" Andrea asked in a frantic voice as Judith propped an extra pillow from the other twin bed behind her. "Could there be a serial killer loose in these mountains?"

"I don't know," Judith replied in all honesty. "I think we'd all better watch out for ourselves from now on."

"Oh, my." Andrea covered her face with her hands. "I can't believe this!" she wailed. "Who would kill a decent little man like Leon? Or Barry, for that matter. It's insane!"

Judith sat down on the other twin bed. "If you have an idea—any idea at all—who'd want to harm them, you ought to say so. This situation is getting more than ugly.''

"But I don't!" Andrea removed her hands, revealing a face drained of color except for a touch of blush on each cheek. "This isn't the Mafia, this is the phone company!''

Neither Judith nor Renie responded immediately. Finally, Renie spoke up. "The others have to be told. Are you up to it, Andrea?''

Andrea frowned, appeared to concentrate, then slumped back against the pillows. "No. In fact, I'd like to be left alone.''

There was no choice. Judith and Renie went back into the corridor. They had barely shut the door behind them when Renie grabbed Judith by the arm. "Coz! That's not Andrea's room! Didn't you notice that there were no female-type items anywhere? When I went into the bathroom, there was a man's shaving kit.'' In her excitement, Renie's voice had started to rise. She quickly lowered her tone, and glanced around to make sure no one had heard her. "There was also a prescription for allergies," she whispered. "It was made out to Leon Mooney.''

Judith usually wasn't so unobservant. But between the shock of finding Leon's body and trying to cope with Andrea, she simply hadn't noticed the absence of feminine articles.

"She was wearing makeup," Judith said, then grimaced. "You think she was having an affair with *Leon?*''

"It's possible. Men and women possess strange attractions for each other that are sometimes hard for the rest of us to fathom." Renie pointed to the door where they'd gotten no response. "I'll bet that's Andrea's room. She was in his, waiting for him. Maybe . . .'' Renie paused and swallowed hard. "Maybe he was bringing them both a piece of cake.''

"Is Andrea married or divorced?" Judith asked, still marveling at the thought of an amorous Leon Mooney.

"Married," Renie responded, beginning to pace the corridor. "Her husband, Alan Roth, is an unemployed computer genius. You know the type." Renie raised her eyebrows.

"I know the unemployed part, but the genius eludes me," Judith replied just as Ward Haugland poked his head out of the door directly across from them.

"What's going on out here?" he demanded, exhibiting uncharacteristic testiness. "Some of us are trying to sleep."

Renie, who disliked being snapped at under any circumstances, turned sharply. "Leon Mooney's been murdered. Pleasant dreams, Ward."

"*What?*" Ward's usual drawl was swallowed up in a single bellow.

Renie had turned her back on the executive vice president, but perceiving what appeared to be both shock and horror on his face, Judith took pity. "It's true, Mr. Haugland. We found his body in the kitchen about half an hour ago. Do you think you could tell the others?"

There was no need. Doors were now opening on both sides of the corridor. Margo, Max, Gene, Russell, Ava, Nadia, and finally Frank Killegrew all peered out of their respective rooms.

Ward delivered the bad news, then waited for the cousins to elaborate. This time, Renie deferred to Judith. "She saw him first," Renie declared in a slightly sulky voice.

Judith explained, briefly, if a bit haltingly. The circle of faces ranged from a distraught Nadia Weiss to a stoic Gene Jarman. Naturally, Frank Killegrew assumed command.

"Let's go down to the lobby," he said, his usually broad shoulders slumped under a bright blue bathrobe. "Nadia, call the police. Again."

"It seems the phone lines are down," Renie said, not without a trace of satisfaction. "It's too bad you don't have underground wiring up here."

Killegrew scowled, then stepped into the elevator, along with Ward, Gene, and Ava. The others waited. Apparently, thought Judith, there was a pecking order even when it came to elevator riding.

"Why the hell would someone kill Leon Mooney?" Max muttered. "That little guy wouldn't step on a bug."

"Mooney's money," Margo said softly. "That's what we've always called the comptroller's shop, isn't it? Maybe he was juggling the books."

"Not Leon," Max responded. "What would be the point? The man had no life outside of the job."

"There's nothing wrong with that," Russell said, on the defensive. "Some of us love our work. Usually." He shot Max a dark glance and rubbed the bump on his head.

Judith hadn't mentioned anything about the weapon that had presumably killed Leon. With a sidelong look at Max, she wondered if he'd used it again, and for a more lethal purpose. But anyone could have used the carving to deliver a death blow. The last time Judith had seen the soapstone Eskimo, it had been in the hands of Margo Chang.

The elevator returned; Russell, Margo, Max, and Nadia got in. The cousins were left alone in the hallway.

"I guess we know where we fit into the scheme of things," Judith remarked. "Dead last."

Renie elbowed Judith. "Don't say things like that."

Judith gave a nod. "Okay. I'll stick to conjecture, guesswork, and speculation. I take it Leon wasn't married?"

"I don't think so," Renie replied as the elevator doors slid open. "Somewhere along the line I heard he lived with his mother until she died a year or so ago."

The doors were about to close when a frantic voice called from down the hall. Judith quickly pressed the "open" button. Andrea dashed inside, still in her robe, but with her hair swept back up on top of her head.

"I heard all the commotion in the corridor," she said in a breathless voice. "I decided I'd better not miss out on what was happening. Did anyone ask where I was?"

No one had, at least not as far as the cousins could recall. Andrea looked relieved, then disappointed. Judith wondered if being overlooked was worse than being chastised.

"How are you feeling?" Renie asked as the car glided to the first floor.

"I'll survive," Andrea replied, but her voice was listless.

The bar had been reopened in the lobby. Nadia, in fact, was carrying more bottles in from the dining room.

"I won't go in the kitchen," she declared, looking mulish. "You'll have to reuse your glasses."

"I'll go in the kitchen," Max volunteered. "I was in 'Nam. Stiffs don't scare me." He stalked out of the lobby, his short plaid robe flapping around his pajama-clad legs.

"I was in Korea," Killegrew said in a troubled voice, "but I don't think I want to see poor Leon." He made a faint gesture in the direction of the kitchen. "The only thing is, we can't leave him there. We have to eat."

But Gene Jarman shook his head. "We can't move the body. We have to wait for the authorities." He turned to Judith and Renie, who had managed to squeeze onto one of the sofas next to Ava. "You didn't touch anything, did you?"

"Only the light switch," Judith said.

Ward leaned forward from his place on one of the other sofas that ringed the big coffee table. "Did you say you knew the chief of police?"

"Ah . . ." Judith hesitated. "Not personally." It was more or less true. Judith had met the chief at various departmental functions, but she doubted that he would recall to whom she was attached.

"See here," Killegrew said, ignoring both Ward's question and Judith's response, "we can't have a dead body underfoot, Gene. I don't care what the rules and regulations are. We've got to keep this ship afloat."

"Frank," Gene began, "we can't take the law into our own . . ."

"The law!" Killegrew made a dismissive gesture. "This is jungle law around here! Some maniac is on the loose, we can't get through to the authorities—though I'm sure that this is only a temporary lapse and service will be restored promptly—and there's no way out until the storm breaks. I'm perfectly willing to take responsibility.''

"I'd like that in writing," Gene murmured.

"What I propose," Killegrew continued, "is that we move poor old Leon down to the basement. There's a safe behind the desk here in the lobby. We'll lock up the so-called weapon in there. I'll do it myself, you can watch me. Then we can restore some semblance of order to this retreat."

"Oh, Frank!" It was Andrea, bursting into tears. "How can you? This isn't normal! This is horrible!"

"Now, now," urged Killegrew, coming over to pat Andrea's heaving shoulders, "there's no point in going to pieces. The telecommunications industry has gone through more terrible times than this—the great blizzard of 1888, the Johnstown flood, the San Francisco earthquake and fire, the Depression, a bunch of wars, strikes, antitrust suits, Judge Harold Greene, and the breakup of the Bell System. It's just that what's happened to us here hits close to home. But bear up, the train's still on track. We have to show our mettle. After all, we're OTIOSE."

The rallying cry did not go unheeded. "Here, here!" Ward Haugland shouted, clapping his hands. "You're darned tootin', Frank. What happened to Barry and now what's happened to Leon is pretty danged bad, but let's face it, we've got a business to run." Somewhat clumsily, Ward got to his feet. "Come on, Gene, let's get Leon out of the way."

OTIOSE's corporate counsel held up both hands. "Sorry, Ward. I won't be a party to this. It's not legal."

Exasperated, Ward turned to Russell. "How about you?"

Russell grimaced. "It's not that I don't want to help, but I'm rather . . . squeamish. I'd rather remember Leon as he was."

"He was one pretty darned homely little bugger, if you ask me," Ward muttered. "I don't reckon that being dead has made him look much worse."

Andrea's sobs grew louder. "I can't bear it! Shut up, Ward! I hate you!"

"Oh, for Pete's sake!" Ward threw up his hands. "I'll get Max. He won't weasel out on me."

Reluctantly, Gene got to his feet. "I'll get the weapon. I'll wrap it in a towel."

Killegrew's expression was uneasy as he watched his second-in-command and his legal counsel depart. "Did anybody bring a laptop?" he asked.

Margo sneered. "You told us to leave everything at the office except our fertile brains. No distractions, remember?"

"Yes, well . . . hmm." Killegrew fingered his jutting chin. "Maybe that was a mistake. In retrospect, of course. We might have faxed somebody for help."

"Using what?" put in Ava. "If the phone lines are down, so are the fax lines. In case you've forgotten, Frank, they use the same wire."

"Of course I haven't forgotten," Killegrew snapped, though his face turned red. "I just thought that with all your gee-whiz expertise, there might be another way." He glared at Ava.

She gave the CEO an arch little smile. "I'm afraid not. We're helpless. We might as well be living in the nineteenth century."

Killegrew turned to Margo. "I hope you're coming up with some ideas about how to keep this from the media. I don't want a scandal. OTIOSE can't afford bad press right now."

"It's a murder case," Margo said. "Two murders. There'll be an investigation. You can't hush that up."

"You damned well better try," Killegrew growled. "It's your job." It wasn't just a reminder; it sounded to Judith more like a threat.

Andrea's sobs had finally subsided. She raised a haggard face and spoke in a surprisingly strong voice. "We've got another, more important job, if you ask me. In case it

slipped everybody's mind, I'm vice president—human resources. We've lost two of those human resources, in a
most inhumane manner. I want something done about it,
and I want to start *now*."

The motherly velvet glove had been thrown down; the
plump iron fist was shaking at Frank Killegrew. He drew
back, looking unsettled.

"Now, now, Andrea, I don't see what we *can* do." Killegrew's glance of appeal fell on Gene Jarman, who had
returned from the kitchen and was cradling a towel that
contained the freezer bag with the soapstone carving.
"What's your considered opinion, counselor?"

"For now, I want somebody to open the safe. I don't
much like holding on to evidence like this," Gene replied.

Killegrew went behind the registration desk. The safe
was in a recessed area below the room slots. "Damn," he
muttered. "It's locked. We don't know the combination."

Judith felt herself wince. In years gone by, she had become adept at figuring out combination locks. It had begun
with necessity, when Dan McMonigle would hide his occasional earnings as a bartender and leave Judith holding
the bag for the household bills. Later, the knack had served
her well when on the sleuthing trail. She preferred not revealing how she'd acquired her skills. Fortunately, no one
asked.

The combination proved remarkably simple. Judith wrote
it down on a piece of lodge stationery and passed it around
to the others. There was safety in numbers, she decided.

With a scowl, Gene handed the towel and the carving
over to Killegrew, who put the items inside the safe after
only a brief, awkward juggling act. "There we go," he
said, dusting off his hands as if he'd accomplished a feat
of derring-do. "Lock it up."

Judith complied. The group reassembled around the
hearth. Killegrew again turned to Gene Jarman. "That's
that. Safe as houses. Now let's hear your words of wisdom
on what we do next."

Gene sat back on the sofa, his brown eyes lifted to the rafters. "I'll have to think this over," he said after a long pause.

"We don't have time for that," Killegrew retorted. "Come on, Gene, for once, forget about all that due caution and deliberate care bunk."

Gene uttered a heavy sigh. "We can do one of two things. We can all keep our mouths shut and not discuss what's happened today. That's what I'd advise. Or," he went on, with a sardonic look for Killegrew, "we can start asking each other a lot of embarrassing questions and try to get to the bottom of this. If we do that—and again, I'm not advising it from a legal standpoint—we might at least get our stories straight before we have to answer to the authorities."

Nadia, who had been mixing Russell Craven a rum and Coca-Cola, stared at Gene. "Are you suggesting that we lie?"

"Of course not." Gene's dark-skinned forehead creased. "I'm saying we pool our knowledge—such as it is—so that we don't end up looking like babbling idiots when we finally talk to outsiders."

Killegrew gave a brief nod. "That makes sense. Okay, Gene, you're in charge."

Max and Ward returned at that moment. They had removed Leon Mooney, not to the basement, but to a room on the third floor. "More homeylike," Ward said. Andrea began to weep again.

After Killegrew had filled Max and Ward in on Gene's alternative plan, Judith noted that the mood shifted. The group was getting down to business, a grisly business perhaps, but they were tackling it in a style they understood. Despite the bathrobes and slippers and cocktails and subject matter, the OTIOSE executives were taking a meeting, and the atmosphere seemed to relax. Even Andrea dried her eyes and reasserted her iron grip.

Judith poked Renie. "We're still here," she whispered. "How come?"

Renie gave a little shrug and a shake of her head, but said nothing. It didn't take long for the question to be answered.

Gene Jarman, who had traded places with Frank Killegrew, addressed the cousins. "It's unfortunate that the two of you had to be present during such a tragic time for OTIOSE," he said gravely. "But we can't change that, and what's even more unfortunate, is that you both seemed to have played big parts in that you found the bodies. We'd better start by going over what happened this afternoon and now tonight. Nadia, would you take notes, please?"

Nadia picked up a notebook and a pen from the coffee table, then slipped her glasses from her bathrobe pocket. "I'm ready," she said through pursed lips.

"Good." Gene turned back to Judith and Renie. "One word of caution—you must never speak of what went on in this room tonight. If you do, the gravest of consequences will follow."

Given what had already happened at Mountain Goat Lodge, Judith could guess that such consequences might be fatal.

SEVEN

IT WAS ALMOST midnight before Judith and Renie finished recounting their stories. Being questioned by Eugene Jarman Jr. was like being on the witness stand. He was precise, exacting, and relentless. The hardest part came when he asked about the items Judith had found at the bottom of the ice cave.

"You actually went inside the cave?"

"Yes. There wasn't much room because of the broken branches, but . . ."

"Why did you go inside the cave?"

"To get a better look."

"At what?"

"The body. And to see if there was anything that might tell us who . . ."

"Aren't you aware that a crime scene should never be touched?"

"Yes, but I didn't know it was a crime scene."

If Gene was taken aback by Judith's response, he didn't show it. "So you went ahead and disturbed the area around the body?"

"I didn't disturb it. I just picked up some things that were lying on the ground. If I hadn't, we would never have known who . . ."

"Come now, Ms. Flynn, surely you realized that the

authorities would eventually search the cave. Why did you feel compelled to do it yourself?''

Because I was freezing to death and my brain wasn't working. Because I was bursting with curiosity. Because I've done it before. But Judith only voiced these thoughts to herself. To Gene and the others, she merely said, "It seemed right at the time.''

Gene's tone reeked of disapproval. "Your heedless actions may cause serious legal problems. Tampering with evidence is a crime. On the other hand, we have only your word for it that Barry Newcombe met with foul play.''

"Oh, come on, Gene," said Margo. "If somebody finds a dead body with something tied around its neck, what do you think happened? I doubt that Barry was making a fashion statement.''

"He did dress well," Andrea noted. "And his shoes were always so nicely shined.''

Gene frowned at both women. "Let's skip the sidebar comments.'' He turned back to Judith. "Tell us exactly what you found near the body.''

Judith listed the items. "That's how we knew who it was.'' Suddenly she gazed around the room with a dumbfounded expression on her face. "I still have those things in my purse. Why didn't any of you ask about them?''

"I thought we did," Killegrew said. "Nadia, didn't I tell you to recover them?''

Nadia gave a little start. "Did you? Goodness, I must have forgotten. I was so upset.''

"Do you want me to get them now?" Judith asked. "They're in my room.''

"Later," said Killegrew. "Let's get on with it.''

Gene Jarman did, posing another thirty or so questions, most of which Judith didn't find relevant to the case. At last, he moved on to the discovery of Leon Mooney's body. There was much less to tell, and Jarman concluded by asking Renie why she'd turned on the kitchen lights.

Renie was miffed. "The better to see him with? Jeez, it

was pretty dark in there. Did you want us tripping over poor old Leon?''

''My point,'' Gene said painstakingly, ''is that the killer might have turned the lights *off*. It's very likely that you smudged important fingerprints.''

Renie's face fell. ''You're right. I didn't think of that.''

Ava had gotten to her feet. ''Are we done?'' she asked in a tired voice. ''It's late, and I don't know about the rest of you, but I'm beat.''

Gene didn't look pleased. ''We haven't gone over any of our whereabouts after the meeting tonight. I think we should get that down while everything is fresh in our minds.'' He glanced at Nadia. ''How are you doing?''

''Fine,'' Nadia replied, though she appeared haggard. ''I'm certainly glad I haven't forgotten my shorthand.''

''All right,'' Killegrew sighed. ''Let's go around the room. It shouldn't take long.''

''Let's start,'' Gene began a bit ponderously, ''by asking who saw Leon last.''

No one spoke. Glances were exchanged, throats were cleared, and drinks were sipped, but nobody responded. Finally, Max Agasias broke the silence.

''He was sitting on that ottoman, the last I remember,'' Max said, pointing to the empty green leather footstool near the hearth.

Everyone followed his gaze, fixated on the spot as if they could see the ghost of Leon Mooney.

''He went up in the elevator with me,'' Margo finally said. ''You were there, too, Russell. Don't you remember?''

''Was I? Did he?'' Russell stared vaguely at the fireplace.

''Yes,'' Margo continued. ''We were the last to leave the lobby. Leon's so quiet that sometimes we don't notice him. Or didn't,'' she added in a softer tone.

''I saw him last.'' Andrea held her head high. ''We'd

decided to share another piece of that delicious angel food cake.''

Everyone stared, and someone snickered. Judith thought it was Margo. "He went back down almost immediately," Andrea said, ignoring the stares and the snicker. "I suppose that was around ten-thirty-five.''

Another silence followed. The wind no longer howled in the chimney, and the room was very still. Judith turned to look outside. She could see nothing but blackness. Perhaps the storm was finally passing.

"I went right to bed," Max finally said.

"So did I," Margo asserted.

"Me, too," Ward chimed in.

"What else was there to do?" Nadia asked, though she darted a quick look at Andrea.

"It'd been a long day," Gene allowed. "I headed straight for the tub.''

"I read for a few minutes," Ava said, pulling up the high collar of her flannel nightgown. "Then I watched the storm through the window.''

"I went over my notes for tomorrow's session," Kille-grew recalled. "We start at nine, with breakfast at eight.''

To Judith's surprise, no one protested the announcement. Nadia, however, sagged in her place on the sofa. "I haven't checked the food supplies," she said in apology. "I'm not sure what . . .''

"We'll do the meals," Judith volunteered. "We might as well make ourselves useful.''

"Thank you!" Nadia's slim shoulders slumped in relief. "Ordinarily, it would be no problem, but so much has happened, and it's getting so late, and I . . .''

"Now, now," Killegrew said, "don't be so hard on yourself. Even I can put a piece of toast in the breader. I mean, bread in the toaster. Ha-ha!''

The few responding laughs were feeble. As before, Killegrew led the first elevator flight, with Ward, Gene, and this time, Margo. Ava had held back, taking Nadia by the arm. The two women spoke briefly, then Nadia joined the others by the elevator.

"She's worn out," Ava said in a low voice. "I told her I'd clean this stuff up. I'm kind of wired anyway."

"I thought you were tired," Renie said.

Ava watched Russell, Nadia, Andrea, and Max get into the elevator. "I am, but I don't think I could sleep. It just didn't seem to me that we were getting anywhere. Gene's first idea was better. What's the point in asking all these questions? This isn't a game of Clue, it's real life."

"You're right," Judith noted as the three women began collecting the dirty glasses. "Nobody has a real alibi. But of course they didn't mention what happened a year ago. Do you remember much about it?"

Ava used her shoulder to open the dining room door. "You mean that Friday afternoon when we presume Barry must have been killed? I've certainly been thinking about it. The problem is, it didn't seem important at the time. It's all kind of fuzzy now."

Entering the kitchen, Ava stopped on the threshold. Her face tightened, the strong, handsome features locked in what might have been grief or horror or both.

"Damn!" she breathed. "You say you found Leon slumped against that counter?"

"That's right." Judith gestured at the dessert plate where angel food cake crumbs lay scattered on the cold marble counter.

"Horrible." Ava took a couple of slow, deliberate steps into the kitchen. "How ruthless—and reckless—can a killer get? It's absolutely terrifying." Her smooth, nut-brown skin took on a sallow tinge as she clutched at her throat. "Sometimes I wonder why I ever went to work for OTIOSE."

"Where were you before this?" Judith inquired, wondering if she dared sweep up the cake crumbs.

"WaCom," Ava replied, making an obvious effort to

calm herself. "I'd been there since it was founded back in the mid-'80s by Jim Clevenger, one of the computer boy wonders. Four years ago Frank Killegrew made me an offer I couldn't refuse." Ava's expression was cynical. "If I'd stayed at WaCom, I'd probably be president now. As you may know, Jim died in a skiing accident last winter."

Judith vaguely recalled the news story, which had made page one of the local papers. Renie, however, was more aware of what went on in the world of commerce. She tipped her head to one side and looked rueful.

"Clevenger was really sharp," she said. "I'm surprised you left him to work for OTIOSE."

"Jim Clevenger was also a jerk," Ava declared. "He was extremely hard to work for, not just demanding, but unreasonable and erratic. It was a relief to come to OTI-OSE. And the money was better. At the time."

Judith made up her mind. She and Renie couldn't work on a counter that was covered with cake crumbs. It wasn't like blood splatter or gunpowder tattooing. As long as the body had been moved, there was no evidence to preserve. She rinsed off the glass plate, brushed the bigger pieces of cake into a garbage bag, and wiped the counter clean. If there'd been fingerprints, more were to come. People, even corporate executives, tended to congregate in the kitchen. The crime scene was bound to be disturbed. This was a working kitchen, and Judith had mouths to feed.

". . . So much competition in the industry these days," she overheard Renie say to Ava. "Which reminds me, what's going on with the Alien Tel lawsuit? I did a project for them last October, and I heard their suits were going up against your suits in court."

Ava shook her head, a despairing gesture that sent her long, dark hair rippling around her shoulders. "I'm keeping my mouth shut on that one. But you're right. It's a matter of record. The case comes up in superior court next month."

"It sounded kind of cut-and-dried," Renie remarked,

loading dirty cocktail glasses into the dishwasher. "Alien Tel likes to call itself 'An Out of This World Telecommunications Company,' but they got caught poaching off of some of OTIOSE's microwave towers. Maybe they should have launched a space satellite instead."

"They're small, they're new, they thought they could get away with it." Ava shrugged.

"I heard from one of their p.r. types," Renie continued, unwilling to let the topic rest, "that Alien Tel agreed to pay for usage along with any fines or penalties. But OTIOSE wants to make a public example of Alien Tel."

"That's possible." Ava had turned her back on Renie and was putting a couple of empty liquor bottles into the recycling bin.

"I never heard of Alien Tel," Judith said, feeling left out of the conversation. "Are they located around here?"

"Their customer base is mostly east of the mountains," Renie replied. "That's where they butted heads with OTIOSE. As I recall, one of the towers was up here near the summit."

Ava didn't respond directly. "I think we've got everything cleared away," she said, dusting off her hands. "I'll make one last check of the lobby, then I'm heading for bed. Good night."

The cousins watched her leave. "Touchy, touchy," murmured Renie.

"I didn't think so," Judith said. "You can't blame her for not tattling about a big lawsuit."

Renie opened the refrigerator door and took out two carrot sticks and a radish. "It's no secret, coz. It's been in the paper. You know, the business section, which you only use to line the bird cage. Except you don't have a bird cage because you don't have a bird."

"I think I call it my mother's apartment," Judith remarked absently.

"Anyway, the whole thing should have been settled out of court months ago," Renie went on, popping the radish in her mouth. "But OTIOSE refused to deal. The Alien folks told me it was a personal vendetta."

Judith, who hadn't been terribly interested in the court case, now focused her full attention on Renie. "You mean Frank Killegrew?"

Renie shook her head. "I mean Gene Jarman. His ex-wife, Sabine Bristow-Jarman, is the attorney for Alien Tel. He's out to get her, and damn the expense. Gene's not really a trial attorney, but he's had some experience and intends to try the case himself."

"Killegrew must support the suit," Judith said, taking one last look around the kitchen.

"Publicly, yes," Renie replied, following Judith through the laundry room to the back stairs. "Now I want to know why Ava wouldn't talk."

"Are you referring to motive?" Judith asked over her shoulder.

"There's got to be one, right?" Renie said as they ascended the stairs. "You got any better ideas?"

Judith made a frustrated gesture with her hands. "That's where I feel at a loss. I don't know these people, and I certainly don't know anything about the business world."

The cousins stopped talking as they proceeded down the hall. It seemed to Judith that an unnatural calm had settled over the lodge. Not only had the wind died down, but there were no noises coming from any of the guest rooms. Yet Judith had a feeling that behind the closed doors, none of the guests were sleeping soundly.

"You forgot your snack," Renie said after they got to their own room.

"I lost my appetite," Judith admitted. "Finding a dead body on the kitchen counter will do that."

Judith and Renie decided to sleep in the bathrobes provided by the lodge. They rinsed out their underwear, then realized that the garments probably wouldn't dry in the chilly room. Renie suggested that they take their things down to the laundry room and put them in the dryer; Judith

told her she wasn't going back downstairs for a million
bucks.

"There's no telling what—or who—we'd find this
time," she said, piling kindling and logs into the fireplace.
"Let's hang the stuff next to the hearth and hope for the
best."

"I'm game," said Renie, flopping down on one of the
twin beds and lighting a cigarette. "Gamy, too, if we have
to stay here very long."

"We can wear the robes and do another load of laundry
tomorrow," Judith said, wishing Renie hadn't decided to
smoke just before they retired for the night. "But we only
do it when other people are around."

"Good thinking." Renie, who had unearthed a glass ash-
tray bearing the imprint of the old Milwaukee Road railway
company, tapped her cigarette. "Bad thinking," she added.

"About what?" Judith had slipped under the covers and
already had her eyes closed. "I really wish you wouldn't
smoke in bed."

"Motive. If Gene's on the spot, he should have been one
of the victims," Renie reasoned. "Why kill a lowly staff
assistant like Barry?"

"You *are* watching that cigarette, aren't you?" Judith
opened one eye.

"Leon Mooney I could understand," Renie continued.
"He controls the budget. If he went to Gene—or Frank
Killegrew—and said 'The window is closed on wasteful
litigation', then Gene might want him out of the way. But
that would only be a temporary stop-gap. Someone would
be promoted almost immediately, and the funds would still
be cut off."

"Once when Dan was smoking in bed, he melted his
Ding-Dong." Judith rolled over, her back to Renie.

"Promotions!" Renie exclaimed. "Who'll get Leon's
job? Nobody here. It'll be some assistant vice president
from treasury or accounting."

"Coz . . ." Judith's voice was pleading. "Will you shut

up, put your cigarette out, and turn off the damned light?''

"Okay, okay," Renie sighed. "It's not like you to avoid a guessing game involving murder."

"It is at one o'clock in the morning when I'm exhausted. Good night."

Renie not only put her cigarette out, she threw it into the grate, checked the lingerie hanging from the fireplace tools, took one last look at the falling snow, and clicked off the bedside lamp.

"Good night," she said to Judith.

Judith was already asleep.

Seven A.M. came far too early. Neither Judith nor Renie felt fully rested. Indeed, the vigor Renie had shown the previous night had degenerated into grouchiness.

"Don't talk to me, and you'll be okay," she snarled when Judith came out of the bathroom.

Judith opened her mouth to express agreement, saw the black look on Renie's face, and clamped her lips shut. The cousins dressed in silence, though Judith had to fight down an urge to complain when Renie lighted her first cigarette of the day.

The sun was almost up, but it was hidden behind heavy gray clouds. The snow was still falling, though not as heavily, and the wind had died down. That was not necessarily good news as far as Judith was concerned. If the wind changed, perhaps coming in from the west, the snow clouds might blow away.

It was Renie who finally spoke, just as they were about to go downstairs. "Don't forget to give Frank or Nadia those items that belong to Barry," she said.

"Right." Judith opened her big shoulder bag while Renie unlocked the door and stepped into the corridor.

"Well?" said Renie, fists on hips. "Let's hit it."

Judith turned a hapless face to her cousin. "They're gone."

"What's gone?" Renie had virtually shouted. She gave

a quick look down the hall, then lowered her voice. "What are you talking about? Barry's ID?"

"All of it," Judith whispered. "Credit cards, notebook, the whole bit."

"Jeez." Renie reeled around the corridor, then shoved Judith back up against the door. "Did you lock up when we left last night to go downstairs?" she asked under her breath.

"No. Did you?"

"No." Renie grimaced. "I didn't think about it."

"Who knew I had the stuff in my purse?"

Renie appeared to concentrate. "Everybody. You mentioned it in the lobby while Gene Jarman was questioning you."

"So I did." Judith slumped against the door. "What's the point?"

Renie grabbed her by the arm. "Who knows? But we can't stand out in the hall and talk about it. Let's go."

The kitchen looked exactly as they had left it the previous night. Judith had planned a simple self-serve breakfast of cereal, toast, fruit, juice, and coffee. But there were eggs in the refrigerator and bacon in the freezer. She decided she might as well improvise.

"It had to be the notebook," Judith said, filling the big coffee urn. "The rest was all the usual plastic."

"But there was nothing in the notebook," Renie noted, apparently jolted out of her early morning mood by the theft. "The pages had been ruined."

"Whoever took it didn't know that," Judith said, measuring coffee into the urn's big metal basket. "I don't think I mentioned how the damp had ruined the notebook."

"You didn't." Renie put two pounds of bacon into the microwave and hit the defroster button.

Judith carried the urn into the dining room. "Tell me everything you know about these people," she said when she got back to the kitchen.

"You didn't want to hear it last night," Renie said in a contrary tone.

"That's because my brain had died of exhaustion. Give, coz."

Renie removed the bacon from the microwave and began laying strips in a big skillet. "I don't know that much. You've already heard about Frank Killegrew—he was a former Bell System vice president who decided to start up his own company. While he claims to be from Billings, Montana, he was actually born and raised in some itty-bitty town about thirty miles away. His background was hard-scrabble, a fact he likes to hide. To his credit, Frank went to college, in Butte, I think, then straight to the phone company after he graduated with an engineering degree. His rise wasn't exactly meteoric, but it was steady. He and his wife—I think her name is Patrice—have two grown children. Patrice is a typical corporate wife—pampered and spoiled. More so than most, because I think her family had money. Frank golfs, skis, and has a big cruiser. They live in one of those plush neighborhoods on the lake and have a summer home on another lake in Montana."

"Good work," Judith said approvingly. "You seem to know Mr. Killegrew quite well."

"Not really." Renie was opening cereal boxes. "I've designed some brochures that featured his bio. Some of the other, more personal stuff I've picked up from the downtown grapevine."

"How about Ward Haugland?" Judith asked as she began to cut up a big Crenshaw melon.

"A native Texan, another engineering degree, another guy who rose through the Bell System ranks," Renie said. "He served as an assistant vice president under Frank, then left with him to form the new company. He also golfs, skis, and has a boat."

"Is that required at the executive level?" Judith asked with a little smile.

"In a way," Renie replied, quite serious. "It's part of the old boy network. If, for example, you play golf with the boss, you're more inclined to get the next promotion. If you golf, ski, *and* have a boat, you're a shoo-in. Or so the passed-over, non–sports enthusiasts would have you believe."

"Is Ward married?" Judith inquired, tackling a cantaloupe.

"Definitely, to a world-class hypochondriac. Helen Haugland has suffered more diseases than the AMA allows."

"Is she also spoiled and pampered?"

"Not to mention coddled and overprotected. I've never met her—she never goes anywhere except to the doctor—though come to think of it, I did meet Patrice Killegrew once," Renie said as she turned the heat on under the bacon. "It was a couple of years ago, at some graphic design awards banquet. She was a stuck-up pill."

"Somebody said Leon had lived with his mother," Judith remarked. "What else?"

Renie shook her head. "Nothing. I think she died not long ago. Leon kept himself to himself, as they say."

"Except when he was keeping company with Andrea Piccoloni-Roth," Judith pointed out.

"So it seems. The odd couple." Renie paused, apparently conjecturing about the unlikely pair. "Andrea and— what's his name? Alan Roth—have a couple of teenaged boys. Roth stays home on the pretext of being a house-husband, as well as the aforementioned computer genius. I saw his picture on her desk once. He's rather good looking, in a lean, pedantic kind of way."

"More of a hunk than Leon Mooney?" Judith started to smile, glanced at the counter where she'd last seen Leon, and immediately regretted the impulsive remark.

"Not a hunk," Renie replied. "Just . . . more attractive."

"How about Gene Jarman? I know he's divorced and his ex-wife works for Alien Tel."

"That's about all I know, too," Renie said. "Gene strikes me as one of those black guys who doesn't want to admit he *is* black. He's very careful about his background, which I gather was an Oakland ghetto."

"That doesn't sound much different than Frank Killegrew hiding the fact that he grew up in Destitute, Montana, or whatever podunk name the town is called."

"No, you're right. As usual, people are people. Maybe Gene seems touchier, because he's an attorney instead of an engineer."

Judith was about to inquire into Margo Chang's background when Margo entered the kitchen. She had come through the dining room and was carrying a mug of hot coffee.

"Thank God," she murmured. "The lifeline is open."

"Dig in," Renie urged, indicating the fruit and the cereal boxes.

Margo shook her head. "Right now, all I need is coffee. God, I was awake half the night. I kept thinking I heard someone trying to get into my room. It was just nerves, but it didn't make for decent rest."

Judith finished culling strawberries and leaned against the counter across from Margo, who'd sat down on one of the tall stools. "My cousin was just filling me in on who's who in the company. How long have you been with OTIOSE, Margo?"

Taking a deep, satisfying swig of coffee, Margo eyed Judith warily. "What is this—a grilling of suspects?"

"No, no," Judith said in her most self-deprecating manner. "I feel lost in this group. Which is kind of scary, all things considered. I'm just curious. You can't blame me for wondering what I've gotten into."

"That's what we're all wondering." Margo made a face. "At the first sign of clear weather, I'm walking out of here, heading for the summit, and ordering a car to collect me. Then I'm going straight home to write my letter of resignation. This is one terrifying phone company."

"I don't blame you," Renie put in. "I wouldn't want to be in your shoes trying to explain all this to the media."

Margo's plain face looked drawn. "The worst is yet to come."

Judith tensed. "What do you mean?"

Margo had set the coffee mug down on the counter, almost in the exact spot where the cousins had found Leon. "I mean, when the killer is unmasked, or whatever they call it in mystery novels." The almond-shaped eyes darted from Judith to Renie. "Until last night, I honestly believed that some outsider murdered Barry. But it's different now that Leon's dead. Nobody could have gotten into the lodge." Her lower lip trembled. "Don't you see? It has to be one of *us*."

EIGHT

IN THE STRAINED atmosphere of the kitchen, Judith felt the full impact of being sealed off from the rest of the world. Yet all three women carried on, perhaps in the hope that their mundane tasks could keep terror at bay. Margo drank more coffee, Judith took a fruit platter out to the dining room, and Renie flipped bacon. The snow continued to fall.

"It was seven years ago," Margo said suddenly when Judith returned to the kitchen. "That's when I joined OTIOSE. I'd been working in p.r. for a public utility company in California. I wanted a change, and L.A. was turning into a zoo." She uttered a brittle laugh. "I should have stayed there. I didn't know when I was well off."

"Were you hired in at the officer level?" Renie asked.

"No. I went to work for Herb Oldman, who had the good sense to die of a heart attack three years later. I got his job, and thought I was on top of the world. Now I feel as if it's caved in on me." Margo held her head in her hands.

"Excuse me." The uncertain voice came from the doorway where Russell Craven stood, his fair hair even more unruly than usual. "May I please have some cream? Real cream, if you have it."

Judith went to the refrigerator. "How are you doing, Mr. Craven?" she asked with an encouraging smile.

"Doing?" He patted the bump on his head. "Not very well. This hasn't been a congenial experience so far."

Judith poured cream into a ceramic pitcher. "No one can be feeling good this morning," she commiserated. "Are you really going to continue with your meetings?"

Russell exchanged a questioning look with Margo. "I suppose," he said. "What else is there to do? We can't leave. I went to the front door just now and when I opened it, a pile of snow fell on me. I could barely close it again."

"Great." Margo set her mug down with a thump. "We should have paid more attention to the forecast. Why do we always assume the weatherman is off-base? And why doesn't somebody come get us? Aren't there search and rescue people around here?"

"They're probably having enough trouble with people stranded on the highway and at the ski areas," Judith said, then went to the phone. "I suppose it wouldn't hurt to try . . ."

The line was still dead. The spark of hope that had appeared in the eyes of the others flickered and died. Judith gave them a rueful look.

"Sorry. But breakfast is almost ready."

Russell and Margo didn't budge. It occurred to Judith that they preferred staying in a group. As if to underscore the conferees' feelings, Max Agasias and Ward Haugland appeared next, entering from the laundry room.

Max went straight to Russell and put a hand on the other man's shoulder. "Hey, no hard feelings about last night. I lost my temper, that's all. Sometimes I get pretty damned frustrated with the second-class way my marketing people are treated."

Russell recoiled slightly, but managed a small smile. "We're all protective of our own shops," he said simply.

"Coffee's ready in the dining room," Judith announced as a furtive Nadia Weiss slipped into the kitchen.

"I saw it," she said in a nervous voice. "But I . . . well, I thought I'd wait." Her blue eyes darted every which way, then came to rest on Russell. "Shall we get coffee now? Or . . . ?"

"We'll all go," Max said.

"I need a refill," Margo chimed in. The five of them trooped off to the dining room.

Judith began cracking eggs in a frying pan. "Take that toaster out and plug it into the outlet with the coffee urn," she said to Renie. "It's almost eight. They'll all be here in a few minutes."

They were, except for Andrea. As Judith dished fried eggs directly onto the conferees' plates, Frank Killegrew opined that his vice president–human resources was probably too upset to come down for breakfast.

"Andrea was fond of Leon," Killegrew said, passing the toast around the table. "I mean, really fond of him. She took his death pretty hard."

"Oh, Frank." Margo was shaking her head.

"What?" Killegrew stared at Margo.

"We're all taking it hard," Margo asserted. "Don't you get it, Frank? Somebody is out to kill us."

"That's extreme," Gene Jarman said quietly. "We mustn't jump to conclusions. Nobody knows for certain what happened to Barry Newcombe."

"We know he's dead," said Ava Aunuu. "That's not a good sign."

Gene's calm brown eyes rested on Ava. "It could have been an accident. Think it through, consider the exigencies. Barry went off to the store or wherever just before a storm like this one hit. He could have returned in the middle of it, lost his way, and sought refuge in that cave or whatever it was. He froze to death. It happens."

"With a leather strap around his neck?" Ava sneered at Gene. "So what happened to Leon? He smothered himself in angel food cake?"

"I thought he was hit on the head," put in Russell, who again fingered his own skull and winced.

"Afraid so," Ward mumbled. "It's a nasty business, all right."

"The point is," Killegrew said between mouthfuls of fried egg, "we might as well carry on. We can't leave, and there are plenty of items left on our agenda. As long as the cabin's still airtight, we can fly."

"You're right, Frank," Ward agreed. "Besides, it'll keep our minds off . . . this other stuff." The second-in-command lowered his eyes to his breakfast plate.

Judith, who was reaching between Nadia and Gene to set a coffee carafe on the table, summoned up her courage. "Excuse me. I have a small announcement."

All eyes veered in her direction. To her acute embarrassment, she blushed. "Someone took Barry's items out of my handbag last night."

"Cripes!" exclaimed Ward.

"Oh no!" cried Nadia.

"Ridiculous," murmured Gene.

"That does it!" Margo threw down her napkin and stood up. "Isn't there some way we can get help? This is a nightmare!"

"Now, now," Killegrew said, though he sounded shaken. "Has anybody tried the phone this morning?"

"I did," Judith responded. "It still doesn't work."

Max Agasias sat far back in his chair, balancing his burly body in what struck Judith as a precarious position. "You see? What do we tell our customers? Go cellular, go wireless—and never leave home without it. I guess only OTI-OSE people are too damned dumb to take marketing's advice."

Margo, who was pacing back and forth in front of the buffet, swung around. "Well? Did you bring your cell phone, Max? Did you take your own bright-eyed advice?"

Max locked his hands behind his head and grinned.

"Hell, no. I followed Frank's orders here, like a good little Nazi."

Russell Craven was shaking his head. "My, my. No cell phones, no laptops, no pagers, no . . ." He stopped and looked somewhat diffidently at Killegrew. "Wouldn't you think," Russell said quietly, "that there would be a battery-powered two-way radio around this lodge?"

"Dubious," Max responded dryly. "Why would they need it? We sell complete communications systems, and old-fashioned battery-driven radios are dinosaurs."

"We could look," Gene put in. "They might have one stored in the basement."

"It's an idea," Killegrew allowed, though he, too, sounded dubious.

"Forget the damned radio," Margo implored. "I want to know how somebody got into Ms. Flynn's handbag."

Judith explained how she had left the bag in their room when the cousins had come down to get a snack. "I didn't discover the theft until this morning," she added, "but it probably occurred before Ms. Jones and I finally retired some time after midnight."

"You said you didn't lock the door?" Gene Jarman had assumed his role of witness interrogator.

"No," Judith replied. "It didn't seem so important to keep people out when we weren't inside."

A silence fell over the dining room. Margo began to pace again, Ward toyed with his food, Russell sat with his chin on his hand, Ava stared off into space, Gene sipped coffee, Nadia twisted her hands in her lap, Max twirled a piece of melon on his fork, and Frank Killegrew grabbed the coffee carafe. Judith went back into the kitchen.

"I eavesdropped," Renie admitted. "Do I detect a note of desperation?"

"Several," Judith said. "Some are louder than others."

The cousins remained on kitchen duty for another half-hour, eating their own breakfasts between treks into the dining room. Shortly before ten, the conferees headed in a body to the lobby. Apparently, it was business as usual.

Judith and Renie were clearing the table when Ava and Nadia reappeared. "We've formed a buddy system," Ava announced. "Nobody goes anywhere alone, including to the bathroom. In fact, we're thinking about sharing bed-rooms tonight. If we're still here."

It was unclear if Ava's reference was literal or—really literal. "Good idea," Judith remarked. "My cousin and I are sticking together like glue."

"If only," Nadia sighed, "Leon had taken Andrea with him last night when he came down to get the cake. Or if Barry had asked one of us to go with him a year ago. I would gladly have accompanied him on his errand. I'm used to fetching and carrying." Only a hint of bitterness was evident in her voice.

"You couldn't guess what would happen to either of them," Ava said, not unkindly.

"I enjoyed talking to Barry," Nadia went on as if she hadn't heard the other woman. "He always had all the news."

"Gossip, you mean." Ava's tone was good-natured. Judith noticed that she looked reasonably rested. Or perhaps it was the rich blue high-necked sweater and slacks ensemble she was wearing. It was the one that Judith had seen in the suitcase, and it was definitely a becoming color with Ava's dark complexion.

"Yes, gossip." Nadia smiled, producing a rather charming effect despite the obvious strain on her thin face. "You see," she said to Judith and Renie, "Barry heard *every-thing*. Staff assistants usually do. And he had this most ingenious way about him. If he had an interesting piece of news—"

"Gossip," Ava interjected.

"If you like." Nadia darted Ava an amused glance. "Anyway, when he heard something truly interesting, he'd call around and ask if whoever he was speaking to had any recent tidbit. If that person—''

''You,'' put in Ava.

''Possibly,'' Nadia agreed, ''but by no means just me. If you—''

''He never called me with gossip,'' Ava asserted.

''You know what I mean.'' Nadia was growing impatient at the interruptions. ''If you had something worthwhile to tell, then he'd reveal what he knew. It was like a game.''

A deadly game, Judith thought, with a quick look at Renie.

''From what I've heard,'' Ava said, nibbling at one of the leftover strawberries, ''most of his so-called news was about who used the Cloud Room.''

''The Cloud Room?'' Judith echoed.

''Now, Ava,'' Nadia began with a reproachful expression. ''Don't go telling tales out . . .''

''Come on, Nadia, you started it.'' Ava waved a contemptuous hand. ''I don't think so-called Cloud Rooms are exclusive to OTIOSE these days. In this case, there are actually two of them, the men's and women's rest rooms on the twenty-ninth floor. It's where employees go to do cocaine.''

''Oh!'' Judith was shocked, even though she knew she shouldn't have been. Joe constantly railed against the onslaught of drug traffic in the city. ''Is this a big problem?''

''That depends on the individual,'' Ava replied, despite a warning glare from Nadia. ''In some cases, it doesn't appear to affect a person's work. In others, it's ruinous. I had to recommend the firing of two people in the past year, and authorize rehab for another half dozen. OTIOSE contracts out with a firm that deals in addiction among corporate employees.''

Leaning against the counter, Renie nodded. ''Newer Resolutions, isn't it? I did some design work for them two years ago. As I recall, in most companies, it's a three-strikes-and-you're-out program.''

"That's right," Ava agreed. "At least it is with OTI-OSE. The company will pay for two rehab sessions, but after that, you're gone and on your own."

"Why," Judith asked, "can't they nip it in the bud? That is, if they know where employees go—to this so-called Cloud Room—why don't they stop the drug use right there?"

"Because," Ava answered, "they'd simply go somewhere else. Our headquarters is a thirty-story building. There are lots and lots of places to do drugs. And that's just during office hours."

"Sad," Judith murmured.

"But true." Ava gave Nadia a gentle shove. "Let's go, we're holding up progress. Frank wants to start the meeting in ten minutes, and we've got to get Andrea down here."

The two women went off through the laundry room to the back stairs. Judith eyed Renie. "What floor are the executives on at headquarters?"

"Thirty." Renie's lips twitched.

"That's what I thought," said Judith.

Judith had just turned on the dishwasher when she heard the screams. Renie jumped and knocked a cereal box off the counter. An eerie silence ensued.

"What was that?" Renie asked in a startled voice.

"It was a scream. Or screams." Judith was trembling. "Where did it come from? And," she gulped, "why did it stop?"

Cautiously, the cousins went into the laundry room, then as far as the bottom of the back stairs. They heard nothing.

"Maybe it wasn't upstairs," Renie whispered. "Maybe it was downstairs, in the basement."

Judith glanced around the small hallway where the top of the basement stairs could be seen near the rear entrance. "Maybe. But I'm not going down there. Let's go into the lobby and find out if anybody else heard anything."

If the others hadn't heard the screams, they now saw a

most alarming sight. Ava and Nadia were huddled in the open elevator, seemingly paralyzed by fear. Just as the door automatically started to close, Ava hurtled into the lobby. Nadia stumbled behind her.

Gene and Max rushed to meet the women. "What the hell . . . ?" shouted Max, grabbing Nadia before she fell.

"It's Andrea," Ava gasped, leaning against Gene. "She killed herself! Andrea's dead!"

NINE

AVA BURIED HER face against Gene's shoulder. Max half-carried Nadia to the nearest sofa, almost bumping into a dazed Russell Craven, who was wandering around the wide hearth, glassy-eyed and muttering to himself. Frank Killegrew and Ward Haugland simply stared at one another. Margo Chang picked up her black suede bag and pulled out a Ladysmith .38 Special revolver.

"If anybody comes near me, they're dead!" she shrieked. "Nobody's going to kill me, nobody's going to drive me to suicide! I'm getting out of here alive!"

"Margo!" Killegrew turned white. "Is that thing loaded?"

"You bet!" Margo swung the gun around the room, taking aim at each of the others in turn. "I know how to use it, too! I go to the range once a month!"

"My God!" Killegrew sank down on the sofa next to Nadia.

"You know," Russell said, no longer wandering around the hearth but edging nervously away from Margo, "firearms are very dangerous. Do you realize you should never point a gun at anyone unless you intend to use it?"

"Shut up, Russell!" She pointed the gun straight at him. "Of course I know that! Furthermore, I've got a concealed weapons permit, a federal firearms license, a long-standing membership in the NRA, and I belong to the local chapter of OFF, the Organization of Firearms for Females.''

"Then you're legal." Gene Jarman shrugged.

"Now, now," Killegrew said without his usual hearty reassurance, "let's not get excited. Andrea's the problem here. I can hardly believe she'd kill herself."

With a wary eye on Margo, Gene led Ava to one of the other sofas. "Brandy would be in order," he said to no one in particular.

Judith started to bolt out of the room, then looked at Margo. "May I?" she asked, feeling childlike and stupid.

Margo lowered the gun. "Go ahead. But don't anybody forget I won't hesitate to use this." She patted the weapon, then slipped it back into her suede bag.

Renie went into the dining room with Judith, where they found two half-empty bottles of brandy. "I don't blame Margo," Renie said in a tense voice. "This is absolutely horrible."

"It sure is," Judith agreed, gathering up some of the other liquor bottles and motioning for Renie to get some glasses. "I'm beginning to feel as anxious to get out of here as Margo is."

"At least she's armed," Renie said. "I wouldn't mind having an AK-47 about now."

Judith gave a little snort. "You'd be lucky not to shoot yourself. Or me."

Giving Judith a hapless look, Renie led the way back into the lobby. Once again, Gene had taken over the questioning, but his manner had become slightly more deferential.

No one refused the brandy. Indeed, Killegrew swallowed his in a gulp, and Nadia inhaled the fumes for such a long time that Judith thought she'd suck the liquor right up her nose.

"Let's begin," Gene said calmly, "with you, Ava. You

mentioned that Andrea's door was unlocked?''

"It was." Ava gave a short, grim nod. "We knocked, of course, but she didn't respond. We thought maybe she was in the bathroom, so we went in." Ava hesitated, lifted her chin, and continued. "Andrea was in bed, and we assumed she was asleep."

"What did you do then?" Gene asked quietly.

Ava glanced at Nadia, as if for confirmation. "I called to her. Nadia had stayed in the doorway."

"And?" Gene prompted.

"Nothing. I knew Andrea was upset about Leon," Ava went on, speaking more rapidly, "so I thought maybe she'd taken something to help her sleep and was really out of it. Frank was anxious to start the meeting, so I went to the bed and gave Andrea a little shake. I couldn't rouse her. Then I saw the pill bottle and the note."

Gene cleared his throat. "Let's back up a moment, please." He turned to Nadia, whose eyes seemed to have grown as large as the big glasses she wore over them. "Does this account agree with what you recall so far?"

"Yes." Nadia's voice was toneless.

"All right." Gene offered Ava a slight smile of encouragement. "Do you have the note with you?"

Ava shook her head. "I remembered what you said last night about not touching anything. I left it on the nightstand."

"What did it say?"

Ava swallowed hard. "It said, 'Leon, I'm coming to join you.' ''

"Did you recognize Andrea's handwriting?"

"Not really," Ava admitted, "but Nadia did. She'd come all the way into the room when she saw I had trouble waking Andrea."

Gene turned again to Nadia. "You're certain it was Andrea's writing?"

"Yes," Nadia answered, still without inflection. "I've

seen it many times. She often sent Frank handwritten notes.''

"What did you do next?" Gene asked Ava.

Ava put a hand to her forehead. "I'm not sure. I think we both realized at the same time that Andrea was dead. We ran out of the room and came down here."

Gene sought corroboration from Nadia, who nodded. "We may have screamed," she said. "It was so . . . ghastly." Nadia shuddered at the memory.

"In other words," Gene mused, "Andrea is still lying up there in bed . . . dead."

"I haven't heard her walking around," Margo snapped. "What's wrong with everybody? Can't this crew accept the *facts?*"

"Sleeping pills," murmured Russell. "Did you say Andrea took sleeping pills?"

"Sometimes she did," Nadia said. "Last night she offered me one, but I have my own prescription. I can hardly blame Andrea for taking something to help her sleep. She was so upset."

Ward stretched out his long legs. "Could it have been an accident?" he asked.

"Not with that note," Killegrew put in. "My God, I had no idea she and Leon were . . . so close. Sometimes," he added darkly, "I wonder what really goes on behind my back in this company. Sometimes I think the caboose is running this ship."

"I think you mean 'train.' " Margo's tone was mocking.

Killegrew glowered at her, but said nothing. Indeed, no one responded until Gene spoke again. "Someone will have to go up there and check things out. I suppose I should do it, since I'm the legal counsel." He grimaced, then uttered a choked little laugh. "Max, would you come along? We'd better stick to the buddy system."

Max, however, demurred. "I already helped cart Leon upstairs, for which the cops are going to jump me. Count me out on this one."

"Remember," said Russell in a small voice, "I'm squeamish."

"I wouldn't go near that room for a billion dollars," Margo declared.

"I'll go." Judith was so surprised by her impulsive announcement that she hardly recognized her own voice.

"I don't think that's a . . ." Ward began.

"Good idea," interrupted Killegrew. "It's probably smart to have an outsider on hand for something like this."

In other words, Judith thought with a sinking feeling, *there'd be someone else to blame.* But she'd opened her mouth and put her foot into it. As a flummoxed Renie watched, Judith accompanied Gene to the elevator.

"This might not be pleasant," Gene said as they moved up to the second floor.

"I've done it before," Judith said without thinking.

"Of course. Leon. And Barry." Mournfully, Gene shook his head.

"Yes," Judith agreed hastily. "Leon and Barry." It wouldn't do to enumerate a few other corpses she'd stumbled across in the past.

The door to Andrea's room was wide open. Judith quickly calculated that it was the same room she and Renie had first tried the previous night. As they had guessed, Andrea had been waiting for Leon in his room.

Gene stepped aside to let Judith enter first. She found herself tiptoeing, but stopped abruptly when she saw Andrea lying peacefully on the bed. The dead woman could have been asleep; only her head and shoulders were exposed. Andrea was on her back, with the silver hair splayed out on the pillow. Her plump face seemed blotchy, perhaps bruised. Remembering that Andrea was a fellow Catholic, Judith crossed herself and said a silent prayer.

"Poor woman," Gene said softly. "Suicide's such a desperate act."

Judith turned sharply. "It is. Andrea didn't strike me as a desperate woman."

"You never know what people are really like," Gene remarked, coming around to study the nightstand that stood between the twin beds. "Ah—here's the note and the empty pill bottle. Halcion, made out to Andrea Piccoloni-Roth last month. It's a popular prescription sleeping drug, I believe."

"Yes." Judith's mind was racing. On the other bed lay the extra pillow, which had been removed from under the spread. "What do you think of that note?" Judith asked, coming around to join Gene.

The company attorney kept his hands carefully pressed against his sides. "It's clear, isn't it?"

"In what way?" Judith queried.

Judging from the scowl on Gene's face, he didn't like being on the other end of questions. "Andrea couldn't live without Leon. What else could it mean?"

Judith said nothing. She stared again at the pillow on the empty bed. "Where's the water glass?" she asked.

"What water glass?" Gene sounded annoyed.

Judith pointed to the pill bottle. "There's no sign of a glass on the nightstand. Why would anyone take a bunch of sleeping tablets without water?" Judith didn't wait for a response, but went into the bathroom. "The glass is in here," she called. "Two glasses, in fact. One's clean, the other has a bit of water in the bottom."

Gene had moved to the bathroom door. The scowl was gone, but he looked puzzled. "What's your point?"

A sudden, paralyzing fear gripped Judith. She didn't know Gene Jarman. He seemed like a diligent, somewhat stiff-necked man who had brought himself up by the bootstraps. Yet his very success was evidence of not just ambition and determination, but perhaps ruthlessness as well. The same might be said of all the OTIOSE executives. And one of them was a killer. It could be Eugene Jarman, Jr.

"Nothing," Judith said in a careless voice. "I was just speculating."

"Is there anything unusual in the bathroom?" he inquired, gazing around the small but economical space.

"No." Judith started to come back into the other room;
Gene stepped aside. "Have you noticed anything we should
report on?" Judith asked in an unusually meek voice.

Gene didn't answer right away. He was standing at the
foot of the bed, staring morosely at Andrea. "She was a
nice woman, if you didn't cross swords with her. Then she
could be a real tiger." He moved between the beds. "I
shouldn't do this, but I feel I must." Carefully, he lifted
the sheet and pulled it over Andrea's face.

"That's . . . better," Judith said, relieved that Gene
hadn't suggested they move Andrea upstairs with Leon.
"Finished?"

Gene said he was. In silence, they returned to the lobby.

The brandy bottles had been emptied, replaced by gin,
rum, vodka, and whiskey. The mood, however, was
scarcely festive. When Judith got out of the elevator, she
noticed the look of relief on Renie's face.

"I think we should make more coffee," Renie whispered. "These people are going to need it once they kill
all the booze."

"Don't use that term," Judith urged, but was quick to
follow Renie out of the lobby. "Did anything happen in
my absence?" she asked when they reached the dining
room.

"No, just a lot of maundering about poor Andrea,"
Renie replied, unplugging the big urn on the buffet table.
"Her husband was a lazy dreamer, she was the breadwin-
ner, all Alan Roth ever wanted was a meal ticket, she
wouldn't divorce him because she was Catholic."

"Sounds familiar," Judith murmured, heading for the
kitchen. "After nineteen years of marriage to Dan, I can
sympathize with Andrea."

"I'll bet you can," Renie said as Judith firmly shut the
door behind them.

"That's not all," Judith said, pressing her back against

the door. "Much as I hate to say this, coz, I think Andrea was murdered."

Renie winced. "I hate to hear you say that," she breathed, "but why am I not surprised?"

"Because we're in the middle of a bloodbath, that's why." Judith closed her eyes for a moment, then squared her shoulders and walked over to the counter where she sat down on one of the tall stools. "First of all, Andrea wasn't the type to commit suicide. Even if she was in love with Leon Mooney—and we don't know that for sure—the Andrea Piccoloni-Roths of this world do not kill themselves."

Renie perched on one of the other stools. "It didn't sound right to me from the start."

"This isn't just amateur psychology," Judith went on.

"I hope not. Bill hates competition," Renie said, referring to her husband's staff position at the university. "Bill says that besides being simplistic and superficial, most non-professionals . . ."

Judith held up both hands. "Stop! Your husband's brilliant, but this isn't the time for one of your long-winded wifely essays. I'm talking *facts* here, coz. As in fact number one—there was an empty Halcion bottle on the nightstand next to the bed. Fact number two—the water glass, which you gave Andrea last night, was in the bathroom. Now who swallows pills in the bathroom with the water glass, and then takes the bottle with them into the bedroom?"

"Is 'nobody' the right answer?" Renie had assumed her middle-aged ingenue's air.

"Right. Fact number three," Judith continued. "The note said what Ava told us—'Leon, I'm coming to join you.' Andrea undoubtedly wrote that, but I'll bet she wrote it last night to slip under Leon's door. It simply meant that she was going to meet him in his room, which is where we found her when we went to tell her about Leon. But now she's in her own room, next door. My guess is that the killer found that note—probably on Leon—and used it to fake a suicide."

"Clever," Renie remarked. "And fortuitous."

"Exactly. Then we get to fact number four—which isn't really a fact, but a conjecture." Judith gave Renie an apologetic look. "The extra pillow that I'd put under Andrea was lying on the empty twin bed. Now it's possible that she removed the pillow herself. But I'm thinking that she came back to her room and simply flopped onto the bed. Under the circumstances, wouldn't you? She was worn out, she was upset, she very well may have taken Halcion to help herself sleep. Why remove the pillow?"

"She didn't." Renie's face was expressionless.

"Of course she didn't," Judith continued, "because . . ."

"Because she wasn't in Leon's room."

"What?" Judith made a face at Renie.

"You said so yourself." Renie lifted her hands, palms up. "The water glass and the pillow you're talking about were in Leon's room, not Andrea's. So what are you trying to say?"

Judith looked blank, then exhilarated. "What I was saying all along. Except that now I'm sure I'm right. The *killer* removed the extra pillow from under the spread of the other twin bed. Andrea didn't die from an overdose of sleeping pills. She was smothered."

Judith and Renie weren't sure how to break the news to the others. It hadn't seemed to Judith that Gene Jarman was suspicious. On the other hand, he wasn't the type to reveal what he was thinking. As the cousins made fresh coffee, they mulled over the problem.

"Andrea must have let in whoever killed her," Renie pointed out, running water from the tap into the urn.

"Of course she would," Judith agreed. "Despite Leon's death, she must have trusted whoever came to her door."

"Which could be anybody," Renie noted. "The only person she really seemed on the outs with was Margo."

"Andrea had probably already taken the Halcion," Judith said, opening the kitchen door for Renie, who was carrying the urn back to the dining room. "She was probably drowsy. Maybe whoever called on her offered to sit with her until she nodded off. Then he—or she—applied the pillow." Judith winced. "I thought her face looked sort of bruised, but then I don't know what effects an overdose of Halcion has on a person."

"I don't know, either," Renie admitted, plugging in the urn. "Didn't somebody say they heard noises during the night?"

Judith stared at Renie. "You're right. It was Margo. She thought someone was trying to get into her room. I'll bet Leon was on one side of Andrea's room and Margo was on the other."

"That's right," Renie responded. "I saw Margo come from that room last night when everybody heard the commotion."

The cousins gazed at each other. "Shall we?" Judith finally said.

"I suppose," Renie said reluctantly. "Our popularity is about to plummet to minus zero."

"Our popularity isn't the issue," Judith said bluntly. "Trying to stop a killer from striking again is what matters."

While not exactly drunk, the OTIOSE crew wasn't quite sober, either. Ava was curled up against Gene; Nadia appeared to be asleep; Ward and Max were arguing good-naturedly; Russell was talking to himself; Margo was sitting with her suede bag—and Ladysmith .38 Special—in her lap; Frank Killegrew was clutching his slide rule and staring off into space.

"Well, well," said Ward as the cousins entered the lobby, "here come the little ladies."

"Persons," Margo shouted, fingers digging into the suede bag.

"Lady persons," Ward chuckled. "Hey, at least they're still alive."

"That is *not* funny," Nadia declared, opening her eyes and glaring at Ward.

Renie had been delegated by Judith to break the news. She lighted a cigarette, took a few puffs, blew smoke in Margo's direction, remembered the gun, and apologized.

"Sorry, I'm kind of nervous. We don't bring good news."

"Oh, my God!" cried Margo. "Is someone else dead?" She glanced around the room, taking a head count. "We're all here," she announced on a sigh of relief.

"It's about Andrea," Renie began, nervously teetering on the flagstone hearth. "We don't believe she committed suicide. We think she was smothered with a pillow."

"My God!" Killegrew seemed incredulous.

"That's ridiculous," Gene said with a faint sneer.

"Don't Catholics go to hell if they kill themselves?" Russell asked in a mild voice.

"Of course she didn't kill herself," Margo asserted. "Andrea was too tough for that kind of cowardly act. And even if she and Leon had something going, I wouldn't exactly call it grand passion."

"What would you call it, Margo?" Ava asked with a smirk.

Color crept into Margo's plain face. "What do *you* mean? All I'm saying is that Leon was probably looking for a substitute mother. Andrea had a maternal air, I'll give her that. But she'd never do anything to ruin her marriage. Hanging on to Alan Roth was her priority." A note of bitterness had surfaced in Margo's voice.

"That's because she was a Catholic," Russell said doggedly. "They don't divorce, either."

"Bull," snapped Margo. "It's because she didn't want anybody else to have Alan."

"Now, now," Killegrew injected. "Let's stop boring holes in this ship's hull." He gazed up at Renie from his place on the sofa. "Excuse me, but I don't see where your opinions come into this situation."

Gene was on his feet. "I don't see how you came to this conclusion, Ms. Jones." He turned to Judith. "I assume this was actually your idea, Ms. Flynn?"

"Well, yes," Judith admitted as all eyes turned in her direction. With scrupulous attention to detail, she went over her reasoning. "The pillow is the key," she said after enumerating her deductions. "If you turned it over," Judith said directly to Gene, "I suspect you'd find traces of lipstick and other makeup on the pillowcase."

Nadia blanched at the implied violence. "That's awful! Who would do such a thing?"

All eyes avoided Nadia. "We *could* check," Gene said, his usual self-confidence slipping a notch.

"Then do it," Killegrew ordered. "We'll all go this time." He stood up. "Come on, let's get this over with."

"No!" Nadia cried. "I'm not going back to that room!"

"Neither am I," Ava declared.

"Dead people make me throw up," Margo asserted.

"I'm squeamish," said Russell.

In the end, Killegrew, Gene, Max, and Ward headed upstairs. The others retreated into the library, apparently in search of a different venue. Judith had tried to prod Renie into joining the upstairs contingent, but there wasn't room for a fifth person in the elevator. Renie suggested that she and Judith take a look at the room later.

"How do we get in?" Judith asked, putting another log on the fire.

"Good question," Renie replied. "Ava said Andrea's door wasn't locked when she and Nadia went up there this morning. As far as we know, the key is still in Andrea's room. I assume someone will look for it now. We'll have to ask."

"With Gene on hand, they won't search the place," Judith pointed out. "Which means they'll have to leave the door unlocked."

"Good point," said Renie, taking a cigarette from her

purse and indicating the bottles on the coffee table. "Dare we?"

"At ten A.M.?" Judith gave a little shake of her head.

"It's ten-thirty," Renie said dryly. "Anyway, who's counting? This isn't exactly a typical Saturday morning in January."

"It sure isn't," Judith began, and then stopped. A strange buzzing noise sounded from somewhere close by. "What is that? A timer?"

"It sounds like my new oven," Renie said. "It beeps at me when the temperature gets up to whatever I've set it for."

The noise stopped. Judith went to the big front windows, gazing out at the snow. "It's drifted so that I can hardly see anything," she said. "I wonder how much fell during the night."

"Three, four feet maybe? Can you tell if it's still snowing?"

"Not from this part of the lodge," Judith responded, glancing toward the big windows where the snow had piled up almost to the top frame. "I don't suppose I dare open the door."

"I wouldn't." Renie finished her cigarette and threw it into the grate. "It's sure quiet around here. At least it is between murders."

But the quiet was broken by the buzzing noise. Judith came back to the sofa, a puzzled expression on her face. "Is it a clock? The electrical system? An intercom?"

The cousins gazed around the lobby. There was nothing to suggest what had caused the sound. "Maybe it came from one of the conference rooms," Renie offered as the noise stopped again. "Somebody might have left a microphone on."

Judith didn't agree. "It's closer than that. It's right here, in this part of the room."

"Weird." Renie stared at the collection of bottles. "To

hell with it," she said, and reached for a fifth of Canadian Club. "I've had too much coffee and I'm not in the mood for my usual daily half-gallon of Pepsi."

"Okay, okay," Judith sighed. "Pour me some of the Dewar's scotch. How's the ice holding up?"

Renie shot Judith an ironic glance. "I don't think ice is a problem around this place, coz. What did you make of Margo's comments regarding Andrea and her husband, Alan?"

"It sounded as if Margo has the hots for Alan Roth," Judith replied, examining her fingernails. "Drat, I wrecked a nail somewhere along the line." She dug into her shoulder bag for an emery board, then continued speaking. "That would explain the flare-up between Margo and Andrea at lunch yesterday. Just now I got the impression that Margo wanted to marry the guy. I mean, why else would she care if Andrea wouldn't divorce him?"

"Exactly," Renie agreed. "Margo may be painfully plain, but she doesn't seem to have any trouble getting men. A regular boudoir bawd, goes the rumor mill."

"She's not all *that* plain," Judith noted, filing her snagged nail. "She has lovely eyes and perfect skin. Not to mention a vivid personality."

"She dresses well, despite the fact she has no figure," Renie said, then tensed as the mysterious noise sounded again. "Damn! What is that? It's really close by."

Judith looked all around the sofa where she was sitting. She dug among the cushions, feeling deep into the sides and back. "Maybe somebody dropped something down here," she said, her voice muffled.

Renie was on her hands and knees, searching under the sofas, chairs, and coffee table. "I don't see anything. Maybe we should get that flashlight." She started to stand up and accidentally knocked over Judith's shoulder bag. Some of the contents spilled out onto the floor. Renie let out a little yip. "It's your pager, you moron! Somebody's trying to reach you!"

At that moment, the elevator opened, and Max, Gene, and Ward entered the lobby. Between them, they were awkwardly carrying an unconscious Frank Killegrew.

TEN

"HE PASSED OUT upstairs," Max announced in a tense voice. "We think he may have had a heart attack."

Russell, Nadia, Ava, and Margo emerged from the library. Nadia in particular looked stricken, a thin hand at her throat and her skin suddenly turning ash-gray. "Not Frank!" she gasped.

Ava, however, seemed less affected. "Is he dead?" she asked in a manner that suggested her CEO's demise wasn't unappealing.

"No," Ward responded, as they carefully placed Killegrew on one of the sofas. "Frank's going to be just fine. He's one tough customer."

"Really," Russell squeaked, "if he isn't, I'd rather be somewhere else. Terminally ill people upset me."

"Buck up, Russell," said Ward. "I've seen Helen through worse crises than this. My wife once had three heart attacks in one day."

"I'll bet," murmured Margo.

Nadia had rushed to Frank's side. "Frank! Frank! Wake up! I'm here, I'll help, I'll do anything! Just say something!"

Frank's eyes remained shut. Nadia started to shake him, gently at first, then with more vigor. "Frank!

Please, please, tell me you're all right! What would I—what would we—do without you?''

Gene put a hand on Nadia's shoulder and firmly pulled her away. "Does anyone know CPR?" he inquired.

"Isn't that for people who are drowning?" Russell said in his usual vague tone.

"I'm not certain," Gene admitted. "We wouldn't want to do the wrong thing and have Frank's heirs sue us."

"Andrea'd know if she weren't dead," Ward murmured. "Her human resources folks are the ones who handle first-aid classes."

Judith, who had learned emergency measures to treat guests, started to speak up just as Killegrew appeared to come around. "Am I all right?" he demanded, blinking rapidly. "Did someone hit me on the head with an Eskimo?"

"No, Frank, certainly not," Nadia responded, her slim shoulders slumping in relief. The antidote to her attack of nerves appeared to consist of making herself busy. She deftly poured out a shot of Scotch and offered it to Frank. "Drink this," she urged. "It's a stimulant."

"It's Scotch," Killegrew murmured, but he accepted the tumbler. "Oh, my God! What's happening to us? This can't be real!" He attempted to sit up; Nadia and Ward each supported his effort.

"What happened?" Judith asked Ward, as the pager went off again in her purse.

No one seemed to hear the sound. "We were sort of moseying around Andrea's room, checking things out—without touching, mind you," Ward added with a quick glance at Gene Jarman, "and then we finally decided we'd better have a look at that pillowcase. Gene allowed as how it probably would be okay as long as we sort of held it up by the corners. Sure enough, there were some marks on it—kind of a reddish one and sort of a blackish one. When Frank saw that, he just keeled over."

"Why wouldn't I?" Killegrew grumbled. "My entire

staff is being wiped out!'' Regaining his usual jocund manner, he gave Margo a belligerent look. ''If I knew which one of you was doing this, I'd use that gun of yours and take matters into my own hands!''

''If you knew,'' Margo said between clenched teeth, ''I'd let you.''

Nadia was leaning into Killegrew. ''Are you all right? You shouldn't get so upset. It's bad for your digestion.''

''Screw my digestion,'' Killegrew growled. Then he put a hand on his chest. ''If I had a heart attack, I'm over it. Whatever it was, nobody can blame me for a collapse.'' He glanced at Ward. ''You're right. I'm one tough customer. Everybody knows that Frank Killegrew is fit as a fiddle and still captain of the good ship OTIOSE!''

''Yes, sir,'' Ward replied with a crooked grin. ''I mean, aye, aye.'' He saluted his superior.

''I think,'' Gene said slowly, ''that one of us has to try to get out of here and seek help.''

''How?'' Margo demanded with a sneer. ''The good ship OTIOSE doesn't have wings.''

''I looked outside from upstairs,'' Gene went on, ignoring Margo. ''The snow is letting up and the wind is down. There are skis in this lodge. There might even be a snowmobile around here someplace. If we could dig a path from one of the entrances, we could get somebody out. Who skis besides Frank?''

''I do,'' Ward responded, ''but it'd take hours to shovel the snow away from the doors.''

''If a path can be cleared, I can get out of here,'' Ava volunteered. ''I ski, so does Margo.''

Margo was still sneering. ''It's at least a mile to the highway. The snow's covered all the landmarks. We'd get lost. Count me out, I'm not going on any suicide mission.''

Russell quivered. ''Don't use that word.''

''Put a sock in it, Russell,'' Margo snapped. ''Andrea didn't commit suicide. She was murdered. Just like everybody else.'' All of Margo's bravado evaporated, and she swayed slightly, but caught herself on the mantelpiece.

"At least we could try," Gene persisted. "This situation has gotten completely out of control."

"You might say that," Ward said, acknowledging the understatement.

"Accidents," Killegrew muttered. "We'll say they were accidents."

"For Chrissake!" Max burst out. "Are you talking about a coverup? That's crazy, Frank!"

"Let's talk about it," Ward said in a calm voice. "It's about time we considered damage control."

"Holy cats!" Renie said under her breath. "Let me out of here. I can't listen to this bilge." She stomped off to the library.

Judith followed, closing the door behind her. "Killegrew can't be serious," she said.

Renie had flopped into a leather wingback chair. "Yes, he can. You'd be shocked by the things that CEOs and other executive types think they can get away with. Have you forgotten Watergate?"

"This is far worse," Judith asserted, sitting down in the mate to Renie's chair. "People are being murdered. If they attempt a coverup, the killer will go free."

Renie rolled her eyes. "You still don't get it, do you? The people—excuse me, the *persons* in the corner offices don't think like the rest of us. They live by a different set of rules and ethics. Try looking at it from Frank's point of view. If they get out of here with most of them still alive, and can actually pass off the three deaths as accidents, then allowing the murderer to go unscathed is a small price to pay to preserve not only OTIOSE's public image, but the company itself. The others would keep their mouths shut in order to keep their jobs. That's the way it works—or can—on the executive floor."

"Margo's already said she's going to quit," Judith pointed out. "She won't keep quiet."

"Maybe not, but it might depend on the package they

offer her when she leaves. It could be very lucrative—and very tempting. Besides,'' Renie went on, ''you'll notice she didn't mention quitting in front of the others. As far as we know, she only talked about it to us.''

Judith mulled over Renie's words of corporate wisdom. It was peaceful in the library, especially to Judith, who had always sought solace among books. Someone had built a fire in the small grate. For the briefest of moments, Judith tried to imagine that she and Renie were having a cozy chat on a wintry weekend in the mountains.

The pager went off again, shattering the illusory respite. ''Damn!'' Judith exclaimed. ''I forgot about that thing! How do I make it stop?''

Renie sighed. ''First off, you look in the little window to see who's calling you. Then you press a button that'll keep it from reringing. Those things are set up so that they keep going off until you acknowledge that you've taken the call.''

''Oh.'' Judith fished the pager out of her purse. ''This is hard to read.'' She held the little device under the table lamp next to her chair. ''Drat. It's my home number. It could be Mother. I wonder what's wrong? How do I answer this?''

''You can't, without a phone,'' Renie said, then brightened. ''This might be a good thing, coz. If it really is an emergency, then maybe somebody will figure out that you can't call back.''

Judith looked askance. ''Meanwhile, Mother is lying on the floor of the toolshed with her dentures wedged in her gullet?''

''Something like that,'' Renie murmured. ''Now if it were *my* mother, she would already have tried to page me about fifty times. It's a wonder she hasn't given me a pager for my birthday or Christmas. I keep hoping she won't figure out how they work. Her half-dozen phone calls a day are already enough to make me nuts.''

Judith was well aware that Aunt Deb's obsession with

the telephone—and with Renie—went to extremes. But Gertrude abhorred the phone and disdained the pager. She wouldn't try to contact Judith unless something serious had happened.

"Now I'm worried," Judith said, getting up and starting to pace around the library.

"That makes a lot of sense," said Renie. "You're worried about something that may or may not have happened and about which you can do absolutely nothing. In the meantime, we're sitting here like . . . sitting ducks."

Judith stopped pacing. "Meaning what?"

Renie laid her head back against the soft brown leather. "Meaning that you and I are not OTIOSE employees. We have nothing to gain by keeping our mouths shut. That, in turn, means that the killer has nothing to lose by getting rid of *us*. Now do you get it?"

Judith got it.

Lunch was a moribund meal. Judith and Renie served sliced ham and turkey, three kinds of bread, four varieties of cheese, what was left of the fresh fruit, and a pasta salad prepared beforehand at Hillside Manor. For the most part, the conferees picked at their food and kept conversation to a minimum. Whatever had gone on during the damage control meeting had markedly dampened their spirits.

"Poison," Judith heard Nadia whisper. "What if we're all being poisoned?"

"We'd have keeled over by now," Ward said, but he closely inspected his ham.

"I don't feel so good," Russell said, and spit out a strawberry.

"Don't be silly," Margo remonstrated. "You're imagining things."

"We have to eat to keep up our strength," Killegrew declared. "Look at me, I'm not afraid." He took a big bite out of his sandwich to prove the point.

Judith returned to the kitchen. A few minutes later, after

the cousins had eaten their own turkey sandwiches, she suggested that they check out Andrea's room.

Renie grimaced. "Must we?"

"It'll be okay. Gene covered Andrea with a sheet. We might as well do it now. When I went into the dining room the last time, it didn't look as if anybody intended to stir for a while."

The cousins used the back stairs. As they'd guessed, Andrea's door was unlocked. Upon entering, Judith and Renie both paused, lost in morbid thought.

"Gruesome," Renie whispered, gazing at the figure in the bed.

Judith was examining the extra pillow, which had been turned over to show the cosmetics smudges. "Andrea had put on fresh makeup for Leon and some of it had gotten smeared when she found out he was dead. But I knew there'd be enough left to make a mark on the pillowcase. This is a vital piece of evidence. I hate to see it left lying out in the open with an unlocked door."

"You wouldn't dare," Renie said faintly.

Judith folded her arms across her bosom. "I would, if I thought it would help convict a killer."

"Aren't we in enough trouble already?"

"Not quite." Gingerly, Judith slipped the case off the pillow.

"Oh, great!" Renie reeled around the room, accidentally knocking Andrea's briefcase off a shelf by the bathroom door. Hastily, she bent down to pick it up.

"Keep that briefcase," Judith ordered.

Renie stared. "You *are* deranged."

"Endangered, not deranged. You said so yourself." Judith began to pull out drawers, then go through the small closet. "We're buying life insurance," she said, opening Andrea's suitcase. "We're taking whatever evidence we can find and we're going to stash it and then we're going to threaten the OTIOSE crew."

"Good grief." Renie had sat down on the spare twin

bed. ''What with? Margo's gun, which we'll wrestle away from her in a dazzling display of martial arts?''

''No, of course not.'' Finding nothing of interest in the suitcase, Judith put it back in the closet. ''We threaten them with the evidence.''

''Which consists of one smudged pillowcase.'' Renie shook her head in a forlorn manner.

''So far.'' Judith pointed to the briefcase. ''We might find something in there. Come on, help me collect the water glasses and the sleeping pill bottle.''

''Fingerprints,'' Renie said doggedly. ''You'll ruin any fingerprints.''

''No, I won't,'' Judith replied from the bathroom. ''I'm very carefully putting the glasses back in the paper wrappers they were set out in by the staff. I'm also going through the wastebasket.''

''I'm going through the window,'' Renie said. ''I wish I'd never mentioned that we were about to be killed.''

The wastebasket yielded nothing except the paper covers for the glassware and an empty plastic garbage bag. ''Let's go,'' Judith said, grabbing Andrea's purse. ''I've checked out everything I can think of.''

Renie was still on the bed. ''I think it's safer to stay here with Andrea. At least she's not babbling like a self-destructive idiot.''

''That's because she already self-destructed.'' Seeing Renie's curious look, Judith clarified her statement. ''I don't mean suicide. I mean that something she did—or more likely something she knew—caused her death. I'm guessing that the same holds true for Barry and Leon.''

Reluctantly, Renie stood up. ''If you're referring to the exchange of gossip, I can see that with Andrea and Barry. But not with Leon. Did he strike you as someone who would sit around savoring juicy corporate tidbits?''

''No,'' Judith admitted, ''he didn't. But I keep thinking of that phrase somebody mentioned—'Mooney's Money.' Money is always an excellent motive.''

The cousins went out into the hall. "We've got to find a good hiding place," Judith said when they were in their own room. "It's too obvious to hide anything in here. Think, coz."

"How about the safe?" Renie said off the top of her head. "You can change the combination. Nobody will know."

Judith beamed at Renie. "Perfect. Let's check out the briefcase and purse before we go back downstairs. If there's nothing of interest, we can put them back in Andrea's room."

They went through the black leather handbag first. Andrea's wallet contained a great many credit cards and even more business cards. There were also several receipts, apparently saved for the purpose of possible returns or for income tax records.

"She hadn't cleaned this out for a while," Judith remarked. "Most of this stuff goes back to November and December. Wow!" She held up a small piece of paper. "Andrea bought somebody a Rolex watch! A Christmas present for Alan, maybe?"

"A bribe's more like it," Renie said, sorting through the rest of the handbag. "Maybe Andrea was trying to buy her husband's fidelity."

"This is kind of interesting," Judith said, holding up another receipt. "It's from Thursday, and it's for lunch at the Manhattan Grill. Andrea filled in all the tax-required info. Apparently, she treated Patrice Killegrew."

"So? I imagine it doesn't hurt to butter up the boss's wife now and then." Renie dug deep into the leather handbag. "Hey, I found another wallet. More keys, too. No wonder this sucker's so heavy . . ." Renie stared at the items in her hand. "This is Barry's stuff!"

Judith put Andrea's wallet down on the bed. "I'll be darned. What about the notebook and the rest of it?"

"It's all here." Renie handed the weathered notebook to Judith.

For a few moments, Judith was silent. "These things were meant to be found," she said at last. "If Andrea was a suicide, and the Leon Mooney affair story didn't wash, then we were supposed to believe that Andrea had killed Barry. Let me see those keys."

Renie handed over the ring that Judith had found in the cave. "Six keys," Judith said, spreading them out on the counterpane. She pointed to the first key on the ring. "House or apartment key, right? The next one's the same type, probably for a second lock. The big one's a car key. It looks a lot like the one to my Subaru. These three smaller ones are—what? A gym locker? A filing cabinet? Luggage?"

"They could be any of those things," said Renie, looking puzzled. "What's your point?"

"Did Barry have a car?"

"How would I know?" Renie sounded mildly annoyed, then snapped her fingers. "He must have. How else could he transport his catering supplies?"

"Okay." Judith seemed satisfied. "So that big key would be his. Where then is the key to the company van he drove to Mountain Goat Lodge?"

"Maybe it's still in the cave," Renie suggested. "You might have missed it."

Judith shook her head. "Not possible. They left in that van, with Nadia driving, remember?"

"Ah." Enlightened, Renie smiled at Judith. "Good thinking. So what you're saying is that the killer made sure he—or she—retrieved the van key from Barry after he was dead."

"That's right. Now we have to find out from Nadia who gave her that key. And why."

"Why what?" The puzzled expression returned to Renie's round face.

"If Barry had supposedly run off, he wouldn't have left the key behind," Judith reasoned. "So how did the killer explain having the key in his—or her—possession?"

"Maybe," Renie said, "we should go downstairs and leave the rest of this stuff until later."

"You mean we should get to Nadia while she's still alive?" Judith thought for a moment. "That's not a bad idea, but I'd like to finish our search so we can return this stuff in case somebody else comes looking for it."

The briefcase was full of what looked like personnel folders along with Andrea's notes, many of which had been taken at the previous day's meetings. "See what you make of these," Judith said, handing the notes to Renie. "I don't speak corporate lingo."

Renie scanned the handwritten pages. "Most of the references are about planning for the future. Frank's vision for OTIOSE, comments from the others, suggestions, ideas, all that sort of thing. It's pretty bland, if you ask me."

"I did," Judith replied absently, flipping through a fat daily planner. Since it started with January first, there weren't many entries, and most of them struck Judith as routine. She did, however, find Patrice Killegrew's name written in three times.

"Isn't this too much buttering up?" she asked of Renie. "Here's dinner with Patrice on Wednesday, January third, lunch on Friday, the fifth, and again last Thursday." Judith sifted through the receipts again. "I can find only the one from the Manhattan Grill. Patrice must have treated on the other two occasions. They lunched both times at that bistro in the public market."

"It might have something to do with Frank's retirement," Renie said, removing several folders from the briefcase. "You know, planning a big bash to honor the occasion."

"Wouldn't Nadia be involved in that?" Judith inquired.

"Well—yes, but sometimes human resources people get sucked in, too." Renie opened one of the folders. It was the same one she had found on the podium in the conference room. "Andrea played the horses?"

"Why not? We do when we get the chance." Judith put the receipts back in Andrea's wallet.

"I suppose she needed a vice besides Leon Mooney," Renie allowed. "He wouldn't make me feel steeped in sin. Hey, this is weird." Renie had turned to the second page of material in the folder. "There's another list, but it's names and titles and companies, along with a bunch of other really strange stuff."

Judith took the sheet of paper from Renie. The first listing read, "Charles E. Fisher, vice president—customer services, S.W. Com.; Oct. 8–10, Cascadia Hotel, Room 608, bouncy blonde or redhead, no S&M."

The cousins stared at each other. "Hookers." Judith formed the word silently. "Look at this—James L. blah-blah, assistant vice present, blah-blah, Plymouth Hotel, blah-blah, Asian or Hispanic, plumpish, into bondage. Here's one that says, African-American dressed as Little Miss Muffet, and right below it is some guy who wants a tall Scandinavian wheat-thrasher."

Renie started to giggle. "Somebody was running a hooker ring out of OTIOSE? That's rich!"

Judith wasn't laughing. "Andrea?" She wrinkled her nose. "It's possible, I suppose. In another life, she could have been a madam."

"No." Renie grew serious. "Not Andrea, not any of these top level female executives. They wouldn't exploit other women. I know I said that the sisterhood is a myth, but there *is* a code. Prostitution isn't part of it."

"So this was planted along with Barry's stuff?" Judith was puzzled.

"Maybe." Renie, who was sitting cross-legged on the bed, rocked back and forth. "Or Andrea found it on the coffee table where we left it and was going to take somebody to task."

Judith leafed through the remaining four pages in the folder. There were more names and descriptions, similar to the ones they'd originally thought belonged to race horses.

"Bronze Beauty—long-legged, aloof, can dominate"; "Crinkles—nicely padded, fun-loving, extensive costume wardrobe, wigs, undergarments, etc."; "Frangipani—exotic, erotic, no funny stuff."

The cousins, however, didn't recognize any of the supposed clients' names. They all appeared to be from out of town, mostly from the officer corps, and almost exclusively connected to the communications business.

"Who?" Judith demanded, handing the folder back to Renie.

"In this bunch? I could only guess, which would get me nowhere, because I wouldn't put it past any of the men." Renie hesitated before putting the folder back into the briefcase. "Evidence? Or not?"

Judith considered. "That folder seems to have a life of its own. Let's leave it and see what happens to it next. As long as we know where it is now, maybe we can learn something if it turns up somewhere else."

Renie complied. "I might exclude Killegrew," she said as they headed back into the hall. "He wouldn't dare dirty his hands with this sort of thing."

"He must know about it," Judith said as they approached Andrea's door.

"Maybe not," said Renie. "Maybe that was Andrea's fatal mistake. Maybe Frank Killegrew was about to find out."

After creeping downstairs, the only items the cousins put into the safe were the pillowcase, the water glasses, the pill bottle, and Barry's belongings. Inside the safe, the Eskimo carving still lay on the towel. Judith breathed a sigh of relief. The remainder of their pilfered collection had been returned to Andrea's room.

The OTIOSE staff, or what was left of them, had retired to the library. "If any more of them get bumped off," Renie said as they cleared away the lunch plates in the dining room, "they can start meeting in the elevator."

"That's not funny, coz," Judith snapped. "You're the one who thinks we're next on the hit list."

Renie sobered. "Not next. Last."

"Swell." Judith paused, holding several coffee mugs against her chest. "We've got to figure this out, coz. I really want to know who is going to try to do us in."

"That'd be nice," Renie admitted, then gave Judith an apologetic look. "Sorry, I didn't mean to be flippant. I just don't know how else to keep the horror at bay."

"Margo's gun might do that," said Judith as they returned to the kitchen. "Maybe we can eliminate some of these people."

Renie was startled. "With Margo's gun?"

"No." Judith gave her cousin a twisted smile. "I mean, as suspects. Russell, for example. Can you see him as a cold-blooded killer?"

"He'd be very cunning," Renie said, again quite serious. "Devious, too. Under that supposedly squeamish, vague exterior lurks genius. He's the R&D man, remember. I never put anything past people who sit around and just think."

"Okay, we leave Russell in," Judith said with reluctance. "If Margo was the killer, would she brandish that gun?"

"Why not? It's a great cover. No one's been shot. Yet."

"I like Ava," Judith said, putting away the uneaten ham and turkey. "Maybe it's because she lent me her clothes. Couldn't we cross her off the list?"

This time, Renie's response didn't come so promptly. When it finally did, it was qualified. "I like her, too, but she's ambitious. Don't you remember what she said about how she could be running WaCom if she'd stayed on? That implies she'd like to be running OTIOSE."

"I thought you said Ward Haugland was a shoo-in for Killegrew's job."

"There are no shoo-ins in the corporate world," Renie

responded. "He's the heir apparent. The key word is 'apparent.'"

Judith began unloading the dishwasher. "How about Ward?"

"Ward's viable. Under that 'aw-shucks' manner there's big-time drive and determination. Of course," Renie added, "he's been very loyal to Frank. I've heard that Ward has turned down a couple of other offers this past year."

"I suppose we can't rule out Max, if only because he has a hot temper and a lot of resentment," said Judith.

"He's strong, too," Renie noted.

"Which Nadia isn't. Could we skip her?" Judith's tone was hopeful.

"She's thin, but wiry. Like me, before I got fat. I'd never trust me. I can be vicious when aroused." Renie finished clearing off the counter. "Nadia's another one who's very loyal to Frank. I could see her committing a crime not for herself, but for him."

Judith stared at Renie. "Is she in love with Frank?"

"I don't know. Naturally, there have been rumors. A man and a woman don't work that closely together without having people talk about them."

"There's Gene," Judith said disconsolately. "Too prudent, too cautious, right?"

"Precisely the kind that can snap," Renie said. "Pressure—you don't understand what it can do at the executive level."

"So we're left with Frank Killegrew." Judith picked up a dish towel, gave it a frustrated yank, and tossed it onto the counter. "He founded OTIOSE. Why would he ruin it by killing off his employees?"

"Good question. To be honest, I can't think of an answer. He *is* OTIOSE. The perfect solution is that someone is out to get him, indirectly. If there was an outsider in this bunch, everything would make sense. But that's not the case, and we're up a stump." Renie heaved a big sigh just as Max and Ward entered the kitchen.

"We're looking for shovels," Max announced. "Crazy as it sounds, we're going to try to tunnel our way out."

"The snow stopped," Ward said on a note of optimism. "We may get a thaw." The two men headed for the basement.

Judith and Renie exchanged curious glances. "Tunnel?" said Judith.

"Thaw?" said Renie. "Don't count on it."

"They can't tunnel for a mile," said Judith. "That's crazy."

"They're desperate," Renie responded.

Judith gave a slight shake of her head. "Aren't we all?"

ELEVEN

MAX AND WARD had decided to go out through the front
entrance because it faced west and the snow might not
be as deep. Judith and Renie joined the others in the
lobby as Gene and Russell attempted to open the big
double doors.

"One at a time!" Killegrew shouted. "We don't want
an avalanche in here!"

The knotty pine door on the left slowly swung inward.
As feared, the snow came with it, spilling onto the flagstones and showering the onlookers with frozen particles.

"Eeek!" cried Nadia. "We'll be buried alive!"

But the pile of snow only reached about four feet into
the lodge. Near the top of the open door, they could see
daylight. Max, with hands on hips, surveyed the task that
lay ahead.

"We're snowed in, all right," he said, stating the obvious. "This is going to take some time."

"Better bundle up," said Killegrew, going over to the
coffee table. "Say, Nadia, could you fix me a Scotch
and soda?"

Nadia busied herself with bottles and glasses. Judith
noticed that the liquor supply was getting low. She wondered if there was more in the basement. Given all that

had happened so far, it wouldn't do to run out of booze.

Max and Ward headed for the elevator, presumably to put on their all-weather gear. Gene and Ava wandered back into the library. Margo and Russell followed Judith and Renie into the kitchen.

"Do we have enough food?" Margo inquired.

"We're fine," Judith assured her. "In fact, I was just wondering about the liquor. Maybe we could all go downstairs and see if there's a backup supply."

"They should have a wine cellar," Margo said. "Come on, Russell. It'll give us something to do."

Russell trailed Margo like a well-behaved pup. Judith and Renie joined them, carefully going down the narrow stairway. The basement wasn't quite what Judith had expected. It was partitioned into rooms. They passed the storage area for outdoor equipment, the game room with billiard and ping-pong tables, a large, well-stocked woodpile, a much larger laundry room than the small alcove off the kitchen, a heating and furnace room, another storage room where extra furniture was kept, and finally what passed for a wine cellar.

The bottles were stored in their original cases. To Judith's relief, there were also boxes filled with every imaginable liquor as well as two kegs containing beer, light and dark. Each member of the foursome grabbed as many bottles as possible and returned upstairs.

The lobby was empty and quite cold. The snow was melting on the flagstones, creating puddles of water. Judith and Renie went in search of a mop and some rags.

"When do we make our big threat?" Renie asked after they were in the supply room.

"I'd like to have more evidence first," Judith replied. "The pillowcase might prove that Andrea was murdered, but except for possible DNA results, it doesn't tell us who smothered her."

They didn't find any rags in the cupboards, so they had to make do with towels. Renie piled such a tall stack in her arms that only her eyes and hair showed. "Hold it. You said we had a life insurance policy. Show them, tell them." Renie bit off the words. "Now, before we expire, right along with your stupid policy. Come on, coz—we can't wait to get more evidence."

"I didn't say *get*," Judith responded, carrying a mop and a bucket. "I said *have* more evidence. Which isn't exactly right, either. What I meant was . . . um . . ."

"You haven't made up the evidence." Renie sighed, balancing the towels and following Judith out of the supply room. "In other words, you're going to tell one of your monster lies."

"I never lie," Judith said, indignant. "I might fib, but only when it's absolutely necessary."

"So what's the fib?"

"I don't know. That's why I'm stalling. You got any bright ideas?"

They were back in the lobby before Renie could come up with an answer. Ava and Nadia were exiting the women's rest room; Russell and Gene were standing in the doorway to the library; Frank Killegrew and Margo were nowhere in sight; Ward and Max hadn't yet returned from upstairs.

The cousins began wiping up the wet floor. Nadia offered to help. The heat from the lobby was causing the snow to melt fairly fast. It was almost impossible to get the flagstones dry.

"I suppose the snow that was up against the building was fairly soft anyway," Judith murmured, more to herself than to Renie or Nadia. "I'm not sure that opening the front door was a good idea."

"It's the only way to get help," Nadia said, down on her hands and knees.

"How's Frank?" Renie asked, wringing out a towel in the bucket.

"He's fine, he's really fine," Nadia replied. "We went to check on one of the smaller conference rooms. Margo's

with him now. We may move our meeting there. It's a bit
chilly in the lobby with the door open.''

''What about the library?'' Judith inquired. ''Isn't that
where you were earlier?''

Nadia made a face. ''Yes. But those big leather chairs
are so . . . comfortable. Russell in particular tended to nod
off.''

Renie, who had also been kneeling, stood up. ''This is a
losing battle. Between the warmer temperature outside and
the heat from the lodge, we're getting a regular little stream
across the floor. Look,'' she said, pointing to the top of the
open entrance way, ''we could see barely six inches of
daylight when the door was first open. Now it's nearly a
foot.''

Judith followed Renie's finger. Her cousin was right. She
could make out a fallen tree branch across the drifted snow,
or perhaps it was a piece of the roof that had blown off
during the blizzard. From what Judith could tell, the afternoon was overcast, but there was neither snow nor rain
falling on the mountainside. Perhaps their prospects were
looking up.

''Where the hell is Ward?'' Max demanded as he exited
from the elevator.

Everyone turned to stare at the marketing vice president
who was bundled up in a red and black hooded lumber
jacket.

''He went upstairs with you,'' Ava said. ''Isn't he in his
room?''

''If he is, he's in the can,'' Max retorted, then pushed
back a heavy glove to look at his watch. ''It's almost two-
thirty. We went up to change just before two. What's taking
him so long?''

Killegrew and Margo were coming from the conference
room area. ''Now, now,'' said Killegrew, ''what's going
on? I thought you and Ward were going to start digging.''
He gave Max an accusing look.

The vice president of marketing's slightly simian features

always looked pugnacious, but now they turned obstinate. "I'm not starting alone. I'll wait for Ward if it takes all afternoon. What's he doing in his room? Taking a nap?" Suddenly Max's big, burly body sagged. "What *is* he doing?" he mumbled.

"What are you talking about?" Killegrew demanded, taking a step forward and looking as if he wanted to shake Max. "Didn't you two stay together?"

Max paled. "We couldn't. Not the whole time. We had to get our gear from our separate rooms. It seemed pointless to change clothes together. Hell, we locked our doors. I mean, I did, and Ward's was locked when I tried it just now. Otherwise, I'd have gone in to see if he was in the can."

"Oh, dear!" Nadia's exclamation was very faint.

"Ward!" Ava clutched at the rolled-up collar of her blue sweater.

Frank Killegrew seemed to be at war with himself. The muscles in his face worked, his strapping body twitched, his eyes darted around the lobby. "We'd better all go," he finally said in a thick, uncertain voice.

Nadia pressed both of her small hands against his chest. "Not you, Frank! You've already had one terrible shock today. Please, stay here. I'll wait with you."

"So will I," Russell chimed in. "I'm squeam . . . ooof!"

Margo had belted Russell in the stomach. "Don't you dare say that again, you chicken! Go ahead, stay down here and cower in the corner. I'm going." She lifted her chin at Ava. "How about you?"

Ava shook her head. "I don't think so."

In the end, it was Max, Margo, and Gene who got into the elevator. The cousins would join them in the hallway, but they'd get there via the back stairs. They'd also bring an ax.

"I don't really want to do this," an unenthusiastic Renie said as they went down to the basement. "What we find isn't going to be nice."

"Probably not," Judith sighed, "but we should be there as witnesses."

"Why?" Renie asked as they headed for the alcove that housed the woodpile.

"Why?" Judith hesitated. "Well, because we need to know everything if we're going to figure out whodunit. More evidence, that's the ticket."

"I thought you were going to make some up," Renie replied in a peevish voice.

"I was, but real evidence would be better." Judith found two axes, but chose the one with the longer handle. "Let's go."

When Judith and Renie got back to the second floor, they saw Margo trying to turn the lock with a paper clip. She wasn't having much luck. Max and Gene hovered behind her. Judith had considered offering her expertise, but thought better of it; perhaps it wouldn't be wise to admit that she could not only crack a safe, but pick a lock.

"I could push it in," Max said. He had taken off his lumber jacket to reveal a heavy olive-green flannel shirt.

"No," Gene said, avoiding Max's gaze. "We don't want a gaping hole. That is, in case . . ." His voice trailed off.

Max saw the ax in Judith's hand. "Then we'll chop around the lock."

Gene nodded. "Go ahead. Let's hope Ward didn't shoot the dead bolt."

Ward hadn't. It took Max almost ten minutes to hack away at the solid pine, but eventually he freed the lock, doorknob, and brass plate from the door itself. Gingerly, Max reached into the opening and swung the door free.

The room looked like all the others that Judith had seen. It appeared to be empty. Max led the way, going to the foot of the twin beds, peering beneath them, checking the small closet, then opening the door to the bathroom. He looked in the tub. There was no sign of Ward.

Renie was shivering. Judith put a hand on her cousin's arm. "Hang in there, coz," she whispered.

"I'm okay," Renie said under her breath. "It's cold in here."

"It is, actually," Judith agreed. She glanced at the small fireplace. The grate was empty.

"I don't get it. I saw him go in." Max scratched his bald head, then went back to the closet. "His parka's gone. So are his ski pants. Look," he went on, pointing to a hanger. "There's the blue shirt and the navy cords he was wearing earlier today. He must have changed."

"Weird," breathed Margo. "What did he do? Go outside?"

"He couldn't get outside," Gene reminded her. "He must have left this room, locked the door behind him, and . . ." OTIOSE's legal counsel turned a bleak face to the others.

"My room's just across the hall," Max said. "If anything had happened out in the corridor, I would've heard it."

The room, with its chilly atmosphere and missing occupant, seemed to have acquired a sinister air. In a body, five unsettled people made for the door. Max closed it behind them, then stared down at the hole where the hardware had been.

"What are we going to tell Frank?" he asked in a dismal voice.

"The truth," Margo retorted. "Frank can take it. Besides, we don't know if anything happened to Ward. He might be wandering around the lodge looking for us."

The suggestion, no matter how overly optimistic, buoyed Max and Gene, who fairly bounded to the elevator. Even Margo seemed more amiable. As Judith and Renie hung back, they heard Margo call to them, "Come on, squeeze in. I'm skinny as a flagpole and you're kind of small, Serena."

"I used to be," Renie murmured, but she and Judith managed to fit into the small car.

Killegrew, Nadia, Ava, and Russell were waiting for

them with an air of dread. "Well?" the CEO demanded when they stepped out into the lobby. "What's happened to Ward?"

"Nothing," Margo replied. "We couldn't find him." Her face fell slightly as she looked around. "He's not here?"

"Of course not," Killegrew growled. "You mean he wasn't in his room?"

"No, he wasn't." Max seemed to topple from his brief elation. "I suppose we could search the basement."

"We went down there to get the ax," Judith said. "We didn't see him. But then we really didn't look. We went straight to the woodpile."

"Let's go." Max was already heading down the hall towards the basement stairs. Margo and Gene followed, but this time the cousins held back.

"We'd have heard him if he was there," Judith whispered to Renie.

"Probably," Renie replied. "But the basement is pretty big."

"Why would he go down there?"

"To get more shovels?" Renie shrugged, then added in a doubtful tone, "I wouldn't think he'd go alone."

Nadia gestured at the flagstones. "It's been melting quite steadily. We'd better mop up again."

"I'll get more towels," Renie volunteered, starting out of the lobby.

"Not alone, you won't," Judith said, hurrying after her.

"I'll join you," Nadia put in, almost running to keep up with the cousins. "Frank's safe. The others are here."

"Goodness," Judith said in amazement she hoped didn't sound feigned, "your devotion to Mr. Killegrew is really admirable. But then I work for myself. When you're your own boss, you can't look up to yourself."

"Frank Killegrew is a very exceptional man," Nadia declared as they reached the supply room. "I was with him when he was a Bell System vice president. In fact, I worked

for him from the time I left my post with the Red Cross in
New Delhi and moved back to the States. Frank had just
made middle management. Twenty-four years. I was teas-
ing him the other day, and saying we had a silver anniver-
sary coming up this November.''

"Really." Judith surveyed the towel supply, which was
beginning to dwindle. "That's a long time."

"We've made a good team over the years." Nadia's
voice was wistful.

Judith started out of the supply room with her stack of
towels, then stopped. "Say, Nadia, I've got an odd question
for you. Remember last year when you were at the lodge?"
She paused for Nadia's faint nod. "You told us you drove
the company van back to town after Barry disappeared.
Where did you get the key?"

Nadia rested her chin on the armload of towels. "The
key? Oh, dear—where did I get it?" She pursed her lips.
"Oh! I found it on the coffee table in the lobby."

Judith's face fell. "You don't know who put the key
there?"

"*Keys,*" Nadia corrected. "There was a small ring with
three, perhaps four keys on it. One was for the ignition,
one was for the storage compartment in the undercarriage,
and the other one—or two—were . . ." She paused. "I'm
not sure. Maybe they were duplicates of the others."

"But you still had no idea who left them on the coffee
table?" Judith persisted.

Nadia shook her head. "No. At the time, I assumed
Barry had left them after he'd . . . gone off." Behind the
big glasses, Nadia lowered her eyes.

"I see." Judith didn't know what else to say. She'd
come up against a dead end. The three women traipsed back
out to the lobby.

"Drat!" Renie exclaimed as they reached the entrance.
"It's snowing again. I can see it coming down by the top
of the door."

"It must have gotten colder," Ava said, getting up from

one of the sofas. "Once the sun—whatever there is of it—starts going down around three or four o'clock, the temperature drops."

"I could use another Scotch and soda," Killegrew called from his place near the hearth.

Nadia set down her stack of towels and hurried over to serve her master. Judith and Renie exchanged sardonic glances. A moment later, Gene, Max, and Margo appeared in the hallway.

"No luck," Max stated, looking disturbed. "We searched every freaking nook and cranny. No Ward."

"That's ridiculous," Killegrew said in a gruff voice. "He has to be somewhere. What about the other rooms?"

Margo gave Killegrew a skeptical look. "Why would Ward be in somebody else's room? That doesn't make sense."

"We know he went to his own," Gene put in. "We saw his clothes."

Killegrew drew back on the sofa, squaring his broad shoulders and tossing his slide rule from one hand to the other. "That doesn't mean he stayed there. For God's sake, use your brains. My executive vice president didn't just evaporate in a cloud of smoke! I say, everybody check out their own rooms. Andrea and Leon's, too. Let's hit it!"

Everyone scurried for the elevator except the cousins and Killegrew, who gave his key to Nadia. Even Russell was dragged along by Margo, despite his squeals of protest.

"We'll go last," Renie said. "We can't all get in the elevator anyway."

"You bet you'll stick around," Killegrew said ominously. "I'm not staying down here by myself. It's not that I'm afraid," he added hastily. "It's just that we agreed on the buddy system. If you don't sail your ship by the book, you'll end up on the skoals."

"That's *shoals*, Frank," Margo called, just before the elevator doors closed on her and Max, Gene, and Russell.

Nadia and Ava decided to take the stairs. Killegrew, with

his fresh drink, put his feet up and stared off into the crackling fire. The cousins returned to their task of mopping up.

"Consider the big picture," Frank Killegrew said suddenly.

Judith and Renie turned curious gazes on OTIOSE's CEO. "Which big picture?" Renie finally asked.

"The future of telecommunications in the Northwest," Killegrew said, sounding sententious. "Where do you see yourselves ten years from now?"

"Paris?" Renie had gotten to her feet.

Killegrew waved a beefy hand, then retrieved his slide rule from the coffee table. "I'm talking about your lifestyle, your quality of communications service, your wants and needs when it comes to . . . ah . . ."

"I think," Renie said slowly, "you need to be more specific."

Killegrew's blue eyes narrowed. "Okay, try this. If OTIOSE goes down the toilet, a whole bunch of other, smaller, less efficient companies will leap into the breach. You think it's bad now with all your different phone bills and companies? If you can't figure out which one can fix your inside wiring or your outside line or even your five different phones, think what will happen then. Rates will go up, quality will go down, you'll be lucky if you can get two tin cans and a piece of string to call your next-door neighbor."

"I don't call my next-door neighbor," Renie retorted. "She hates me."

Killegrew didn't try to hide his exasperation. "Don't act stupid. You get my point." He waited, his eyes moving between Renie and Judith. "How much will it cost us to keep the two of you from shooting your mouths off?" he finally said.

"Let's start the bidding at three point five million and stock options," Renie replied. "That's each. Our silence isn't merely golden, it's platinum."

"Too much." Killegrew's chin jutted.

Renie flicked a wet towel at the air. "It's not negotiable.

Remember, I want to be in Paris in ten years.''

Ava and Nadia returned via the elevator. "No luck," said Ava in a grim voice. "The others are checking the . . . deceaseds' rooms now.''

Judith nudged Renie. "Our turn," she said under her breath.

In the elevator, Judith expressed her shock over Kille- grew's offer. "Is he serious? Does he think he can bribe us?''

Renie shrugged. "The idealistic stuff about OTIOSE got nowhere. What else did you expect?''

"This is terrible." Judith leaned against the rear of the car. "You were right. He's unscrupulous.''

"I've been trying to tell you, they all are," Renie said as the doors slid open to reveal the second floor. "Most of them, anyway.''

Max and Gene were coming out of Andrea's room while Russell quavered in the hallway with an irritated Margo at his side. "No Ward in any of the rooms," Max said in a morose voice. "Try yours.''

The cousins' room was empty, too. "What about the third floor?'' Gene asked.

"Why the hell would Ward go up there?'' Max de- manded. "The only thing of interest is Leon, and he's stiff as a board.''

"It was a thought," Gene said apologetically.

Max sighed. "I suppose we'd better look. Come on, Gene. The others can go back downstairs.''

Along with Margo and Russell, Judith and Renie took the elevator to the lobby. No one spoke during the brief descent. As soon as they stepped out of the car, Killegrew made a request.

"We could use some appetizers to go with these drinks," he said, looking put upon.

Margo sneered. "You're the only one who's drinking, Frank. I don't think the rest of us have much of an appe- tite.''

"There's some cheese and crackers," Judith said. "If you like, I can make up a tray."

Killegrew nodded. "As I said, we have to keep up our strength."

The cousins trekked off to the kitchen. Russell Craven was at their heels, hemming and hawing.

"I don't mean to trouble you, but . . . ah . . . er . . . I would enjoy a cup of tea. Um . . . often, in the afternoon around this time, my secretary, Ms. Honeythunder, brings me a nice hot cup."

"It's no bother," Judith assured him. "I'll put the kettle on right away."

"Soothing," Russell said with a little sigh. "Refreshing. Bracing. Hot tea." He started to sit down on one of the stools, then jumped back as if he'd been stung by a bee.

"Is that . . . ?" Jerkily, he pointed to the counter.

"More or less," Renie said. "Go ahead, sit down. What Leon had isn't contagious."

"But it is." Russell's fair, rather weak features were filled with despair. "One by one, we're . . . doomed."

The remark was unsettling. Judith opened her mouth to contradict Russell, considered what had happened thus far, and kept quiet. Renie squirmed a bit before taking Russell by the hand and leading him to a stool on the opposite side of the counter.

"If you really believe that," Renie said, at her most solemn, "then you must try to help us. Do you know why your people are being killed?"

Russell chewed on his lower lip. "I've been thinking about that. Of course, that's all I ever do—I think."

"And you get ideas," Renie said encouragingly. "Often, they're brilliant ideas. How about now?"

"Well . . . um . . ." Russell ran a hand through his unruly hair. "It had occurred to me that someone was trying to get Frank's possible successors out of the way to make room for himself—or herself. Naturally, the ultimate decision is always up to the board of directors." Russell uttered

a nervous little cough, perhaps embarrassed by his uncharacteristic loquaciousness. "But you see, I don't think Andrea or Leon was being considered—though you never
know. And that young fellow—what was his name?—he
was from the lower ranks. So that doesn't seem likely, does
it?"

"No," Renie agreed. "It doesn't. I understand that Ward
and possibly Ava and maybe you are the prime candidates."

"Not me!" Russell held up both hands as if to ward off
the corner office. "I'd never take such a pressure-packed
position! I'm perfectly happy where I am! I'd make a terrible CEO!"

Judith, who had gotten out a big oval tray and placed it
on the counter next to Russell, began opening boxes of
crackers. "Can you think of another motive?" she asked
in a quiet, composed voice.

Russell sighed. "I try to avoid getting involved in office
politics. I always have. I've spent my whole career in research and development, starting with Bell Labs right after
I graduated from college in the East. Since I came to OTI-
OSE eight years ago, I've concentrated solely on new products and applications. I pay no attention to what goes on
in other departments. That's why Max got so mad at me
last night. Maybe he has a point. But I abhor distractions."
Russell uttered a small, embarrassed laugh. "I guess that's
why my wife told me I could come out here by myself.
Emmy felt as if *she* was a distraction. Poor girl, maybe she
was."

Judith was slicing cheese. "Your wife remained in the
East?"

Russell nodded. "She still lives in New Jersey. Our children are grown, and on their own. More or less."

"Less is not more when it comes to children," Renie
murmured. "You live alone, Russell?"

"I do. It's fine." He gave both cousins a diffident smile.
"No distractions."

The tea kettle whistled. Judith hadn't been able to find a tea pot, so she poured the hot water directly into a mug and added a tea bag. "Then you can't think of any reason why someone might be killing your co-workers?"

Sadly, Russell shook his head. "As I mentioned, power is very attractive to certain people. Persons, I mean. But it doesn't seem to be the case here. Especially under the revised circumstances."

Renie jumped on the phrase. "What revised circumstances?"

Russell drew back on the stool. "Well . . ." His fair skin flushed. "I can't actually say. It's just that . . . er . . . ah . . . the future isn't as clear as it once was."

Renie leaned closer to Russell. "For OTIOSE in general?"

He fidgeted on the stool. "Not . . . um . . . well . . . It's too complicated, and I shouldn't have mentioned it."

Remembering that Russell liked cream, Judith poured some into his mug. "You should if it would save lives," she said in her sternest voice.

For one fleeting moment, the stark expression on Russell Craven's face indicated that he was about to unburden himself. But he shook his head, and spoke with unusual firmness. "No. I can't betray a trust. Besides, I honestly don't believe that there's any connection between these awful murders and . . . my point of reference."

Judith's shoulders slumped in discouragement; Renie turned her back on Russell. A strained silence fell over the kitchen.

At last, Russell cleared his throat. "Excuse me . . . Could I have some sugar, please?"

Judith gave Russell the sugar and a baleful look. Seeing that he would not leave the kitchen without them, Judith hurried through her task. She found some olives and pickles in the refrigerator, added them to the tray, and headed for the lobby.

Renie and Russell followed. Killegrew was not the only

one who was drinking by the time Judith put the appetizer tray down on the coffee table. Max and Gene had returned after a fruitless search of the third floor. They each held a martini glass, as did Nadia and Ava. Margo was drinking straight Scotch from a shot glass.

"I have hot tea," Russell said in a shy voice, though it was impossible to tell if the statement was made to assert his virtue or to prevent an offer of alcohol.

"Gene and I are going to start shoveling after we polish these off," Max said, indicating his cocktail. "We can't wait around all day for Ward, especially now that it's started to snow."

"I can't think where Ward would be," Nadia said in a fretful voice.

"Who can?" Margo snapped. "You've already said that forty times."

Judith glanced at the flagstones near the entrance. The water was getting deeper and wider. "We'd better get back to work," she said to Renie. "Otherwise, we're going to be at flood stage."

"Great," Renie murmured. "I can't swim."

The cousins returned to their seemingly endless chore. They could hear the pressure of the snow against the lodge, causing creaks and groans in the structure. Despite the new flakes, there was yet more daylight showing at the top of the doorway. Judith noted that the branch or piece of roof or whatever it was that had fallen onto the drift was moving downward and forward.

"Watch out for that thing," she said with a warning poke for Renie. "It's starting to slide. It might be something heavy."

It was. As Judith and Renie watched with a sickening sense of horror, they saw the body of Ward Haugland skid from the top of the snowbank and fall on the flagstones with a dull, dead thud.

TWELVE

EVERYBODY SCREAMED. GENE spilled his drink on the Navajo rug, Margo reached for her gun, Max dropped a gin bottle, which smashed on the flagstone hearth, and Frank Killegrew leaped from the sofa so fast that his pants ripped. Ava slid off the footstool, just missing the broken glass from the bottle that had slipped from Max's hands. Nadia and Russell swayed in their respective places with eyes shut tight and expressions frozen in grotesque masks.

"Ward!"

"Is he . . . ?"

"God!"

"No! No! No!"

"How . . . ?"

"Save us! Somebody, please!"

"I'm going to throw up now."

Bedlam reigned for the next few minutes. Judith and Renie scrambled out of the way, slipping and sliding on the wet floor. Ward Haugland stared at them from wide, lifeless eyes. The cousins finally staggered toward the cluster of sofas.

Gene, whose normal composure now seemed completely shredded, took a few hesitant steps towards the latest victim. "Madness," he muttered. "Where will it

161

all end?'' He stopped, some ten feet away from Ward.

Max joined Gene. ''What the hell . . . ?'' Max said under his breath. ''I don't get it.''

''His room,'' Judith said thickly. ''Where is his room?''

Max and Gene looked at her as if she'd lost her mind. Maybe, she thought dazedly, she had. ''His room,'' she repeated, more clearly. ''Wouldn't Ward's room be above the front entrance? It's in the middle of the second-floor corridor.''

Comprehension dawned on Gene. ''I see. You mean . . .'' He stopped, then shook his head. ''That's terrible.''

''What are you jabbering about?'' Killegrew demanded. ''Speak up, dammit!''

Gene turned to face his CEO. ''Ward's room is right above the entrance. Whoever killed him must have pushed him out the window.''

''That's why it was so cold in there,'' Renie said under her breath. ''The window had been open.''

''Ridiculous,'' scoffed Killegrew. ''Ward must have jumped. It's another suicide.''

''Jeeesus!'' screeched Margo. ''Who would try to commit suicide by jumping out a window into a snowbank? Get over it, Frank—Andrea didn't kill herself and neither did Ward.''

''Then how did he die?'' Ava asked, clinging to the footstool.

With small, creeping steps, Max and Gene moved forward. ''We really shouldn't touch the . . .'' Gene began.

''Stick it up your backside,'' Max growled. ''We have to find out what happened and we can't leave poor old Ward lying here like a doorstop.''

''Close that door!'' Killegrew ordered in a savage voice. ''We're never going to shovel through that stuff! It's getting dark, it's too late. Besides, this place is a mess. Look at that floor!''

Naturally, everybody looked at Ward. ''Gee, Frank,''

Margo said, at her most sarcastic, "you're right, as usual. Having Ward's corpse cluttering up the flagstones is pretty darned unsightly. How come we can't keep this vessel ship-shape and trim-tidy?"

"Margo," Killegrew roared, "I've just about had enough out of you!"

"You sure have," she shot back. "All my speeches, all my words, all my vast vocabulary. If it weren't for me, you'd be reciting catch-phrases off of gas station reader boards."

"Good God Almighty!" The words were torn out of Max's throat as he and Gene bent over the body. "It's a garrote! Just like—" He jabbed a finger at Judith and Renie. "—they said about Barry!"

Several people gasped, including Judith, who edged forward. Bending down to peer between Gene and Max, she saw what looked like a leather belt twisted around Ward Haugland's neck. But something was missing. There was no stick. Judith said nothing, but she had to wonder why.

The unease in the lobby was palpable. Every person in the room seemed to be casting wary glances in the direction of everyone else. Margo was hugging her suede handbag, but fear flickered in her dark eyes.

"Close that door, I said." Frank Killegrew's voice sounded hoarse. "Now! I feel a draft!"

"It's the hole in your pants, Frank," said Margo. "Aren't you a little old to have pictures on your underwear?"

Killegrew turned crimson. "Close that door!"

Nobody moved. Gene cleared his throat. "We have to face facts. One of us is a killer. There's no one else here."

"Did any of you hear me?" Killegrew roared. "For the last time, close that damned door!"

Max finally went to the door and gave it a tug. "I can't," he said in a helpless voice. "There's too much snow blocking it."

Someone laughed. The sound did not come from the

lobby. It came from outside, drifting in over the snowbank and echoing off the knotty pine walls.

The listeners inside the lodge were too stunned to scream, too scared to move. They just stood there, open-mouthed and terrified.

Then, their little world became suddenly, ominously silent.

Judith and Renie had taken their very stiff drinks into the library. "They think we did it," Judith said. "They think we have an accomplice outside."

"Do we?" Renie saw Judith's puzzled expression, and continued. "I mean, is someone out there who might be the killer?"

Judith propped her chin on her fists. "It's possible. But hasn't the lodge been locked until now? And how would anybody get through the snow? If we can't get out, who could get in?"

"It's crazy," Renie responded. "But somebody's out there. Who the hell is it?"

Wearily, Judith shook her head. "I can't imagine. The caretaker? He'd have keys."

"His place is a half-mile from here," Renie said. "Keys or no keys, he'd still have to get through the snow. And what would bring him out in this awful weather when he's been ordered to stay away?"

Judith didn't answer immediately. In the lobby, she knew that Max and Gene were removing Ward Haugland's body and taking it up to the third floor to join Leon Mooney. Frank and Nadia had gone upstairs so that she could mend his pants with her sewing kit.

"Who *is* the caretaker?" Judith finally asked.

"I don't know," Renie responded, stoking up the fire which had been about to die out. "Somebody hired by the lodge, I suppose."

"His place is a half-mile which way?" asked Judith.

"I don't know that, either." Renie was getting crabby.

"Let's find out," Judith said, taking a big swig of Scotch.

"How?" Renie was still irritated.

"We'll ask somebody. Maybe Frank. Or Nadia. Didn't you say that . . ."

The pager went off. Judith jumped, then groped around in her shoulder bag. "Now what?" She peered in the little window. "Damn—it's my home number again."

There was a phone on the desk in the library. "Try it," Renie said, apparently making an effort to overcome her annoyance. "Maybe the brief lull in the weather freed up the line."

To Judith's surprise, she heard a crackling noise when she picked up the receiver. Jiggling the disconnect button, she tried to get a dial tone. Nothing happened. "They could be working on it," she said as she hung up.

"Could be," Renie said. "We don't know where the problem is. It might be clear down the pass or even back in the city."

"It must be Mother trying to reach me," Judith murmured, drinking more Scotch. "I'm not sure I ever mentioned the pager to Joe."

"It's Saturday, Joe's home," Renie pointed out. "If something happened to your mother, he'd know about it."

"Joe might be working overtime. He could be running errands. He may have gone somewhere with Bill." Judith's voice grew increasingly agitated.

"They may be snowed in, too," said Renie. "You know how it is on Heraldsgate Hill—three inches, and we can't budge. Heck, it's so steep in our neighborhood that we can't even get out of the garage."

"Y-e-s," Judith admitted, then finished her drink. "Come on. It's time to present the evidence."

Renie looked skeptical. "Which is?"

"Just follow my lead."

Sidling up to the coffeetable, Judith poured herself a small measure of Scotch. The OTIOSE group appeared to be in wary, desultory conversation. They all seemed to tense when Judith and Renie joined them.

"Excuse me." Judith rattled the ice cubes in her glass. "*Excuse me*," she repeated, somewhat louder. Nadia and Russell were still talking to each other. "Thank you," Judith said when everyone had finally turned anxious faces in her direction. "I have a small speech."

"Hunh," snorted Margo. "Somebody's giving a speech I didn't have to write for them? How bizarre!"

Judith tried to ignore Margo. Indeed, she also tried to ignore the malevolent stares from the OTIOSE employees. "My cousin, Serena, and I are in a very awkward position," Judith began, her voice sounding unnaturally high. "While Serena knows some of you slightly, I'm a complete stranger. Therefore, I wouldn't blame any of you for being suspicious of us."

"Damned straight," said Max.

"You're outsiders," said Ava.

"Why shouldn't we be suspicious?" demanded Killegrew.

"I'm not suspicious," Russell maintained. "They made me a nice cup of hot tea."

"Thank you, Russell," Judith said with a small smile. "As I was saying, we understand your concern. It appears to be on two levels. The first is that some of you may think we perpetrated these heinous crimes." Judith paused, waiting for comments. There were none, though anxious glances were exchanged. "The second," she continued, "is that you may be afraid that we're going to rush off to the media and reveal everything that's happened here."

"You wouldn't dare!" cried Nadia.

"Don't try it," warned Killegrew.

"We can get an injunction," murmured Gene.

"Talk your heads off, who cares?" said Margo.

It occurred to Judith that the threat of exposure by the cousins posed a greater danger to most of the OTIOSE crew than did the possibility of Judith and Renie carving them up with a chainsaw. Taking their reaction as confirmation, Judith resumed speaking.

"The fact is, we haven't harmed anyone nor do we intend to. Not in any way." Again she paused, this time for emphasis. "However, we will do our civic duty. It so happens that we have acquired certain evidence which points to the killer. Not only has this evidence been placed in safe hands, but so has a note stating that if anything should happen to either of us, those damning proofs will be turned over as soon as humanly possible to the authorities."

"Evidence?" Ava wore a bewildered expression.

"You're bluffing," Killegrew declared.

"Is this *physical* evidence?" Gene queried.

"Most definitely," Judith responded, wondering if Gene had an inkling about the pillowcase. "Several pieces of evidence, in fact. They're all in safe hands."

"Wait a minute," Max said with a deep scowl. "Who did you give this stuff to? There's nobody here but us." Despite his statement, everyone turned toward the entrance where the door still stood open.

Judith was quick to squelch speculation. "We don't know where that laugh came from any more than you do," she said to the group in general. "As for the evidence— and the note—we gave everything to the one person we know did *not* commit any of these crimes. You know who you are, and that you are sworn to secrecy. You also know that we have a note from you, making the same kind of statement to ensure your own personal safety." Judith's gaze floated somewhere above the gathering. "That's all I have to say. Thank you."

Max raised a hand. "Hey! What about Q&A? We always have Q&A after a speech."

"We always have cookies," Russell put in.

But Judith had withdrawn to the other side of the room, where Renie stood with an inscrutable expression on her face. "Shall we mop?" Renie asked out of the corner of her mouth.

"I'm tired of mopping," Judith asserted in a low tone. "I'm tired of this lodge, and these people, and the whole damned thing." She took another big swallow of Scotch.

"What about dinner? It's going on five."

"Don't tell me you're hungry."

Renie shook her head. "Not really. But I assume the herd will want to graze."

"Let them. I quit."

"Hm-mm. You're getting testy, coz. Is it the booze or the company?"

"Both." Judith nudged Renie in the direction of the dining room. "Let's go in there. We can actually talk above a whisper."

Once the doors were shut behind them, Renie grinned at Judith. "That was brilliant, coz. You even managed to stun me with that part about the note to one of the OTIOSE gang."

"It'll keep them guessing," Judith said. "I had to come up with something."

"I wish we *could* trust one of them," Renie said, her grin fading. "What about Nadia? Could she push Ward Haugland out a window?"

"You said yourself she's wiry." Judith sat down at the banquet table reserved for the conferees. "If you know how to use a garrote—I gather there's an art to it—you need surprise rather than strength. In fact, it would be easy if the killer somehow first rendered the victim helpless. As for pushing Ward out the window, that would depend on where he was standing when it happened."

"He was a fairly big guy," Renie pointed out, sitting down next to Judith.

"Tall, yes, but lean and lanky. A hundred and sixty pounds, I'd guess. It could be done, even by someone like Nadia. The real question is, who flunked the buddy system?"

Renie's eyes widened. "You're right. Unless it was Max

who was also alone in his room upstairs, somebody got loose.''

"I've been trying to think back to when we returned to the lobby after Max and Ward went upstairs to change. How long were we gone collecting towels in the supply room? Five, ten minutes at most?''

"About that,'' Renie agreed. "But before we went there, we'd been in the basement getting more liquor.''

"That's right.'' Judith drummed her nails on the bare table. "Margo and Russell went with us. They took the bottles out to the lobby. Where were they when we finally got there?''

Renie's face fell. "I don't remember. Nadia and Ava were coming out of the restroom, though.''

Judith nodded. "Have you ever noticed how long other women take to use a stall at a public restroom?''

Renie chuckled. "I figure they must be completely dressing and undressing. Maybe they put their clothes on backwards, and then switch them around. It beats me, but I sure get tired of standing in long lines at the theater or the opera or a ball game.''

"That's what I mean,'' Judith said. "It's conceivable that a woman—let's say Ava, just for the heck of it—could go into a stall at the same time as another woman—like Nadia—and come right out, leave the restroom, then return five, even ten minutes later, without the other woman knowing she was gone.''

"It's a stretch,'' Renie said with a frown.

"Try this—one of them says she forgot her purse. The other one is already in the stall. She waits, because she feels it's safe, the other woman will be right back.''

"Okay, I'll mark 'slim' by that one,'' Renie conceded. "What about the rest of them?''

Judith concentrated on her memory of the lobby as she had seen it upon her return from the supply room. "Russell and Gene were talking by the library. But we know they hadn't been together long because Russell had been with us in the basement. Who had been Gene's buddy before that? Was he alone for a few minutes before Russell came along?''

Renie snapped her fingers. ''Frank and Margo had gone to check on one of the conference rooms. That's why they weren't there.''

''You're right, but nobody could see them. Did they stick together?'' Judith made a face. ''It's impossible to figure out unless we interrogate them separately. That won't be easy.''

''How about impossible? The buddy system, remember?''

Judith grimaced. ''That's true. You and I will have to be their buddies, I guess.''

''Gack.'' Renie finished her Canadian whiskey. ''You mean, we each take one of them aside and pump away?''

''You got it. It should be kind of subtle. I'll take Margo, Ava, and Nadia. You get Frank, Max, and Gene. Russell's up for grabs.''

''Hey!'' Renie wagged a finger in Judith's face. ''How come you get all the women?''

''Because women can always talk to women, no matter what their backgrounds. On the other hand, men don't open up so easily. But,'' Judith went on in an attempt at flattery, ''you're used to corporate types. You have a knack.''

''Twit,'' said Renie. ''Don't pull your soft soap act on me. I get the tough ones. Thus, you get Russell. He likes you best. You made him tea.''

''Fine.'' Judith finished her Scotch and stood up. ''Let's go separate a couple of them from the herd.''

''How do we manage that?'' Renie asked with a dubious expression.

Judith gazed in the direction of the kitchen. ''I guess we'll have to make dinner after all. I'll cook, you mop.''

''Jeez.'' Renie wasn't pleased. ''So I get Frank to help me swab the decks while you and Margo peel potatoes.''

Grinning, Judith tipped her head to one side. "I like that. Frank will like that. It's right up his cliché alley."

"No, thanks. I'll ask Gene. Lawyers are used to cleaning up after other people." Renie led the way back into the lobby.

At first, Margo was reluctant to join Judith. But after some coaxing, the p.r. vice president patted her suede bag and agreed to accompany Judith to the kitchen. Meanwhile, Renie managed to secure Gene's help with what was becoming a rather alarming situation in the entranceway. The water was edging toward the near walls and creeping up on the Navajo rugs in the sitting area. Russell suggested that they search for an indoor-outdoor vacuum in the basement.

"Good thinking," Renie said. "They must have something like that because of all the skiers trooping in and out. Come on, Gene, let's go look."

A sense of trepidation stole over Judith as she watched her cousin and Gene Jarman head for the basement. But she herself had been alone with Gene earlier. Nothing alarming had happened. Surely Renie was safe. The cousins had issued their insurance policy.

Margo seemed to be studying Judith closely. "I'm not much of a cook," she said, still holding the suede bag. "Why me? Why not your cousin? Or Nadia?"

"My cousin and I are getting a bit sick of each other's faces," Judith said glibly. "As for Nadia, it seems to me that she always gets stuck with the grunt work. Why not spread it around?"

"Because I'm a vice president and Nadia's not." Abruptly, Margo looked contrite. "Sorry. That was arrogant. In any event, I don't expect to be a vice president much longer."

Judith was removing a dozen stuffed Cornish game hens from the freezer. "Here," she said to Margo as she placed the frozen birds one by one on the counter. "You can unwrap these and thaw them in the microwave. Dinner's go-

ing to be a bit late.'' She paused for just a fraction. "So
you still plan to quit?''

"You bet. Whatever's going on in this company is too
gruesome for my tastes.'' Margo finally put the suede bag
down, but kept it close at hand. "Besides, this scandal
could ruin OTIOSE. I don't intend to stick around for the
fallout.''

Judith shut the freezer. "You don't think the company
could survive if the story gets out?''

Margo opened her mouth to give a quick reply, then
hesitated. "I'm not sure. There have been other phone company scandals over the years involving just about any sin
you could imagine. You wouldn't believe some of the wild
stories, despite the pristine, even dull, cachet associated
with the phrase 'phone company.' But underneath, there
were the same rampant human emotions that exist in more
flamboyant, glamorous corporations. Greed, ambition, sex—
the whole gamut. Once in awhile they played out in some
highly unusual—and ghastly—ways.''

Judith gave Margo a curious look. "I don't ever recall
reading about such things in the paper.''

Margo's expression was ironic. "You wouldn't. That's
what people like me get paid to do—cover it up. Oh, I'm
not saying that the old telecommunications industry was
rife with scandal, but given the millions of people who
worked in it during the glory years, there was plenty that
had to be swept under the corporate rug. Now, with divestiture, and the sprouting up of new companies all over the
place, you have a whole new breed of so-called phone company people. They're smarter, tougher, and much more
ruthless.'' Margo glanced at her suede bag. "This weekend
proves my point.''

"Goodness,'' said Judith, aghast. "Do you think power
is what this is all about?''

"Yes.'' Margo tucked her bag under one arm and carried
four game hens to the microwave. "What else?''

Judith began uncovering the green bean and mushroom

dish she had prepared at Hillside Manor. "Yet there's a chance OTIOSE might survive?"

"It's possible," Margo allowed, waiting for the microwave to turn off. "But I don't want to be the one who has to shuck and jive with the media. Not to mention that I couldn't go on working for the company after all this. Good God, somebody on the executive floor is a killer!"

Judith gave Margo a rueful smile. "Then you don't think it's my cousin or me?"

"Hardly." Margo removed the first four game hens and put the next batch in the microwave. "Unless you're a couple of hired assassins, I don't see the point."

The concept made Judith laugh. "We're not. We're exactly what we seem to be—a couple of Heraldsgate Hill housewives who run their own businesses on the side."

"Housewives," Margo repeated. "What a quaint term." Unexpectedly, she added, "I like it."

Involuntarily, Judith's eyes strayed to the digital time display on the stove. It didn't tick, but something did, and Judith guessed that it was Margo's biological clock.

"Has your career gotten sort of . . . redundant?" Judith couldn't think of a better word.

Margo sighed. "I'm virtually at the top of my profession. I make good money, I'm well respected, my life's my own." She stopped, staring gloomily at the microwave.

"But it's not enough." There was no query in Judith's words. "Everyone has holes in their lives, it's part of human nature. But some of them can be filled."

Margo looked at Judith with something akin to awe. "You do understand. Somehow, I thought you were . . ." She fumbled for words; Judith thought Margo didn't do that very often.

"You thought I was a pinhead because I'm not in the business world," Judith said with a little smile. "The real world is down on the ground, not on the thirtieth floor. I've spent my life with my feet planted firmly in the earth. Believe me, there've been many times when strong winds threatened to knock me over. But I've kept standing there, as if I'd grown roots. I may not have been a career woman, but I *have* worked—and it's easier to leave your troubles behind you and head off to the job. On the other hand, except for the paycheck, there's not much real payoff. At least not the kind that really counts.''

Margo nodded gravely. "Success—even money and power and sex—aren't enough. I want to make somebody happy. And I want one of those little people to rock in my arms." She gave Judith an embarrassed, rueful look. "Have I made a complete fool of myself or should I go on?''

All her life, Judith had been accustomed to people opening up to her. Maybe it was her sympathetic face, her friendly manner, or her innate understanding of human nature. Whatever the reason, she was never surprised when virtual strangers unburdened themselves.

"If it hadn't been for my son," Judith said grimly, "I'd have probably poisoned my first husband in the first five years of our marriage." She slapped a hand to her mouth. "I don't really mean that," Judith added lamely.

Margo uttered a truncated laugh. "Life's tough. I thought I was tough. I'm not. I found that out this weekend, but I have to pretend.''

"We all do," Judith said, opening one of the double ovens. "Tell me—who do you think is the killer?''

"Oh, God." Margo held her head. "I've tried to figure it out, especially now that Ward is dead. How did anybody—any of *us*—get upstairs to kill him?''

"Good point." Judith began lining up the game hens in a big roasting pan. "After you and Russell took the liquor bottles to the lobby, what did you do next?''

Margo removed the last four game hens from the microwave. "I've thought about that. When Russell and I got to the lobby, Frank and Nadia had gone to check out the conference rooms. Ava came out of the library and asked if I'd go to the restroom with her, but I didn't need to, and just then Nadia came back and said she'd go if I'd stay with Frank. I tracked him down and we checked the mikes and rearranged the chairs and then we came back to the lobby. Max was there, wondering what had happened to Ward. I honestly don't remember what the others were doing.''

Judith did, having gone over the scene with Renie. ''How long was Frank alone in the conference room?'' Judith asked.

Margo spread her hands. ''A minute? Two minutes?''

''Oh.'' Judith was disappointed. Something Margo had said suddenly struck her. ''If Ava was going to the restroom, where was Gene? They'd been in the library together.''

''Gene?'' Margo looked blank. ''I don't know. I didn't see him after I came back from the basement.''

The basement, thought Judith, panicking. Renie was in the basement with Gene. They'd been gone an awfully long time.

''Let's see how my cousin and Gene are doing,'' Judith said, trying to keep the anxiety out of her voice.

But just as the two women headed for the stairs, Renie and Gene appeared, wrestling with a large and cumbersome contraption.

''We found it,'' Renie announced, short of breath. ''It was in the heating room.''

''Good.'' Judith felt pale and drained. ''I'm . . . glad.''

Renie and Gene rolled the big dry-wet vacuum through the kitchen and out toward the lobby. Margo eyed Judith with an inquisitive expression.

''You thought Gene had offed your cousin?''

''Well . . .'' Judith tried to evade the question, but finally gave in. ''It crossed my mind.''

Margo nodded. ''Mine, too.''

Judith stared at Margo. ''You actually suspect Gene?''

Margo gripped her suede bag. ''I suspect everybody. Don't you?''

THIRTEEN

AFTER THE GAME hens and the bean dish had been put in the oven, Judith and Margo returned to the lobby. Ava was next on her list of people to interrogate, and the easiest way to get her alone was to ask her to take over for Margo and help set the dining room table.

Ava balked. "I'm tired," she complained. "After dinner, maybe I'll get my second wind and go on cleanup duty."

Cleanup of another kind was going on near the entrance. Renie and Gene had turned on the vacuum, which was sucking up the water. Killegrew shouted to them, saying that if they also sucked up some of the snow, maybe they could get the door closed. It was, he asserted, pretty damned cold.

Interrupting Nadia's attempts to soothe her CEO, Judith asked the administrative assistant to help get dinner on the table. Nadia started to demur, then grudgingly acquiesced.

As Judith and Nadia left the lobby, Renie and Gene were attacking the encroaching snow. To Judith's surprise, Killegrew's suggestion seemed to be working. Bemused, she wondered if it was a seemingly lame-brained idea like this one which had sent Frank Killegrew to the top of his profession.

"I cannot think," Nadia began as she randomly opened cupboards in the kitchen, "why I'm such a wreck. It isn't as if this is the first crisis I've faced."

Judith was startled. "Including multiple murders?"

"No, no, not murder," Nadia said, still searching in the cupboards. "But especially at work on Friday afternoons. It seems as if there's always a crisis that has to be resolved before five o'clock. You wouldn't believe how stressful that can be."

Judith, who had been setting out silverware, observed Nadia's rummaging with curiosity. "Are you looking for plates? They're right here, on the counter. I've already unloaded the dishwasher."

"Plates?" Nadia turned, pushing her big glasses up on her nose. "No. I thought . . . I wondered if perhaps there was some cooking sherry in the kitchen. I wouldn't mind a little pick-me-up."

It seemed to Judith that Nadia had picked herself up so often with the liquor in the lobby that she ought to be floating on air. But the administrative assistant's drinking habits were none of Judith's business.

"I think there's a bottle in that tall narrow cupboard on your left," Judith said. "It's in with the various kinds of vinegar."

"Ah." Nadia had to stand on tiptoe to reach the sherry. "As I was saying, Friday afternoons can be absolute hell. A negative news story in the early edition of the evening paper. A decision handed down by the state utilities commission. A disaster with a member of the board. One of the worst happened just recently. Do you recall the Santa Claus debacle?"

Judith's interest was piqued. "You mean when Santa ran off with Barry Newcombe?"

Pouring sherry into a juice glass, Nadia shook her head. "No, no. That was over a year ago. This happened during the recent holiday season. We'd offered a nine-hundred toll number so that children could call Santa. Of course there's a charge for nine-hundred numbers. Quite a few parents became upset because their children ran up rather large phone bills. The story made the newspapers, and OTIOSE was referred to as a Grinch or a Scrooge or just plain *greedy*, when in point of fact, those irresponsible parents should have exercised some control over their ill-behaved children. Some of them actually made obscene calls to Santa, and we had at least two adults who complained that he didn't sound like the real one. But the most unfortunate part was that when the article came out that particular Friday in December, none of the officers were around. I never could figure out where they'd all gone, but I was the one who ended up having to field the media's questions. It was horrible.''

But not as horrible as murder, thought Judith. Or maybe it was, to Nadia Weiss. "Tell me about the board," Judith said, picking up the silverware and indicating for Nadia to bring the plates. "Do the members actually control the company?"

"There are twelve directors," Nadia replied, following Judith into the dining room. "Three are OTIOSE officers— Frank, Leon, and Ward. It's traditional that the president, the executive vice president, and the chief financial officer sit on the board. The rest of the members come from throughout the region. They include only the most prominent names in business, education, and private endeavor."

In other words, the usual stuffed shirts, Judith thought, laying a fresh cloth on the table. "But you're short two members," she pointed out.

"What?" Nadia looked up from the pile of dinner plates. "Yes, yes, we are." Her mouth, which seemed to accelerate with every swig of sherry, turned down. "It's incredible, isn't it? Two vacancies to fill. Four, really. Ray Nordquist of Nordquist's Department Stores is about to retire, and William Boring Jr. of the Boring Airplane Company feels he's overextended."

"So," Judith said slowly, "one-third of the board will

have to be replaced. Will Ward and Leon's successors automatically become members?''

''Probably, though in the past sometimes the vice president–legal counsel has served instead of the chief financial officer.'' Nadia carefully set the plates down on the table.

''Does the board wield much power?'' Judith asked as they returned to the kitchen.

Nadia uttered a small laugh. ''Some say they're merely a rubber stamp for Frank and the rest of the officers. But that's because our executives know what's best for OTI-OSE. Once in a great while, however, the other members go off on a tangent and become quite obstinate. Then it's up to our gang—if you want to call them that—it's more like family—to dissuade them.''

The term ''family'' struck Judith as wildly inappropriate; ''gang'' was more like it. She recalled Joe's despair over teenagers who joined gangs. Maybe it wasn't so different with grownups. Everybody had to belong to something or someone, and at the corporate level, co-workers could become like family. Maybe for someone like Nadia, who seemed to be alone in the world, OTIOSE filled a deep need. Maybe she wanted to be ''one of the gang.''

Judith handed water glasses to Nadia, whose attitude about the murders was disturbingly blasé. ''It must be terribly hard on you to have three of your co-workers die in your midst. You seem to be holding up rather well.''

''Oh, no!'' Suddenly, Nadia was aghast. ''I'm utterly shattered! Not to mention frightened out of my wits! But I can't let it show. Why do you think I feel so stupid when my nerves give way? On the executive floor, someone has to keep calm. A steady hand at the tiller, as Frank would say. Often, it's up to me.''

''I see,'' said Judith, and for once she did. Frank Killegrew, and perhaps the other officers, relied on Nadia. She was the axle to their big wheels. ''Like with the Santa Claus phone calls.''

''Exactly.'' Nadia drank deeply from the juice glass. ''Of

course that was by default. When the news story hit, the officers simply . . . disappeared.''

"Including Margo," Judith said.

Nadia gave a nod of assent. "Including Margo. Even though it was a situation that fell into her shop. I ended up coordinating the p.r. effort.''

"Speaking of disappearing," Judith said, jumping at the chance to change topics, "have you any idea how one of your group could have gotten cut off from his or her buddy at the time Ward was killed?''

The implication made Nadia wince. "Are you suggesting that . . . ?''

"Yes, of course. Aren't we all in agreement that somebody in this lodge is a killer?''

"I'm not sure." Nadia turned sulky. "What about that person laughing outside the lodge? We've all tried to look from the upper windows to see if anyone is there, but it's impossible to see very far. Yet we all heard that awful laugh. Surely that could have been the killer.''

"It's possible," Judith admitted, "but I don't see how. Of course if we could be sure that each person inside the lodge was with someone else, then we'd know we're all innocent.''

Behind the big glasses, Nadia's eyes narrowed. "I thought you and your cousin knew the killer's identity.''

"What I said was that we have evidence *pointing* to the killer. That's not quite the same," Judith hedged. "It will take a forensics expert to actually pin the murders on this . . . person.''

Nadia took a moment to sort through Judith's ambiguous statement. "You haven't eliminated *me*," she finally said. "I don't have your note or your evidence.''

Judith said nothing. Nadia drank more sherry. In silence, the two women carried the remainder of the table settings out to the dining room. When they were back in the kitchen, Judith rephrased her original question.

"Do you know where everyone was around the time that Ward must have been killed?"

"Frank and I were in the lobby," Nadia replied, not looking at Judith. "Then we went to check on the smaller conference rooms. I had to use the restroom, so I asked Margo to stay with Frank. Ava accompanied me to the bathroom. I wasn't alone—nor was Frank—for more than a minute." At last, she gave Judith a defiant stare.

There was no way to prove or disprove Nadia's story. It seemed to mesh with Margo's account. Perhaps Frank Killegrew would have a different version.

Nadia finished her sherry while Judith checked on the game hens and the bean dish. Then the two women returned to the lobby. The interrogation of Ava would have to wait until after dinner.

Renie and Gene had removed enough snow so that the door could be shut. They were just turning the lock when Judith joined them. Renie was panting from exertion and Gene was mopping his brow.

"We had to pour all the melted water down the restroom toilets," he explained, then pointed to the wet-dry vacuum. "We filled that thing eight times."

"Good work," Judith remarked before turning to Renie. "I could use your help in serving."

"I'm pooped," Renie said, then caught the meaningful glint in Judith's eyes. "But so what? I'm a glutton for punishment." She took a cigarette from her purse and lighted up.

"I think I liked it better when you were just a glutton," Judith murmured, leading Renie not to the kitchen, but to the restroom. "Let's stop in here first."

"I've been here a lot," Renie said, but followed Judith. "Gene and I were so buddy-buddy that he came with me into the women's restroom to empty the water."

Judith made a quick check of the six stalls; they were vacant. "So what did you find out from Gene?" she asked, entering the stall at the near end of the row.

''He knows we have the pillowcase.''

Judith blinked several times at the closed door. ''He does? And how did he learn that?''

''I don't know,'' Renie responded over the sound of running tap water. ''It was a slip on his part. He said something to the effect that, 'Physical evidence consists of more than proof of foul play.' Thus, I deduced that he was alluding to the pillowcase—which you had mentioned to him when you were in Andrea's room—and to the fact that we had removed it.''

Judith emerged from the stall. ''Was he guessing? Or did he know?''

''I don't think Gene Jarman guesses,'' Renie said, drying her hands on a paper towel. ''It's not his style.''

''Coz,'' Judith began, dispensing liquid soap into her palm, ''do you see what that means?''

''Of course. Gene has been in Andrea's room since you were there with him. Either he went with someone—or he went alone,'' Renie said with an impish expression.

''Brilliant deduction,'' Judith remarked. ''So which was it?''

Renie was in front of the mirror, brushing her hair. ''I tried to get a run-down on who he was with at the time of Ward's murder. Gene had gone into the library with Ava, but he was very evasive about how long they were there. It made me wonder what they were doing. Do you remember yesterday afternoon when we thought we heard somebody in one of the smaller conference rooms? I've noticed a certain intimacy between Gene and Ava. How about you?''

Digging a lipstick out of her shoulder bag, Judith gave Renie a bemused look. ''Why not? They're single, they make a good-looking couple. It's nobody's business but theirs. However,'' she went on, waving the lipstick at Renie, ''they didn't stay in the library during that whole critical time period. Ava came in here with Nadia, and Gene and Russell were seen talking outside the library. At some point, they separated, if only for a very brief . . ."

The pager went off again. Startled, Judith dropped the lipstick which rolled across the floor and under the fourth stall. Renie chased the lipstick while Judith checked the pager.

"My number," she sighed. "Do you suppose Mother is dead?"

"Not a chance," Renie replied, crawling around on the floor. "My guess is that she wants you to go to the store and bring back a fifty-pound bag of Goo-Goo Clusters. She's probably forgotten you're out of town. Meanwhile, my mother is . . ." Renie stopped, the lipstick in one hand and something else in the other. "It's a note someone dropped," she said, standing up.

The note had been folded several times into a quarter-inch thickness. Renie smoothed the paper and held it so that Judith could read over her shoulder. It appeared to have come out of a daybook and was a list of things to do for Thursday, January 11.

Take Frank's suit to cleaners—grease spot on left
   lapel
Stop at post office to get change of address forms
Change Frank's appointment with Hukle, Hukle,
   and Huff
Call cable company re Frank
Go to liquor store

"Nadia," Judith breathed.

"Dogsbody," Renie said. "Which, some might say, is another word for wife."

"But she's not," Judith noted. "On the other hand, she acts like one."

"Interesting," Renie remarked, and pointed to the notation about Hukle, Hukle, and Huff. "Roland Huff is the city's leading divorce attorney."

Judith respected Renie's knowledge when it came to local law firms. Her mother, Deborah Grover, had been a legal secretary for almost fifty years. Still, Judith had a quibble.

"So what kind of law do the Hukles practice?"

"Mostly estate and insurance." Renie held up a hand before Judith could interrupt. "I know what you're thinking—Frank Killegrew's appointment could have been with Burton or Kay Hukle. Still, it's intriguing."

"Maybe." Judith, however, was gazing not at the items on the list but at the paper itself. "What intrigues me is why this was folded so small and ended up on the restroom floor. What do you do with memos to yourself after you've polished them off?"

"I toss them," Renie replied. "But this came out of a daybook. People don't usually rip out the pages, they just move on to the next one. I write my reminders on whatever spare piece of paper I can find."

"Good point." Judith refolded the list and put it in her shoulder bag. "I think I'll hang on to this. Maybe something will come to me."

The cousins entered the kitchen from the back way, through the laundry room. "We should wash our clothes after dinner," Renie said. "I don't think we're getting out of here tonight. It's still snowing, but not as hard."

Dolefully, Judith shook her head. "Meanwhile, Mother is dangling by her thumbs from one of the coat hangers Aunt Ellen made out of macaroni for Christmas presents."

"Macaroni?" Renie frowned. "The ones my mother got were fusilli. They're kind of brittle."

Judith opened the oven. "I got a wreath shaped from manicotti."

"Mine was a lampshade of egg noodles. It melted when Bill screwed in a hundred-and-fifty-watt bulb."

"Joe took the wreath to work and hung it in the deputy chief's office. He ate it."

Renie giggled. "He did not!"

"I only know what Joe tells me. Aunt Ellen's a dear, but

she does send the strangest presents.'' Judith removed the bean dish and set it on the counter. "Speaking of Joe's co-workers, I wonder if anyone from the department has tried to get hold of Frank Killegrew.''

"We wouldn't know if they had,'' Renie pointed out.

The cousins busied themselves with dishing up dinner. It was almost six-thirty when they announced that the meal was served. Ava suggested that Judith and Renie join them.

"There's plenty of room at the table,'' Ava said in a sardonic tone.

Judith felt like asking if she could charge for overtime, but thought better of it. Getting out in one piece seemed like her greatest priority. She exchanged questioning glances with Renie, then decided they might as well sit with the others. At first, there was little conversation except for requests to pass the salt and pepper.

Judith chose to enliven the atmosphere. "Have any of you ever met the lodge's caretaker?''

All eyes regarded her with curiosity, but it was Margo who responded. "How could we? This place is off-limits during the retreat.''

"I heard he was an odd duck,'' Max put in.

"Who told you that?'' Killegrew demanded.

Max looked blank. "Ward? I think he mentioned it when we were here last year.''

"That's right,'' Ava chimed in. "Ward said he was a Korean War vet who'd gotten his brains scrambled.''

"How would Ward know?'' Killegrew grumbled. "Ward never served our great country.'' He jabbed a thumb at Gene. "Neither did you. Weren't you a draft dodger during the Vietnam conflict?''

"I was 4-F,'' Gene replied with dignity. "I suffered from asthma until I was in my early twenties.''

Killegrew turned his hostile gaze on Russell. "Then you're the one who went to Canada.''

"I was a conscientious objector,'' Russell asserted. "I served as a medic.''

Killegrew harumphed. "If I'd known that when I hired you, I wouldn't have. Hired you, I mean. Is that in your personnel file?"

"I don't know," Russell responded, looking affronted. "Andrea kept all our files. I never bothered to check mine. Those things aren't important to me."

"What difference does it make?" Margo asked in a vexed voice. "That's ancient history. How did we get off on this stupid subject, anyway?"

"The caretaker," Judith said meekly. "I was wondering if the laugh we heard this afternoon might have been him."

No one seemed very comfortable with the suggestion. "It better not be," Killegrew said, still irked. "He's supposed to stay away."

"Then who was it?" Ava inquired. "Ms. Flynn has a point. *Somebody* was out there."

Nadia, who had poured herself a glass of white wine, waved a slim, dismissive hand. "It's a moot point. We can't see outside, so we don't know what's happening. It could have been the ski patrol."

"We might see from upstairs," said Max. "When Gene and I took Ward to the third floor, we got a better view, at least to the east. I didn't see anything. Did you?" He turned to Gene.

Gene shook his head. "I didn't look. All I wanted to do was get out of there. It's not pleasant being in a room with corpses."

"Rudy Mannheimer." It was Max who spoke. "That was the caretaker's name. Ward told me he's been up here for several years. He's an antisocial S.O.B., and this is a perfect job for him."

"We can see to the east and west," Killegrew noted, his manner more amiable. "From our rooms on the second floor, I mean. Not now, though. It's dark."

Judith frowned at the non sequitur. There wasn't an opportunity to dwell on it; Max wanted to know where Nadia had gotten her wine.

"Over there," Nadia replied, indicating a mahogany cabinet that reached almost to the ceiling. "That's where they keep several types of wine, including some rather nice French vintages."

Gene, Margo, and Ava fairly galloped to the cabinet. A supply of glasses filled one shelf. Amid the extraction of corks and pouring of wine, Frank Killegrew requested "something reddish but not real dark." Nadia found a rosé, and refilled her own glass. Russell shyly asked if he might have a sweet wine, perhaps with blackberries. Max said to hell with it, he wasn't much of a wine drinker, and went off to the lobby to mix another martini.

"He went alone!" Nadia gasped, handing Russell a blackberry cordial. "Do you think . . . ?"

Judith found Max quite safe, unless the double he was pouring construed a potential danger. "I'm the one who was on the second floor with the killer, remember?" he said when Judith expressed concern. "Whoever it was went for Ward, not for me. I figure I'm safe."

"I'm not sure anybody's safe," Judith said. "It doesn't pay to get careless."

Max took a big drink from the martini glass. "It doesn't seem to matter, does it? Whoever our killer is somehow manages to get the job done." He waved a big paw at the collection of bottles. "You want something? You're Scotch-rocks, right?"

"Yes." Judith smiled, surprised that Max would have noticed. But of course he was a marketing man; such types were paid to acquaint themselves with the habits of potential customers and thus to win their hearts, minds, and new accounts.

"Here," he said, deftly pouring the whiskey over a half-dozen cubes. "How come you aren't cowering in a corner?"

"I don't work for OTIOSE," Judith replied. "Besides, my cousin and I have our insurance policy."

Max downed the rest of the double, then began mixing

another. "We've all seen the garrote, the empty pill bottle, and the pillowcase. They don't add up to much, if you ask me." He loomed over Judith, his hazel eyes glinting dangerously. "What else have you got? It must be something you saw or heard."

Judith backpedaled a couple of steps. "We've seen and heard quite a bit," she said in a small voice. Then, because Max's size and stance were so intimidating, she blurted out one of her more outrageous fibs. "We saw someone in the corridor about the time of the murder. It must have been the killer."

Max Agasias recoiled, spilling some of his drink. "Who did you see?" he demanded.

Judith clamped her lips shut. Max used his free hand to grip her shoulder. "Who? Tell me, dammit! Who was it?"

There was no right answer, yet Judith had to say something. Judging from Max's frantic attitude, she realized what he expected—or was afraid—to hear.

"You," she gulped. "But someone else, too."

"Besides me?" Max let go of Judith. "Who?" he asked again, now more bewildered than agitated.

She shook her head in a helpless manner. "I'm not sure. It was shadowy in the corridor. The lights had dimmed, ever so briefly." The fib was growing, taking on a life of its own, mutating into a colossal lie. "It could have been . . . anyone."

Somewhat glassy-eyed, Max was staring off into space. "You're right. It could. Except maybe . . ." He stopped, suddenly asserting a modicum of self-control.

Judith relaxed a bit. "What were you doing in the corridor?" It took nerve to inquire, but the Scotch gave her false courage.

Max's broad shoulders slumped. "I was looking for something in Andrea's room. It belonged to me."

Judith made a quick mental inventory of the items that she and Renie had returned. "Did you find it?"

Dejectedly, Max shook his bald head. "It was gone. Somebody got there ahead of me."

Judith stiffened. Was Max referring to Barry Newcombe's belongings? But no one knew they'd been stolen from Judith's shoulder bag. No one, Judith reminded herself, except the person who had stolen them . . .

"Are you okay?" Renie had poked her head around the corner.

Judith offered her cousin a tentative smile. "Yes, we're fine. We thought we'd have a quick drink. How about you?"

"Are you kidding?" Renie asked. "Most of our fellow diners are already ripped. Somebody has to stay sober. I nominate me."

"I'm not ripped," Judith murmured as she and Max returned with Renie to the dining room. "But we need to talk. Let's clear the table."

"Unh-unh," said Renie. "Ava's going to do that. You need to talk to her, remember?"

"Trade you Ava for Max," Judith whispered as they approached the table. "I already did him."

"We'll see," Renie hedged, sitting down in her place between Gene and Margo.

"Fiber optics, my butt!" shouted Margo. "Until you give customers more underground wiring, they won't give a rat's ass if . . ."

"Too many numbers, not enough numbers," muttered Ava. "Everybody has to have a private line, a fax line, a cell phone. Before we know it, it'll take forty-seven numbers just to dial your . . ."

"If you can't beat 'em, sue 'em," Gene mumbled. "I love lawsuits. They get me out of the office."

"Analog, digital," Russell said in a sing-song voice. "Digital, analog. Diggity-do, loggity-dog, we're all lost in a big thick fog."

"That's it!" Frank Killegrew bellowed, getting to his

feet in an unsteady fashion and brandishing his slide rule like a sword. "You're out of order! All of you! Be positive! Keep the ship on the rails! How did I ever think I could turn this company over to such a bunch of whimpering nincompoops?"

Nadia put up a restraining hand. "Please, Frank—you're getting very red in the face. You don't want to have another . . . spell."

Killegrew shoved Nadia's hand out of the way. "Spell? I didn't have any damned spell! I was shocked, that's all. I'm as hale and hearty as a nuclear sub." Despite his protests, he sat down abruptly.

"Hell, Frank," Max said, finishing his second double martini and filling his glass with red wine, "you ought to be glad that some of us are still alive. If you ask me, this weekend has put a whole new meaning to downsizing."

Killegrew's face was still red. "That's not funny. If you're all so damned smart, why don't you figure out who's killing us off?"

Margo pointed to Judith and Renie. "They have. Maybe we should hire them to replace Ward and Andrea and Leon."

"But there are only two of them," Russell said, replenishing his blackberry cordial. "Mmm—this is very sweet. I like it."

"Numbskull," Killegrew muttered. "I'm surrounded by numbskulls and pansies."

"Pansies?" thundered Max, pounding on the table with both fists. "I'm no pansy! I was in 'Nam!"

"Right," Killegrew said on a grudging sigh. "You were a real hero. How come you never made it past Private E-2?"

"Hey!" Max began, but Margo hit him over the head with her empty plate.

"Shut up, Max! Let's not get on the old war horses again! I'm sick of it! Who gives a damn?"

"Some people don't like war," Nadia said quietly, then

peered at Gene over the rims of her glasses. "You were a protester at Berkeley, weren't you?"

Gene drew back in his chair. "So? That was in my undergraduate days at Cal."

"You were a member of SDS." Nadia gave Gene an arch little smile.

"I was not!" Gene shouted. "I kept away from all those radical movements!"

Nadia wasn't backing down. "But you protested the Vietnam war."

"That's different," Gene retorted. "Everybody did that at Berkeley. Once I got into law school at Stanford, I stayed clear of politics."

Nadia's thin face took on a conciliatory expression. "Maybe you shouldn't have. Given your background in an Oakland ghetto, didn't you feel a need to help your so-called brothers and sisters better themselves?"

"My . . . ?" Gene looked on the verge of apoplexy. "I'm middle class! I was always middle class! I'm more than middle class, I'm a lawyer!"

"Who are in a class by themselves," Margo murmured. "Calm down, Gene. You made it. Nobody cares about your beginnings."

Ava leaned across the table towards Nadia. "What about your origins? You never talk about your background, Nadia. Is it true that Frank found you under a cabbage?"

Nadia's nostrils flared. "That's silly! Why don't you tell us how you got here from Samoa?"

A spurt of anger crossed Ava's face, then she composed herself. "I took a plane. That's all anyone needs to know. But," she went on, "maybe this is the time to make an announcement." Getting to her feet, she glanced at each of the others in turn. "I was going to save this for the last day of the retreat. Considering how this weekend has gone, several of us have already seen our last day, period." She paused, noting the sobering effect of her words. "Thursday afternoon, I received a call from a former employee of mine at WaCom. Next week, they're going to tender a merger offer with OTIOSE.''

A stunned silence enveloped the dining room. Max was the first to speak, his usual resonant voice unsteady.

"That's not a merger—that's a takeover!"

"We'll fight them in court," Gene asserted, but he was obviously shaken.

"Cutbacks, layoffs, early retirement," Nadia whispered. "Just like the divestiture era. Oh, my!"

"Geniuses," said Russell. "Hordes and hordes of geniuses at WaCom. They have more ideas than I could ever think of!"

"Who cares?" said Margo.

Judith gazed at each speaker, noting that all of them were—as usual—self-absorbed and isolated from one another. Finally, she looked at Frank Killegrew, who had said nothing.

He was facedown in his game hen carcass.

FOURTEEN

UNDER THE CIRCUMSTANCES, it was natural for everyone to assume that Frank Killegrew was dead, either by accident or design. As Nadia finally noticed her superior's collapse, she screamed and began shaking him. The others watched in horror until Margo grabbed Russell by the shirt collar.

"You said you were a medic in 'Nam," Margo shouted. "Do something!"

"I never went to 'Nam," Russell said, quaking in his chair. "I was assigned to NATO in West Germany."

"Ohhh . . . !" Margo gave him a hard shake. "Do something anyway, you little twerp! You're still a medic!"

"I was discharged in 'sixty-nine," Russell insisted. "I can barely find the Band-Aids in the official OTIOSE first-aid kit."

"No wonder you didn't know what CPR is," Margo railed. "You're the most worthless, futile . . ."

But Frank Killegrew didn't appear to need medical help. He had lifted his head and was beginning to sputter.

"Oh, my," Ava remarked, "he's not dead after all. What a relief."

Judith thought Ava sounded more sarcastic than relieved, but the CEO was now sitting up and blustering mightily while Nadia wiped white and wild rice stuffing from his face.

"I'm fine, I'm fine," he asserted. "It's just another damned shock I didn't need." As Nadia finished her task and resumed her seat, Killegrew glowered at Ava. "Why didn't you mention this sooner?"

Looking weary and wan, Ava hesitated before replying. "I tried to, Frank, when we were alone after the first session yesterday. But somehow, I never got the chance." She lowered her eyes and folded her hands. "I'm sorry."

"WaCom can't do this," Killegrew declared. "The state utilities commission won't allow it. Gene, you jump on this first thing when we get back. Alert our public affairs people, have them get the lobbyists in gear. It's one thing for WaCom to gobble up other computer companies, but they won't get their greedy mitts on us."

Max, who was feeling his bald head to see if Margo's plate had left a lump, turned to Ava. "Who runs WaCom since Jim Clevenger's out of the picture?"

Briefly, Ava's dark eyes met Max's gaze. "Dick Freitas, the second-in-command, took over as acting president and CEO. WaCom's been on a year-long talent search. They want someone new, a fresh face, an outsider. I don't know if they've made a final decision yet or not."

"They have." Margo looked smug. "On Tuesday, they'll announce that their new chief is Alan Roth."

Judith and Renie couldn't stand the clamor that ensued after Margo Chang's announcement. After the first five minutes of incredulous shrieks and outraged wails, the cousins retreated to the kitchen.

"Andrea's husband?" Judith was as disbelieving as the OTIOSE executives. "Does that make sense?"

"Maybe he really is a computer genius," Renie said, clearing her plate into the garbage. "Just because he didn't have an official job doesn't mean he wasn't working. He might have been some kind of consultant to WaCom.''

Judith sat down on one of the tall stools. "I don't get it. Shouldn't a CEO have organizational and administrative skills?"

Renie smirked. "Look at Frank. Does he strike you as a managerial wizard? His strength is delegating. Maybe Alan can do that, too."

"You know," Judith said, still looking perplexed, "if OTIOSE is an example of how the world of commerce runs, I'm beginning to wonder how any companies or businesses keep from going belly-up."

"You'd wonder more if you had to deal with them like I do," Renie said. "Management has no loyalty to employees and employees have no loyalty to the workplace. Common sense seems to have gone out the window years ago. Everybody spends more time in useless meetings than getting things done. And everybody brings their private lives to the office, which becomes a group therapy session. Boy, am I glad I work for myself. I'm a lousy boss, but I know how to take criticism. I just tell myself to shut up and get down to business."

"Hillside Manor is such a quiet, nonpolitical, uncomplicated place," Judith sighed. "Sure, I get crazy guests and my mother drives me nuts and it's hard work, but compared with what goes on downtown, I've got it made."

"Me, too," Renie agreed. "Working for yourself is the only way to go. I'm sure that's why Bill and Joe are anxious to retire. They can't be their own bosses. Joe's got a tough chain of command with the police department, and even though people who don't know any better think professors live in an ivory tower, it's covered with thorns. There's a hierarchy, politics galore, and all kinds of budget crises, especially at a state university."

"At least Joe and Bill accomplish something," Judith pointed out. "Joe may get frustrated, but he does protect and serve. If you save only one life in the course of a year, that's a huge contribution."

Renie nodded. "You bet. And Bill may feel as if most of his students are only slightly smarter than your average artichoke, but every so often he realizes that he's made a big impression on someone that will last a lifetime. How many other people can say that about their so-called careers?"

Judith blinked at Renie. "Yes," she said in an odd voice. "How many people can?"

"What?" Renie regarded Judith with curiosity, but there was no chance for an explanation. Ava entered the kitchen, looking somewhat sheepish.

"My bombshell has sent everyone back to the bar," she said. "Margo didn't help things, either. I had to get away. Let me help clean up."

"Go ahead, coz, take a breather," Judith responded, still sounding unlike herself.

Renie looked uncertain, but headed for the lobby. Judith and Ava returned to the dining room. It was a shambles, with overturned chairs, spilled wine, and scattered food littering the tablecloth and floor.

"They were very upset," Ava said in apology. "No one who knows Alan Roth—except Margo—can believe he's qualified to run WaCom."

Judith began collecting dirty plates. "Andrea must have known about this, don't you think?"

"Probably," Ava agreed, picking up silverware. "She and Alan had their problems, but they were still married. If he was about to be given a big job like the one at WaCom, he must have discussed it with her."

"But Andrea didn't tell Frank," Judith pointed out, heading back to the kitchen.

"Obviously not." Ava had grown thoughtful. "Nadia was right—a merger will mean cutbacks and layoffs and all the rest of it. Andrea would know that, which means . . ." She stopped, staring at the silverware she'd just put into the dishwasher.

"What?" Judith asked.

Ava's expression was wry. "Where did Nadia get all that information she was spouting at the dinner table? Especially the old stuff about Gene and Max and Russell? She was about to start in on me, as well. Where did she get her data, and why bring it up now?"

Judith thought back to the conversation, though the word was only a euphemism for wrangling. "Frank was needling people, too. Surely military records would be common knowledge."

"It doesn't work that way," Ava said. "People lie on their resumes, they omit things they'd rather not have in their files, they add accomplishments that didn't happen. But somewhere along the way, particularly when someone is being considered for a big promotion, a company will do a background check. It's usually done by the security people who fall under human resources at OTIOSE." Ava gave Judith a meaningful look.

"So Andrea would have been privy to all the dirt?" Judith asked.

Ava nodded. "That, and what she'd pick up from rumor scavengers like Barry Newcombe. But my point is, *why now*? Did Andrea bring her files with her? Did Nadia get a look at them and pass the information on to Frank?"

Judith tried to recall what she and Renie had found in Andrea's room. There *had* been personnel files, but they had been so thick that the cousins hadn't taken time to peruse them. Judith, however, couldn't admit as much to Ava; no one must know they'd searched Andrea's belongings.

"If that's true," Judith temporized, "Nadia must have found those files after Andrea died."

Ava gave a single nod. "The question is, how soon after she died?"

Judith's eyes widened. "You think Nadia is the killer?"

Ava made a helpless gesture with her hands. "No. Not really. Unless . . ." She bit her lower lip.

"Unless what?"

"Nothing. It's all so . . . difficult." Ava started for the dining room. "Let's finish cleaning up this mess."

Judith decided she might as well change topics. "You started in on Nadia's background," she remarked, removing glassware from the table. "I take it you weren't referring to the personnel files."

"I wasn't," Ava responded. "The story I've heard is that Frank met Nadia when he went back for his tour of duty at AT&T. It used to be that anyone from the associated companies who was on the rise spent a couple of years at headquarters in New York. Nadia was a clerk-typist in what they called the plant department then. Frank was already married, but his wife didn't move to New York with him. Patrice Killegrew came from a wealthy family, and could afford to fly back and forth to join him for long weekends. They had children in school, and she didn't see any point in uprooting them and moving back east for what would be a relatively short time. As you might guess, the inevitable happened."

Judith kept pace with Ava as they walked back to the kitchen. "Frank and Nadia had an affair."

"Exactly. It wasn't a mere fling, it was serious," Ava continued. "But as I said, Frank and Patrice had small children, and she was rich. Not only that, but in those days, divorce was frowned on by the upper echelon. Potential officer candidates were supposed to be solid citizens, untouched by scandal. Frank couldn't possibly dump Patrice."

"So he brought Nadia with him when he was sent back to the West Coast," Judith said.

"That's right. He promoted her every time he moved on, and eventually she became his administrative assistant." Ava turned rueful. "I've often wondered if he did her any real favor. She might have been a bigger success on her own."

Judith didn't understand. "Meaning—what?"

Ava turned on the dishwasher, then leaned against it.

"Nadia came along at a time when women were beginning to rise in the Bell System. Oh, sure, there's still a glass ceiling and all that, but she's smart, she has drive, she's got the makings of a good manager. Sometimes I feel she really runs the company instead of Frank."

"That crossed my mind, but I don't know much about the corporate world. Tell me," Judith went on, recalling how frantic Nadia had been when she thought Frank had had a heart attack, "are they still . . . intimate?"

"Define intimate." Ava laughed, a faintly jarring sound. "Let's put it this way—Nadia is more of a wife to him than Patrice ever was. You can see that from the way they behave. She does everything for him. And if you're referring to sex, my guess is that they still have that, too. Patrice is a very cold woman."

"Nadia's not exactly warm and fuzzy," Judith noted.

"You haven't met Patrice. She could give those icicles outside a run for their money."

"But . . . Frank and Patrice stay married?" Judith couldn't keep the question out of her voice.

"Of course." Ava's manner was ironic. "If Patrice knows about the relationship between Frank and Nadia, she ignores it. Mrs. Killegrew—and it is definitely *Mrs.*—enjoys being the wife of a CEO. Money and status are her substitutes for love and sex. Besides, Frank could never risk a divorce."

"Times have changed, though. Unfortunately," Judith added.

"Not so much in the old boy network," Ava said. "For the most part, Frank's peer group is still extremely conservative and old-fashioned."

"Well." Judith tried to absorb everything Ava had told her. The folded piece of paper with the notation about Hukle, Hukle, & Huff didn't necessarily indicate that a Killegrew divorce was in the offing. And while Ava's account of Frank's domestic triangle was interesting, Andrea's personnel files might have a more immediate bearing on the week-

end's events. Had Max been looking for them? How and
when had Nadia slipped away to Andrea's room?

The folded piece of paper. It suddenly dawned on Judith
why it was important. "Ava," she said as the other woman
started back for the dining room, "how long were you in
the bathroom with Nadia this afternoon?"

"What?" Ava looked at Judith as if she were crazy.

Judith felt embarrassed. "I don't mean . . . It sounds stupid, but . . . Really, I have a very good reason to ask."

Ava's expression grew serious. "Are you talking about
the time period when Ward was killed?"

"More or less, yes."

"Oh, let me think." Ava cocked her head to one side.
"Five minutes? I don't know. However long it takes. I'm
not much for primping."

"Are you sure it didn't take longer than five minutes?"
Judith persisted.

"Yes." Ava now seemed more definite. "Ask Nadia.
She was with me. We were chatting between the stalls. I
suppose we each wanted to make sure the other one was
okay."

Judith's bright idea was dashed. "Before that, you were
with Gene in the library, right?"

Ava was starting to look vexed. "Yes, I was. And no, I
won't answer any more questions about *that*."

Judith gave up. In silence, the two women cleared away
the dirty tablecloth, swept the floor, and finished tidying the
kitchen. As Ava was about to leave, Judith apologized.

"I'm sorry, I didn't mean to be impertinent. I was only
trying to figure out who was where when Ward was murdered."

Ava gave Judith a tired smile. "We're all trying to figure
that out. Frankly, it's impossible."

Judith frowned. "Why do you say that?"

Ava began ticking off the names on her fingers. "Margo
and Russell had gone to the basement with you and your

cousin. But after they came back to the lobby, Margo went to find Frank. Nobody knows where Russell was at that point, though he claims to have stayed put. But how long did it take before Margo met up with Frank? What was he doing while Nadia was heading for the restroom? What was Nadia doing after she left Frank? And what took Max so long to figure out that Ward was taking forever to change? Don't you see? Only Gene and I can alibi each other.''

Given what appeared to be a romantic relationship between Ava and Gene, Judith didn't think that was much of an alibi. ''You can't alibi Gene while you were in the restroom,'' Judith said.

Ava's face fell. ''You're right. I can't.''

As far as Judith could see, nobody had an alibi.

Ava obviously agreed. ''You were with your cousin?''

''Yes, in the kitchen.''

''See what I mean?'' Ava said with an ironic smile.

She was right, Judith thought. The cousins didn't have much of an alibi, either.

No one seemed inclined to stay up late that night. Russell and Ava were the first to announce that they were headed for bed. Gene and Margo followed. Nadia badgered Frank to get his rest; he'd had a very trying day, she said.

''Is she kidding?'' Max snarled after the pair had gone upstairs in the elevator. ''This is worse than 'Nam! At least over there you knew who the enemy was. Well,'' he added, staring at the floor, ''most of the time you did.''

''How's your head?'' Judith asked.

Max fingered his smooth pate. ''Okay. Margo didn't hit me very hard. I suppose it was only fair after I whacked Russell with that damned carving.''

Judith had decided that a frontal attack was best. ''Were you looking for Andrea's personnel files this afternoon?''

Max's chin jutted, then he slumped against the sofa. ''Yes, but I never even saw them. Everything had been cleaned out except her notes and a daily planner.''

''Does the phrase 'Scandinavian wheat-thrasher' mean anything to you?'' Judith inquired.

At first, Max looked puzzled. Then he held his head. ''It means my ass,'' he said, then peered at Judith between his fingers. ''How did you know?''

Renie edged forward on the footstool. ''We found the folder in the conference room yesterday. We put it here, on the coffee table. Somebody must have picked it up.''

''It's not mine,'' Max said, his long arms dropping to his sides. ''It's got to be somebody in my department, so I'll take the fall. That damned file's been missing for over a year.''

Judith sat up very straight. ''How do you know if it's not yours?''

''Because,'' Max explained, cracking his knuckles, ''I found it back then when I was going through some year-end stuff for the annual report. I'd guessed something like that was going on, but I wasn't sure who was responsible. In marketing, we entertain a lot of outsiders. Somebody wanted to go beyond wining and dining to win new clients. I left the file where I found it with a note to see me, ASAP. All these months, nothing happened. Then, last night, Andrea started making hints about 'prostituting ourselves' and 'women who took things lying down.' She kept looking at me, and I realized she must know. There was no chance to talk to her alone, so I went to her room last night. She wasn't there. I had no idea she was waiting for Leon in his room. That's when you must have seen me in the corridor.''

Judith felt surprise register, but desperately tried not to let it show. ''Last night. Yes, that's what we must have seen.'' She flashed a warning glance at Renie.

Max stretched his long legs out towards the hearth. ''I suppose she was going to show the file to Frank. Or maybe she was just going to hold it over my head. Blackmail comes in some weird forms.''

"Why would Andrea want to blackmail you?" Renie asked.

"Well . . ." Max seemed genuinely puzzled. "I honestly don't know. Like everybody else in the company, she felt marketing types aren't real telecommunications people. We're mavericks, and as vice president, I get to wear the black sheep label. Plus, my wife, Carrie, and I've been having some problems. We fight a lot, we always have. Carrie hates company functions. She's a master gardener and has her own career. Playing the part of corporate helpmate makes her puke. As you might guess, a wife with an attitude really pisses off women like Patrice Killegrew. It pissed off Andrea, too. She liked to fit everybody into their own little niche."

"What about Mrs. Haugland?" Judith inquired. "I understand she's too sickly to take part in company social gatherings."

Max waved a big hand. "That's different. Helen Haugland thrives on sympathy. She got plenty of it from poor Ward, and most of the others. Oh, some of them saw through her, but Helen can pull the wool over lots of eyes. I wonder what'll happen now that Ward's dead. She might have to get off her dead butt and *do* something."

While Judith was interested in Max's assessment of his colleagues and their spouses, she realized he hadn't answered the original question. "You mentioned blackmail," Judith said. "Do you mean that Andrea would have used the hooker ring files to make you do something you otherwise wouldn't do?"

Max seemed to consider Judith's somewhat garbled suggestion. "Maybe originally. She and Alan have a couple of kids. One of them is out of high school, I think. It might be that she wanted me to hire him. Anyway, that can't be true now. I mean, Alan's going to run WaCom, right? And WaCom wants to merge with OTIOSE. So now I figure that Andrea was going to use that file to get me canned."

Renie leaned forward on the footstool. "And replace you with someone hand-picked by Alan? That makes sense."

"I'm afraid so." Max assumed a brooding expression as the lobby grew silent.

The silence was short-lived. A sound came from somewhere, unexpected and distant. Judith, Renie, and Max all tensed.

"That's an engine," Max said, getting up and inclining his bald head. "Where's it coming from?"

"The basement?" Renie offered.

"I don't think so," Judith said, straining to hear. "It seems to be coming from outside."

The sound grew fainter. Max jumped off the sofa. "Come on! We're going upstairs! Maybe we can see something from the second-floor windows!"

They raced from the elevator to Max's room, which was closer than the cousins'. But once inside, they could see nothing. It was dark, and the snow, which now consisted of big, wet flakes, obliterated the landscape.

"Damn!" Max tugged the window open and leaned out. "Listen!"

Judith and Renie practically fell over each other trying to get close to the open window. Sure enough, they heard the sound again.

"An engine, a motor," Judith breathed.

"Look!" Renie was halfway over the sill, snow soaking her sweatshirt. "A light!"

Judith and Max barely glimpsed the faint amber glow before it disappeared. The sound died away, too. The trio continued to watch and listen. Close to five minutes passed before anyone spoke.

"Damn!" Max swore again. "I don't get it." He gestured in the direction where they'd seen the light, then closed the window with a rattling bang.

Judith recalled where she and Renie had seen the light the previous night. Their room was down the hall from Max's, at the end of the corridor. "We saw a light on this side of the lodge last night," said Judith. "Is there a road in that direction?"

Max looked thoughtful. "I think so, to the caretaker's place. But it's got to be impassable. The only way you could get through is with a snowmobile. They can go in just about any conditions."

"You wouldn't need a road," Renie said, more to herself than the others.

"That's right," Max agreed. "If there'd been one here in the lodge, we could have gotten out by now."

Judith was wearing a curious expression. "There are skis and all sorts of other winter sports equipment in the basement. I assume they're rentals. Why isn't there a snowmobile?"

Max shrugged. "Liability, maybe. They can be dangerous if you don't know how to handle them. Some models go up to a hundred and ten miles per hour."

Judith took one last look out the window. All she could see were the big, white flakes, falling softly onto the drifted snow. It was very quiet.

But someone was out there. Judith's logical mind told her it couldn't be the killer. The lodge had been locked up the entire weekend. The blizzard had cut off access to all but the highest windows. Yet nothing was impossible, not to someone with murder in mind.

With a sudden jarring tremor, Judith wondered if they had been looking for the killer in the wrong place.

FIFTEEN

"WHO ELSE WAS in the corridor last night?" Judith asked Renie some two hours later after the cousins had done their laundry and retired to their room. "Did you catch the part about Max seeing someone when he tried to talk to Andrea last night?"

Renie nodded. "You, of course, never saw him or anyone else, you big fibber. Are you thinking Max may have seen the mysterious stranger?"

"I'm not sure who—or what—Max saw," Judith replied. "Andrea's room is at the far end of the hall. The lighting's pretty dim. Max seemed uncertain. I got the impression that maybe he sensed rather than saw someone. It might have been anyone, including the alleged outsider."

"It could be done," Renie asserted. "If someone climbed up the side of the lodge, they could get in through one of the second- or third-floor windows. A ladder, snowshoes, ropes—whatever. If someone was determined to get in, they could probably do it."

Judith was sitting on the bed, chin on fists. "What's the risk factor? If seen inside the lodge, a stranger would automatically become the prime suspect."

"But no one's seen this phantom," Renie pointed out. "This is a big place, and for the most part, we've all tended to congregate together in two or three rooms. Look,'' Renie continued, perched on the edge of her twin bed, ''Leon and Andrea were probably killed within a couple of hours of each other last night. Ward was murdered this afternoon. Why couldn't the killer have come in late last night, hidden on the third floor or in the basement, and committed all three murders before heading out again? The first time we saw the light was early evening yesterday. We all heard the laugh this afternoon, after Ward was killed. Now, mid-evening, we see another light, but not in the same place. During the time the murders were committed, nobody—that we know of—heard or saw anything outside. What does that suggest?''

''I see your point,'' Judith agreed. ''Which is reassuring in that it means the murderer may have finished his—or her—grisly business. However,'' she added on a heavy sigh, ''it also means that if the killer is an outsider, you and I don't have the foggiest notion of who it might be.''

Renie made a face. ''Better to have an unknown homicidal maniac wandering around the mountains than one of the OTIOSE gang prowling the halls. I like outside; I really hate inside.''

Judith got up and went to the honor bar where she removed a Pepsi for Renie and a diet 7-Up for herself. ''I understand your reaction. But it doesn't work for me.''

Renie looked mildly offended. ''Why not?''

''Because,'' Judith said, sitting back down on the bed, ''it doesn't fit. I've been thinking this through for the last couple of hours, and much as the outsider theory appeals to me, the rest of the pieces don't mesh. Barry was killed a year ago, during the retreat. We find Barry, and suddenly other people start dying. I'm convinced there's a connection. Except for the conferees, who could know we'd found his body?''

''Whoever is out there,'' Renie replied.

''I don't think so,'' Judith said, though there was a tinge of doubt in her voice. ''We didn't see any tracks in the snow when we went back the second time. And after that, it started to snow pretty hard. I'm sure that little cave has been covered up again. No, coz,'' Judith said with a sad shake of her head, ''it doesn't wash. I still think the killer is in the lodge.''

''You want the killer to be inside,'' Renie accused. ''Otherwise, you couldn't figure out whodunit.''

''Don't say that, coz!'' Judith shot Renie an angry look. ''I'm trying to use logic. Does it make sense that somebody follows the OTIOSE conferees to Mountain Goat Lodge two years in a row and starts killing them?'' She didn't wait for Renie's response. ''Of course it doesn't—it would be easier and safer to do away with them in the city. If we knew why Barry was killed in the first place, then we'd know why the discovery of his body meant that Leon, Andrea, and Ward also had to die. What is the common link between the four of them? That's what we should concentrate on.''

Renie sipped her Pepsi and considered. ''First link— OTIOSE. They all worked for the same company, never mind at what level. Second link—each other. They knew each other.''

''Hold it.'' Judith gestured with her soda can. ''That's not precisely true. Barry worked for two different departments, human resources and public relations. Except for his occasional catering jobs and driving the conferees to the lodge last year, how would the others have known him? Russell doesn't even seem to remember Barry.''

''Russell's a dreamer,'' Renie responded. ''People aren't important to him, only ideas matter. A week from now, Russell won't remember *us*. As for the others, Barry would have had contact with all of them. Human resources and p.r. deal with all the other departments. He certainly knew Nadia, and therefore, no doubt came into contact with Frank and Ward.''

''The files,'' Judith murmured. ''Andrea's personnel files have disappeared—according to Max—and there must be a reason.'' She set down the soda can and clapped her hands. ''That's it! That's the link! Barry and Andrea worked in human resources. Andrea had all the dirt. Barry loved dirt, he traded bits of gossip. As a staff assistant, wouldn't he have access to her files?''

Renie nodded. ''To her official files, yes. But Andrea may have had CYOA files, too. She may have kept them in a safe place.''

Judith looked blank. ''What's a CYOA file?''

Renie grinned. ''It stands for 'Cover Your Own Ass,' excuse my French. It's anything you keep that you can use to protect yourself or hold over someone else. It can be as simple as a phone message you received from somebody who might later deny they called you. Or it can be photographs of your CEO in bed with a donkey.''

Judith's excitement returned. ''That's good. That's great. Like I said, the files are the link.''

''Maybe.'' Renie was definitely dubious. ''How do they link up with Ward and Leon?''

''I haven't figured that out yet, but they must,'' Judith insisted.

Renie finished her Pepsi. ''Sleep on it. I'm tired, let's turn out the lights.''

Judith regarded Renie with wonderment. ''You're not afraid?''

''You're the one who dreamed up our insurance policy.'' She glanced at Judith with alarm. ''Don't tell me you think it lapsed?''

''So far, so good.'' But Judith got up and started moving one of the two armchairs to the door. ''Just in case the policy expires,'' she said with a sickly smile. ''And to make sure that we don't.''

''What about the windows?'' Renie asked.

Judith glanced across the room. ''They're latched from the inside. We're okay. Oh!'' She put a hand to her head. ''Which is another reason why an outsider couldn't have gotten in.''

Renie went to one of the windows and jiggled the catch. "It wouldn't take much to break this. Besides, we don't know what the third-floor windows are like."

"Forget it," Judith said with finality. "It's after eleven, you're right, we're tired. Let's go to sleep."

Renie was still fiddling with the window catch. "Let's take turns sleeping."

"Fine. You stay up first. Wake me around eight." Judith got into bed.

"To hell with it." Renie got into bed, too.

The cousins slept.

They were awakened by an explosion. Judith jumped up, got entangled in the bedclothes, and struggled to free herself. Had someone set off a bomb? She panicked, but finally managed to extricate herself and looked in every direction.

Renie was wrestling with the pillow, trying to cover her head. "Stupid Bulgarians," she muttered. "Why are they always working on their damned condos across the street? Why don't they build something back home in Blagoevgrad?"

Judith was at the door, shoving the armchair out of the way. "Wake up, you're not on Heraldsgate Hill, you're at Mountain Goat Lodge." As she cautiously opened the door, another explosion sounded. "It's outside. What now?" She rushed to the windows, then gaped. "It's raining! Maybe that was thunder!"

"It's the Bulgarians," Renie repeated, her voice muffled by the pillow. "Ignore them and go back to sleep."

Judith ignored Renie. A glance at her watch told her it was just after seven-thirty. The morning was very gray, with rain pelting the snow. Judith waited for a flash of lightning, but heard only another loud, shuddering noise.

"That's not thunder," she said. "What could it be?"

Renie finally removed the pillow and struggled to sit up. "Damn. You're determined to annoy me." She rubbed her eyes, yawned, and stretched. "Okay, you win. What explosions?"

Judith turned away from the window. "Didn't you hear them?"

Renie yawned again. "I heard something, or else I wouldn't be awake. I told you, it sounds like the Bulgarians across the street from our house. They're always renovating or adding on or digging up or tearing . . ."

A fourth explosion interrupted Renie. "That's not the Bulgarians," Judith declared.

"Probably not," Renie agreed, cocking her head. "It's the avalanche crew."

Judith was startled. "What avalanche crew?"

"You said it's raining?" Renie yanked back the covers and sat on the edge of the bed. "Then it's gotten much warmer during the night, which, after a heavy snowfall, means there's an avalanche danger. To prevent disasters, the crews set off explosions to break up the snow. I thought everybody knew that."

"If I did, I'd forgotten," Judith murmured, moving away from the windows. "Great—now the roof will cave in. What next, plague and locusts?"

"Floods," Renie responded. "Maybe fires." She reached for a cigarette.

"Oh, no! Not this early!" Judith railed. "Haven't you run out of those things yet?"

Renie shook her head. "I brought a whole carton with me. Why do you care? Your mother still smokes. Joe has his cigars. What's wrong with Little Renie's little weedies?"

"They stink," Judith retorted, waving away a cloud of smoke. "Mother shouldn't smoke. She's so forgetful, but when I try to talk to her about it, she gets ornery. The last time I caught her putting a lighted cigarette in her housecoat pocket, she pulled it out and tried to stick it in Sweetums's mouth. I swear I saw Sweetums inhale."

"Ghastly," Renie remarked, puffing away. "Are we doing breakfast?"

"Not for *them*," Judith said, jerking a thumb in the direction of the corridor. "I've changed my mind. I'm tired
of waiting on those spoiled brats."

"There might be fewer of them this morning," Renie
noted with an ominous look.

"Don't say that," Judith shot back. Suddenly she went
back to the window. "Look," she called to Renie, "the
snow outside the sill has melted a good four or five inches.
Do you think we might get out of here today?"

"Not if there are avalanche warnings," Renie replied,
stubbing out her cigarette and heading for the bathroom.
"They'll close the pass. They always do."

As soon as Renie disappeared, Judith opened both windows to air out the room. The explosions had stopped. Judith wondered where the blasts had been set off. Perhaps
at the summit, where the main ski areas and the private
chalets were located. Though loud, the booms hadn't
sounded very close. Maybe there was no danger around the
lodge.

But there was danger inside, Judith reminded herself
grimly. Half an hour later, she and Renie were in the
kitchen. It was a shambles. Coffee had been spilled all over
the counter, egg yolk dripped down the front of the stove,
there was burned toast in the sink, and a broken cereal bowl
lay in several pieces on the floor.

"Pigs!" Judith cried. "Look at this mess!"

"It's not *our* mess," Renie pointed out. "Shall I tell
Frank Killegrew to come in here and clean up?"

"Yes." Judith folded her arms across her chest. "Yes,
I'd like to see that. I'm sick of these jerks."

Renie started to shake her head, then straightened her
shoulders and marched out to the dining room. Vaguely
astonished, Judith followed.

"Okay," Renie barked, "we're padlocking the kitchen

unless you lazy swine get off your dead butts. You have five minutes.''

Judith saw the seven disbelieving faces stare at Renie. *Seven,* she thought. *They're all still alive and eating breakfast. Why am I surprised?*

Nadia got to her feet. "Of course we'll tidy up. I always tidy up. Ava, Margo, let's all pitch in.''

Margo held onto the edge of the table as if she thought it might levitate. "Screw it, Nadia. One of the men can help. Why should Ava and I get stuck with so-called women's work? Why should you, for that matter? Stand up for yourself for once.''

Nadia looked shocked. "It's no trouble. Really, Margo . . .''

"I can wash dishes," Russell offered with a sheepish expression. "I do it whenever I run out of plates.''

Margo snapped her fingers at Russell. "Then do it here. Get going.'' Russell scurried away, while Nadia started to follow him. Margo, however, put out a restraining arm. "No, you don't. Let one of these bozos go with Russell.'' Her withering glance took in Killegrew, Max, and Gene.

"Why not?'' Gene said with a shrug. "I'm single, like Russell. I have to fend for myself sometimes.''

Margo dropped her arm but kept her attention on Nadia. "What are you going to do when Frank retires? You're not yet fifty, you're too young to retire. Are you going to hang on with OTIOSE and be a slave for the next CEO?''

Nadia lifted her pointed chin. "Frank's not going to retire. How can he, after all this?''

"Isn't that up to the board of directors?'' Max's expression was puzzled as he regarded his chief.

Killegrew held his head. "Of course it is. I'll be sixty-five in June, which is the mandatory retirement age. Of course,'' he continued in a thoughtful voice, "the board could change the by-laws.''

"Maybe they will.'' Ava's tone was bland. "Why not, Frank?''

"Well . . ." Killegrew scowled at Ava, then brushed toast crumbs from his plaid shirt. "If WaCom really plans to attempt a merger with us, it wouldn't be a bad idea to keep the same skipper at the helm of the S.S. OTIOSE."

Max was now looking more worried than puzzled. "Are you saying you won't fight the merger, Frank? Hell, you won't officially retire until June. This deal's supposed to come down next week."

"I haven't charted our course yet," Killegrew replied. "How can I, without a first mate? Ward's . . . gone."

"Name someone to fill his spot," Margo said, finally sitting down again. "The board can ratify the appointment later. You can exercise emergency powers. If," she added dryly, "there ever was an emergency, this weekend is it."

Judith thought that was an understatement. Still standing by the door, she peeked into the kitchen. Somewhat to her surprise, Russell and Gene were hard at work. The vice president–research and development was scrubbing the stove; the company's legal counsel was sweeping the floor. Judith quietly closed the door.

"We should discuss this," Killegrew said. "Formally, I mean. Nadia, bring my coffee into the game room. We'll take a meeting there. Get Gene and Russell out of the kitchen."

Five minutes later, the OTIOSE contingent had adjourned to the game room. Renie surveyed the mess they had left behind in the dining room. "So much for my big mouth," she said. "Now I suppose I won't get the graphic design consulting contract."

"Do you still want it?" Judith asked, forcing herself not to start clearing away the table.

"Sure," Renie answered, heading for the kitchen. "If I turned down jobs from all the corporate types I thought were unethical or arrogant or even criminal, I'd go broke. As long as their money doesn't have pictures of Bugs Bunny on it, I'll take it straight to the bank."

The kitchen, at least, looked almost clean. Judith and

Renie made toast, fixed bowls of cereal, and poured coffee.

"I guess we won't be going to church this Sunday," Judith said in a wry voice.

"I guess not," Renie agreed. "I wonder if Father Hoyle has ever heard an excuse like ours for missing Mass?"

"You mean, 'I didn't attend church last Sunday because I was trapped inside a mountain lodge during a blizzard and possible avalanches with three dead bodies and a homicidal maniac?'" Judith laughed, a slightly bitter sound. "As excuses go, it's not bad. Let's hope Father Hoyle believes us."

"He will," Renie said, opening a jar of boysenberry jam. "I'm sure he recalls a rather lethal Easter Bunny a few years ago at Our Lady, Star of the Sea."

"Don't remind me," Judith said. Given their current situation, she wasn't in the mood to think back to the deadly doings in her home parish. "Hey," she burst out, knocking the spoon out of her cereal, "let's go exploring."

Renie's eyes widened. "Where? Not the third floor—I don't need to see any more bodies."

"The files," Judith said. "Somebody must have them. What do you bet that most of these people don't lock their doors after they leave their rooms? We didn't."

"They would if they had the files," Renie countered. "If they haven't destroyed them, they'd stash them somewhere no one else would think to look."

"Good point." Judith was momentarily subdued. "Do you really think they'll talk Frank into not retiring?"

Renie narrowed her eyes. "What do you think?"

"He doesn't sound like a man who wants to retire," Judith said after a brief pause. "I've never heard him mention a single thing about what he plans to do. Joe's already sending away for information on fishing trips."

"He should have asked Bill," Renie said. "My husband's got a suitcase full of fishing brochures, not to mention cruises, Amtrak trips, and half the hotel-casinos in Vegas."

Abruptly, Judith stood up. "Let's go."

"You're serious." Reluctantly, Renie set her coffee mug on the counter.

Judith nodded. "Two points—first, would whoever stole the files keep them or burn them? Second, whoever *didn't* take them might not lock their doors. We can get rid of some suspects."

"Somebody's already doing that," Renie remarked, but she followed Judith to the back stairs.

Andrea's room wore a desolate air. But it had definitely been disturbed since the cousins had searched it. The daily planner was lying on the spare bed and the personnel files were gone.

Max's room was also unlocked. It looked virtually the same as it had when Judith and Renie had gone with him to look out the windows. There were no items of interest, and it appeared that nothing had been burned in the grate except logs and kindling.

The same was true of Russell's room. Indeed, it was so Spartan that it might never have been occupied. The cousins moved on to Ava, who, they recalled was staying next door to Russell. Somewhat to their surprise, Ava hadn't locked her door, either.

"I suppose there's no point," Judith mused. "They're all together during the day, or at least in pairs."

"True," Renie agreed. "If they don't have anything to hide, why bother?"

Judith scanned the top of the bureau where Ava kept her personal items. There was a hairbrush, a mascara wand, an emery board, and a packet of birth control pills.

"Maintenance or prevention?" Judith inquired with a sly smile.

"Either one. Both. Lots of women take the pill for reasons other than contraception," Renie noted.

"That's so." Judith opened the small closet. The only items hanging there were a yellow flannel nightgown, a black bathrobe edged with white piping, and the red jewel-necked sweater and woolen slacks Judith had borrowed. "Odd," Judith said under her breath.

"What's odd?" Renie came to stand next to Judith.

"Why hasn't Ava worn that red outfit? All three days, she's had on either the blue or the green ensemble. Wouldn't you change clothes if you had any?"

"Sure," Renie responded. "Maybe Ava doesn't want to wear that one because you did. No offense, coz," she went on, poking Judith in the ribs, "but some people are funny about things like that. Besides, Ava said she didn't care much about clothes."

"Yes, she did," Judith said, giving the red outfit one last curious look.

They moved on, but the next room they checked was locked. "Who is it?" Renie asked. "Gene?"

"I think so. I'm trying to remember who came out of where when we brought the latest gloomy news."

"Gene would lock up," Renie said. "He's a lawyer."

Judith pointed to the damaged door across the hall. "That's Ward's room. Shall we?"

"Well . . ." Renie hesitated.

Judith didn't. She opened the door, but everything seemed the same as it had been when she'd accompanied the others in their futile search for OTIOSE's executive vice president.

"No sign of a struggle," Judith murmured. "Do you realize that Ward must have been lying outside those windows while we looked around for him in here?"

Renie grimaced. "Why didn't anybody look outside?"

"It never occurred to any of us, I guess. Besides, Ward's body must have sunk into the snow before it slid inside the lobby." Judith checked the grate, the closet, the bathroom, then went to the windows. The rain was still pouring down and the snow had melted another two inches. The dull, gray morning light cast a pall over the landscape.

"At least we can see something out there," Renie noted. "Not that there's much to see except melting snow."

Judith, however, wasn't looking at the gloomy scenery. She opened one of the windows which, like the others in the guest rooms, swung inward. "Stand here, coz. I'm going to try to kill you."

"Oh, goody," Renie said, but complied.

Judith approached Renie from behind. "Lean out over the sill, as if you were looking for something."

"Okay." Renie leaned, bracing herself on the window frame.

Judith contemplated her cousin's bent-over form. "This isn't working. I can't kill you because you're too short. Let's change places. You sneak up behind me and put a garrote around my neck."

"I don't have a garrote." Renie gazed around the small room. "Wasn't Ward killed with a belt?"

"Yes. His own, presumably." Judith sighed. "I'm getting soaked. Use a towel."

Renie grabbed a bath towel. "Here I come," she said. "Ooof!" Her assault on Judith went awry. Renie collapsed on top of Judith. "I can't reach your neck," she complained. "I may be too short, but you're too tall."

Judith backed up, sending Renie into the bureau. "My point exactly," she said, closing the window. "I'm five inches taller than you are. Ward was about six-one. Maybe we can eliminate Russell and Nadia. She's not as tall as you are, and Russell can't be much over five-eight."

"Margo's no taller than that," Renie noted, regaining her balance. "What if Ward was sitting down?"

"Where?" Judith looked around. The armchairs were at the other side of the room.

Renie pointed to the space between the windows. "On the honor bar. Heck, anywhere. Whoever killed him must have had to push him out the window."

"That indicates strength," Judith said, running her hands through her hair which had gotten quite wet while she hung out of the window. "Oh, shoot—we've been through all this. An adrenaline rush can accomplish just about anything.''

Renie was heading for the door. ''I've had a good time, but this wasn't it,'' she said. ''Let's finish our fruitless search.''

''Okay,'' sighed Judith, then stopped next to the bureau. ''Did you see this?''

''What?'' Renie sounded impatient.

Judith bent down. ''It's some kind of pin. You must have knocked it loose when you fell against the bureau. It says, 'Bell System—twenty-five years service.' ''

Renie examined the pin and nodded. ''So who has twenty-five years of service before coming to OTIOSE? Ward comes to mind. It's probably his.''

Judith's shoulders sagged in disappointment. ''Oh, well. I was hoping it would point to somebody else.'' She took the pin from Renie and placed it on the bureau.

It didn't surprise the cousins to find that Margo had locked her door. Nadia's was open, however. Unlike the other rooms, hers was cluttered. Clothes, cosmetics, notebooks, paperbacks, perfume, and enough lingerie to last through an arctic winter filled every nook and cranny. But none of it seemed pertinent to the murders.

''This must be Frank's room,'' Judith said, nodding at the door next to Nadia's.

It was also unlocked, and if not cluttered, it was messy. Frank Killegrew was obviously not a man who was used to looking after himself. The bed was unmade, the cap was off the toothpaste tube, the sink was full of whiskers. But except for evidence of being spoiled, the cousins found nothing.

''That's it,'' Renie declared. ''We flunked. I think I'll go downstairs and smoke a lot.''

Judith started to trudge after Renie to the elevator, then called to her cousin to wait up. ''Leon—we forgot about him.''

"He's eminently forgettable," Renie responded. "Alas, poor Leon."

The room was unlocked. The bed, where Andrea had waited for the man who never came to share his angel food cake, was still in disarray. The extra pillow, which Judith had put behind Andrea's head, remained in place.

The only difference was that Nadia Weiss was lying on the spare bed, and she was obviously quite dead.

SIXTEEN

"THIS . . . CAN'T . . . BE . . . happening," Judith gasped.

Renie was stunned. She neither spoke nor moved, but simply stood at the foot of the bed and stared at Nadia with unblinking eyes.

"Coz . . ." Judith began, but also found herself at a loss for words.

Nadia Weiss lay on her side, the right arm extended, the left curled around her stomach. Her face was contorted and her stockinged feet dangled over the edge of the bed. She was fully clothed, though her large-rimmed glasses lay carefully folded on the nightstand.

Judith knew it was useless, but she finally moved closer and tried to take Nadia's pulse. "She's still warm." Judith let Nadia's right arm fall away.

"Of course she's still warm," Renie murmured. "We saw her downstairs not more than an hour ago."

Judith gazed at the spectacles, then noticed the glass and the pill bottle. "Good grief! It's the old sleeping pill trick, just like Andrea. Or almost," she added on a more thoughtful note. "Look, coz."

Edging closer, Renie's foot struck something under the bed. "Hold it—what's this?" With her toe, she nudged the obstacle into plain view.

It was an empty pint of gin. "An added attraction?" Judith remarked, then turned her attention back to the pill bottle. "Triclos. 'Take one capsule before bedtime. Do not mix with alcohol.' The prescription is dated last week and made out by a Dr. Robert Winslow for Nadia Weiss. The pharmacy is located above downtown, in the hospital district."

Renie nodded. "Nadia mentioned having her own sleeping pills, and she told me once that she's lived forever in one of those elegant older apartments within walking distance of downtown. But this time the killer was more thorough." Renie pointed to the empty water glass, then to the gin bottle. "Maybe the stuff's more lethal if you mix it with booze. The killer might have known that and added the gin for effect."

"Maybe." Judith seemed distracted as she gestured at the fireplace. "Why light a fire? No one's staying in this room."

Renie turned. "That *is* odd. It's not much of a blaze, though. It's practically out."

Rushing to the hearth, Judith all but shoved Renie out of the way. "Look! There's no sign of a log in the grate. Kindling, maybe—and paper." She gazed at Renie, who had joined her in front of the fireplace. "What do you think got burned in here? Andrea's files?"

Renie grabbed the poker and leaned down. "There's not much left, but I see some charred paper clips and those metal fasteners that hold files together." She stood up. "You're right, maybe Nadia burned the files."

"Why?" Judith's dark eyes scanned the room. "Did she take them from Andrea's room? Did they include the so-called hooker files? Look, coz," she continued, pointing back to the grate, "there's not a lot of paper in there. Andrea's files were two, three inches thick, which is why we didn't take time to go through them."

"Maybe Nadia only wanted to burn certain incriminating data," Renie suggested.

"Incriminating to whom?" Judith asked, beginning to pace the small room.

Renie shrugged. "I don't know. Herself, maybe. Or whoever killed her."

"This is wrong," Judith declared, making a slashing motion with her hand. "This seems all out of kilter."

"I don't know what you're talking about," Renie admitted.

"I don't either. That's the problem." Judith bit her lower lip and scowled.

Renie started for the door. "Shall we go break the latest bad news?"

Judith shook her head. "Not this time."

"What?" Renie was flabbergasted.

"No. We'll go back downstairs, as if nothing's happened. Let's see how the rest of them—what's left of them—react."

Renie gritted her teeth. "Okay—if you say so. I'm not much of an actress."

"You'll manage," Judith said dryly. "Just play dumb. I know you can do that."

Upon reaching the game room, the cousins discovered a fragmented contingent. Max Agasias was furiously hurling darts at a board on the far wall. Ava Aunuu was lying on the pool table, crying her eyes out. Gene Jarman, Jr., stood under mounted elk antlers, chewing on his knuckles. The rest were nowhere in sight. The big windows that ran along most of one wall showed nothing but snow, a bleak, suffocating sight.

Of the three who remained in the game room, Gene seemed the most approachable. "What's going on?" Judith asked in a hushed voice.

Gene recoiled as if Judith had slapped him. "Nothing," he said sharply. "Nothing you need to know."

Judith backed off. Renie had gone to Ava, gently prodding her heaving shoulders.

"Go away," Ava blubbered. "Leave me alone."

With a puzzled glance for Judith, Renie withdrew. Max was still throwing darts, going dangerously wide of the target. Margo entered the lobby from the direction of the women's restroom. She looked absolutely furious.

"I hate everybody," she announced. "I wish I could shoot you all." For good measure, she jiggled her suede bag, then glanced at the elk antlers, as if she were envisioning one of her co-worker's heads in the same place.

"There must be a reason for your hostility," said Renie in a strange, strangled voice. "You might feel better if you talked about it." She turned to Judith, speaking in a whisper. "Do I sound like Bill?"

"You sound like hell," Judith shot back. "But go for it."

Ignoring Renie, Margo stalked past the cousins and went to the near wall which was decorated with Haida masks and jewelry. With her back to the others, Margo stood rigidly, one hand clenching at her side, the other clutching her suede bag.

"What happened to the buddy system?" Judith murmured.

Renie shook her head. "I don't know. Who's missing? Frank and Russell?"

She'd hardly finished speaking when both men entered the game room. Frank Killegrew looked distraught and Russell Craven appeared miserable. Max whirled around, unleashing a dart that sailed between the two men's heads.

"We've got to calm down!" Killegrew cried, jerking around to watch the dart land out in the hall. "A mutinous crew can cause a shipwreck."

"Sorry," Max mumbled. "That was an accident."

Margo turned her head. "The ship has sunk, Frank. Glub, glub, *glub*. That was my point. That's why I'm quitting. Don't you get it? I'm not going down with your stupid S.S. OTIOSE."

"Now, now," Killegrew began, "you're considering just the short term . . ."

"Don't start again!" Ava cried. "I can't stand it!" She buried her face against a side pocket.

"I'm confused," Russell said in a disconsolate voice. "Margo, I thought you liked Alan Roth. I'm the one who should be upset. I *am* upset. My career is over."

"Now, now," Killegrew repeated, "you don't know that for sure, Russell. If the board agrees to change the by-laws and I stay on as CEO, it won't matter if we merge with WaCom. I'll still have an oar in the water."

"But you won't!" Ava declared, attempting to sit up on the pool table. "That's what I'm trying to tell you! That's why it doesn't matter if you name me as Ward's successor. Do you think Alan Roth will want any of us working for him after what happened to his wife this weekend?"

Judith and Renie glanced at each other. "Ava as executive vice president?" Judith said under her breath.

"Why not?" Renie whispered. "She's very capable."

Killegrew had assumed an authoritative stance in front of the dart board. Max's homely face was belligerent, but he set the last two darts down on the wet bar. Gene moved out from under the antlers while Margo finally turned all the way around to face the others.

"It may be," Killegrew said, hooking his thumbs in his suspenders, "that this weekend—as tragic as it's been— could work in our favor." Seeing the dismay and even horror on the faces of his employees, Killegrew held up a hand. "Now, now—don't get me wrong. Nobody is more upset by what's happened here than I am. But there's always an upside. Ava's got the right idea about Alan Roth. He may not want anything to do with us now that Andrea's . . . passed away. But that might mean WaCom will scrap the whole merger idea. This crew has scurvy, right? We're contaminated. There are other telecommunications companies out there to merge with." Killegrew looked at Gene. "What about Alien Tel? Settle the damned suit out of court and let WaCom gobble *them* up."

Gene Jarman stiffened. "I can't do that. I won't do that.

It's a point of . . . It's a legal point." Gene turned away.

Killegrew jabbed a finger at his legal counsel. "You'll do it if I tell you to! We can't afford a personal . . ." The CEO swung around to Margo. "Well? What can't we afford?"

Margo sighed. "The word's 'vendetta,' Frank."

"Vendetta?" Killegrew wrinkled his blunt nose. "Okay, we can't afford that. So drop it, first thing."

Gene said nothing; his face was expressionless.

Max picked up a pool cue and broke it in two. "So where the hell does that leave me?"

"Right where you belong," Killegrew shot back. "You and Russell both. If we can get out of this WaCom deal, your departments stay as they are."

"*If*," growled Max. "That's a damned big word, Frank."

"We'll see." Killegrew moved toward the wet bar, which someone had stocked with the dwindling number of liquor bottles. "It's almost eleven. I guess it wouldn't hurt to run up the cocktail flag a little early. Nadia, mix me a Scotch and soda, will you?"

The request seemed to echo off the plate glass windows and disappear among the high polished beams of the ceiling. Judith and Renie had moved close together, scrutinizing each of the six remaining conferees. Ava, who had dried her eyes, glanced behind her; Gene's stance became less rigid as he looked around the room; Margo moved closer to the group and frowned; Max, looking curious, rested the broken pool cue pieces against his thigh; Russell sat on a chessboard, oblivious to the pieces he had knocked over, including the bishop that was poking into his backside. It was only Frank Killegrew who showed immediate dismay, and for all the wrong reasons.

"Where'd Nadia go? I said I could use a drink. What's wrong with that woman? Doesn't she know who signs her checks?"

"Leon used to," Margo said. "As chief financial officer, he signed all our checks."

Killegrew glowered at Margo. "You know what I mean. Didn't Nadia go with you to the restroom a while ago?"

Margo shook her head. "She left the game room before I did, Frank. You asked her to get you a coffee refill."

"Which," Killegrew declared with great umbrage, "she did not do. Where's her sense of loyalty?"

Ava struggled to get off the pool table, while Gene began to shift nervously from foot to foot. Margo swung the suede bag in an ominous gesture and Max started for the dining room.

"She may still be in the kitchen," Max said over his shoulder. "I'll check."

"Not without a bodyguard," Gene called out, and hurried to join Max.

Russell swerved on the chessboard, sending several pawns and a rook onto the floor. "Where's Nadia?" he asked in a vague, bewildered voice.

"Russell . . ." Margo began, but she sounded weary and went mute.

Ava was hugging herself, her chin sunk into the high rolled neck of her navy sweater. "I can't . . . she couldn't . . . Oh, God!"

Max and Gene returned via the corridor that led through the laundry room to the kitchen. "She's not anywhere we could see," Gene announced in a tense voice. "Should we look in the basement?"

"Why," Killegrew demanded, "would Nadia be in the basement? There's no coffee pot down there." But the usual bluster had gone out of him; he sounded frightened and unsure.

Judith was beginning to doubt the wisdom of keeping the others in the dark. She plucked at the sleeve of Renie's sweatshirt and drew her back towards the lobby entrance.

"Maybe we should tell them," she whispered.

Renie shook her head. "It's too late. Let it slide."

Margo was staring at her watch. "How long has Nadia been gone? Half an hour?"

"More than that," Killegrew responded. "It wasn't quite ten when I asked her to get me some more coffee. It's bang-up eleven now. Six bells," he added, but his voice broke on the nautical reference.

Taking in Killegrew's obvious distress, Gene Jarman joined his chief on the hearth. "Let's divide ourselves into threes," he said, then apparently remembered Judith and Renie. "I mean, fours. Half of us will search the rest of this floor and the basement. The other half will go up to the second and third floors. Ava, Margo, Max—will you come with me?"

Max stepped forward at once, but neither woman seemed anxious to take part. Briefly, they stared at each other, and some sort of understanding must have passed between them. Margo actually gave Ava a hand to help her down from the pool table.

"Why," Margo murmured, "didn't I resign last week?"

"You had no reason then," Ava said.

"Yes, I did." Margo trooped out of the lobby with Ava, Gene, and Max.

The cousins were left with Frank Killegrew and Russell Craven. "I don't think I can do this," Killegrew declared in a weak voice. As he reached for the Scotch, his hand shook. "I never dreamed it would come to this."

"To what?" asked Russell, who was still sitting on the chess board.

But Killegrew didn't reply. He sloshed Scotch into a glass and drank it down in one gulp. "Okay," he said, squaring his shoulders, "let's go."

The foursome took the elevator to the second floor, which meant that they would begin their search at the opposite end from Leon's room. Judith tried to think of a way to curtail the suspense, but nothing came to mind. Renie was right. It was too late to admit they'd found another body. Judith didn't dare tip her hand.

They started with the cousins' room, checking the bathroom and under the beds. This time, they remembered to look out the windows. It was still raining hard, and the snow had melted another three inches. Through the steady downpour, Judith could see into the distance. There was nothing but the tops of trees, some of which now showed bare branches. The wet, drooping evergreens look dejected in the rain.

Down the hall they went, finding everything the same as when Judith and Renie had made their search earlier in the morning. Or so it appeared until they reached Gene's room. It was now unlocked. Killegrew strode inside, calling Nadia's name.

Judith glanced around. There was an open briefcase on the bed, a cardigan sweater hanging on the back of one of the ubiquitous armchairs, an empty glass on the nightstand, and a half-filled laundry bag on the floor. There was, of course, no sign of Nadia.

Margo's room was still locked. Killegrew swore under his breath, then knocked hard three times and again called for Nadia. With a shake of his head, he led them on.

As before, Leon's was the last room they checked. Killegrew turned the knob, opened the door, started to mouth Nadia's name, and staggered.

"No! No! Nadia!" he cried in anguish. "Oh, my God!" He fell to his knees, leaning against the side of the bed where Nadia's stockinged foot still dangled. Lifting his head, Killegrew grabbed Nadia by the shoulders in a futile attempt to rouse her. "Wake up, Nadia! Wake up! It's me, Frank! Please, please, wake up!" He collapsed on top of her lifeless body.

"Oh, dear!" Russell exclaimed. "Is she . . . ? Oh, dear!"

Killegrew's shoulders were heaving. Russell, with a hand over his mouth, rushed into the bathroom. The cousins could hear him being sick, but their concern was focused on Frank Killegrew.

"Mr. Killegrew," Judith said softly, "come away. There's nothing you can do."

He continued to sob for several seconds. Then, suddenly, he turned his head and stared at Judith. "I *can* do . . . I can *do* . . . I can do . . ." His entire body sagged as he slipped off the bed. "I can't do," he breathed in an incredulous voice. *"I can't do."*

For Frank Killegrew, it appeared to be a revelation.

It took a great deal of coaxing and soothing for the cousins to get Killegrew and Russell out of Leon's room. The bereaved CEO rejected Judith's suggestion that Max and Gene carry Nadia up to the third floor where the other bodies lay at rest. Killegrew adamantly refused to have Nadia moved. Judith understood, and backed off.

The others had already returned to the lobby from the basement. Since Killegrew appeared to be in shock and Russell still claimed to feel sick, the burden of making the tragic announcement fell on Renie, who hurriedly consulted with Judith.

"The four of us found Nadia Weiss dead in Leon Mooney's room. Cause of death can't be determined without an autopsy."

Ava began to cry again, Margo collapsed in a side chair, Gene held his head in his hands, and Max exploded with a stream of obscenities. It was clear that the OTIOSE contingent had completely fallen apart.

"There's no logic to this!" Gene exclaimed. "It's irrational, insane, beyond understanding! I can't deal with it anymore!" He whirled around, looking as if he were trying to escape.

Ava stopped crying and raised her head. "It's not a cut-and-dried legal issue you can find in one of your RCW law books," she said, compassion evident in her voice. "But it *is* real, Gene. What's so horrible is that I can't see beyond the next few minutes. It's like the future has been canceled for all of us."

"It sure as hell has for some of us," Max declared savagely. "Who's next?" His homely face was a mixture of fury and fear.

"Not me," Margo averred, gripping her suede bag. But for once, she didn't sound very confident.

Killegrew, who was now drinking straight from a bottle of Scotch, turned bleary eyes on the others. "It had to be suicide," he mumbled.

"Can it, Frank," Margo said wearily. "We know better. Stop kidding yourself."

"I don't blame her," Killegrew said, as if he hadn't heard Margo. "I feel like jumping off a cliff."

"Oh, please don't!" Russell begged. "Really, this is all so . . ." Slumped on the footstool, he ran a hand through his disheveled fair hair. "It's exactly what Ava just mentioned—it's *real*. I don't know much about real things, only ideas and theories and concepts. But," he continued, hiking himself up to a full sitting position, "I do know how to conjecture, it's part of my job. I saw that pill bottle on the nightstand in Leon's room. It was given to Nadia by the company physician, Dr. Winslow, who is somewhat old-fashioned. Triclos—or triclofos or chloral hydrate, to call it by its more common name—is not often prescribed any more. I recall this from my days as an army medic. It can be lethal, of course, especially if it's taken with an alcoholic beverage. There was also an empty gin bottle on the floor by the bed. I must assume—or conjecture, if you will— that whoever murdered poor dear Nadia must have put the chloral hydrate tablets into the gin."

A little gasp went up around the lobby, but the usually reticent Russell Craven hadn't finished. "You see, I *have* been thinking. It's what I do. And I've come to one unalterable conclusion. The deaths have not been caused by any of us. We've wondered a great deal about an outsider committing these crimes. That can be the only answer.'' From behind his round, rimless glasses, Russell stared at Judith and Renie. "It must be those two women. They are the killers, and we must act at once.''

SEVENTEEN

JUDITH AND RENIE both started to protest, meanwhile backpedaling across the lobby. But no one actually came after them. The OTIOSE executives appeared depleted, as if the latest horror had sapped their collective will.

"We can't stop them," Killegrew finally said in a lethargic voice. "It's inevitable. We've come here to die."

"It's like the Nazis with the concentration camps," Ava said in wonder. "You get on a bus, you think you're simply being sent to some harmless place, but you never come back."

"My grandparents were slaughtered by Mao's henchmen," Margo said, her grip slackened on the suede bag. "They thought they were being taken to a political meeting in another village."

"My family fled Armenia during the First World War," Max said in a toneless voice, "but some of our relatives were massacred by the Turks. It was a bloodbath."

"I had two great-grandfathers who were lynched," Gene said, staring into space. "One in Alabama, the other in South Carolina. My uncle was almost beaten to death during the freedom marches in Mississippi. In Oakland, two white cops gave my father a concussion for no reason. Nobody knows the trouble I've seen.''

"Really," Russell said in a huffy tone, "none of you are showing much spunk. All we have to do is lock them in their room. Then we'll be safe until we can get out of here."

The suggestion was met with apathy. Slowly, the cousins moved back towards the others.

"Russell," Judith began in what she hoped was a reasonable tone, "you're off base. If you're relying on logic, let's put it to the test. For openers, we weren't here last year, which is when all this may have started. We have nothing to do with OTIOSE or any other telecommunications outfit except for my cousin's tenuous connection through her freelance design business. I was asked to fill in for some other caterer at the last minute, as at least some of you may know. Why on earth would either of us come to Mountain Goat Lodge and start killing people? It makes absolutely no sense."

Russell adjusted his rimless glasses. "Killing often doesn't. People go on rampages."

"We don't," Renie declared. "Margo, I've worked with you before. Have you ever had any reason to doubt who and what I am?"

Margo's expression was unusually vague. "No—I guess not. But then I never pay much attention to consultants as individuals. They come in, do their job, and leave."

Renie sighed. "Yes, I understand that part. But if we'd wanted to kill you, we've had ample opportunity. Why didn't we poison your food?"

"Too obvious," Max responded.

"Poison can be extremely subtle," declared Judith, who'd had experience with its cleverly disguised lethal effects. When the others regarded her with wide-eyed alarm, she hastened to explain. "I read a lot of mysteries. There are poisons that can't be detected, poisons with delayed reactions, poisons that can be masked in various ways."

"That's true," Margo said glumly. "I read mysteries, too."

"So what do we do?" Max asked, automatically turning to Killegrew.

The CEO scratched an ear. "I don't know. Eat lunch, I suppose." Somehow the callousness of his remark was diluted by his desolate manner.

Margo got to her feet. "Ava and I'll make lunch." Seeing the startled expressions on the men's faces, she waved an impatient hand. "Okay, so it's women's work, but this is different. It's like . . . a safety precaution."

Russell pointed a bony finger at Judith and Renie. "What about them?"

"Lock them in the library," Margo retorted as she and Ava started for the kitchen. "Let them read some more mystery novels. If they're so smart, maybe they can figure all this out."

The cousins didn't protest their incarceration. "What a morning," Renie sighed as she and Judith sank into the library's wing-back armchairs. "So much for gratitude. I guess Russell forgot about that hot tea you made for him." She sighed again, gazing at one of the two tall windows which were flanked by muted plaid drapes. "I wonder how long it will be until the snow has melted enough that we really can get out of here?"

Judith shook her head. "It'll take a while. And don't forget the avalanche danger."

Looking glum, Renie didn't respond right away. "Somebody out there knows we didn't do it," she finally said.

"That's right," Judith agreed in a strange voice.

Renie's eyes narrowed. "Do you know who it is?"

Now it was Judith who didn't answer immediately. "I've got a hunch," she admitted at last. "Do you?"

Renie nodded slowly. "I think so, yes."

"We have no proof," Judith remarked bleakly. "Those files might help us, if we could find them."

"You don't think they've been destroyed?"

Judith shook her head. "I don't think the killer has found them. Damn," she cursed under her breath, "I have to go to the bathroom. Do you think they'll let us out?"

"Pick the lock," Renie said. "You can do it."

Judith brightened. "Maybe I can. It's worth a try." Just as she fished into her shoulder bag for something that would trip the lock, the pager went off again. "How annoying! I don't need that thing bothering me right now. I feel like throwing it out the window."

"Stop worrying about something you can't help," Renie advised. "We've got more urgent problems here."

"You're right." Judith hauled an oversized paper clip out of her purse and began straightening it. "Let's hope these locks aren't as daunting as they look. The ones on this floor are obviously much newer than the ones on the guest room doors."

Renie watched while Judith plied the paper clip. The library door had a sophisticated lock, and presented a serious challenge. After almost five minutes, Judith was forced to give up.

"We'll have to knock and yell to get out of here," she said, tossing the now useless paper clip into a wastebasket made of woven branches. "I hope they can hear us."

Renie began pounding on the door and shouting. Nothing happened. "I don't hear any hurrying feet," she said.

The cousins suddenly heard something else.

The library telephone was ringing.

Judith snatched up the receiver. "Hello? Hello?" she virtually yelled into the mouthpiece.

"Goodness!" exclaimed Arlene Rankers. "Why are you shouting, Judith? You practically broke my eardrum!"

"Arlene!" Judith collapsed into one of the armchairs. "What's wrong, Arlene?"

Renie hovered over Judith, who held the phone away from her ear just enough so that her cousin could hear, too.

"I've been paging you for two days," Arlene said in an irritated voice. "I found your pager number on the bulletin board in the kitchen. I didn't even know you *had* a pager, Judith."

"Ah . . . Neither did I. I mean, I forgot. But the phones have been out up here at the lodge and . . . Never mind, what's the problem? Is it Mother?"

"Your mother?" Arlene laughed. "Of course not! Your mother is wonderful, as always. She had such a nice time going to Mass and out to breakfast with us. She said you never took her for rides in the snow any more."

Judith's head was spinning. Gertrude hadn't attended Mass for almost three years, claiming that she was too feeble. She managed, however, to get to her bridge club meetings around the hill and occasionally, to the church itself for a bingo session. Judith considered her mother a fraud.

"It's snowing at home?" Judith inquired. "I don't usually drive in the snow."

"It doesn't bother Carl," Arlene declared. "But of course we're midwesterners and know how to handle it. Now tell me, Judith, how do I get into your computer program for future reservations? I've been doing them all by hand."

"The computer!" Judith felt giddy. "That's all?"

"*All?*" Arlene sounded irked. "I can't get into the cancellation program, either, and there have been several of those, what with this bad weather and people being so timid about getting around in it. Honestly, you'd think that just because the planes have been grounded and some of the roads are closed and the metro buses have been taken off their runs . . ."

Judith and Renie exchanged startled looks. "How much snow *is* there, Arlene?" Judith interrupted.

"Mmm . . . Two feet? Your statue of St. Francis in the backyard is completely covered. The poor birds have nowhere to land."

"Oh, my. That's quite a lot of snow for us in town,"

Judith said. "Okay, let me tell you how to get into those programs . . ." She jiggled a bit in the chair, fighting off nature's urges. When she had finished her instructions, most of which required questions from Arlene, Judith asked if Joe was home.

"Poor Joe." Arlene's voice dropped a notch. "Poor man. Poor soul. He's fine," she added on a far more chipper note.

Accustomed to her friend and neighbor's peculiar contradictions, Judith grimaced only slightly. "Is he home? Can I talk to him?"

"No. Yes. I must run, Judith. I've got a million things to do, since Carl and I are leaving next week for . . ."

"Wait! Do you mean he's home but I can't talk to him or he's not home and I can . . . That is, I can't . . ."

"He's at work," Arlene broke in. "He's been at work since the snow started Saturday during the night. He got called in late Friday on a very big case. Then he got stuck downtown. It's really terrible here, Judith. We're completely marooned."

"But . . . you said . . ." Realizing it was pointless to argue, Judith sighed. "Okay, Arlene. Thanks for all your help. We may be able to get out of here by tomorrow. It's melting fairly fast."

"Not here," Arlene said. "The wind changed last night, coming from the south. We got another four inches, with more coming tonight. Take care, and say hello to Serena." Arlene rang off.

Judith stared at Renie. "The phone works. Who shall we call?"

"The bathroom?" Renie said with a quirky little smile.

"I forgot about that," Judith admitted. "I can wait. Let's start with the police."

"Which police? As I recall," Renie said dryly, "that was our first obstacle."

"*My* police," Judith responded, punching in digits. "At least Joe will be able to tell us who we should contact."

"Oh, God!" Renie cried. "Are you going to tell him about our body count?"

"I have to," Judith said, then held up a hand as someone answered at the other end. "Joe Flynn, please . . . He's not? But I thought . . . Oh . . . Oh, I see. All right. Yes, please have him call me at this number. This is his wife." Judith replaced the receiver. "Joe didn't get stuck downtown," she said to Renie. "He and Woody are out in that snazzy neighborhood between downtown and the lake. That's where their victim was found."

Renie recognized the neighborhood. "They've got tons of little hills and short, narrow streets," she said. "It's not as steep as Heraldsgate Hill, but it'd be really difficult navigating in the snow."

"At least Joe's in a classy part of town," said Judith, and then she laughed, a rueful sound. "I guess he's stuck with a stiff, too." Suddenly, she jumped out of her chair. "The bathroom! We've got to get to the bathroom!"

"So you mentioned," Renie smirked. "How about using that wastebasket?"

Judith stared at Renie. "I don't mean that," she responded, going to the door. "Help!" she screamed. "Help! Help!"

"What in the . . . ?" But Renie was at her side, pounding on the heavy pine panels.

The cousins were almost hoarse by the time Margo and Gene came to the rescue. "We thought the yelling came from outside," Margo said. "What's wrong?"

"Outside?" Judith blinked at Margo. "No, it was us."

Their captors didn't argue when Judith and Renie asked to be locked up in their own room. They needed access to a bathroom and also wouldn't mind if someone brought them a couple of sandwiches. After escorting the cousins upstairs, Margo and Gene promised to deliver food.

"You didn't tell them the phone worked," Renie said after the cousins were alone. "How come?"

"Because," Judith explained, scurrying into the bathroom, "I wanted to stall for time. Obviously, the OTIOSE gang was in the dining room when the phone rang and they didn't hear the kitchen extension."

"So what good does it do us?" asked Renie. "Now we're shut up in here."

"With a much simpler lock," Judith called out over the flushing of the toilet. "The only problem is, we don't have access to a phone on this floor. I forgot about that."

"Crazy," Renie muttered. "What did you mean when you said 'bathroom'?"

Judith was washing her hands. "What? I can't hear you."

"Never mind." Renie collapsed onto the bed and lit a cigarette. "I'm sure I'll find out."

Judith entered the bedroom. "I'm glad Mother is okay. It sounds as if I'll lose some money with the cancellations, but I can't do anything about that. And, as usual, Arlene is coping very well."

"It's a good thing this is a three-day weekend," Renie pointed out. "Bill doesn't have to teach and nobody has to work. Maybe by Tuesday, things will get back to normal."

A knock sounded at the door. Ava and Max had arrived with chicken salad sandwiches, chips, and the carrot and celery sticks Judith had cut up early Friday morning. Only two days had passed since then, but to Judith, it felt like much more.

The cousins thanked Max and Ava, who both seemed extremely subdued. "How's everyone doing?" Judith asked, her usual compassion surfacing.

"Lousy," Max retorted. "Honest to God, we have this sense of impending doom."

"But Max," Ava said, giving his sleeve a little tug, "it *is* melting. By tomorrow morning, I'll bet we can get out of here."

"Tomorrow's a long way off," Max replied in a grim voice. "I won't go to my room tonight. I'll stay up, and insist that everybody else does, too. We can take turns sleeping on those sofas in the lobby. Three on guard duty, three catching some Z's. The buddy system was a bust.''

''That's because we're not used to doing things in pairs,'' Ava pointed out, then turned to the cousins. ''I mean, we're executives, we're used to being independent and going our separate ways.''

''No teamwork, huh?'' said Renie. ''Every man—sorry, every *person*—for him or herself.''

''Well,'' Ava said lamely, ''we do tend to think mostly in terms of our own departments. You have to. Otherwise, you'd get shortchanged on personnel, budget, even floor space and office equipment.''

''Don't I know it?'' Max muttered, starting back into the corridor. ''As Frank would say, you have to chart your own course.''

''But he also says we have to row together,'' Ava countered, following Max down the hall. ''When you're at the top, like Frank is, you can see the big . . .''

Renie closed the door. ''I can't stand another word of that crap,'' she declared. ''They've got dead bodies all over the place, the company may be in ruins, they're all scared out of their wits—and they still talk the corporate line. It's sickening.''

Judith wasn't really listening to Renie. After taking a couple of bites of her sandwich, she asked her cousin to make sure the coast was clear in the corridor.

Renie opened the door again. ''They're gone. So what?''

Judith gave Renie a baleful look. ''They didn't lock the door. Either Max and Ava don't think we're dangerous, or they know we're not. Let's go.''

''Go where?'' Renie was looking blank.

''The bathroom, remember?'' Judith breezed past her cousin.

''What bathroom? I thought you—oh, never mind.'' Renie trotted behind Judith as they covered the length of the corridor until they reached Leon's room.

In the struggle to get Killegrew and Russell out of the

room and away from Nadia's corpse, no one had thought
to lock Leon's door, either. Judith marched right inside,
though Renie lingered briefly on the threshold.

"How many times do we have to view the body?" Renie
asked.

"Avert your eyes," Judith called over her shoulder as
she went into the bathroom. "At least they already moved
Andrea upstairs."

With a sigh of resignation, Renie followed. Judith was
pushing back the nylon shower curtain.

"Don't tell me . . ." Renie began with a gasp.

Judith shook her head. "No body. Just . . . the files."

Several folders covered the empty tub. Judith picked
them up, handing the first batch to Renie. "They had to be
somewhere," Judith said. "It dawned on me that along
with Andrea, Nadia knew Barry Newcombe fairly well.
Let's say that Barry was privy to some of the items in
Andrea's private files. He worked for her, didn't he?"

Renie nodded. "Barry might have snooped. Clerks often
do."

"Okay. So Barry might have passed something juicy on
to someone else. Why not Nadia? Since he was in the business of bartering gossip, she'd be a likely client because
she'd know what was happening on the executive floor.
Let's say Nadia got an inkling that more was to come—
except Barry never got the chance to pass the rest of it on.
In the normal course of events at work, Nadia couldn't get
at Andrea's private files. But once Andrea was dead, Nadia
seized an opportunity. That must be who Max saw in the
corridor Friday night. Nadia must have beaten him to the
punch by just a few minutes."

Renie was looking skeptical. "How did Nadia know Andrea had those files with her?"

Judith waved a hand. "Andrea was dropping hints, especially about the hooker files. I suspect she was passing
tidbits on to the others as well. Gene and Russell and even

Nadia were being clobbered with some of that data. It had to come from somewhere.''

The files were somewhat damp, but otherwise appeared to be intact. The cousins gathered up the folders and hurried back to their own room, and this time, they locked the door from the inside.

''The hooker file!'' Renie cried. ''It's right on top!''

''Good,'' Judith responded, fingering the tabs on the other folders. ''There are files for each of the conferees, including Andrea. Does that strike you as odd?''

Renie, however, shook her head. ''I'll bet it's full of stuff she heard people say about her. Not true necessarily, but potentially damaging.''

''Corporate paranoia and skullduggery never cease to amaze me,'' Judith marveled. ''Shall we start with Ward? He's first.''

On a gray, wet January afternoon, what little light there was began to die away shortly after three o'clock. The cousins had to turn on the bedside lamps before they completed the dossiers on Ward, Gene, Nadia, Russell, Max, Margo, Leon, Ava, and Andrea's own much slimmer folder. Judith and Renie had learned very little that they hadn't already heard.

''So what if Ava had had a youthful, unhappy marriage before she left Samoa?'' Renie shrugged. ''Russell collects dead bugs. Big deal. Margo supposedly slept with everybody. Naturally, Andrea would want to believe that. Ward's wife was an albatross. Andrea had fingered Max for running the hooker ring. No surprise there, either. I'm getting bored.''

''Leon was devoted to his mother,'' Judith said, flipping through the chief financial officer's file. ''He was very secretive about his personal and his professional life. Obviously, the latter was a sore point with Andrea. She's written a note on this one page that says, 'Why can't he tell me?' 'Me' is underlined three times.''

''They were sleeping together,'' Renie said. ''Like most

women, she probably felt they shouldn't have secrets from each other. Like most men, Leon may not have agreed.''

Judith looked up from the file. ''There's a page missing.''

''How can you tell?'' Renie inquired. ''Most of the entries are fragmentary.''

''Not all of them.'' Judith tapped what appeared to be the last page in the folder. ''Andrea has written what must have been the equivalent of a teenaged girl's diary. She goes on at length about some staff meeting and an independent audit and how Leon stood up to Frank and refused to be badgered and acted like—I quote—'*a real man.*' Then she writes that Frank brought up the audit later . . . and that's it. The sentence stops, and the last page starts in mid-sentence about how much Leon liked the annual report cover with the photo of the sun setting behind the microwave tower.''

''It was a cliché shot, though,'' Renie said. ''I did some of the interior graphics for that report and . . . Whoa! That's the end of Leon's file?''

Judith nodded. ''That's it. Why?''

''Because that was last year's annual report.'' Renie frowned, then started looking through some of the other files. ''Coz, this is weird. Check the last pages of the other folders. See if you can tell when the final entries were made.''

Surprisingly, Andrea had been haphazard about dating her material. Still, Judith could find nothing more recent than the previous January.

''That's very strange,'' Judith remarked. ''Why would she stop keeping her personal files a year ago?''

Renie had no explanation. ''We haven't gone through Frank's,'' she pointed out. ''Let's see if his file ends abruptly, too.''

Frank Killegrew's file was thicker than the others. He'd been born in Molt, Montana, served as a U.S. Army Ranger in Korea, attended Montana School of Mines in Butte, and gone to work for Mountain States Telephone Company in Helena. His mother's name was given as Kate Killegrew; no father was listed. Instead, there was a picture of a cat sitting on the roof of a house, and a notation that read, "Ha Ha!"

"What does that mean?" Renie demanded.

Judith smirked. "What it shows." Her dark eyes glittered. "Frank was born in a cat house. No wonder he's ashamed of his origins."

"Woo-woo," Renie said under her breath. "That's funny."

"No, it's not." Judith, who had flipped through the rest of the pages, suddenly turned serious. "Well, maybe it is, but the unfunny part is that Frank's file stops long before last year. There's nothing after his years with the Bell System."

Renie grabbed the folder out of Judith's lap. "You're right," she said in wonder. "There's no mention of OTI-OSE."

Rubbing at her temples, Judith got up from the bed and looked out the window. The rain continued to come down, a steady sheet with no hint of wind to shift the dark clouds. "The snow's still melting . . ."

Judith screamed. Renie ran to join her cousin.

There was a man at the window, and he was holding a high-powered rifle.

EIGHTEEN

JUDITH AND RENIE flattened themselves against the wall, hopefully out of the line of fire. "What do you want?" Judith cried, finally finding both her courage and her voice.

In answer, the man slammed the butt of the rifle into one of the smaller panes. Glass shattered onto the floor. Judith and Renie held onto each other, both shaking like leaves. The man, who was on the top rung of a tall aluminum extension ladder, reached through the broken pane and tried to unlatch the window. Judith looked around for something to hit at his fumbling fingers, but there was nothing within reach. The window opened, and the man scrambled into the room. Raindrops and wet snow flew in every direction.

"What's going on?" he demanded in a rough voice.

Judith blinked several times. The man wore a heavy parka over ski pants, and rested the rifle butt on the floor next to his all-weather boots. He had a gray beard and a weathered face, but wasn't much taller than Judith.

"Who are you?" Judith asked in a faint voice.

The intruder's initial reaction was hostile, then he frowned at the cousins. "Mannheimer, who else?"

"Mannheimer?" Judith echoed the name. "Do we know you?"

"Hell, no." Mannheimer shook off the moisture that had accumulated on his person. "Rudy Mannheimer, Mountain Goat Lodge caretaker. Who the hell are *you*?"

"The caterers," Judith replied, stretching the truth a bit. "We got marooned. Where have you been?"

Mannheimer gestured with his head, causing the hood of his parka to slip down and reveal overlong gray hair. "Back at my place. Where else?"

"Um . . . Nowhere," Judith said. "That is, the weather's been terrible. Ah . . . Why are you here now? I thought you had orders to stay away."

Mannheimer lowered his head, as if to charge the cousins. Instead, he answered the question in his ragged, jerky voice. "It's my job, dammit. Orders can change. Like when a blizzard hits. Guests are still my responsibility. Safety first. Couldn't get through since Friday. The first floor's still snowed in. I saw a light up here. I thought I'd give it a try."

"You might have asked first," said Renie, her usual spunk returning. "You didn't have to break the blasted window."

Mannheimer snorted. "You're not real friendly. So tell me. Is everything okay?"

"Oh, brother!" Renie twirled around, holding her head.

"Actually, it's not," Judith said with regret. "There's been some . . . trouble."

"Trouble?" Mannheimer's close-set blue eyes bulged. "What kind of trouble? Frank doesn't like trouble."

"You know Mr. Killegrew?" Judith asked in surprise.

Mannheimer flipped the rifle from one hand to the other. "Sure. We go way back. To Korea. Same platoon. So what's up?" Mannheimer glowered at the cousins.

"I think," Judith said in an unusually high voice, "you ought to talk to Frank. He'll tell you."

"So where is he?" Mannheimer's head swiveled, as if he expected Killegrew to pop out from behind the bathroom door.

"Downstairs," Judith answered promptly. "Go ahead, we'll stay here." She gave Mannheimer a phony smile.

"Okay." The caretaker headed for the door, the rifle now cradled in his arms. He paused on the threshold, unlocking the door the cousins had secured behind them. "Don't worry. I'll fix that window. It's my job." Mannheimer left.

Renie sat back down on the bed. "I wouldn't mind hearing what happens when Frank tells Mannheimer what's been going on."

"And so you shall," Judith said, moving to the door. "Give him a minute to get downstairs."

The cousins used the back stairs. They tiptoed through the kitchen, down the hall, and edged toward the lobby. Judging from the sound of Frank Killegrew's voice, the OTIOSE contingent had regrouped in the game room.

". . . real brave of you, Rudy," Judith heard Killegrew say to the caretaker. "What are our chances of getting out of here?"

Mannheimer must have been standing further away. His response was muffled. "Melting . . . trouble . . . what . . . ?"

Killegrew's laugh was forced. "You might say we've had some nasty accidents. The blizzard, the heavy rains, the avalanche warnings." He laughed again. "Then you get into stress and tensions and all sorts of heavy seas that can rock the boat. Not to worry, Rudy, old man, we're managing."

"Frank!" Judith recognized Margo's anguished cry.

"He has to know." Gene's voice could barely be distinguished.

"I don't like this," Russell muttered. "He has a gun."

"What Rudy needs is a drink," Killegrew declared. "Come on, let's adjourn to the lobby. I wouldn't pass up a stiff shot of Scotch myself."

Judith heard voices muttering and feet shuffling. The sounds died away. "Let's cut back through the kitchen and listen from the dining room," Judith whispered.

Just as they entered the kitchen, the phone rang. Renie sprang for it, catching the receiver before the final "brrng" stopped.

"Joe!" Renie cried. "Thank God! Here, I'll let you talk to Judith!"

Judith suddenly felt close to tears. "Where are you? Arlene said . . . Never mind, is everything all right?"

"Yeah, it is now," Joe replied, though he sounded harried. "Woody and I finally got somebody with a four-wheel drive to get us out of that place by the lake. What's going on with you? Are you stranded up there?"

"Yes," Judith answered. "It's raining, though. Maybe we can get out tomorrow." She took a deep breath. "Meanwhile, there's something you should know."

"If it's about that body you found, forget it," Joe said, sounding increasingly irritable. "The deputy chief talked to some bozo or some bimbo up there Friday, and that accidental death you mentioned isn't our problem. Have them call the park service. They have jurisdiction."

"Oh. That's good. I'll tell them right away." Judith took another deep breath. "While we're on the subject, I should come clean about . . ."

"Clean? Sorry, somebody's trying to talk to me at this end. Hold on." Joe must have put his hand over the receiver; Judith could hear only muffled voices. "Yeah, I need clean underwear," he said, coming back on the line. "Your goofy cleaning woman didn't come Friday because she was afraid it would snow. I couldn't find any dark socks yesterday. Where does she put the clean stuff after it comes out of the dryer?"

Judith always marveled at her husband's inability to find any of his belongings, even when they were right under his nose. Or, as had occasionally happened, in his hands. "Phyliss," she said, referring to her daily help, "keeps three separate baskets in the basement. The blue one is for the B&B laundry, the green is for our personal linens and towels, and she puts our clothes in the yellow one. They should all be lined up by the washer and dryer, which, in case you've forgotten, is in the basement laundry room.''

"Hey!" Joe barked. "What's with the sarcasm? I not only get called in on a weekend, I get stuck with a stiff in a house that hardly has any food in it. Plus, I have to share a bed with the M.E. who snores like a steam engine and smells like . . . well, like an M.E. Woody was smart—he grabbed one of the twin beds in the master bedroom.''

"Why didn't you take the other one?" Judith asked.

"Because the stiff was lying on it." Joe sounded as if he were gnashing his teeth.

"Oh." Judith's urge to tell Joe about the other murders faded. "I'm sorry about that. Really. Will you be able to get home?"

"I don't know." Joe now sounded glum. "Even with four-wheel drive, it's almost impossible to get up Heraldsgate Hill in snow this deep.''

"Maybe we'll both be home by tomorrow," Judith said with what she hoped was optimism.

"Maybe." Joe obviously wasn't convinced. "I've got to go. There's a pile of paperwork on my desk.''

"Okay. Be careful. Please.''

"Right. You, too.''

"Bye.''

"Bye.'' Joe rang off.

"He's in a bad mood," Judith said, replacing the receiver and looking for the telephone directory, which he finally found under a turkey roaster.

"He'd be in a worse one if you'd told him about the other bodies," Renie pointed out. "Who'd he say to call?''

"The park service.'' Judith ran her finger down the listings under federal government. "Here's the number.''

Renie's round face was troubled. "Why you?''

"What do you mean?''

"It's their problem." Renie jerked a thumb over her shoulder. "Tell them to call. Why get involved?''

"We *are* involved," Judith countered. "We'll be questioned, we'll have to give statements."

"So? Deal with that when the time comes. But for now, have one of the survivors out there call. Better yet, tell Mannheimer. He's the caretaker, it's his job."

Judith put the receiver back in its cradle. "Okay, I will. Let's see how the rest of them are faring."

They weren't faring particularly well. Having reopened the liquor bottles, the distraught OTIOSE executives had now degenerated into a maudlin state. Frank Killegrew was feeling very sentimental and was exchanging old war stories with Rudy Mannheimer, who appeared to have gotten drunk rather quickly.

"... out on patrol ... cold as a well-digger's ... then these gooks came ..." Killegrew's voice was lost in a maundering mumble.

"*Gooks?*" Margo sounded indignant, though she lacked her usual fire. "What kind of language is that?"

"Slopes," Mannheimer said, his voice thick with whiskey. "North Korean S.O.B.s. Hell, honey, you're too young. You don't know nothin'."

Judith and Renie were hiding next to the French doors that led to the lobby. They could hear, but not see the speakers.

"Screw Korea," Max declared. "That was a picnic compared to 'Nam. Jungle, heat, bugs, civilians loaded with grenades ..."

"Bull," Mannheimer retorted. "You ain't fought a war till you freeze your nummies off at Pyongyang."

"War's horrible," Ava said, her voice shaking with conviction. "Killing is horrible. Death is horrible. Life is ... horrible."

The cousins heard footsteps hurrying from the lobby. "Ava," Judith breathed. "Let's head her off."

Judith and Renie ran back through the dining room, the kitchen and the laundry room. Down the hall, they could see Ava getting into the elevator. The cousins raced up the backstairs, arriving just as Ava stepped out onto the second floor.

"Don't!" Judith yelled. "Wait!"

Ava ran, too, heading for her room which was two doors down from the elevator. She nipped inside, but couldn't close the door before Judith put a shoulder against the solid pine.

"Stop it, Ava!" Judith commanded. "Let us in! Please! Don't do anything else foolish!"

Ava and Judith were about the same size and build. As each woman put her weight on opposite sides of the door, it appeared that the younger and more physically fit Ava had the advantage. But Judith had Renie. The cousins finally managed to triumph.

Ava turned a ravaged face on her pursuers. "Why do you want to stop me? It's none of your business!"

"Yes, it is." Judith spoke through taut lips. "Unlike the rest of you, we're not indifferent to the sufferings of other people. Besides, OTIOSE got us mixed up in all this. We couldn't get out of here free and clear if we wanted to."

Ava, who had been backing away from the cousins, shook her head. "I don't care. It still has nothing to do with you. Not really. Leave me alone."

"No." For emphasis, Judith sat down on one of the twin beds while Renie closed the door. "Why waste your life? It's not worth it. OTIOSE isn't worth it, and," Judith went on, raising her voice, "neither is Frank Killegrew."

Ava's dark eyes widened. "It's not about Frank!" she shouted.

"Oh, yes it is," Judith said. "You know it is. It's always been about Frank. Given what I've come to understand about the corporate world, it couldn't be about anybody or anything else."

"You know?" The words were whispered as Ava collapsed into one of the armchairs.

Judith nodded. "I didn't really figure it out until today, when I saw how Frank reacted to Nadia's death. He was truly devastated. I realized then that Nadia had in fact killed herself. She'd taken the sleeping pills along with the gin and committed suicide.''

''No!'' Ava covered her face with her hands.

''Yes.'' Judith nodded solemnly. ''And you were about to do the same thing. How, Ava? With a broken glass to slash your wrists?''

Slowly, Ava's hands fell away. ''How did you guess?''

''There aren't any more lethal medications around—that I know of—and I didn't think you could wrest Margo's gun away from her. You might have had better luck with Mannheimer's rifle, though it would have caused a scene.'' Judith paused, waiting for Ava to regain some measure of calm. ''Do me a favor, will you? May I see your neck?''

Ava's hands flew to the big collar of her blue sweater. ''Oh! How . . . ? You couldn't have . . .'' She saw the determination on Judith's face and slowly pulled the collar down to reveal dark bruises.

Judith nodded. ''When you loaned me your clothes, you insisted that I take the red outfit, which had a much lower-cut neckline than either the blue one you're wearing now or the green one you wore earlier. It was a small but curious point. Then I remembered that Friday, in the conference room, Renie and I overheard something. We thought it was lovemaking, but that was far from the truth. You were being strangled by the same person who killed the others. At that point, you suspected that Barry Newcombe was dead even though we hadn't yet found the body. You had a good idea about who had killed him. Tell me, Ava, *how did you get Frank Killegrew to stop*?''

For a long, tense moment Ava didn't answer. At last she got up and went to the honor bar where she took out a can of fruit juice. ''I told him OTIOSE couldn't survive without me. That meant he couldn't survive, either.'' Ava turned a dreary face to the cousins, then sat down again. ''I had my informants, I not only knew the changes OTIOSE would

have to make in the future, but what WaCom and many of
the other companies planned to do to beat the competition.
Most of all, I could accomplish these goals for OTIOSE.
I'd also learned about the pending WaCom merger, and
while I didn't tell him outright then, I'd hinted that it might
come up soon. Frank realized I was indispensable.'' Ava
made a rueful face.

"None of the old-line telephone types have my background in computers,'' she continued. ''Russell deals with
ideas for applications and products, what customers need
and want, rather than the actual means of making these
things possible through technology. Frank's never understood the whole computer concept—he's still living in the
sixties. Anyway, he tried to pass off his attack as a fit of
temper. Maybe he heard you outside the conference room—
I had no idea anyone was there, I was too horrified. But
something suddenly stopped him. That was when he promised me Ward's job.''

Renie, who had settled into the other armchair, nodded.
"A bribe. But what about Ward?''

Ava leaned her head back in the chair. ''The implication
was that Ward would succeed to the corner office. But I
knew better. Frank wasn't going anywhere, he had no in-
tention of retiring. His whole scheme was to get the by-
laws changed and stay on for at least another five years.
Frank, you see, couldn't let go of OTIOSE. It was his company, he'd founded it, he'd staked everything he had on its
survival.''

"And something he didn't have,'' Judith said wryly.
"Money. He'd used his wife's fortune to bankroll OTIOSE,
hadn't he? Is that why Patrice was going to divorce him?''

Ava sighed. ''I'm not sure about that. Andrea and Patrice
were rather close. They'd gotten together several times
lately, apparently so Patrice could vent her rage.''

Judith thought back to Andrea's daily planner noting the
luncheon and dinner dates with the boss's wife. Though

Patrice Killegrew was a shadowy figure, Judith could imagine the woman's fury.

Ava continued. "Andrea told me that Patrice only recently discovered how little money she had left. Mrs. Killegrew was the kind of corporate wife who did nothing for herself. A housekeeper, cook, maid, chauffeur—the whole bit, including, of course, financial advisors to handle her fortune. The Killegrews could afford all the help they wanted, because in the beginning, they relied on her wealth, and later, when Frank became a CEO, his base salary was around three hundred thousand a year. But Patrice's mistake was letting Frank hire the advisors in the first place. In effect, he handled her money, and ended up robbing her blind. When she found out—I think it was at the end of the year when she actually got off her elegant behind to talk to their accountant—she went crazy. Patrice couldn't bear to be poor. It was one thing to have Frank be unfaithful to their marriage, it was something else for him to steal from her. I guess she threw him out."

"I guess she did," Judith said. "We found some notes Nadia had written to herself. There were references to someone moving. It wasn't her—she'd lived forever in an apartment above downtown, and still did, according to the address on the sleeping pill prescription. Thus, I assumed that Frank was the one who was moving, and the logical conclusion was that his wife had given him the thumb. He also had an appointment with a law firm that specializes in divorce. Gene knew about that, didn't he?"

Ava, who had taken a sip of her juice, looked startled. "Yes, I told him. How did you guess?"

Judith gave a modest shrug. "The slip of paper I mentioned that belonged to Nadia had been left in the women's restroom on purpose. I thought at first it was used to jam your stall. You recall that I asked how long you were in the bathroom?" Seeing Ava nod, Judith went on. "Then it occurred to me that someone had purposely put the note on the floor of the restroom. It needn't have been a woman. My guess was Gene, because he's an attorney and would realize the significance of Frank's appointment with Hukle, Hukle, and Huff. Gene wanted everyone to know that Frank's marriage was on the rocks, but because he's such a cautious man, he felt compelled to act in a covert manner."

Ava looked impressed. "My God, I didn't realize we'd hired a sleuth as a caterer!"

Judith eschewed the compliment—if indeed that was what had been intended. "Identifying the killer shouldn't have been too hard. In fact, I'm kicking myself for being so slow. Everything pointed to Frank all along. But so many bits and pieces only fell into place in the past few hours. Like Rudy Mannheimer."

"Rudy?" Renie and Ava both echoed the name, like a shrill Greek chorus.

"That's right," Judith replied. "Frank's personnel records showed he was a Ranger in Korea. That was the old name for Special Forces, which utilizes all sorts of dirty tricks, including a garrote. Sad to say, the Rangers were trained to be ruthless killers. In fact, if I recall correctly, they themselves suffered tremendous casualties in Korea. I suppose some of them never quite got over the killer instinct—and the fear of being killed."

"Paranoia?" Renie put in. "Or self-defense? Bill would say that in cases like Frank's, where killing is not only legal, but condoned by . . ."

"A bit of both," Judith interrupted hastily before Renie could go off on one of her tangents. "But we digress. Frank used to be in partnership with the previous owners of Mountain Goat Lodge. He and Rudy go back to Korea. Rudy seems like an odd duck, and I can't help but wonder if Frank didn't get him the job up here. If so, Rudy's in his debt. I also wonder if Rudy knew about Barry Newcombe but kept his mouth shut. It wouldn't surprise me if Rudy Mannheimer helped hide Barry's body. Still, I don't think it will be easy to get Rudy to open up."

"Barry," Ava murmured. "It's strange how we keep forgetting him."

"Not really," Judith said with a touch of irony. "Barry wasn't in upper management. That made him a nonperson. But last year when he was hired as caterer, this whole series of tragic events was set in motion. Barry must have swiped Andrea's private personnel files. I've no idea what he intended to do with them—blackmail, perhaps? Or just a bit of clout to get some financial support to start his own catering business?"

"I don't know." Ava's response seemed candid. "I wasn't lying when I said I didn't know Barry very well."

"Whatever the reason," Judith continued, "it was a terrible mistake on his part. He must have told Frank, who looked at the files and saw certain things that could never be made public. Barry might not have recognized their significance, but Frank did, especially the part—which has turned up missing—about using Patrice's personal funds to help set up the company. Leon Mooney knew all about it, he had to as chief financial officer, and no doubt altered the books under duress. But Barry had signed his own death warrant. Everyone knew he was a notorious gossip and wouldn't hesitate to barter his juicy tidbits. Unlike Andrea and Leon and the rest of you, Barry couldn't be manipulated by threats of losing a prestigious position. So Frank killed Barry and hid his body by the creek. He also hid the files there."

Renie's head swiveled. "What? You never told me that!"

Judith gave her cousin an apologetic look. "Sorry. It didn't dawn on me until you mentioned that I should piddle in the library wastebasket. Then I remembered you found an empty plastic garbage bag in Andrea's wastebasket. Why would she have such a thing? It was incongruous. Andrea wasn't the type to carry her belongings in a garbage bag. But more to the point—why had we uncovered Barry's body so easily? The answer had to be because someone had already been rooting around in the snow by the ice cave. Frank had disturbed the hiding place earlier in the day when he went to retrieve the files.'' Judith gazed at Ava. "But you already knew that. That's why Frank tried to strangle you."

Ava nodded. "I saw him go out to the creek. I couldn't figure out what he was doing, so I followed him partway. He was digging around in the snow, and then he had something in his hands—the garbage bag—and I kept watching while he tried to cover up the place where he'd been searching. Suddenly I had this sinking feeling. Since we'd only arrived an hour earlier, I knew whatever Frank had found must have been there much longer. Like from last year. I thought about Barry, and after our afternoon meeting, I confronted Frank. That's when he tried to kill me."

Renie looked stunned. "That was terribly risky, Ava. Why didn't you wait until you were back in town?"

Ava's fingers twisted around the juice can. "I don't know. I felt compelled to act. Maybe I thought Frank would confess and turn himself in and that would be that. In retrospect, it was a very stupid thing to do."

"You're right." Renie grew thoughtful. "I suppose Frank originally intended to leave the files there with the body, but realized he could use them against the others. That's why there were no entries for an entire year."

"That's right," Judith agreed. "Those files took on a life of their own. I suspect Frank planted them in Andrea's room after he killed her. Then Nadia stole them—or Frank did later. Either way, they were meant to be found. Ward and Leon's vacancies on the board would have to be filled, probably by Gene—and you." Judith inclined her head at Ava.

Ava gingerly touched the bruises on her neck. "So any dirt about us could be used to coerce us into changing the by-laws. And Leon was killed because he knew how Frank had bankrolled the company. But Ward . . . He was so loyal to Frank. Surely he'd have gone along with Frank's wishes *not* to retire.''

Judith offered Ava a sad little smile. ''Maybe so. But Frank had promised you Ward's job. Ward had to go.''

In distress, Ava ran her fingers through her long black hair. ''That's what I was afraid of. Everything suddenly crashed in on me this afternoon. I couldn't work for a murderer. And I felt guilty, too. You're right—Ward's blood is on my hands.''

''You put your career ahead of justice,'' Renie said quietly. ''I'm afraid it's true—lives might have been saved if you'd acted sooner.''

Ava dropped her hands into her lap. ''It's like tunnel vision up there on the executive floor. They talk about career pathing. It's literal. You travel down that path and you never look left or right. All you see is that title or that salary or those perks at the end of the tunnel. Nothing else matters. It's horrible when you stop to think about it.''

A silence followed, as Ava wrestled with her special demons. Renie finally spoke up, breaking the tension. ''What about Andrea? Why kill her?''

''Because,'' Judith said, ''she not only knew he'd fleeced Mrs. Killegrew, but that Leon had been forced to juggle the books. There was a missing page in her private files that followed a discussion of an independent audit. I suspect that page—which Frank destroyed—contained incriminating information about Frank's financial dealings. He burned that page—probably along with Leon's own records—in Leon's room. He couldn't do it right after he killed Leon in the kitchen because Andrea was waiting in Leon's room. When we noticed the fire in the grate this afternoon, at first we thought the entire set of folders had been destroyed. Then we realized there weren't enough ashes. So what else had to go? The phrase *Mooney's money* came to mind. Someone had mentioned it, and it stuck. Money is always a serious motive when it comes to murder. It dawned on me that the real financial records had been burned, as opposed to the fraudulent ones that Leon had been forced to make public.''

"Good grief." Ava had paled and was holding her head. "How did Frank think he could get away with it?"

Judith uttered a bitter little laugh. "Frank thought he could get away with anything. His corner office mentality made him believe he was different from other people, that he was above the law, that he could do anything he wanted because he was a CEO. Oh, I realize not all powerful people go on a homicide spree. But they kill in other ways—they demean their subordinates, they stifle them, they control them—and often, they fire them. You can destroy other human beings without violence. In the isolated corner office, someone like Frank becomes so disassociated that he lives in a different world, a false world where the only values are the ones he makes up."

Renie nodded slowly in agreement. "Not only that, but he'd invested his entire life in OTIOSE. Oh, he may have had a boat and played golf, but those were just extensions of his executive persona. Unlike other people—like my husband and my cousin's husband—he had nothing outside of his exalted position. He was a shell of a man, hollow inside, and incapable of living anywhere but in the corporate world. When reality touched him in the form of retirement, he went over the edge. As my psychologist husband would say, Frank Killegrew . . . went nuts."

"My God!" Ava clapped a hand to her cheek. "Will I be like that? Am I already there?"

"Let's hope not," said Renie. "You're still young. This weekend, you've seen how corporate thinking can cause total devastation. Follow Margo's example—get out before it's too late."

Ava didn't respond. She seemed to sink into deep thought, her eyes on the brightly striped rug beneath her feet.

"My cousin's right," Judith chimed in. "It was too late for Nadia, which is why she killed herself. She had nothing but Frank—and OTIOSE. That was her family, her gang, where she belonged. She was utterly devoted to him, as much as any wife is to a husband. In fact, she acted just like an old-fashioned wife, waiting on him, fetching and carrying, soothing, selfless. If his horrible schemes were uncovered—as Nadia knew they would be—he'd face disgrace and ruin. He'd go to prison, and she'd lose him. Nadia couldn't bear that. Nor could she face what might happen to OTIOSE, which was her real home. Don't make the same mistake as Nadia did, Ava. Find a life—a *real* life—while you still have the chance."

Ava was still staring at the carpet. "I have no family here. Everyone is in Samoa. But I have some friends outside the company. Maybe I could start to . . ." Her voice trailed off.

"We need your help," Judith said abruptly. "We have to trap Frank."

Ava's head jerked up. "What are you saying? There's no evidence? I thought you had . . ."

Judith slowly shook her head. "We have next to nothing. These were virtually bloodless crimes. There will be fingerprints, yes, but not just Frank's. We've all been in and out of the guest rooms, either in groups or as individuals. For all we know, Frank wore gloves. There may have been a struggle with Ward—I suspect there was. We found a Bell System service pin on the floor in his room, which may have come loose when he tried to fight Frank off. But that doesn't prove anything. None of it does. All of his victims trusted him—he was the boss. I imagine Andrea drank whatever Frank gave her without a qualm. No doubt he told her it would be good for her. Whatever Frank said was law. It's the way you corporate people think."

"Good Lord." Ava took another sip of juice, then rose from the chair. "What do you want me to do?"

"First," Judith said, also standing up, "we're going to call the park service. Their law enforcement personnel have jurisdiction at Mountain Goat. Then we're going to restage that little scene with you and Frank in the conference room. Are you game?''

Ava grasped her throat. ''I . . . I don't know. It was terrifying at the time. Just now, before you stopped me, I was about to . . . But I really . . .'' She lowered her face into her hands and began to sob.

Judith bit her lip. Ava, like the rest of the OTIOSE executives, had been stripped of all surface emotions. The weekend had pared them down to the bone. Judith saw the bruises on Ava's throat, and understood how deeply the young woman had been wounded.

''Never mind,'' Judith said. ''I'll do it.''

''Whoa!'' Renie grabbed her cousin by the arm. ''Don't you dare! It's not your fight!''

''Yes, it is,'' Judith said grimly. ''I threw down the gauntlet. Let's go.''

Renie was still arguing when the three women reached the kitchen. Judith, however, had made up her mind. ''I know, I know. It's a dirty job, but someone's . . .''

''Why you?'' Renie demanded. ''What about me? I've got the corporate connection. Let me stick my neck out for once. Literally.''

''No. Absolutely not.'' Judith picked up the phone and dialed the park service number. ''Let's see how fast they can get here.''

A woman, instead of a recording, answered the park service phone this time. She sounded flabbergasted when Judith informed her what had happened at Mountain Goat Lodge. It was clear that she initially thought Judith was playing a practical joke.

''Look,'' Judith said, at her most earnest, ''if you send some of your police personnel, they'll be able to see the bodies for themselves. Or is it impossible to get someone into Mountain Goat until the snow melts some more?''

''Of course it's not impossible,'' the woman huffed. ''We can have someone there within the hour.''

Judith frowned into the receiver. "You can? But the first floor here is still mostly snowed in."

"Drifts," the woman said, not sounding quite as suspicious. "The lodge is out in the open. There's no real windbreak. It's a problem, all right, but the caretaker and the staff should have seen to it."

It was pointless to try to explain that the lodge was off-limits to anyone but the conferees. "So the roads are passable?" Judith inquired.

"For the most part," the woman responded. "The highway crews have been working through the weekend. How else," she added on a note of exasperation, "do you think the phone company got through?"

"The phone company?" Judith echoed.

"Yes. I understand they restored telephone service late yesterday. Didn't you see or hear them?"

Judith had. Noise. Lights. Laughter. Real phone company people doing real work. The outsiders had been insiders. Even as the highly paid OTIOSE executives had created mayhem at Mountain Goat Lodge, the humble craft technicians had come through. Maybe, Judith thought, the spirit of service was still alive, even if some of the officers weren't.

Judith finally convinced the woman to send at least two park service police officers and a couple of rangers to the lodge. While still dubious, the woman had finally allowed that it wouldn't hurt to check on the situation, but it might be up to an hour before the personnel arrived at the scene of the alleged crimes.

"We'll have to stall a bit," Judith said to Renie and Ava, then glanced at the digital clock. It was going on five. "Maybe we should get dinner."

"I can't cook," Ava declared. "Shall I set the table?"

Before Judith could answer, Margo charged into the kitchen. "Ava! Where have you been? We've been worried sick!"

"I've been with them," Ava replied, gesturing at Judith and Renie. "How's . . . everything?"

Margo blinked at the cousins but didn't question their liberation. "Awful," she replied, making a face. "Frank and that horrid Mannheimer are drunk as skunks. If you ask me, that caretaker is an alcoholic. Gene and Max have hardly said a word in the last half-hour, and Russell just stares off into space."

Judith frowned. The last thing she wanted was to have Frank pass out. "We'll make coffee," she said quickly. "Ava, Margo, you start pouring it down all of those men as soon as it's ready. And keep them away from the liquor."

By five-thirty, Margo reported that Frank and Rudy were still drunk, but in upright positions. Refilling the men's coffee mugs, she hurried back to the lobby.

Grimly, Judith turned to Renie. "You're going to have to let the park personnel in through the second floor. They can use Mannheimer's ladder. I'll be with Frank in his room. Remember, it's opposite ours—the other corner room."

Renie nodded. "I don't like this. What if they don't come?"

Judith grimaced. "Then you'll have to rescue me."

"Oh, swell!" Renie twirled around the kitchen, hands clasped to her head. "How do I do that?"

"With Margo's gun," Judith said, pointing to the suede bag that Margo had left on the counter before carrying out the coffee refills. "Take it now."

"Oh, good grief!" Renie reeled some more.

"Do it quick, before she comes back."

With a big sigh, Renie opened the suede bag and removed the handgun. "I haven't fired a gun since my dad took me target shooting forty-odd years ago. It was up at the family cabin, and I blew a hole through Uncle Corky's picnic ham."

"Better than blowing a hole through Uncle Corky." Judith gazed at the gun. "Is it really loaded?"

Renie checked the chambers. "Yes, ma'am. And so's Frank. Now what?"

Judith squared her shoulders. "Now we nail him. This may be our finest hour."

She didn't say that it could also be their last.

NINETEEN

FRANK KILLEGREW WAS sulking. "Sh'almost shix," he mumbled. "Who drinksh coffee at shix? Time for martoonis and shotch. Cocktail time, cockroach hour, cock-a-doodle-doo!"

"Chicken if you don't," Judith said with forced cheer. "Frank, I'd like to talk to you for a minute. Do you mind? Dinner's almost ready."

"I'm the cock of the walk," Killegrew declared, trying to get up off the sofa. "I can do anything I damned well . . ." He fell back, but was given a hand by Max.

"There you go, Frank," Max said. "I think you've got a customer with a complaint. Turn on the service-is-us charm, okay? *You big dumb moron*," Max added under his breath.

"Customer? Complaint?" Glassy-eyed, Killegrew gazed at Judith. "So what's the problem, little lady? Not enough lines? Interference on toll calls? Equipment not up to Western Electric standards? Well, let me tell you, ever since we started letting those little yellow people over there in Chinkville build phones, we've had . . ."

"Frank!" Margo screamed right into the CEO's ear. "Stop it! You're the most bigoted man I ever met!"

"Hey!" Killegrew whirled on Margo. "I hired you, didn't I? And Gene and Ava and . . . and a bunch of other ethnic types. Get off my back before I fire your scrawny Asian ass!''

''I already quit!'' Margo yelled back. ''You're a disgrace, Frank! You embarrass everyone, especially yourself!''

''Awww . . .'' Killegrew waved a hand in disgust. ''Got to see what this little lady wants. Need to set things straight. Service, that's what counts. Where's m' slide rule?''

Judith finally got Killegrew into the elevator. She was filled with doubts about her proposed plan. In the CEO's current inebriated state, she wondered if he'd even remember his terrible crimes, let alone be incited to act in a manner that would incriminate him.

''I thought,'' Judith said in an uncertain voice as they moved slowly down the second-floor corridor, ''we might speak privately in your room. I'd prefer not to have anyone overhear what I have to say.''

''Privacy,'' Killegrew murmured, his speech no longer slurred. ''Confidential. No letters to the editor, no complaints to the state utilities commission, no calls to the FCC. That's the way it ought to be, just one-on-one, as if you were a real person.''

''Yes,'' Judith agreed, though Killegrew's ramblings weren't uppermost in her mind. ''Here we go—your room, right?''

''My room. My corner room. My beds. My . . . stuff.'' He staggered inside, allowing Judith to close the door behind them.

''Well.'' Judith put her hands together in a prayerful attitude. ''Do you remember when my cousin and I told you about our insurance?''

''Insurance?'' Killegrew's expression was puzzled. ''Wait a minute—are you selling insurance?''

Judith shook her head. This wasn't going to be easy, she thought. Maybe she had miscalculated. ''I'm speaking of the insurance we have regarding the killer. We know who has killed all these people, Mr. Killegrew.'' She paused, taking a deep breath. "We know it was *you*."

Frank Killegrew's gray eyes narrowed. And then he laughed. It was a hearty sound, full-bodied and rich. "That's good! I killed Andrea and Leon and Ward! That's *damned* good! Ha-ha!"

"You left out Barry." Judith's tone was solemn.

"Barry?" Briefly, Killegrew again looked puzzled. "Oh, that clerk. He was queer. I don't get it. Why do people want to be queer?"

Judith wasn't about to explain homosexuality to Frank Killegrew. Indeed, she was beginning to think she couldn't explain anything to him. "You didn't kill Nadia," she said, hoping to strike close to the heart. "She killed herself because she couldn't bear to see what would happen to you when you were found out. She really loved you, Frank. And, in your own weird way, I think you loved her."

"Nadia." Killegrew spoke the name with a certain reverence. "What'll I do without her?"

"Life, with no possibility of parole," Judith retorted. "You're crazy, Frank, drunk on power and prestige."

Killegrew tipped his head to one side. "Well . . . I am a little drunk. But you're the crazy one." He held the slide rule in one hand and tapped it against his leg as his gray eyes hardened. "Your insurance isn't worth ten cents. Where's your proof?"

With a flash of insight, Judith glanced at the slide rule. "In your hand. You used that stupid slide rule to garrote Barry and Ward by twisting the leather thong and the belt around their necks. Oh, I'll admit it would be impossible to prove in court. But circumstantial evidence *is* admissible, Frank. You'll be charged and brought to trial. Any hope you've had of staying on as CEO is doomed. The other members of the board will vote you out even before you're due to retire. It's over, Frank. You're cooked."

"Uh-uh." Killegrew swung his head from side to side, and suddenly he looked quite sober. It dawned on Judith that maybe the wily CEO hadn't been drunk in the first place. "*You're* cooked," Killegrew roared, raising the slide rule and starting to bring it down on Judith's head.

Judith ducked, feeling the slide rule cut into the air above her. Killegrew was a big, powerful man in more ways than one. Judith knew she couldn't elude him for very long. *Where were the park rangers?*

"Coz!" she yelled as Killegrew swung again and she felt her hair being ruffled.

The door burst open. Two national park service rangers stood on the threshold, their weapons drawn. Killegrew turned around, then dropped the slide rule. "Thank God!" he shouted. "This woman was trying to kill me!"

"Let's all calm down," said the older and taller of the rangers. "What's going on here?"

Killegrew moved swiftly to the two men, putting a hand on each of their shoulders. "Frank Killegrew, president and CEO of OTIOSE. By God, I'm glad to see you! This woman is a crazed customer who thinks that Martians have invaded her telephone system. It happens all the time. Take her away, boys!"

The taller officer, whose name tag read "R. Westervelt," stared at Judith. "Who are you?" Westervelt asked.

"Judith Flynn, the caterer. But I . . ."

"The caterer!" Killegrew roared with laughter. "You see—these people will use any excuse to come after the phone company! My God, we've been a target of every crank and crackpot for years! If your life is all screwed up and you're playing with a half a deck, go after the phone company! It's an easy target, we're under government scrutiny! Would you like to see our nut file? It's full of people like her!"

Westervelt turned to his partner, a square-built young man with crinkly red hair. "Nunnally, we've got a situation."

Nunnally nodded. "Didn't somebody mention bodies?"

Returning his gun to its holster, Westervelt looked at Judith. "On the phone, someone referred to possible homicides. Where are the victims?"

"All over the . . ." Judith began, but was interrupted by Killegrew.

"Victims? Now, now," he bellowed, shaking a finger at Judith who was trying to peer into the hall in hopes of catching sight of Renie, "that's an exaggeration, isn't it? We've had a couple of nasty accidents. Look, fellows," he continued, putting an arm around each of the officers, "you don't have to get mixed up in this. I've already got a call in to the chief of police in town. He's flying back from Hawaii, and he'll get everything straightened out. We may be on your turf, but it isn't really your responsibility. Why make trouble for yourselves? Eh?" He gave each of the officers a nudge.

"Well . . ." Westervelt looked again at Nunnally. "This *is* our jurisdiction."

"So?" Killegrew seemed amused. "You're in the business of stolen skis and drunken picnickers and people who pick wildflowers and attacks by bad-tempered bears. This is phone company business, big city stuff, and we'll sort it out with the chief." Killegrew winked. "He's a pal—know what I mean?"

Westervelt's long face was a mask of uncertainty. "That's . . . fine, but we still need to check out any complaints . . ."

"Complaints!" Killegrew threw his head back and roared with laughter. "That's it! Complaints! You can't get half as many as I do! See here, fellows, we'll turn this poor soul over to our p.r. vice president and get everything squared away. Ms. Chang knows how to handle these people. Now how about coming down to the lobby and having an adult beverage or two?"

Westervelt cleared his throat. "Well . . . sorry, we can't do that, sir. We're on duty. But maybe we should talk to the others."

Killegrew slapped Westervelt on the back. "Good idea! They'll set you straight." Halfway to the door he stopped and turned back to Judith. "What about her? Shouldn't you arrest her now before she does something really dangerous?"

The officers exchanged dubious glances. "Well . . ." Westervelt scratched an ear. "We really should search the lodge in case the homicide story is true. Meanwhile, are you pressing charges against this woman, sir?"

"You bet!" Killegrew snapped his fingers. "Assault, attempted murder, whatever it takes! My God, I'm lucky to be alive!"

Judith bridled. "Wait a minute! This is absurd! *He's* the one who tried to attack *me!* He's the one who murdered four people and caused the death of another one! He's a maniac, a psychotic, a man without a conscience!" Frantically, Judith tried to look out into the hall. *Where the hell was Renie?*

Killegrew was chuckling indulgently. "You see? She's raving. They always do. Come on fellows, let's put this plane in the hangar. Haul her away, and we'll keep in touch."

Killegrew started to leave the room, but Westervelt detained him. "Sir," Westervelt said in a deferential tone, "hold on just a minute. We have two other rangers downstairs. Let's wait here for them. They can take the prisoner to our vehicle."

The CEO rocked impatiently on his heels, the slide rule protruding from his back pocket. "What?" Killegrew frowned. "Oh, yes, why not? If there's been any trouble around here, she caused it."

"Shall I cuff her?" Nunnally asked, reaching for his belt where a pair of handcuffs dangled.

"Well . . . Okay, that sounds right." Westervelt gave an ambiguous nod.

"Hey!" Judith put both hands behind her back and retreated to the window. "This is a terrible mistake! How can you believe him and not me?"

The officers again looked at each other, but it was Killegrew who spoke. "Because you're nobody. And I'm OTIOSE!"

"Well . . . He's right, you know," Westervelt said to Judith. "Mr. Killegrew is a well-known businessman. I've even seen him on TV."

"You're darn tootin'," Killegrew said. "Come on, come on, let's get going."

"But . . ." Judith felt miserable, frustrated, depleted. Was it really impossible to combat Frank Killegrew's corporate reputation and civic image? Was he actually above the law? Was Judith really a *nobody?*

Though Nunnally looked vaguely apologetic, he grasped Judith by the forearms and forced her to turn around. She flinched, hearing the click of the handcuffs. But before the officer could lock them in place, she heard an unexpected, yet familiar voice call to her.

"Mom!"

"Mike!" Surprise and shock made Judith limp. She gaped at her son, then turned to the others. "You see?" she said in a voice that shook with emotion. "I *am* somebody after all. *I'm his mother.*"

Renie, who had been hiding Margo's gun under a dishtowel to prevent the rightful owner from attacking her, was right behind Mike. "He'd been told to stay in the lobby with the others because he's not a law enforcement ranger," Renie explained, tossing the towel aside. "When none of you came downstairs, I had a heck of a time convincing his partner that we ought to see what was happening."

While mother and son embraced, Frank Killegrew blustered. Judith's newly found cachet of giving birth to a park ranger lent her credibility. Nunnally went up to the third floor to see if there really were bodies stashed in the dormer rooms. Westervelt found Nadia lying on Leon's bed, then called for backup and several ambulances. Killegrew continued to bluster.

Mike, who had been filled in on the situation by his aunt, spoke sharply to the CEO. "The less you say, mister, the better. I may not be a police officer, but at least I know that much. Stick it, will you? You're getting on my nerves."

Killegrew looked astonished. "You! You're just a punk kid! Do you know who you're talking to?"

Mike turned to Renie. "Who'd you say this guy was?"

Judith regarded Killegrew with unconcealed loathing. "He's a captain whose ship has been torpedoed. He may not admit it, but he's just about to hit rock bottom."

Renie started to say something, but Killegrew hurled himself between her and Mike. Wrenching the gun out of Renie's hand, he flew into the bathroom. Mike started after him, but it was too late. A sharp report and a flash of light stunned them all. Killegrew's body fell to the floor with a sickening thud.

"Jesus, Mary, and Joseph!" Renie whispered, crossing herself.

"Don't look," Mike ordered, and kicked the bathroom door shut.

Judith had slumped onto one of the twin beds. "I'm . . . sick," she said in a weak voice.

Westervelt and Nunnally came rushing in from the corridor where they'd been conferring about the carnage the younger officer had found upstairs. Mike assumed responsibility, succinctly explaining what had just occurred.

"Maybe he *was* guilty," Westervelt said in amazement. "My God!"

Nunnally offered Judith his apologies. "I'm kind of new on the job, ma'am, and when you run into some big, important guy like Mr. Killegrew, you tend to . . . ah . . . um . . ."

Judith was trying to pull herself together. "I know, I

know. You tend to think he's right because he's got a corner office. Don't worry, you'll learn better as you get older. Power and privilege have absolutely nothing to do with virtue and goodness.'' She turned a wan face to Mike. ''Can we get out of here?''

''Sure.'' Mike gave his mother a hand and raised her from the bed. ''You'll probably have to answer a bunch of questions, though.''

''Not here,'' Judith said with a definite shake of her head. ''Anywhere but here. Park headquarters, the ski lodge at the summit, a gopher hole—I don't care, just so it's not here. I don't ever want to see this place or what's left of these people again.''

Mike grinned, the slightly off-center, engaging expression that Judith loved so well. ''I don't blame you. It must have been quite a weekend. Hey, Aunt Renie, would you really have used that gun if you'd . . .''

The caterer, the graphic designer, and the park ranger quickly cleared the cousins' belongings out of the guest room across the hall. Ten minutes later, they were in Mike's official park service four-by-four, heading for the pass. Judith never looked back.

Joe was soaking his feet in a galvanized tub and watching the eleven o'clock news when Judith finally arrived home that Sunday night. He barely looked up when she came into the third-floor den.

''Hi,'' she said, trying to sound cheerful despite her state of exhaustion.

''Hi.'' Joe's gaze was riveted to the TV screen.

Judith leaned down and kissed his forehead. ''I got back sooner than I . . .''

''Shh!'' Gesturing at the TV, Joe cut her off.

''. . . Leading national park service law enforcement officials believe that Killegrew may have killed at least three of his employees in an attempt to retain his position as president and CEO of OTIOSE.'' The pert Asian anchor-woman was shown against a stock shot of Mountain Goat Lodge and an inset black-and-white photo of a smiling, benign Frank Killegrew. ''While rumors spread this week-end that WaCom plans to merge with OTIOSE, it is not known how the tragedy in the mountains will affect the independent telecommunications company's future. An un-identified spokesperson told KINE-TV this evening that customer service should not be affected, however.''

The screen changed to highway footage, showing snow-plows working along the interstate. Joe hit the mute button.

''Good Lord,'' he said, staring at Judith. ''Why didn't you tell me?''

Judith sank down next to him on the couch. ''I started to, then I lost my nerve. You sounded so grumpy.''

''I was.'' Joe put an arm around Judith. ''It was a rough weekend. But not as rough as yours.''

''They forgot Barry.'' Judith bit her lip and pointed at the silent TV.

''Barry?''

''The staff clerk, the body we found by the creek. Kil-legrew killed him, too.''

''Jeez.'' Joe shook his head. ''Want to make us a couple of drinks and tell me all about it?'' He indicated his soaking feet. ''I'd do it, but . . .''

Judith grinned. ''Yes, you would. You're not like some men, who have to be waited on.'' She got up to fetch their nightcaps.

They had finished their drinks by the time Judith got to the part about Mike's unexpected arrival. Naturally, Joe was astonished.

''Mike and Kristin got their transfer midweek,'' Judith explained. ''Because of all the snow and avalanche danger in the pass, they were shipped out of Idaho right away. They'll both be working in the national park, just an hour away. Isn't that wonderful?''

''It's great,'' Joe enthused. ''You see, Jude-Girl? You

worry about all kinds of things that don't happen.''

"I know." Judith snuggled against Joe. "I worried tonight I wouldn't get home, but the driving wasn't bad at all. Of course the rangers who brought us home knew what they were doing. The worst part was when we got to Heraldsgate Hill. We came up on the north side, to drop Renie off first. That's much easier than coming up the south side. It's so steep. The only problem is, Renie tried to drive the Chev.''

"I thought she didn't drive in snow," Joe said.

"She doesn't. The Chev's piled into a gas station pump at the summit. I'm afraid it's totaled. Bill will be awfully upset.''

Joe grimaced. "I don't blame him. I remember when you ran your Nissan into the wall at Falstaff's Grocery.''

"Maybe Bill won't retire, now that they have to get a new car," Judith mused. "Have you thought any more about it?''

Joe gave a single nod. "Sure. I'm not changing my mind. Bill won't either. Hell, we've both earned retirement. Why not?''

Judith started to say something, nebulous thoughts about financial uncertainty, changes in lifestyle, the future of the B&B—but she kept silent. Joe and Bill looked forward to retirement. Frank Killegrew had feared it, hated it, fought it—and left a path of death and destruction behind him. Retirement wasn't a dirty word, it was a new experience. For men like Joe and Bill, who had paid their dues and invested not in corporations but in family, the work place was no magic kingdom.

"You could cook," Judith said suddenly. "You've always been a good cook.''

Joe moved away just enough to look into Judith's face. "Cook what?''

"You know—some of the meals for the B&B guests. Breakfast, of course. You do wonderful eggs.''

Joe laughed. "Only to serve you in bed. Which sounds like a good idea."

"What? Eggs?"

Joe shook his head. "No. Bed." He clicked off the TV where the weatherman was showing lingering snow clouds.

"Bed." Judith repeated the word and smiled. "You're right, it's a good idea."

"Shall we?" Joe got up, stepping out of the tub.

Judith's dark eyes danced. "Shall we what?" she asked coyly.

"You know what," said Joe.

They retired.

CHECK INTO THE WORLD OF MARY DAHEIM

WHAT COULD BE could be more relaxing than a well-deserved respite at Hillside Manor, the charming bed-and-breakfast inn set atop Heraldsgate Hill? Well, for Judith McMonigle Flynn, the ever courteous proprietress, hand-to-tentacle combat with an irritated octopus might, on occasion, seem like a quieter pastime than running her beloved inn.

Daily worries for Judith include whether she'll be able to pay the utilities bill, whether she'll be able to keep the inn at full capacity during the busy season, whether her supply of hors d'oeuvres will satisfy her guests, whether her crotchety mother will keep out of the way, but most importantly, Judith always worries where that next body will turn up. . . .

It's not that she goes out in search of murders to solve—after all, she doesn't deliberately try to compete with her husband, Homicide Detective Joe Flynn, on his own turf—it's just that murder and mayhem seem to find her. And what's a gal supposed to do?

Grab her ravenous and reliable cousin Renie and hit the trail after the latest killer, before this energetic and entertaining hostess is put permanently out of business.

JUST DESSERTS

A WIDOW OF three years, Judith McMonigle decided to convert her family home into the charming—and therefore destined to be successful—Hillside Manor bed-and-breakfast, which will provide her with a steady income (she hopes) and a place to live for herself and her not-so-gracefully aging mother, Gertrude. In business for just over seven months, Judith suddenly wishes she hadn't gone out of her way to accommodate the Brodie clan . . . except for the fact that the corpse in her dining room, which may put her out of business, also brings the local police onto the scene. . . .

Judith, who barely noted the battling Brodies, had also become quite shaky and needed to lean against the little table for support. Her whole world, built with such hard work and cold cash, seemed to be crumbling. She could already see the quotes in the guidebooks:

"Hillside Manor—Avoid due to homicidal mania."

"Skip this particular establishment unless you're dying for a good time."

"Sleep like the dead here. You won't be the first."

"If you thought the crab dip was bad, wait until you taste the cream puffs!"

Renie sidled up to Judith, who knew her cousin could

read her mind exactly: "Look at it as positive publicity," counseled Renie. "People are morbid. You'll be famous, and thus, rich."

"Bunk," muttered Judith, trying to rally. "I'll be finished, and thus, broke."

Renie's further attempts to soothe her cousin were thwarted by the arrival of four uniformed policemen. "Lieutenant Flynn is on his way," announced one of them, a stolid black man with a walrus moustache.

Judith blinked. "Flynn?"

The walrus moustache barely moved when the policeman spoke. "Joe Flynn. Homicide. Very sharp."

"Oh." Judith didn't dare look at Renie. "Joe Flynn," she echoed in a voice that sounded dangerously giddy. *"Joe Flynn!"*

Renie had purloined Otto's Courvoisier when the medics weren't watching. "Drink this," she whispered, sloshing brandy into an empty glass from the little bar. Judith obeyed and sat down on an armless rocker, a relic of Grandma Grover's era.

Across the room, Otto was bickering with Oriana. "That's not my tea, I had sugar in it. Mine's the one with the fruity-looking flowers. Where the hell did it go?"

"That was Madame Gushenka's," Renie put in, a hand steadying Judith's rocker. "It's still on the table, but I don't think we'd better go into the dining room just yet."

"Bull," contradicted Otto, "that was my tea. Oh, hell," he exclaimed, throwing up his hands, "I'd rather have a stiff scotch anyway."

Ever obliging, Gwen made a rush at the bar, but was stopped by the firemen at the archway. "Please, Daddy needs a little something," she begged, all fluttering eyelashes and rippling wool jersey.

But the stalwart men in uniform could not be coerced. Kinsella and the others were conferring over the body, checking forms, and using the phone in the kitchen. Dejected, Gwen backpedaled straight into Renie, who was holding the almost-empty brandy bottle aloft.

"Here," offered Renie, "let Daddy polish this off. It's his, anyway." She gave Gwen a genuine smile, reminding herself that no matter how bizarre the Brodies might be and how disastrous the evening had become, Judith was still the hostess and needed all the cousinly support Renie could muster. And when Joe Flynn showed up, Renie would have to be prepared for just about anything. Like nuclear war, but not as nice.

At the moment, however, Judith was trying to appear benign. She couldn't prevent her gaze from sliding in the direction of the entry hall, and the rocker moved in jerky spasms, but otherwise she hoped she was exhibiting a calm exterior. Inside was another matter: What, she wondered, would he look like after over twenty years? Would he even recognize her? Did he know her married name? Would he give a rat's ass? She swallowed more brandy and braced herself as the front door swung open.

For Judith, the years rolled back at a dizzying pace, to bouffant hairdos, stiletto heels, and the Good Wool Suit; to picnics on the Ship Canal Bridge, the sun coming up at the city zoo, and driving a sports car on the pedestrian overpass at the university; to sourdough bread flown in fresh from San Francisco, Moscow Mules made out of lab alcohol, and root beer floats at four A.M.

What Judith actually saw was a red-haired, middle-aged man with a receding hairline and just the hint of a paunch. His shoulders were still broad, the charcoal-gray suit was impeccable, and the green eyes still held those gleaming gold flecks. Magic eyes, she thought, and felt her stomach hop, skip, and jump. At the moment, those eyes were registering the entire tableau, the cluster of Brodies, the medics hovering over the body, the police and firemen on the alert. At last, Joe Flynn's gaze came to rest on Judith McMonigle.

"I'll be damned," he said without inflection, "it's Jude-girl."

BANTAM OF THE OPERA

AS TIME GOES on, the bed-and-breakfast continues to do well, gaining a reputation that keeps Judith hopping for most of the year. In fact, Hillside Manor has begun to draw some high caliber celebrities, including obnoxious opera star Mario Pacetti, who threatens to eat Judith out of house and home. Judith's attempts to satiate the significantly statured songster seem of minor significance once the threats on his life draw his attention away from his next meal—which could possibly be his last. . . .

Bruno Schutzendorf was guzzling more wine; Amina Pacetti had polished off the cheese; Winston Plunkett had finally deigned to try the pâté; and Tippy de Caro was balancing a black olive on the end of her nose. Just as Judith was wondering if she should try to renew any sort of civil conversation, Mario Pacetti made his entrance. He still wore his smoking jacket and seemed faintly unsteady on his feet.

"The motion," he explained, clinging to the balustrade. "So long on the road. I grow dizzy."

"Of course," soothed Amina, who had gone to meet her husband at the foot of the stairs. "I, too, am uncertain in the walking. We are like sailors, again on the shore.'' With a wide smile, she led Pacetti to the depleted hors d'oeuvres table. ''Now, eat, Mario *mio*, you must keep up your strength for tomorrow.''

''Eat *what?*'' cried Pacetti, staring at the almost-empty platter and plates. ''Where is the calamari, the olives, the many fine cheeses I was promised?'' He waved an anchovy under his wife's nose. ''I could starve to death! Where is the pasta?''

A faint groan escaped from Judith's lips. No one at the opera house had suggested piles of pasta as an appetizer. She was about to forage for more food when a knock sounded at the front door. *Another pest*, she thought, since only guests and solicitors used the front entrance. Friends, neighbors, and family all tended to come in the back way.

As she hurried across the entry hall, she wondered if the bell was broken. It was unusual for anyone to knock instead of ring.

Dusk was settling in on Heraldsgate Hill. The evening air held the ripe smell of damp and decay. Over the rooftops, Judith could make out a narrow stretch of the bay, and the hazy outline of the mountains beyond. But she could not see anyone on the front porch. The cluster of pumpkins and the tall cornstalks that would serve as holiday decor until Thanksgiving stood innocently between the front door and the porch railing. Puzzled, Judith started toward the four stone stairs that led to the walkway. She had taken only a single step when she stubbed her toe. Stifling a curse, she bent down to examine the obstacle in her path. It was a rock, about six inches in diameter. Judith picked it up and turned it over in her hands.

Musical notes, carefully replicated from what looked like a score, were painted on the rough surface—along with a much more crudely drawn skull and crossbones. Uttering a small gasp, Judith stared at the object, then gazed more intently out into the cul-de-sac. Except for the lights in the Porters' house across the street, she could see no sign of life. Turning, she gave the bell a quick, experimental poke;

it echoed inside the house. Judith frowned. Perhaps whoever had delivered the rock hadn't knocked, but had merely
thrown it against the door. Sure enough, there was a sharp
dent in the screen that Joe hadn't yet replaced for the winter. Still frowning, Judith went back indoors.

If she had hoped to ditch the rock before her guests saw
it, she was disappointed. Tippy de Caro and Winston Plunkett were standing in the entry hall, their eyes fixed on
Judith's hands.

"The bell sounded . . ." Plunkett began, then halted
abruptly as he caught sight of the skull and crossbones.
"Good Lord, what's that?"

"Oh—kids, I suppose," said Judith vaguely. "A practical joke. Maybe they're rehearsing, too. For Halloween."
She gave Plunkett and Tippy a weak smile.

But Tippy, surprisingly, wasn't put off. "That looks
nasty to me. Let's see." Her enormous earrings jingled and
swayed as she bent her head.

The Pacettis and Schutzendorf had joined the others in
the entry hall. Judith surrendered the rock and closed the
front door.

"Ooooh!" cried Tippy, pushing the rock at Plunkett as
if it were a hot potato, "this is ugly! It's like . . . a *threat!*"

"Really, my dear," murmured Plunkett, "as Mrs. Flynn
says, it's probably just a . . ."

"Aaaargh!" The cry was wrenched from Mario Pacetti's
golden throat. He toppled backward, falling against Schutzendorf.

"Dio mio!" shrieked Amina, clutching at her husband's
flailing arm. "We are lost!"

Schutzendorf, who was supporting Pacetti, craned his
neck for a better look at the offending rock. *"Vat?* A stone
with drawings? So *vat?"*

"No!" shouted Pacetti, still limp and allowing Amina to
fan him with her handkerchief. "It is much more! See! The
music!"

"A singing skull," murmured Tippy, now eyeing the

rock with a keener gaze than usual, "like on an MTV video. Maybe it's an ad."

Plunkett, looking puzzled, turned the rock in his thin hands. "There are only a few notes," he said in a baffled voice.

"But such notes!" Pacetti was finally struggling to right himself. "The three in the treble—they are Alfredo's notes! The first ones he sings in *Traviata! 'Mar-che-se . . .'* " The stricken tenor sang the word, *sotto voce*. "He is meeting the guests at Violetta's party in Act I . . . I am doomed!"

Everyone, including Judith, stared at Pacetti. Plunkett made a clucking noise in his throat, Tippy squealed, Schutzendorf rumbled, and Amina had gone quite pale under her makeup.

"Brandy," mumbled Judith. "I'll get brandy." She started for the kitchen just as the water for her cauliflower boiled over onto the stove. Reaching for the burner with one hand and groping in the liquor cabinet with the other, she could hear the wails of Amina, the groans of Pacetti, the rumbles of Schutzendorf.

And Joe Flynn, coming through the back door, breezily asking if dinner was ready.

MURDER, MY SUITE

EVER SINCE JOE Flynn walked back into Judith's life and finally married her, Judith has begun to breathe a little easier. Life is good for Judith, who loves being surrounded by her devoted husband, her delightful son, her bosom buddy of a cousin, Renie, and even, in a rare tender moment, her mother. That is, until life takes a devilish turn when gossip columnist Dagmar Delacroix Chatsworth descends on Hillside Manor with a flurry of lackies and her yappy lapdog Rover, who seems to think he owns the joint. But Judith is ever the professional, gritting her teeth and bearing the barrage, even when things become fatally frenetic. . . .

The phone rang, and Judith chose to pick it up in the living room. She was only mildly surprised when the caller asked for Dagmar Chatsworth. The columnist already had received a half-dozen messages since arriving at Hillside Manor the previous day.

While Dagmar took the call, Judith busied herself setting up the gateleg table she used for hors d'oeuvres and beverages. At first, Dagmar sounded brisk, holding a ballpoint pen poised over the notepad Judith kept by the living room extension. Then her voice tensed; so did her pudgy body.

"How dare you!" Dagmar breathed into the receiver. "Swine!" She banged the phone down and spun around to confront Judith. "Were you eavesdropping?"

"In my own house?" Judith tried to appear reasonable. "If you wanted privacy, you should have gone upstairs to the hallway phone by the guest rooms."

Lowering her gaze, Dagmar fingered the swatch of fabric at her throat. "I didn't realize who was calling. I thought it was one of my sources."

"It wasn't?" Judith was casual.

"No." Dagmar again turned her back, now gazing through the bay window that looked out over downtown and the harbor. Judith sensed the other woman was gathering her composure, so she quietly started for the kitchen.

She had got as far as the dining room when the other two members of Dagmar's party entered the house. Agnes Shay carried a large shopping bag bearing the logo of a nationally known book chain; Freddy Whobrey hoisted a brown paper bag which Judith suspected contained a bottle of liquor. Another rule was about to be broken, Judith realized: She discouraged guests from bringing alcoholic beverages to their rooms, but a complete ban was difficult to enforce.

The bark of Dagmar's dog sent the entire group into a frenzy. Clutching the shopping bag to her flat breast, Agnes started up the main staircase. Freddy waved his paper sack and shook his head. Dagmar put a hand to her turban and let out a small cry.

"Rover! Poor baby! He's been neglected!" She moved to the bottom of the stairs, shouting at Agnes. The telephone call appeared to be forgotten. "Give him his Woofy Treats. Extra, for now. They're in that ugly blue dish on the dresser."

Judith blanched. She knew precisely where the treats reposed, since she had discovered them earlier in the day, sitting in her mother's favorite Wedgwood bowl. Anxiously, Judith watched the obedient Agnes disappear from the second landing of the stairs. Rover continued barking.

"I thought the dog was a female," Judith said lamely.

Dagmar beamed. "That's because he's so beautiful. Pomeranians are such adorable dogs. Rover is five, and still acts like the most precious of puppies. Would you mind if he came down for punch and hors d'oeuvres?"

Judith did mind, quite a bit. On the other hand, the dog would be under supervision. "Well, as long as he stays in the living room." Judith's smile was now strained.

Out in the kitchen, Phyliss Rackley was finishing her chores for the day. Usually she was gone by three, but Rover's destructive habits had provided more work for the cleaning woman, as well as for Judith.

"All those feathers from the down comforter," Phyliss grumbled as she gave the counters a last swipe with a wet rag. "Now my allergies are acting up. I found one of your old quilts to cover the bed."

Judith, in the act of taking a bottle of Benadryl from the windowsill above the sink, snatched her hand away. She wasn't about to get into a discussion of allergic reactions with Phyliss.

"That's fine, Phyliss," Judith said with an appreciative smile. "I'm sorry things were in such a mess today. Let's hope they keep that blasted dog under control until they leave tomorrow morning."

Phyliss was rummaging in her large straw shopping bag. "What's with the strongbox upstairs? It's heavy. I had to move it to get under the nightstand next to the bed. The dog did something truly nasty there."

Judith shook her head. "I've no idea. Dagmar's got a typewriter, too. I'd figure her for using a laptop, but apparently she's the old-fashioned sort."

"Filth," Phyliss declared, removing an Ace bandage from her straw bag and deftly wrapping it around her right ankle. "The woman writes filth. I don't know why a family newspaper runs such trash. Decent people wouldn't read it.'' On her way out, she banged the screen door for emphasis.

Judith grabbed the Benadryl just as Agnes Shay crept into the kitchen.

''We're out of bottled water,'' Agnes said in her wispy, anxious voice. ''I'm so sorry . . . Do you have any in the refrigerator, or should I walk up to the grocery store?''

Judith had no qualms about drinking from the tap, and did so before answering Agnes. Since many of her guests preferred a more purified form of water, she always kept a supply on hand.

''There's both plain and flavored,'' she replied after swallowing her allergy pill. ''It's too hot to walk up to the top of the Hill. Take what you need.'' Judith gestured at the refrigerator with her glass.

''Oh . . . thank you!'' Agnes's round face glowed with gratitude. Like her employer's, Agnes's age was difficult to guess. Thirties, Judith figured, but with a naive air that made her seem younger. On the other hand, her appearance added extra years. Agnes was small, with drab brown hair, a smattering of freckles across her plain face, and a shapeless figure. ''You're so kind!'' she exclaimed, turning to face Judith. She clutched at least a half-dozen bottles against her insignificant bosom.

Judith gaped. ''Ah . . . do you really need *all* of those?'' It looked to Judith as if Agnes had commandeered the entire inventory.

But Agnes nodded. ''Oh, yes. They'll last only until morning. It's this warm weather, you see. Rover gets so thirsty.'' On scurrying feet, Agnes padded out of the kitchen.

A few minutes later, Judith was dividing her purchase of smoked salmon between the hors d'oeuvres platter and the open-faced sandwiches when Freddy Whobrey breezed into the kitchen.

''Rocks,'' he said, then planted himself expectantly next

to the sink. He had been wearing snakeskin cowboy boots upon his arrival at Hillside Manor; now his feet were shod in alligator shoes. Judith suspected that they contained lifts. Freddy probably wasn't more than five feet two in his stocking feet.

"Rocks?" Judith used the back of her hand to wipe the perspiration off her forehead.

"Ice." Freddy's beady black eyes were fixed on the refrigerator door. "I could use a glass, too."

"I'm making punch," Judith responded a bit crossly. "It'll be ready in about twenty minutes."

"Punch!" Freddy guffawed, revealing very sharp teeth. "That's for old ladies like Dagmar and old maids like Agnes! I never drink anything but the real McCoy."

Judith eyed him with distaste, then remembered her manners as a hostess and forced a smile. "I prefer that guests don't drink upstairs," she said, keeping her voice pleasant.

"No problem," he retorted. "Downstairs, outside, inside—you name it, sweetie. Where's the rocks?"

Resignedly, Judith got out a highball glass and shoved it under the ice dispenser. "Here," she said. "To your health."

Freddy gazed up at her with admiration. "Say, you're a big one! Nice. I like tall women. Got some curves, too." Apparently noticing Judith's black eyes snap, Freddy held up the hand that didn't hold the highball. "No offense— I'm giving you a sincere compliment. I may be small, but I'm perfectly formed. You got good features, I can see that. Strong, even, all of a piece. I'll bet you can go the distance. A mile and a sixteenth wouldn't bother you at all, huh?"

Judith favored Freddy with an arch little smile. She noted that he was beginning to bald on top, though he had carefully combed his dark hair over the offending spot. "It wouldn't bother me," she replied, looking over his head to the back door, "but it'd make my husband mad as hell. Hi, Joe. Shoot anybody today?"

"Only one," Joe replied. "He's in intensive care." Joe

threw his summer-weight jacket on the peg in the entryway by the back stairs and unfastened his holster. "Hi, Freddy," he said, putting out his free hand. "How about a game of William Tell? If you've got the apple, I've got the gun."

Freddy ran out of the kitchen. The swinging door rocked behind him. Rover barked and a woman screamed. A hissing sound followed. Furniture fell. More voices were raised in alarm. Judith started for the living room, but Joe caught her by the waist.

"Relax," he said, his round, faintly florid face close to hers. "These people are crazy. I'm not. How about a hug?"

Judith obliged. With gusto.

NUTTY AS A FRUITCAKE

WITH ALL THE comings and goings around the bed-and-breakfast, Judith finds it comforting to know that, should her aging mother require her assistance—beyond the meals she serves her every day and the errands she runs—Gertrude is right on the property, living in the converted toolshed. Although Judith and Gertrude have their moments, this mother-daughter relationship is an affectionate one, depending on how you look at it. . . .

"They're questioning the neighbors," Naomi said in a breathless voice. "First, Mrs. Swanson, then the Rankerses, and finally, me. Nobody else is home—except your mother."

"My mother?" Judith gaped at Naomi, then jumped out of the car to look down the driveway. She saw nothing unusual, except Sweetums, who was stalking an unseen prey in the shrubbery.

"They're questioning her now," Naomi added, backpedaling to her own property. "Don't worry, Judith. I'm sure she'll be treated with respect."

That wasn't what concerned Judith. With a half-hearted wave for Naomi, she all but ran to the toolshed. There wasn't time to think about the awful things Gertrude could say to the police, especially about Joe Flynn. Judith yanked the door open.

Patches Morgan was standing by the tiny window that looked out onto the backyard and the Dooleys' house. With arms folded, Sancha Rael leaned against a side chair that had originally belonged to Judith and Dan. Gertrude was sitting on her sofa, smoking fiercely, and wearing a tiger-print housecoat under a lime-and-black cardigan. She glared as her daughter came into the small sitting room.

"Well! Just in time, you stool pigeon! What are you trying to do, get me sent up the river?"

Judith's mouth dropped open. "What? Of course not! What's happening?"

With his good left eye, Morgan winked at Judith. "Now, now, me hearties, this is just routine. But," he continued, growing serious, "it seems that certain threats against Mrs. Goodrich were made by Mrs. Grover. You don't deny that, do you, ma'am?" His expression was deceptively benign as he turned back to Gertrude.

Gertrude hid behind a haze of blue smoke. "I make a lot of threats," she mumbled. "It's my way. I can't remember them all."

Judith stepped between Gertrude and Morgan. "Excuse me—who told you that my mother threatened Enid?"

Morgan's good eye avoided Judith. "Now, I can't be revealing my sources, eh? You know that anything we might regard as a threat has to be investigated when there's a homicide involved."

"It was years ago," Judith said, then bit her tongue. "I mean, it must have been—*I* don't remember it. Either," she added lamely, with a commiserating glance for Gertrude.

Sancha Rael stepped forward, a smirk on her beautiful face. "This threat involved a family pet. It had something to do with"—she grimaced slightly—"sauerkraut."

Gertrude stubbed her cigarette out. She shot Morgan and

Rael a defiant look. "I forget. I'm old. Senile, too. Maybe I've got Alzheimer's. Who are all you dopey people anyway?" Her small eyes rested on Judith. "You, for instance—I've never seen you before in my life. Are you the maid? You know, the French girl who comes in with a short black skirt and a white doily on her head and dusts with one of those feather things."

Judith didn't know whether to grin or groan. She did neither. "Look," she said to Morgan, "this is silly. I can't believe you're wasting the city's time interrogating my mother. Does she look like the sort of person who'd take a hatchet to somebody?"

Morgan eyed Gertrude closely. "In truth, she does," he said. "Where were you Wednesday morning, December first, between seven and eight-thirty A.M.?"

The menacing expression on Gertrude's face did nothing to dispel the unfortunate image she'd given Patches Morgan. "Here—where else would I be? Do you think my lame-brained daughter ever takes me any place? As for that worthless son-in-law of mine, he'd like to put this cardboard box of an apartment on wheels and send me right down Heraldsgate Hill into the bay. The only time they'll let me out of this dump is when I go sticks up."

Judith was now getting angry. "Mother, you know that's not true! You play bridge, you go to bingo, you get out to dinner with Auntie Vance and Uncle Vince . . ."

Gertrude's face went blank. "Bridge? Bingo? Who are Auntie Vance and Uncle Vince? Where am I? What happened?" She began to hum, a tuneless rendition of "Mademoiselle from Armentieres."

In exasperation, Judith threw up her hands. "Do you mind?" she said to Morgan. "Leave her alone. She's . . . difficult."

Gertrude took out her dentures. She smiled, a fearsome sight.

Morgan surrendered. "We can come back," he said under his breath, motioning to Rael. "Let's talk to Ms. Flynn inside the big house."

"The big house?" Gertrude echoed in a singsong voice after replacing her teeth. "Am I going to the big house? Oh, my! I'll have to wear a striped suit and one of those funny hats shaped like a custard cup and a ball and chain and . . ."

Judith softly closed the door on her mother's irksome rantings. "I'm sorry," Judith said tersely. "As I told you, she can be difficult."

Murder Is on the Menu
at the Hillside Manor Inn
Bed-and-Breakfast Mysteries by
MARY DAHEIM
featuring Judith McMonigle

BANTAM OF THE OPERA
76934-4/ $5.99 US/ $7.99 Can

JUST DESSERTS 76295-1/ $5.99 US/ $7.99 Can

FOWL PREY 76296-X/ $5.99 US/ $7.99 Can

HOLY TERRORS 76297-8/ $5.99 US/ $7.99 Can

DUNE TO DEATH 76933-6/ $5.99 US/ $7.99 Can

A FIT OF TEMPERA 77490-9/ $5.99 US/ $7.99 Can

MAJOR VICES 77491-7/ $5.99 US/ $7.99 Can

MURDER, MY SUITE 77877-7/ $5.99 US/ $7.99 Can

AUNTIE MAYHEM 77878-5/ $5.99 US/ $7.99 Can

NUTTY AS A FRUITCAKE
77879-3/ $5.99 US/ $7.99 Can

SEPTEMBER MOURN
78518-8/ $5.99 US/ $7.99 Can

WED AND BURIED 78520-X/ $5.99 US/ $7.99 Can

SNOW PLACE TO DIE
78521-8/ $5.99 US/ $7.99 Can